WIDOW'S FLAME

Printed in Australia
First Printing: September 2022
Shawline Publishing Group Pty Ltd
www.shawlinepublishing.com.au

Paperback ISBN 978-1-9228-5003-4
eBook ISBN 978-1-9228-5012-6

A catalogue record for this
work is available from the
National Library of Australia

WIDOW'S FLAME

JESS McFARLANE

Dedication

To Alec – the Wilson to my Tom Hanks.

Acknowledgements

I would like to acknowledge the Darkinjung people as Traditional Custodians of the land on which Widow's Flame was written. I want to extend that acknowledgement to the Awabakal people as Traditional Custodians of the land where I continue to write and reside. I pay my respects to Elders both past, present and emerging.

I want to thank my two best friends, Rebecca Larke and Kellie French, for being some of my first ever readers and supporting me since I was 14. I've come a long way since then and your support let me enjoy it every step of the way. Your encouragement lead me to this wonderful relationship I have with creating worlds, characters and their stories, and I'll be forever thankful.

To my sister, Jasmine Clough, and my mum, Cathy Clough – you two have always read little snippets and never gave me a big head about my prose. Your constructive criticism was incredibly helpful (even when it was sometimes downright blunt) and it let me evolve as a writer. That is a huge gift for a writer to have, so thank you.

To my future mother-in-law Bryony Cooke, who was the first person to read the draft of Widow's Flame. If it wasn't for you, this book probably never would have been published, and if it had it would have taken a heck of a lot longer. Thank you for pushing me to force aside my self-doubt and "just send it in already!"

To Bradley Shaw and the entire team at Shawline Publishing, thank you. From the bottom of my heart, I cannot put into words how thankful I am to be given this opportunity. This is a life-long dream come true and your faith in me helps soothe that niggling self-doubt.

To my partner, Alec, who isn't a big reader, but who I spy reading over my shoulder when I'm writing on the lounge, I love you. You've always made a big deal about my writing and my dream, even when I didn't. You've been with me through a lot and I'm excited that you're with me in this next stage of life.

And, finally, to my readers and to any aspiring authors. I respect you, I see you, I hear you. I cannot wait to read your stories, which are so deserving to be shared with the world. Thank you for picking up this book. I hope you devour it, I hope that some parts stay with you. And I hope it to be the first of many to come.

12th November, 1892

My darling wife,

Good news from Wyoming! The house on the property is well underway and there are plans to build a barn once the fences are sorted. I have very good men working with me and we are out building from sun up until sun down most days as the weather permits. We hope to be finished before winter and the snows become too heavy — luckily these pre-cut houses are quite a breeze! I cannot wait for you to see it all. Cheyenne, the city only a few hours' ride from here, is an extravagant and loud place, full of culture and rich, yet gentle folk. You would get along with the ladies here, my darling and I believe they would find your Galway accent quite exotic. Not only that, but they are honest and educated women, such as yourself, and funnily enough, this grand old state has allowed them rights to vote! America is a wondrous place, that is for sure.

I know you may not find the time to reply to this letter, being busy with the business and all. I hope everything is running smoothly for you and please, give my regards to Martin.

I will send word once winter has ended and, hopefully then we can plan to see one another soon. I miss you!

Your husband,
Thomas

1

I'm drinking strong whiskey in the ramshackle Salmon Leap pub when I feel something inside me break. A perfect click at the base of my spine brings a wash of sudden dread over me, dark and overwhelming in such a way that at first, I sit in the wooden chair, staring into space, unsure what to do. I feel my fingers tighten against the glass in my hand, the other unoccupied hand balling into a fist on my lap. And then a feeling of complete and utter anguish sweeps through me. I know this feeling well. I have become mortal enemies with this feeling; sensing it on lonely nights in my bed, banishing it from my house and only letting it dwell in the dark recesses of my mind. This anguish is a monster, a dark and looming creature with sharp claws that dig into the backs of my eyes as it whispers horrible truths inside my ear.

Thomas is dead. Murdered. You are alone.

A bead of sweat trickles down my spine. I let in a breath through my nose, slow to move unless the creature notices and pounces. The familiar roar of the Salmon Leap's patrons is inside my ears, slowly drowning out now that panic has gripped me, but I try to focus on it once more, needing to ground myself within the present. I let my eyes move around the room. There aren't many women here, just fishermen, labourers and farmers. Their wives are at home, either cooking dinner or not expecting their husbands' return anytime soon.

There's a man talking at a table across from mine, using his hands wildly to describe whatever story he's telling his friends. He's grinning, his eyes wide and his face is so expressive that I use his presence to bring myself back. Slowly, the feeling inside me fades. The tingling in my fingers begins to dissipate.

'It was big! Bigger than I ever saw!'

'You say that every time you see a fish out there, Larry.'

Larry shakes his head, the grey hair under the brim of his hat flipping about his jowls. I've seen him many times in the Salmon Leap and I know his friend is right; he *does* say that every time he sees a fish out on the Atlantic.

I pour myself another drink and finish it off, letting the burn of whiskey punish my throat. The room spins. Half a bottle is inside my blood already. Nothing I'm not used to, but tonight is no longer the night for drinking. I need to go home and go to sleep. Whatever just happened inside me has put me off and the patrons inside the pub are getting louder and louder, pounding in my ears. I feel a headache coming on and my mouth starts to turn dry. The residual panic inside me hasn't faded yet and I get frustrated by it, blaming my body for being so bothersome when all I want to do is drink in peace.

I stand up and put on my coat. As I'm heading for the door, I notice a tall man standing at the back of the pub, near the bar where Benjamin is serving drinks, his kind, wrinkled eyes tired. When I look to where the man was, he's gone. The shadow of his appearance lingers in my mind and I can think of only one name.

Thomas.

⊷—◦—⊶

'Thomas,' I said, faintly exasperated.

He lifted his dark head and glanced at me across the room. He was always getting lost in his thoughts, a faraway look to his eye behind the glass of his spectacles. He smiled at me, seeing the expression on my face and shifted his seat in his usual chair by the hearth's fire.

'Sorry, darling Blair,' he murmured. 'What did you say?'

I lifted the metal pot in my hand. 'Coffee?'

'Yes.' He nodded. 'Please.'

'I don't know how Mr O'Hughe manages to work with you.'

I shook my head, giving him a slight smile as I brought him his cup of coffee. The room was warm, filled with the comforting smell of a hearty breakfast cooking on the stove. I took pleasure in cooking for my husband, using the culinary skills my mother taught me before she passed away.

'You manage just fine. Martin can take it on the chin, as he always has.'

Before I could move away, he grasped my hand and pulled me down onto the arm of his chair. I sat down with a little laugh as he wrapped an arm around my waist, kissing the sleeve of my dress. I turned my head towards his and he kissed my cheek softly. I enjoyed the rasp of his moustache against my skin and the softness of his lips, warmed by the heat of the coffee.

'What were you thinking about just now, husband?' I asked him quietly.

He slowly took his arm from my waist and continued to drink his coffee in silence for a moment. I got up and started to serve the food once it was ready.

'This and that,' he finally said.

I didn't take offence to his vagueness. Thomas had the habit of unintentionally playing coy with me — downplaying any idea or thought in his brain if it was still new to him. Never did I question him further if he didn't answer me the first time. I'd known him long enough to know that his thoughts were his and if he stewed upon an idea, I'd eventually know about it when it was time. Many times it was Martin O'Hughe who got to hear the marvellous workings of my husband's mind and not me.

Any ideas he came up with for the distillery, any recipe for a new method on distilling his family's whiskey, any sort of way of getting more and more bottles out to the local pubs or further across Ireland, he took to his cousin and fellow business partner.

I handed him his plate of beans, fried bacon and bread.

'Well, let this fuel more thoughts of *this and that*,' I ordered.

'Ah, my lovely Irish wife,' he sang, making me laugh as he waved his hands about, 'what am I but a mere Englishman, undeserving of such love and support?'

———○———

I keep moving and head outside. It's well past sundown and the wind that batters at my face when I step out is wet from rain and seawater. All I can smell is salt from the Atlantic and the smoky hint of peat fires burning within the city's cottages, drifting across the River Corrib. The smell reminds me of home; of Clifden and my father, his large hands marred by the sharp scales of fish, lifting me up off the sand as he sang songs of old. This monster inside me, with its great claws and long, gleaming tongue, has brought with it a shroud of memories I've tried to push aside for three years.

The river is a thunderous, vibrating roar beneath my feet as I head across the bridge. During the summer, it's hard to get to the other side of the Corrib when the bridge is crowded, full of people peering over the side to watch the salmon fight their way upstream. Men stand in the shallower parts or hang off the edges of small boats to grab at the fish with their hands, laughing and shouting as the crowd above applauds them for their catch. As a younger woman, full of hope and new love, I used to adore the months of April through to July, watching the salmon fight through the current and past grasping hands to reach their spawning grounds up in the Lough. Their silvery bodies, wriggling against the rush of white foam and clear water, used to be an almost magical sight, an honour to witness and a spectacle that brought one back to earth, giving them perspective on the wonders of nature.

But the bridge tonight is silent and the river below is absent of those silver scales, just a churning of water and city muck. Whatever love and hope that had been inside me in those days, died the very day Thomas did, buried with him six feet under the ground somewhere in a part of the world strange and foreign to me. A place I have grown to resent.

I keep my fists in my pockets, shielding them against the gale blowing through the streets. There are people going about their nights, keeping to themselves as I walk past. Some older men, faces weathered from years out at sea, nod my way, recognising me from the Salmon Leap. Others know me by name and some just as the woman who runs one of the whiskey distilleries in town, sour-faced and scornful at the world after her husband's death and too young to be so. However they see me, I don't see them and I haven't for years.

Home is a ten-minute walk from the Salmon Leap. It sits in one of Galway City's many streets, the Atlantic close enough to be heard at night or on a quiet day and seen from the attic. I head inside and take off my coat, grateful for the warmth of the hearth in the kitchen. My mind is still hazy from drink and with the effort it's taken to push away the emotions that came flooding in as soon as whatever inside me snapped. I go upstairs, the house groaning underneath me with a complaint about how late it is. I reach my bedroom, shutting the door and shutting out the world.

⊷•◦•⊷

Martin O'Hughe wakes me early in the morning with a knock on my door. I get up and go downstairs in my gown, a headache pounding in my left temple as I stumble down the steps. Martin's tall, lanky figure is shadowing my doorway when I open it up and I'm at first greeted by the smell of the strong aftershave he always wears. Being Thomas' older cousin, he looks similar to my dead husband in a few ways — the same dark hair and the same moustache, if not a little thinner. Where Thomas' eyes were blue and bright, his are dark and lined by circles that say Martin O'Hughe is not the sleeping sort, not when there's work to be done.

'Good morning, Martin,' I mutter, letting the exasperation I feel towards this man show in my voice. He knows full well how I feel about him, just as I know how he feels about me. The man and I have never and will never get along. 'What can I do for you?'

'You were supposed to supervise yesterday, Ms Ryan.' He puts his hands on his hips as if to accentuate the fact he's annoyed with me. 'Where were you?'

'In town.' I blink at him.

'Ms Ryan, you—' He stops and looks about the street. Amongst the fog of the morning, there are several people about. 'How about we go inside and have some coffee? You look like you need it.'

I don't say anything, only press myself against the wall to let him through. He knows his way about the house and lets himself into the kitchen. He's already going about preparing coffee when I come in after closing the door. I cross my arms in my gown and watch him silently, jaw tight. The sight of Martin O'Hughe inside my kitchen is something I have never gotten used to. I feel protective over my house and its cracked walls and cold flagstone floors. Even more so over the chair that now sits in the corner, away from the heat of the fire where it always used to sit.

Martin doesn't pay me any mind. At least he already knows I growl and claw like a lioness protecting her cubs if anyone chooses to even look at the chair in the corner of the room.

It's old oak and one of the legs is now uneven, making it rock back and forth with the slightest change of weight. The embroidered cushion upon its seat is faded and torn. Such a sorry-looking chair would be thrown away without a single thought in another household, but not this chair. Not *his* chair.

'I was in Dublin the other week,' Martin says, bringing me from my thoughts.

'Mm?'

We sit down at the table when he brings me a cup of coffee and he taps his fingers on the tabletop beside his cup, agitated.

'Six distilleries,' he cries, as if those words mean anything to me. 'We're not even licensed. Our trade is only local. Purchases from the city and Salthill are keeping our heads above the water, but other than that, we're only just scraping by. Dublin, Belfast… even bloody Cork. Their distilleries aren't just selling their whiskey in Ireland, they're selling them all over the damned world!'

'Good for them.'

Martin stares at me for a long time. I take a sip of coffee. He's made it very strong and I feel the bitterness all the way down my throat.

'Ms Ryan…' His voice is low and he speaks slowly, keeping his eyes on mine. 'You weren't at work the other day when you were supposed to be. The men are good at their jobs and luckily rarely need supervising, but if something went wrong—'

'*What* could go wrong, Martin? The safety measures Thomas' family has always held are well above standard.'

He squints his eyes at me. 'Have you been drinking again, Blair?'

My gut twists and I don't know whether it's from the coffee or shame. 'Don't—'

'*Have you?*'

I say nothing. I gaze down at the tabletop, at the scratches and nooks dug out from years of use. Thomas and I took this table from my parents after my mother died. This table has been with me all my life. It knows me well; the goings on of my childhood are etched into its very surface.

'Blair, it's been three years.'

'The men weren't found, Martin,' I spit out suddenly.

A shudder racks through my body and I stare up at Martin's face again, tears in my eyes. Those feelings that came to me last night are standing beside me now, looming over the table like ghouls waiting for a feast. They tell me to scream at him, to tear at his face with my hands until he understands the pain I've been in, the trauma and loss that I feel and have pushed away.

'I read the letter from the marshal,' he snaps back, tense in his chair. 'I know what happened. And I know the pain you're going through because I felt it too. I've dealt with it, however, I've healed and I'm moving on. You—'

'You *know* the pain?' I cry. Those feelings explode inside me and tears are burning my eyes, scratching at my throat. 'Those men murdered my husband — shot him in the head as if he were a lame horse! You don't know *anything* about the pain I've felt these past three years. *Anything.*'

'You're fragile at the moment, I understand, but I didn't come here to talk about this. I came here to talk about the business. We must do something. If you do not feel as if your commitment to the distillery is in everyone's best interest, perhaps you should start to consider selling your share.'

I rub my face with shaking hands. I hear what he's saying, but the distillery was Thomas'. He loved it more than anything. He was proud of it and wanted to continue carrying it throughout his family, to hand it down to the children we never had. The air is thick and heavy around us, the fire within the hearth suddenly too hot, suffocating. I push my cup to the side and see Martin's eyes follow its tracks along the tabletop.

'I didn't want to have to do this,' he continues when he sees I'm making no move to speak.

I cannot speak, there aren't any words inside me other than screams and wails. I am nothing but the banshee he always used to call me, jokingly, but still with a hint of resentment in his eyes. Now that the alcohol from last night has worn off, I'm stuck inside a sober mind, full of pain and disorder, with no numbness to calm it. But with this sobriety I'm seeing clearer the shift my body has taken, a displacement like an eroding cliff edge, close to collapsing. I see it and I'm no longer so afraid of that monster with the grinning mouth full of the sharp teeth of truths.

'I want to see them hang,' I say quietly. My voice is deadly, not mine.

Martin stops talking, in the middle of giving me gentle advice on what to do, how to cope. He stares at me and when I lift my eyes to his face, I can see fear there. Uncertainty. And still a residual form of the resentment he's always held for me.

The woman that got in the way of business. The woman who inspired Thomas to go out to America and get himself killed.

'Those men in that gang… what were they called?'

My mind scrapes through the memory of receiving the marshal's letter. I'd collapsed to the ground in the middle of the street outside the post office after reading it.

It grieves me to write this to you, madam, as there is no easy way to tell you. Your husband was murdered by an outlaw gang at his ranch just outside of Cheyenne, Wyoming, approximately around midnight, 24th June, 1895.

People had come to my aid, asking me what was wrong, and I had had no voice to tell them that my husband had been murdered, that I was now a widow, alone in a world full of death.

'Gaitwood.' Martin's voice is weak. 'The Gaitwood gang.'

I nod slowly. 'The leader… and his men. I want to see them all hang.'

Martin licks his lips and looks away from me, letting out a breath through his nose. 'I do, too. But there is nothing we can do about that, Blair, not now. It's been three years and the marshal still hasn't found them.'

'He's not looking hard enough. Or he's not even looking at all.'

I can see Martin has given up trying to talk to me. He's watching me quietly with his dark eyes and the way his mouth is pursed slightly reminds me of Thomas and I feel a lurch inside my chest. After several more minutes of silence, he gets up and bids me a good day. I attempt to tell him I'll try to make it to the distillery in the morning, but we both seem to know my words are lies and they die on my lips before I've even finished the sentence. When Martin's gone, I begin to clean up. There's a sensation inside my body that's peculiar to me and I try to ignore it as I go about cleaning the kitchen, but it keeps nagging at me. A sense of needing to run somewhere, to go somewhere far away and keep on running until my legs give out underneath me. Whether it's to run from the monsters at my shoulders or to run at their request, I do not know.

<hr />

Galway City is foggy and cold tonight. There's no rain when I make my way to the Salmon Leap pub, but the wind has picked up and the chill to the air seeps into the wool of my coat. I only wear a plain dress and stockings underneath. My boots are old and worn and the leather is so thin my toes are starting to cramp from the cold. But I don't mind it. Growing up on the western coast of Ireland has toughened me up like a weathered hag. The bogs at the city's doorstep and the Connemara Mountains further along were my playing grounds as a child. Clifden isn't far from Galway City. It too has a river in town and if one were to hop into a boat and follow it, they would end up out at sea, just like my father used to. Fishing is not only in my blood, but in the blood of everyone in this place. One is only to walk along the water's edge of a morning to smell the brine and see the flocks of seagulls snooping about the markets set up along the rocks and sand; their cries piercing the still air.

Benjamin looks even more tired tonight when I step in. He nods at me and hands me a bottle of whiskey. I see Ryan's up on the wall behind him. He knows I don't drink it and instead gives me the cheapest on the menu, made by a fellow distillery in Salthill. I take two glasses to start me off and slide the coins across to him.

'Will there ever be a night where I don't see you here, Ms Blair?' he asks me.

'When I'm dead, Benjamin,' I tell him.

He gives a slight snort and shakes his head at my joke, yet a part of me doesn't feel like I'm joking.

'*Sláinte!*' one of the men at the bar says, raising his glass. A few of the others beside him murmur it too, marginally raising their glasses before gulping down their beer.

'*Sláinte,*' I reply quietly, finishing one of the glasses of whiskey.

Benjamin fills the glass again and I give him the coins for it. I then take the two glasses to my usual table in the corner of the pub, beside the window that faces out onto the dark street. It looks like it's now blowing a gale out there and I see fishermen struggling to keep their hats on as they make their way home from work. A few of them come into the pub for shelter and stay a little while, the strong smell of spirits and cigarettes drawing them in. The Salmon Leap is not everyone's usual go-to place to drink. Only a handful of patrons regularly visit the place, myself included. The rest of them are tourists from other parts of Ireland or England or somewhere else in the world, here to see Salthill and its sandy beach, or marvel at the Connemara, or view the Aran Islands through a telescope from the shore. You can tell them from a mile away, skulking into the place with wide eyes as they take in the dank, one-roomed pub, lit only by four lanterns along the green wallpaper. Only then to sit at the mahogany bar, tainted by stains and scratches. Benjamin himself isn't really a sight to behold. With his bulging gut and grey, receding hair, he looks more like a butcher than he does a barman. They generally dress much nicer than they need to — the men in three-piece suits, pressed and starched, hair slicked back, faces clean shaven; the women in vibrant dresses, holding parasols and wearing rouge. I admire them from my window seat every time they come in. Admire them and resent them for having a better life than I. For having one another.

'Do you really have to go, Thomas? Is this really what you want?'

He stared at me, his eyes analysing my face as he leant over where I lay on the bed. 'Whatever do you mean, darling Blair?'

I shrugged, blinking. For so long, he'd been talking about the idea of moving to America, of starting anew and getting away from Ireland. Away from the memories of death and Clifden.

'It's going to be a long time... until I see you again.'

He smiled, moving down to kiss my mouth. I leant up towards him, holding my lips against his for a little longer before he could pull away.

'It'll be good for us,' he murmured against the skin of my cheek, bringing my body closer to his. 'We can start a family.'

'We'll have American children,' I warned.

He laughed. 'American brats, all running about the ranch with dirty feet and missing teeth.'

I pulled away from him to look at his face, serious again. 'You don't paint a very wonderful picture.'

'I know I already have for you,' he replied with a smile, his eyes crinkling at the sides. 'You wouldn't have agreed to it otherwise.'

'I love you,' I said, because I had nothing else to say, no other argument. My husband was leaving to go build a life for us in a new land and there was nothing I could do to stop him. He had the idea in his head, fully flourished and filled to the brim with hope. That was all he needed to have his mind set.

'I love you, Mrs Ryan.'

⊷⊶⊙⊷⊶

'Is that even legal?'

'Probably not, but it hasn't been stopped yet. I swear I've seen some of the constables betting there, anyway!'

I come out of the memory and take another drink of whiskey, trying to burn away the thoughts with the mind-numbing alcohol. The whiskey I drink is nothing close to Ryan's. It's like motor oil more than anything else, most likely distilled with mouldy hay. It's a punishment to drink and that's exactly why I drink it. I look over at the two men who are talking at the bar. Benjamin is standing in front of them, watching them both disapprovingly as they continue to spill beer over the ruined mahogany with their excitable gestures.

'So no one's beat him, huh?'

'No! I watched him knock a man out in less than thirty seconds the other night.'

A fisherman at the end of the bar perks up and yells out, 'What was 'is name again? I'll be sure to put me life savin's on 'im.'

'They call him the American Outlaw!' the first one says.

I feel my heart stammer in my chest.

'Bigger and meaner than an American bison!' the second one adds with a laugh.

I down the last of my drink and get back up with my two glasses, carefully making my way back to the bar. I pay Benjamin and he fills them both up for me while my attention is on the two men. One of them sees me watching and he grins at me, beady eyes on my face.

'Interested in making a few extra bob?' he asks me.

I don't say anything, watching him over the rim of my glass as I drink.

'She's a lady, Brian. Why is she gonna want to go see men fight?'

Brian frowns at his friend. 'I think anyone will wanna watch them if it means making a lot of money.'

His friend grasps him on the shoulder to try and turn him away from me. They're both swaying in their seats, drunk and sweaty old men.

'We're not even supposed to be telling people about this! Don't go spreading word now or there'll be a huge crowd next time we go!'

'Keep a secret for me,' Brian slurs in my direction. 'Head to St Brigid's pub in Salt Hill.'

As the men go back to their conversation, I continue to drink at the bar, silent. I can feel my heart beating rapidly inside my chest, trapped and wanting to burst from the news I've just heard. I don't know quite what to make of it. I'm trying to turn the thoughts over in my brain and I realise again I have the uncomfortable sensation of needing to run, needing to escape and get out. I let out a deep breath through my nose. The glass I'm holding shakes in my hand.

'You alright there, Ms Blair?' Benjamin asks me, cleaning a glass with a rag that should have been thrown out years ago.

'Yes,' I say, but my voice is tiny and I'm not alright.

The American Outlaw.

'When are the fights held?' I suddenly blurt out towards Brian and his friend.

They both turn and look at me, stunned. The friend gives Brian a slap on the shoulder and the man flinches.

'I told you!'

'Oh shoosh,' Brian says to him. He looks at me, jowls jiggling at the quick movement of his head. 'Late afternoon, every afternoon.'

I nod and finish my last drink. I say goodnight to Benjamin and make my way back home.

2

A horse-drawn tram from Eyre Square takes tourists inside of Galway out to Salthill for a day visit in the summer. It runs every other day as well and for a small fee and a short trip, it's the easiest way to get out of the main city and into the colourful little town with its long promenade along the water's edge. Salthill isn't too far from the city and in fact, the city's buildings can easily be seen from the sandy beach, the Aran Islands out amongst the waves in the other direction. The bogs and mountains, so similar to the ones of my childhood in Clifden, sit out to the west of town and on a clear day, it's easy for one to think they could reach out across the bay and brush their fingers across the Clare hills, they appear so close. I've been to Salthill several times in my life. Thomas used to love the bars and shops along the promenade and in the summer, the beach was the perfect place to swim. I know most days aren't clear and the rain that sleets down onto the city of Galway is just as depressing as the rain that sleets down onto Salthill.

I get off the tram when it stops at the station and move with the crowd onto the streets. St Brigid's pub is near the outskirts of town, close to where the buildings give way to farmland and the green scenery of my country takes over. Horses and wagons litter the streets and I dodge past them as I continue along. The place smells like a farm and like the sea and burning peat.

I'm met with so many sights and smells and sounds, so familiar to the city and yet so different at the same time. I make my way towards the outskirts of town. It's getting later in the day and, behind the cloud cover, the sun is slowly sinking into the depths of the horizon.

St Brigid's is a large, limestone building with red windows, the paint cracked and fading a slight off-pink. It sits on a dirt road, amongst the majority of streets in Salthill that aren't paved. A wooden sign hangs out the front, a crude depiction of Saint Brigid herself, painted on the wood and it's swinging wildly in the wind. It isn't raining at the moment, but the windows are fogged on the inside and even over the sounds of the city behind me I can hear the roar of patrons. The pub is so secluded from the rest of the town, I hardly believe any tourist will come accidentally walking in and that's most likely how the patrons want it.

As I'm standing outside looking at the building, I suddenly realise I'm actually there and I've taken steps to find this American Outlaw. It makes me wonder why. Whatever thought process my mind did, it did it without me and controlled my body until I was here, at the doorstep. I know what I want — I suppose I've always known. It seems silly of me to expect the illegal fighter inside this very building is going to help me reach my goal, but I know I must try. I need purpose. I need the belief that Thomas didn't die in vain; I know that now.

The door opens and a few men step out, cigarettes dangling from their bottom lips. They hold the door open for me and I thank them quietly and step in past them as they leave. I'm bombarded with noise and smells. The front room is large and filled with tables, which in turn are filled with people. The Salmon Leap pub has never been this busy. I've never seen so many people in one space, drinking and laughing. A cloud of cigarette smoke hangs about the roof, an accumulation of everybody's smoking looming over their heads like an incoming storm. There's a man going about the room yelling orders — I see him even from the doorway. He's so loud and stands out because he wears a top hat and a fine emerald green waistcoat. He's holding a book and pen, followed by a younger, blonde man, who's carrying a cloth sack.

'Place yer bets!' the man's yelling. 'Place yer bets, people!'

People put their money into the sack and he writes down their names and who they're betting for or against. I bite my lip and step towards him, weaving through the tables and crowds until I'm close by. I dig into the pocket of my coat and draw out my coin purse. I pull out one pound and when the man reaches me, I place it in the cloth sack. The blonde man holding it raises his brows, but the man in the emerald waistcoat simply asks for my name.

'Ms Blair Ryan.'

'Who are you betting for or against, Ms Ryan?'

'For the American Outlaw.'

He gives me a quick nod and keeps moving through the room.

'Where's the fight held?' I ask the blonde man before he moves away.

'Out the back,' he says, jerking his head to a door on the far wall, voice deep. 'In the pit.'

I go to the door and head outside. There's a small, sheltered area at the doorway that leads to what I can only guess is "the pit" the man spoke of — a circle of dirt surrounded by a wooden fence. It's stopped raining, but the ground is muddy and filled with puddles. Already people are gathering around, waiting for the fight to start. I can hear the excitement in their voices. There aren't many women, only a couple of working girls clinging to the arms of fishermen and workers alike. I see some upper-class men smoking cigars and keeping to themselves. One of them pulls out a gold pocket-watch from his waistcoat and looks at it, grumbling under his breath to his friends. I turn my head away when he looks up and slowly make my way to where the crowd is beginning to circle around the pit. I make sure I'm close enough to see properly as the man in the emerald waistcoat comes out, announcing the fight is about to begin.

'If you have not yet placed yer bets, now is the last time to do so! Danny is standing just off to the side there. Go see him!'

Another door at the back of the building opens and a few men come out, but I can only just see over the heads of people. Emerald Man is yelling unintelligible words and the crowd is whistling and applauding. A topless man walks into the pit, his hair a fiery red. He's quite short, but his build is solid and he lifts his hands in the air as people cheer. His fists are wrapped in bandages, big as cinder blocks. Emerald Man yells his name again and this time I hear it, *The Crimson Fist*.

And then another man steps into the ring and the crowd hollers and boos, deafening me. This man is tall and broad, muscles solid under his fair skin. I immediately notice the circular scars on the front and back of his left shoulder, stark white and gnarled, as if they were hastily mended. His brown hair hangs around his eyes as he steps in. He looks grim, his eyes downcast, his mouth a hard line under a thick beard. He doesn't seem to take any notice of the crowd, but he raises one wrapped fist when Emerald Man calls his name, *The American Outlaw*.

My heart begins a drumbeat in my chest. I almost turn away and leave, revolted at myself for even being here in the first place. But I stand firm and stay, watching on, jaw clenched tight. The fight starts and the first hit makes me jump. I watch The American Outlaw as he moves around the pit, throwing punches. He fights savagely, without remorse, each hit sounding out with a sickening thud. There's a fluidity in his movements that is almost hard to believe for a man of his stature. He's so swift, so quick to dodge and land a parry. His opponent has no chance.

It's easy to see this within only seconds of the fight. The Outlaw doesn't seem to mind. He lets The Crimson Fist land a few hits, as if wanting it; wanting the pain and the blood that sprays out of his nose and mouth. It trickles into his beard and down his neck. Soon enough, his chest is covered in it. His fists are the epitome of his opponent's name. And yet his opponent is worse for wear, stumbling about the pit, falling into the crowd weakly as they roar and push him back in. No matter how vicious and deadly the Outlaw fights, he gives his opponent a break, watching him as he struggles. And when The Crimson Fist gets back up and throws another punch, he goes back in for more. It's two minutes and The Crimson Fist is in the mud, out cold. The crowd is screaming; most men throw their hats off into the mud in defeat, swearing at their at bad fortune. I realise I've just won a sum of money, but I don't care. I'm looking at the Outlaw, heart hammering, both intrigued by him and disgusted at the same time.

I hire a room at St Brigid's for a week. It's a dingy little room containing a small bed with an itchy coverlet, thin walls with cracking and peeling ugly red paint and a dusty window that looks down onto the fighting pit. The Outlaw fights every second night and I watch him every time, jostled on both sides by the writhing crowd as they scream and shout for his opponent. As each night passes, the betters come to realise his skill and my winnings lessen in number as they turn their attention to him, calling his name from behind the pit's fence. Every time he defeats his opponent, his face tells me nothing, his eyes downcast as if hiding. He doesn't respond to the calls and jeers from the patrons. Doesn't seem to notice they're even there.

Over the course of those few nights, I begin to resent him, to hate the violence he inflicts on other men for the sake of money and fame. I begin to shudder at the thought of how he gained the name "Outlaw" and my mind can't help but pin him in the same group as the men that killed Thomas. Just as I want to see those men suffer, I want to see the Outlaw suffer, or at least for him to acknowledge the pain he's caused. I don't know his story, I hardly know if he's even American, but there's a fury inside me that twists up my guts and a demon sitting across my shoulders, whispering hateful words into my ear about him. I can't help it. I hate the man and yet, the longer I watch him, the more I wish to speak with him. The more I begin to believe he may be able to help me with the plan that's been slowly stewing inside my mind ever since that night at the Salmon Leap.

On the sixth night, I see him sitting at his usual table inside St Brigid's. He's sat there every night since I've been here and I've stuck to the back of the room, drinking my whiskey quietly, constantly watching him out of the corner of my eye. I've started to notice he doesn't seem like a man who enjoys his fame. People come up to him to talk or buy him a drink and he always declines. They'll sit at his table and speak to one another and only on the odd occasion will he add something to the conversation and it's usually if he's asked a question. The men will bellow out their words and laugh raucously, but he'll continue to sit quietly in his chair, smoking a cigarette and slowly working his way through a bottle of whiskey. On the fourth night I saw him drinking Ryan's and almost said something, but stopped myself before I could. The working girls have already learnt he declines every invitation they offer him and yet some still continue to try and coax their way into his bed. I guess they like the look of him.

But tonight I've drunk more than I have in a while and I feel a spike of courage. I stand up and grab my glass and the bottle that's been sitting on my table, almost empty. I move through the crowded room towards his table and when I reach him, I stand beside his chair until he glances up at me and meets my gaze.

He has a dark bruise under his right eye, but other than that, he looks more presentable than he ever has in the fighting pit. His shirt is simple, collared, the sleeves rolled up to his elbows. His hair hangs around his face and sits above his shoulders.

I motion to the chair opposite his. 'Can I sit?'

I hear the anger in my voice, but I can't help it. I'm drunk and I'm furious at this man that I don't even know. The Outlaw nods his head once and I can see him watching me warily, wondering what a drunken Irishwoman is doing wanting to sit at his table. But perhaps I'm not the first drunken Irishwoman that has asked to sit at his table. I ignore the look he's giving me and set my bottle and glass down. His eyes go to the whiskey's label and I see his nose crinkle slightly at the sight of it as he rolls up a cigarette. The man must've tasted all the whiskeys St Brigid's has to offer to know my choice is the worst. He lifts the rolled-up paper to his mouth and licks a line along it, sealing it closed and his eyes raise up to me when he realises I'm watching him, scowling at him.

'Cigarette, ma'am?' His voice is deeper than I expected, kinder. His accent immediately stands out. So it's not just a name — he is American.

'No... thank you.' I'm somewhat taken aback by him and my mind is so foggy from drink that it's hard for me to recover from it.

The Outlaw doesn't ask me what I want from him and neither does he tell me to piss off. He starts to smoke his cigarette, having lit it with a match that he struck against the edge of his boot. I finish my drink off and refill my glass. He looks at me again.

'You been enjoying the fights, ma'am?'

'They're a little too violent for my likes,' I say honestly.

He gives me a slight smile, but it's grim and it makes him look incredibly sad. 'I'll admit, they ain't meant to entertain ladies.' His eyes pass over the room. 'But some still enjoy it... The women in this country are a little hardier than the women in mine.'

'That so? And what of the men?'

He takes a sip of his drink, not meeting my gaze. 'Jury's still out.'

The demon on my shoulder digs its claws in and suddenly takes a hold of me and I begin to tell him everything, knowing I need to, that this is its request. I know I'm rambling and I know that as every second passes by, I can see him looking for an escape, wishing he hadn't started a conversation with me. People in Galway City know what I'm like. Most of them give me a wide berth these days, but this man doesn't know me, didn't know to avert his gaze and pretend I didn't exist when I approached him and for a moment I feel sorry for him.

'My husband went to Wyoming,' I say, voice trembling. 'To build a ranch... close to a city called Cheyenne.'

He nods, frowning. 'Heard of the place.'

I raise my chin at him, hating the tears that are scratching at the back of my throat. 'He died. Murdered by a gang.'

The Outlaw is silent for a moment. Perhaps he's trying to figure out why I'm telling him all this. I'm not in control. Drink has clouded my mind and the demon is still hissing its request in my ear.

'Sorry to hear that,' he finally says, raising his gaze to meet mine. 'My country's beautiful, yet it can be mighty unforgiving.'

I don't wish for his pity and neither do I want to hear his words. I clench my teeth and my voice wavers out from behind them.

'Were you in a gang, sir? Is that why they call you the Outlaw?'

It's like he finally connects the dots and I see him shift in his chair. He leans back and takes a long drag of his cigarette, the end flaming red for a good few seconds. He breathes out, but it's more like a sigh and smoke plumes above his head.

'What's your name, ma'am?' he asks me.

'Ms Ryan.'

He nods. 'Ms Ryan, I think you should go home. Go to sleep and forget about ever coming here.'

'No.'

The Outlaw watches me intently. I see his jaw tense underneath his beard. I'm ready for a fight. I'm ready to spit and claw if I have to. I sit up straighter in my chair, preparing myself.

'What d'you want, Ms Ryan?'

There it is.

'I want to see the men that killed my husband, hang.'

His eyes tense at the sides. 'What do I have to do with that?'

I know I'm drunk and I know I'm not making much sense to him because I'm not making much sense to myself. But I'm filled with emotions and a motive so strong I can't ignore it any longer. That demon is at my ear again, growling out an order.

'I want to go to your country. I want to find these men and make sure they meet their justice. I want you to come with me.'

The Outlaw stares at me. It looks like he's almost about to laugh or burst out in a fit of anger. My fingers clench against my knees under the table.

'Why not just ask a sheriff or a bounty hunter when you're over there? That's what they're there for,' he finally says.

'The authorities over there have done nothing in three years. If you're an outlaw, you would have ridden with other outlaws, yes? You know them, you know how they think and where they might hide and when backed in a corner, you know how they'd react.'

He picks up his glass of whiskey and finishes it in one go. And then he puts it back down with a loud thud and stands up, his chair almost knocking over underneath him.

'Have a good night, Ms Ryan. Go get some sleep.'

He starts to turn away and I stand as well, going after him.

'Wait!'

He ignores me, weaving through the crowd.

'Sir!'

We've caught the attention of a few of the patrons in the bar and they begin to snicker and mutter, but I'm too far gone to care.

I reach the Outlaw before he gets to the stairwell that leads to the rooms upstairs.

'Stop!'

He puts one foot on the first step and turns, looking at me. I'm breathing hard, my head spinning. I can barely stand up without feeling the need to sit back down, so I reach out and grasp onto the railing of the stairwell to steady myself. He looks at me and I see pity in his eyes and I hate it. I hate him. I want to strangle him and force him to come with me, force him to be a good person for once in his life. I sniff, pushing back tears and close my eyes.

'I don't want to have to beg.'

'Ms Ryan…' I open my eyes and look at him. 'Go and get some sleep.'

Without another word, he makes his way up the stairs and I stand there staring after him, the tears I've been desperately trying to hold back, breaking through. I force back a sob and head up the stairs to my room. When I'm inside, I fall onto my bed and weep until I can weep no more.

3

I don't know what I was thinking. To believe that an American man who may have once been an outlaw would agree to help me hunt down and bring justice to the men that killed Thomas. I must be mad. The grief I've been keeping at bay for three years must have slowly curdled my brains, turning me into nothing but a sorry excuse for a woman, scornful towards the world and everything within it. There is no other explanation because to have such an outlandish expectation of a complete stranger is only something a mad person would conjure up.

The tram home is only a short ride back and yet it feels like I've entered another world — a world familiar and yet incredibly painful to me. I don't go home immediately and instead walk along the Corrib, watching the water rush below, tumultuous and rapid. I feel stupid. I feel so incredibly stupid and embarrassed. Whatever monsters and demons put ideas inside of my aching and drunk head, they are nothing but negative thoughts, backwards and empty. I know I went about everything the wrong way and made a fool of myself, but I can't help but continue to believe I cannot be content until the Gaitwood gang is hanging by a noose from the gallows. I want to see it with my own eyes and something keeps telling me that is the only way I'm going to find peace over Thomas' death. That every day I go on feeling sorry for myself, I am doing him a disservice because he continues to die in vain each day that goes past where I do nothing. Those thoughts inside my head are as tumultuous as the rapids beneath my feet, a bumbling mess, constantly divided between what's the best thing for me.

Each time I think about the Outlaw, my stomach feels sick and my mind revolts at the thought of him, immediately wishing to think of something else. I regret even asking him, showing such a weakness in front of a man I disliked as soon as I set eyes on him. That was never my intention and I can't help blame myself for being so messy, letting myself get to a point where I was close to begging a total stranger for help.

I rub my face with my hands, feeling how cold they are against my cheeks that burn with shame. When I make it home, I go inside and take off my coat and light the hearth. I'm not hungry and yet my stomach rumbles. I make myself a cup of coffee and while the pot is heating up, I go over to Thomas' chair and slowly drag it back over to the fire. When my coffee is done, I sit down in my husband's chair and drink, watching the flames.

⊢•─◦─•⊣

He traced a pattern across my bare shoulder, gazing down at my face with a small smile on his lips. I looked at his hair, relishing in the fact it was messy and not smooth and perfectly set like it always was. We'd made love just as the sun was beginning to rise outside our window and we lay there afterwards, sweating limbs tangled under the sheets. He always held me after, murmuring sweet nothings and watching me as if I meant the world to him. And I knew it was because I did.

'How is it that you're so beautiful?'

'How is it that you're so full of shite?'

He laughed and kissed my nose. And then he kissed my mouth softly, his smile slowly fading against my lips. 'You know I'll send word, don't you? When it's time for you to move over?'

'I just don't see how I can't come with you now,' I murmured, my heart wrenching in my chest. I hated that he'd reminded me of his departure in such a lovely, quiet moment. For just that moment, I'd forgotten he was leaving me and it had felt beautiful, like when we were younger.

'We need someone to look after the business, darling Blair.'

'That's what Martin is for.' I grabbed the back of his neck and pressed my forehead to his, my fingers entering his hair. I kissed him. 'We can build the ranch together. It'll be an adventure.'

'We would be living in a hotel room for a year,' he laughed. 'It would be horrible and uncomfortable and you would end up hating me. Martin needs help here. I'll be fine.'

'I've heard the natives don't very much like people like us.'

'The Indians?' he asked.

I nodded.

'As far as I can tell, they've been put into encampments across the country. The government keeps a firm grip on them.'

'That doesn't sound very nice.'

He shook his head, mouth turned downwards in a grimace. 'It doesn't. If anything, we should be more worried about the people of our own race than the natives.'

'*You* should be worried,' I corrected. 'I'm not going there yet.'

He grinned at me and kissed me once more. 'When you sweep in, they'll have naught but their dignities left to defend themselves against your wrath.'

'You're wrong, Thomas dear,' I said, accepting his kisses and drawing him closer to me with my thighs, 'their dignities are what I go for first.'

Ryan's Distillery is only a few streets away from home. It's an old brick building, tall and large, taking up almost a block on the street it towers over. Seeing it puts a heavy stone in the pit of my stomach, but I gather myself and head up the metal steps at the side and go in through the door. The place smells the way Thomas used to smell coming home from work, only stronger and it immediately makes me remember holding him in my arms, burying my nose into his shoulder. It's a mixture of peat smoke and something sweeter, honeyed and smooth across the back of the palette. My stomach twists as I make my way across the metal mezzanine and to the office where I can see Martin through the window, sitting at his desk. I go in and take off my coat, setting it on one of the chairs at the desks that crowd the office.

Martin glances up from the ledger he's been inspecting and I see the surprise on his face when he realises it's me.

'Decided to come in, hm?'

I nod. 'Not really sure why, to be honest with you, Mr O'Hughe.'

'Where have you been this past week?'

'Salthill.'

He blinks. 'Having a holiday?'

'Just needed to get out of the city.'

He doesn't say anything and closes the ledger with a sigh. 'Well, it's good to see you're alright. You know Thomas would have wanted me to look out for you and that's why I'm always on your back about things—'

I hold up a hand, tired. It's strange how this man can drain my energy almost as soon as I come into contact with him. 'You don't need to explain yourself, Martin.'

He closes his mouth and shrugs. After a moment's silence, he waves his hands about the place, agitated.

'Well... you know what to do. And a lot needs doing.'

<hr />

The Salmon Leap is quieter than usual tonight. I don't mind it as I have a headache from dealing with Martin and all I want to do is sit at my table in the corner and drink whiskey much more terrible than the one I've been brewing all day. How Thomas would laugh at me to see me stooping so low. Benjamin would give me a bottle for free if I drank Ryan's but I cannot bring myself to. It's too much like Thomas; the flavour, the smell, the name. So many memories in every one of those bottles we sell, none that our customers will ever come to understand.

I drink by myself until well past midnight and then I head home, blurry-visioned and numb.

⊷⊶

Three weeks pass without me even realising. I go to the distillery on most days and supervise the men there, keeping the books up to date and ignoring Martin as much as possible. After work, I go to the Salmon Leap and each day is exactly the same; a mess of complete and utter banality that I can hardly tell the difference between Tuesdays and Sundays.

I manage to notice that spring seems to be coming to an end. More and more tourists flock to Galway City and I see them every day riding the tram out to Salthill; their hats bright, outfits colourful, faces full of smiles. Even the salmon show up and the sounds of the crowds laughing and cheering on the fishermen and fish alike can be heard all over the city. It's a sound I used to love, a sound I used to be a part of, standing on the bridge and looking out at the silver bodies in the water. But now those laughs and cheers might as well be wails and screams. It brings that much pain.

I find myself skipping work one day and staying in the house. I clean it up as best I can and cook myself a lunch of fried fish and potatoes with thyme. It crackles and spits in the pan on the hearth and I take comfort in the smell of it, reminding me of the days when I used to cook all the time. I finish my lunch and tidy the kitchen up. I'm scrubbing down the bench when there's a knock at the door and I curse under my breath at Martin for being so pedantic about my whereabouts. I'm sweating from my work, sleeves rolled up to my elbows, my hair falling out of its clip around my face, but I don't bother to present myself for him. Lord knows he's seen me in a much worse state than this. I go down the little hallway towards the front door and open it.

The man standing on my doorstep isn't Martin at all. He's wearing a coat and hat this time and it's a type of hat I've never really seen before, made with fine leather. It's marred by obvious years of use and there's a circular hole in the brim at the back.

'Ms Ryan,' the Outlaw says to me, flicking the brim of his hat in greeting.

My defences go up immediately, hackles rising. A very small part of me is glad to see him, but the other part, the larger part, wants to tear out his eyes and curse him for thinking it was acceptable to come to my house like this.

'How do you know where I live?' I ask without returning his greeting.

'It seems Ryan is a popular name in Galway City.' He looks around the street and then back at me, pressing his lips. His face is so serious, as if etched into stone by a meticulous artist. 'Sorry, I don't wanna intrude.'

'Well, you're doing just that,' I growl. I realise I'm furious with him and it makes me angrier to realise I'm also furious with myself about what happened between us. I go to close the door, wanting to block it all out, but he raises a hand and stops me.

'Ma'am, I ain't here to do anything other than offer my help.'

I laugh. It sounds so ridiculous. 'No, sir, you made it very clear at St Brigid's that you didn't wish to give it.'

'I changed my mind.' We stare at one another for a moment. I feel a drop of sweat roll down my spine under my dress. 'I did some thinking and... I'll help you.'

'Why?'

He squints at me under the brim of his hat. There's a length of braided rope tied around the middle of it, worn and fraying at the ends.

'Let's talk,' he says finally. 'Preferably somewhere that ain't your doorstep.'

I raise my brows at him, but I can feel myself considering it.

At least hear what he has to say.

I lick my lips and reply, 'Come in, then. But if you try anything funny, I'll have you tied up across Salmon Weir Bridge by your entrails for all those damned tourists to see. You have my word on that.'

His smile is grim and tiny. He nods. 'Yes, ma'am.'

I close the door behind him when he steps inside and warily lead him into my kitchen. He must immediately notice the chair that I've pulled up before the hearth fire because I see him watching it, taking in its dilapidated silhouette. I grumble something about sitting at the dining table and he follows me to it at the back of the kitchen. The room is hot and stuffy, so I open the shutter to the window by the table and a cool, slightly damp breeze comes in from outside. The Outlaw has sat down already, but I haven't yet and I can see him taking me in, eyes intent. I go to the stove and put on a pot of coffee. I don't really wish to treat this man like a guest, but my instincts have kicked in before I can even consider denying him my hospitality.

'Coffee?' I say from the stove without looking at him.

'Please.'

There's a tense silence between us as the pot bubbles by the flames, the metal lid clanking as it begins to shake. When it's ready, I pour out two cups and take them over to the table. I sit down across from him and start to drink, silent. I don't know what to say to him. I suppose I don't have to say anything as he's the one that's come all the way from Salthill to tell me something. I'm about to look at him expectantly, telling him I don't have all day, when he glances up from his cup and clears his throat.

'You caught me at a bad time when you saw me at St Brigid's.'

'Clearly.' I don't wish to leave any room for manners towards this man.

His eyes harden slightly at my venom, but he doesn't comment on it and instead says, 'Or maybe the thought process I went through after you left addled my brains.'

'What was that exactly?' I ask him. 'This thought process?'

He takes his time to answer. It makes me wonder whether he really knows it himself. I can't help but notice how whatever he's thinking about has completely changed his demeanour. His shoulders slacken and his eyes grow dark, mouth turning downwards as if he's tasted something bitter.

'I guess I felt sorry for you,' he says honestly after a moment.

My gut wrenches with fury and shame. 'I didn't go to Salthill seeking your *pity*, sir.'

'I realise that,' he murmurs, shaking his head. 'There are other reasons why I wanna help you now, but they're personal and they ain't particularly any of your business.' His brows raise slightly. 'All I wanna know is whether you're still needing my help, that's all.'

I consider it. I wonder what saying yes will bring. A trip to America — a purpose in life, finally. Whatever will happen, I'll make sure I see the Gaitwood gang go down.

'Trips to America aren't cheap,' I say quietly.

'I know. I came from there.' His eyes watch me amusedly. 'Fighting at Brigid's has gotten me a pretty sum of money. I won't have any issues.'

'You'll need to pay for yourself.' I stick my chin up defiantly. 'I know I'm asking for your help, but I don't wish to spend my life savings on myself as well as you.'

'Fair.'

'We might be gone a while.'

His eyes narrow on my face. 'Am I hearing correctly, ma'am, or are you tryna talk me outta helping you just after asking for it in the first place?'

'No,' I growl defensively. 'I'm only just starting to consider how big this decision is.'

'Your husband died, yeah?' he asks, voice quiet now, gentler. 'Killed by a gang?'

I nod sadly. Anything I was going to say to him dies at the back of my throat.

He's watching me and I can see the sorry he was talking about before in his eyes. I want to reach across the table and slap him across the face.

'I think y'know what you need to do, ma'am, but I ain't gonna be the one to tell you what's what.'

He's right. It is up to me whether I really want to go through with this. I think about the past three years wasting away, drowning my sorrow at the Salmon Leap and hating the world for taking away the only man I've ever loved and every aspect of hope with him. I know what the right thing to do is, or at least the thing that my heart is telling me to do. An anxiety I've never felt before suddenly dawns on me and my heart stutters in my chest. I can feel my fingers drumming on the table beside my cup of coffee, playing a rhythm to that anxiousness. The Outlaw's eyes go to them. His eyes are so intent — every time he looks at me, it's like he's looking *into* me, seeing everything that has shaped me. And maybe that's why he agreed to help, because he saw me for what I am, a sorry excuse for a woman with nothing behind her but a life that she can no longer enjoy. Not until those men are dead.

'What's your name, sir?' I ask him, breaking from my thoughts.

I still don't even know who this man is other than he fights at a pub and wins. If I'm going to be going to America with him,

I might as well know his name, if not anything else, about him.

'McCarthy,' he says. 'Colin McCarthy.'

An Irish name.

'Well, Mr McCarthy,' I say. 'Let us go to America and see what that sorry place brings us.'

4

We buy our tickets for room on a ship that will leave Galway Bay and sail to Ellis Island in New York in a week's time. In that week I plan our trip, pack my bags and slowly tidy the house, packing away things of Thomas' that I never thought I'd pack away. Mr McCarthy stays in a hotel in the city close by and I seldom see him in that week, not really wanting to either. I notice him one night drinking at the Salmon Leap, but I don't go and talk to him and neither does he come over to my table and strike up a conversation. Even though we're going on a trip to America together, we treat one another like total strangers, simply because we are total strangers. I gain a little bit of respect for him, glad he's at least on the same page as I am and that, if anything, gives me hope this trip with this man might not be as difficult as I thought.

Martin visits three days before I leave. He doesn't want to know much about my intentions on leaving and what I expect to do over there. I think he can't stand the thought of me going to avenge his cousin's death with nothing but my crazed wits and sharp tongue. He probably finds it amusing in a dark way, and yet he doesn't object.

'Do what you want to do,' he says tiredly. 'I'm done with trying to stop you, trying to protect you. If Thomas is looking down on this, yelling at the both of us, so be it.' He waves a hand dismissively.

I've only just let him into my house and he already looks ready to leave.

'I have to do something, Martin. That damned marshal has done nothing for us. Thomas can't rest in peace while those men are out there. *I* can't—'

'I know.' He shakes his head at me. 'I no longer have the energy to care, Blair. Do what you must. I will hire someone to help me supervise the business in your stead while you're gone.' He sighs and adds in a small voice, 'If we can bloody afford it.'

'I'll send word,' I promise him. *Or maybe I won't. Who knows?*

I could die out there, just like Thomas did, and Martin would be none the wiser. Even the man I'm going with could kill me without a single thought. My body left in a ditch on the side of the road out in the middle of nowhere, a feast for vultures, and nobody would know. I try not to think of that. This trip, this task that I've set out for myself, has given me a purpose in life that I haven't felt in three years. I must do it, whether I die trying or not, I must have the men who killed my husband hang.

⊶◦⊷

The day before the ship is supposed to leave, Mr McCarthy knocks on my door again. I've covered all the furniture with sheets of cloth, including Thomas' chair, and he looks about the barren kitchen as if he's stepped into another realm. I offer him a cup of coffee, mostly because I don't know what to say to break the silence between us, but he declines.

'Just here to find out when and where to meet ya,' he explains. He hasn't taken off his hat indoors and the shadows of the room are playing over the shadow the hat has cast across his face, so I can barely see it without squinting.

I go to where I've put the paperwork on the kitchen table and flick through it. The tickets are there, mine and his.

'The liner will be sailing out of Dún Aengus dock,' I explain, 'at six forty-five in the morning. I'll meet you at the dock, say about six?'

He nods. 'Sounds good.'

There's a short silence between us again and I don't know what else to say. But then he nods his head once more and taps the brim of his hat with his finger, giving me a quiet *ma'am* before heading back out to the door. I watch him leave, the tickets still in my hands. All I can think of is, how am I going to get along and trust this man? I start to wonder whether I've made the right choice and yet I know it's too late. I'm in this and I have to remind myself I'm doing it for Thomas. It *has* to be done and the fact that nothing has been done for three years means I must be the one to do it. I know I can't be content until these men are dead.

The morning brings fog and a slight rise in humidity so that my walk down to the docks is uncomfortable. I try to say goodbye to the familiar streets, the old and looming buildings I've come to know as silent friends, even the people whose faces have grown familiar to me after all these years, but the fog is so thick and the bags in my hands weigh me down. I'm soon sweating under my coat.

Luckily it's only a short walk to the docks and I see the ship we're leaving upon, *The Sovereign*, as tall as the dock's buildings and yet grander, more formidable. People are dashing about the place, passengers and workmen alike and there's already a line starting at where the ship has pulled down its gangplank. Men in uniform stand about and some of them are already taking bags from passengers and double-checking cabins on their tickets.

And then I see him by a building that's closest to where the ship is docked, away from the crowds. He's leaning against the stone wall, smoking a cigarette, his eyes intent under the brim of his hat on the goings-on of the people we'll be spending more than a week with on board. It's as if he senses me coming towards him, as he throws his cigarette to the ground and uses the heel of his boot to grind it into the floor, looking up at me just before I reach him. I see only one bag at his feet and my eyes lift to his face. The bruise that was under his eye when I first met him has faded completely now. There's no more damage to his face because he hasn't been fighting and I'm a little surprised by this, having imagined him to be a man constantly gripped by bloodlust, seeking it wherever he went. Mr McCarthy pulls a pocket-watch out of the pocket in his waistcoat — a simple linen piece that's as plain as all the other clothing I've seen him wear — and flips it open, checking the time. Perhaps he thinks I'm a few minutes late.

'You ready?' he asks me, putting the watch away.

'I think so.'

'Got the tickets?'

I've never known a man so eager to shorten his sentences as much as Mr McCarthy. It's as if time is precious to him and he sees no use in wasting it by saying a few more words to appear more intelligent, or at least a man of leisure and conversation.

'Yes, they're here.' I drop a bag to pull them out of my coat's pocket and he reaches out to take them, but I move them away from his grasp. 'I'll hold onto them if you don't mind, Mr McCarthy.'

He watches me for a little while and then he says quietly, 'Not at all, ma'am.'

There isn't any need for me to prove to him I don't trust him, but at the same time I'd rather he knows. I'm sure he doesn't trust me either and that is fine, too. As long as we can get to America and get done what needs to be done, I don't care if he hates me by the end of it. We're not going across the Atlantic to become friends and to come out the other side of this task as trusting allies. We're going on my terms and my terms only. And avenging Thomas' death is what we'll do, nothing else.

We join the line that starts at the gangplank and weaves all the way down the side of the dock. Steam is pluming out of *The Sovereign*'s three chimneys. There are tall masts on either end of the ship and on them fly the colours of our countries — an Irish flag at the stern, an American flag at the bow. The line starts to move as people begin to board. I notice horses, crates of cargo and a few wagons are being loaded at the back of the ship, into a cargo hold at the centre. When we reach the steward, we're shown where we need to walk to find our rooms and then Mr McCarthy and I are guided up the gangplank. The inside of the ship is mostly creams and whites and red carpeted hallways that weave this way and that, lit by electric lights that buzz and flicker on the walls. The rooms are numbered with plaques and we move through the crowded hallways until we reach the numbers we've been given. Mr McCarthy and I are in the same room and when we go in, there's an elderly couple already unpacking their bags inside. They look up and Mr McCarthy greets them quietly.

'Oh, it's good to meet you both,' the old man says happily. He introduces himself as Miles Howell and his wife as Agnes. An English couple headed out to visit their family in New York. They've taken both the bunks on either side of the walls and are already using the cabinet that's been provided for our clothes. 'Is it alright if Agnes and I use the bottom bunks? I'm afraid we're not as young and chipper as you both to climb all the way to the top.'

'Of course,' I say. I put my bag on the top bunk, above where Agnes is sorting through her bags.

'Sorry, they don't give us much room in here,' she laughs. 'The cabinet—'

'It's alright. Ms Ryan and I are happy to live out of our bags for the next week,' Mr McCarthy says.

I look at him, mouth screwed. I would rather sort through my bags and have a clear order of them, but I relent and say nothing, giving them a small nod.

'So what are a couple like you going to America for? Off to start a new life in the New Country?' Miles asks, smiling.

'Something like that,' Mr McCarthy says before I can answer.

The room is tiny and already it's beginning to feel too crowded for me. I move out, telling them I want to watch my country as we sail away. I weave my way through the hallways until I notice a sign pointing to a set of stairs that will take me up onto the deck. There are already people up here, looking out over the edge of the ship as it blows its horn. I find a spot by the railing, facing towards the city and gaze out at it. I can see the smoke rising above the buildings in the direction of the distillery and my gut clenches.

I'm doing this for you, Thomas.

There's a rumbling noise as the propellers begin to turn and I can see the water frothing and licking at the side of the boat. *The Sovereign* begins to slowly move out of port and I can see people standing at the dock, waving up at us as they smile and cheer. People beside me on the ship wave back and yet I have no urge to lift my hand in farewell. My heart feels sore and all of a sudden I feel close to tears. Someone stands beside me at the railing and I smell the smoke from a cigarette.

'Didn't think I'd be going back again,' Mr McCarthy says, voice low.

I don't say anything, too overcome with a mixture of emotions to form any words. Even if I could — if my throat didn't feel so constricted by tears — I don't think I know what I'd tell him. As Ireland grows further and further away, people begin to lose interest in the novelty of saying goodbye and leave, going about their activities aboard the ship. But Mr McCarthy and I stand there for much longer, as the sun rises further and further into the sky, and until Ireland is nothing but a speck upon the glowing horizon.

I find the bar easily after lunch, where we ate in the large dining room, served with corned beef and vegetables. The bar sits in the middle of the ship, a floor above where Mr McCarthy and I will be sleeping for the next week. I lost him just before lunch time and haven't seen him since, not really caring where he is. I don't trust him, but I trust him enough to not run off on me after the agreement we've made. I don't see any point in him going back home just to run away from me when he came all the way out to Ireland in the first place.

The bar is a small, dim room filled with a cloud of cigarette smoke. It's all mahogany and dark wallpaper and there's a woman singing with a man playing the piano in the corner to entertain the people having after lunch drinks. I spot Mr McCarthy immediately, sitting up at the bar, leaning against it, a glass of whiskey cradled in his arms. His hat is still on and his head is bowed as if in deep thought. I feel somewhat taken aback seeing him and then a rush of annoyance towards the man hits me. I wished to drink in peace and now, I won't be able to. The barman greets me when I walk up and I slide him a few coins when I order. I see Mr McCarthy's head lift in the corner of my eye and I know he's watching me now. Perhaps he wonders if I've even seen him, but I don't look his way and take my drinks to a table at the back of the room. The woman is still singing and her voice is light and airy, circling the room, hand-in-hand with the smoke from cigars and cigarettes. I drink. My stomach cramps, upset over how little I ate.

It doesn't take Mr McCarthy long to decide to come over to me. He sits down in the chair across from mine. I keep my gaze on my glass, ignoring him. He finishes his drink and then goes about rolling up a cigarette.

'What's the plan?' he asks me once he's got the cigarette lit and is breathing smoke out of his nostrils like some mythical creature.

I'm playing with my glass on the tabletop, rolling it between my fingers as I watch the golden liquid inside roll about languidly. I ordered an American whiskey and was glad to see Ryan's isn't on the menu. The whiskey is different to anything I've tasted. It's smooth and like honey, but with a spicy tang and a residual heat that sits at the back of my throat when I swallow.

'We'll go from New York to Chicago. And from Chicago to Cheyenne. That's the route my husband took.'

'You wanna see your ranch first?'

I nod. 'I want to see what could have been... and the place where he was killed. And... the marshal said he's buried in Cheyenne's graveyard. I wish to pay my respects.'

'How you gonna find these men if the marshal can't?'

I look up at him finally. His eyes are squinted slightly and his mouth is pressed in a firm line. I see the doubt written all over his face and it offends me so greatly that I feel a rage begin to bubble at my chest, burning deep within.

'*You*,' I tell him, 'that's why I'm bringing *you* with me. We'll speak to the marshal and he'll be able to tell us where these men were last seen.'

'What if he can't?'

'Then I'll tear up the countryside until I find them,' I growl. 'I know the name of the gang and I'll keep asking until I find them. The Gaitwoods are going to be history when I'm finished with them.'

I see something in his face change, but he ducks his head before I can tell what it is. He shrugs his shoulders a little and takes a drag on his cigarette. Two plumes of smoke rise up past both sides of his hanging head. A thought strikes me, brought on by his sudden different demeanour and alarm bells start to ring inside my head.

'Do I have to be worried, Mr McCarthy?' I ask him. 'About you?'

He looks up at me. 'What d'you mean?'

'*The American Outlaw,*' I gesture to him with my hand. 'Why were you in Ireland? Are you running away from a bounty or what?'

I don't know why I've waited until we're on the boat to ask him this, but it's too late now.

'You don't have to be worried, ma'am.' He neither confirms nor denies. That's all he says.

I narrow my eyes at him and he continues to watch me, as if challenging me with his stare. The rage inside me stirs again, I can feel it in my chest. I finish off the drinks sitting in front of me and stand up.

'If you make me regret bringing you with me, I will make sure you hang right alongside these Gaitwood men. You have my word on that,' I tell him, voice deadly.

'I said I'd help you.' There's an edge to his voice that stops me. He meets my gaze, eyes dark. 'So I'm gonna help you. Just keep your nose outta my business, lady.'

'Don't *lady* me, you bastard,' I hiss. A few people look up, surprised by my outburst, but Mr McCarthy doesn't even flinch. I go to turn away, but then I remember one more thing that annoyed me from before. 'And don't let people think we're a couple here, out to fetch a life together in the *New Country*. I don't exactly wish to be seen as a woman who'd be dumb enough to marry the likes of *you*.'

I leave before he can fire back, not that I see on his face that he intends to. I keep walking, my head pounding and my heart aching in my chest, until I'm at the other end of the boat, looking out at the ship's wake. It's a turmoil of water and foam, waves crashing into one another and it reminds me of the Corrib, of home and of Thomas. I want to scream. I want to close my eyes and block out everything in the world, including my thoughts. Especially my thoughts. I no longer want to be Blair Ryan — a widow who has nothing left in her life but a business that is too painful, too full of memories to manage. Jumping off the end of the boat and drowning myself amongst the rapids would be easier. Even letting myself get sucked into the propellers would take the weight of the world off my shoulders and my life with it. I've thought about it before, back in Galway City, especially when the wound from Thomas' death was still fresh. Finding a gun and shooting myself, running out in front of a wagon in the street or even making my way out to the Cliffs of Moher and walking straight off their rocky edge.

My hands grasp the railing. It would be so easy to climb over the other side and leap into oblivion. But a small voice inside me tells me I can't. That I have things to do and such a long life ahead of me if I only keep trying. I must take it day by day, as I have been ever since Thomas died. I must keep pushing on because no matter how hard dealing with the pain is, it's a reminder I'm lucky enough to still be breathing and Thomas isn't. To take my life would be to insult his memory.

5

On day three into the trip, the skies are clear and the ocean is smooth. The ship cuts quickly through the water like nothing I've seen before and the boat seldom rocks amongst the waves. I've gained my sea legs easily and I wonder whether it's due to years of going out on the boat as a child with my father that has attributed to the skill. I know Mr McCarthy is feeling ill, but he doesn't show it and neither do I really care. I'm still livid at him over the words that passed between us. But not just that. I feel like I've always had a sense of resentment towards the man without really knowing why, other than having the basic knowledge that he's most likely killed and thieved before in order to obtain the name *The Outlaw*. He isn't really a man I want to know and yet he was the man I chose to help me catch the Gaitwood gang and he agreed to do so. I must put aside any hatred towards him and focus on my goal.

Sleeping in our cramped little room with the Howell couple is no luxury. Mr Howell snores and his wife hardly sleeps at all, getting up several times during the night to go to the bathroom. The sound of her shuffling about, opening and closing the door to the cabin, gets on my nerves, but I say nothing as I know even if the room were quiet, I'd still lie awake thinking. I don't know whether Mr McCarthy sleeps or not. He's always silent in the bunk across the room from mine, still as a granite statue while Mr Howell rattles the framework of the bunk with his snoring from below. Other than that, the couple are nice enough and they often invite me to eat our meals together. They invite Mr McCarthy too and on the odd occasion he accepts, but often he's gone in the morning before they're even awake. I know he keeps his distance from me because I have requested it, with the way I look at him and treat him. For now, it's easy enough being on a large ship as we are, but I know eventually he'll be beside me at all times, while we travel across America and there won't be any escaping him. I'll have to get used to his quiet presence.

On day five I'm breakfasting with the Howells in the dining room. Light is filtering in through the windows from outside and the deck is lit up by sun. People walk along it, men wearing hats and women holding parasols to give them shade. There's a lovely salty breeze coming in through some of the open windows and the air is relaxed, the ocean smooth as glass beneath us. I've gotten myself a plate of eggs and toast with a cup of coffee, finally having an appetite to eat. There's a bowl of fruit on the table between us and Mrs Howell takes little nibbles of her sliced pear. Mr Howell smokes a pipe, sitting across from me. He's a stout man and the hair that's left on his head is grey and curly. Mrs Howell is just as stout and grey, but her eyes are a deep brown and they look younger than her wrinkled skin.

'Will you be staying in New York for long?' she asks me. I've already told them about our plan of getting to Cheyenne, but nothing more than that. They most likely believe Mr McCarthy and I are a couple, looking to start a life together out in the middle of the country. They don't question why I wear a Claddagh ring — the wedding ring Thomas gave me — or why Mr McCarthy and I have different last names. They're too polite to ask.

'I don't think so,' I say honestly.

'It would be lovely if you two came and met our family there,' she adds. 'We're planning on having a big get-together and the more the merrier, as they say!'

I smile as kindly as I can at her and take a sip of coffee, not too sure what to say. I don't really want to go meet with a bunch of strangers when I have better things to do. I've never been good with people, always more of a recluse and liking it that way and I don't know what Mr McCarthy is like either. He seems charming enough and the Howells appear to like him a lot, but even then, he has an air that's frightening and would most likely put civilised folk on edge.

'Mr McCarthy and I are unfortunately on a strict schedule. We'll most likely be getting the first train out of New York to Chicago,' I explain. 'As much as we appreciate the offer.'

'Ah, speak of the devil and he shall appear!' Mr Howell exclaims, gripping the pipe with his teeth as he does.

I turn and see Mr McCarthy coming towards us. He looks better today than most of the days I've seen him aboard the ship. Perhaps he's looked out to the horizon and gotten his bearings. Mr McCarthy nods in greeting to us and sits down in the available seat next to mine. We don't meet one another's eye and to the Howells, we most likely look like shy lovers. It makes me sick to even think this, but I guess having them think we're together is better than having them know a young woman is travelling to another country with a strange, most likely dangerous man.

'How are you feeling today, dear?' Mrs Howell asks him. 'You looked a little green yesterday.'

'Better, thank you, ma'am,' he says.

She chuckles. 'Oh, I could never get used to that accent. So charming.'

Mr McCarthy takes a spare cup from the table and pours himself coffee out of the pot. I watch him out of the corner of my eye as I eat. He's still wearing his hat and his arms are sun-kissed all the way up to where his sleeves are rolled to his elbows.

'Settle, Agnes,' Mr Howell says, amused. 'We were just offering Ms Ryan here a night at our daughter's place when you reach New York,' he tells Mr McCarthy. 'It'll be a jolly event.'

Mr McCarthy glances at me. 'Well, that's up to Ms Ryan here.'
The couple nod their heads, looking at me expectantly.

'We'll see,' I end up saying, because I'm sick of them asking when I barely know what we're going to do when we step on American soil myself. All I want is to get to Cheyenne as soon as possible.

I eat a slice of apple, the sweetness clearing my palette. I want something stronger. My stomach clenches for whiskey. But I keep sipping at my coffee in silence as Mr McCarthy and the Howells chatter.

'So where in America were you born, Mr McCarthy?' Mrs Howell asks him.

'Missouri, ma'am.'

'How old are you, dear? Did your mother live through the war?'

He's silent for a moment and then he says, 'Yes ma'am, she did. I was born in 1863, in the midst of it all.'

Mr Howell is smoking on his pipe thoughtfully. I'm still watching Mr McCarthy out of the corner of my eye. He's rigid in his seat and I can tell he wants to change the subject. But I'm also surprised to find out Mr McCarthy is seven years my senior. He appears to be older than his thirty-five years.

'The weather outside is nice today,' I say quickly. 'Perhaps you would benefit from a walk out on the deck in the sunshine?'

'Only if you come along with us,' Mrs Howell says with a smile.

I nod my head. Anything to get out of the chair beside Mr McCarthy, who's still sitting there as if awaiting trial. We rise from the table after we've finished eating and head through the doors onto the deck. The sun is warm and the breeze is cool enough for it to be a comfortable temperature to go for a walk. The Howells walk in front of us, arm in arm and Mr McCarthy and I follow at the rear.

'Thank you,' he says suddenly, voice quiet.

'Don't mention it... really.' I glance at him. 'I hardly care for sitting about a table at breakfast learning about your life when I could be outside enjoying the fresh air.'

'It appears we have that in common.' There's a hard edge to his voice now, as if he's tasting something bitter just by being in my presence. 'I'm not the type to go sharing my story with strangers.'

'Good,' I say defensively. 'I don't think many people *care*.'

'Mrs Howell obviously does, for her to ask.'

'She was just being polite. Have you not heard the questions she asks me? She barely pays attention when I'm answering them. Same goes for you.'

'You can despise me all you like, Ms Ryan, but I do wanna help you. I'm not going back to the country I ran away from for any other reason.'

'I find that hard to believe.' I stop walking and he stops too. We look at each other. He's taller than me and wider and so much more imposing, but I stand my ground easily. He doesn't scare me. 'There must be some secret motive of yours to agree to it. I've begun to believe no man in his right mind would accept such a request from a widow.'

'And no woman in her right mind would request such a thing, *ma'am*.'

I smile bitterly. 'Ah,' I say. 'That's just it. I'm not in my right mind, Mr McCarthy. And at least I can admit that.'

The Howells are walking in front of us arm-in-arm and they haven't noticed we've stopped, glowering at one another. I can see the look in Mr McCarthy's eyes has changed and there's a small semblance of pity in them and it makes me hate him even more.

'We're gonna get nowhere if we don't trust each other.' His voice is low, as if he's afraid people walking past us will hear.

'Yes,' I agree. 'But I trust you enough not to run off on me and that's as much as I can give for now.'

'Yeah, well, we can't continue to be strangers, ma'am. As much as we both don't like it, you're gonna eventually get to know me.'

I stare up at him, my stomach rolling around the food I've just eaten. 'Just help me find these men. That's all I ask of you. I don't care about anything else.'

Before he can reply, Mrs Howell is calling out to us and I turn away and catch up to them, giving the couple a tight smile as they continue to talk. My mind is whirling over the conversation I've just had with Mr McCarthy. I don't really know what to think. I don't like him trying to reach out to me, trying to reason with me whenever I am being unreasonable. The only reason I have him with me is because he is a man who is going to understand the men I wish to see hang. He is a man who has experience with violence. Anything else about him, I could care less.

The seas have been kind to us. We're told by crew we'll be sailing into New York Bay on the seventh day. The trip has been smooth, the passengers just as calm and friendly as the waves beneath our feet. I'm filled with a mixture of dread and excitement at the prospect of sailing into the bay and having my feet on steady ground once more. I want to get to Cheyenne as soon as possible and see the ranch. To see Thomas again and rest my fingers against his gravestone and tell him I won't let his death be for nothing.

I'm packing my suitcases in the room when Mr McCarthy comes in. The Howells have gone off to eat supper. I'm not hungry and I plan to spend the rest of my night in the bar until it's time for bed. Mr McCarthy nods silently at me when I meet his gaze. I say nothing and continue to pack my bags. We've been given a list of questions by crew members on a sheet of paper to answer and I see the list in Mr McCarthy's hand as he sits on the edge of Mr Howell's bed. There's a frown on his face as he goes through the questions and I'm surprised he even knows how to read. I've already answered mine — silly questions such as, *Have you been around anyone with an infectious disease in the past three weeks?* I've answered them all honestly and as close to fact as I can, as they've requested.

'It's not that hard,' I tell him when I see he's still sitting on the same question.

He doesn't say anything for a moment and I clip up my suitcases and sniff, propping them on the floor at the base of the bunk. The ship lurches over a wave and I grip onto the bed to steady myself. Mr McCarthy's face turns green and his eyes close. I smile to myself. It's been a week and he still hasn't gotten used to the movement of the ocean.

'I was worse on the way to Ireland,' he says when he sees my amusement, eyes tense. 'Couldn't even get out of my bunk... Mind you, the ship was filthy and I was surrounded by people vomiting and defecating. So that didn't help at all.'

I square my jaw and say nothing. I nod my head to the piece of paper in his hand.

'What question are you struggling with?'

'Nothing, I'm not stuck on any.'

I go to look at the question I know he's been reading over and over. I see it just before he pulls it out of my reach, glaring at me.

Have you been involved in any illegal activities prior to your trip to America?

'You bastard,' I tell him. 'If you put my trip into jeopardy, I'll—'

'I *won't*,' he bites back. 'Relax.'

I know he's called *The American Outlaw* for a reason, but I didn't think he'd be stupid enough to come back to his country if he was scared of getting arrested as soon as he set foot on

American soil again. There's a tense silence between us and I realise I'm breathing heavily, staring at him angrily.

'Don't tell me to relax,' I finally say.

He shakes his head, staring down at the paper in his hands. 'I know what I'm doing, ma'am.' He meets my gaze then and says, 'I wanna help you. When are you gonna believe me when I say that I'm not gonna try nothing? I may look dumb, but I ain't.'

'*Anything*,' I correct angrily. 'And I'll believe it when I see it, Mr McCarthy.'

I head for the door. I need a drink. His voice stops me on my way out.

'Your eyes need to be open to see it, ma'am.'

Your eyes need to be open to see it.

I'm drinking whiskey in the bar and I can hear his voice repeating those words in my head again and again and I hate it. I hate him. I want to strangle him or throw him overboard or smash a bottle over his head. The alcohol I'm drinking is doing nothing to soothe the fury inside me. I don't know why I've been so stupid to put my faith in him. I've blindly gone along with this man with the foolish hope he'll help me because he's experienced with men like the ones that killed Thomas. But how am I to know for sure? He's agreed with me, so he must have, but how am I to know?

Grief has driven me mad. That's the conclusion that I come to as I sip down liquid fire, burning my throat and lungs. Every time I breathe it hurts, but I keep drinking because it's the only thing I know now. The only thing I'm good at. I've been slowly self-destructing for three years and I'm not going to stop now. Maybe when those men are all dead, swinging limply from the gallows. And I'll lift a bottle towards their lifeless bodies and drink to Thomas.

The blood was what scared me the most. I was used to bleeding every month since my thirteenth summer, but never like that. Never with such pain and anguish, a gush running down my legs as if my insides themselves were weeping. It happened so fast and so suddenly that for several moments I thought I must have been dying. That whatever happiness had been growing inside me was not happiness at all, but death. My monthly cycle hadn't stopped because I was with child, but because I was ill and on death's doorstep.

The wooden boards in the upstairs room where we used to store our things was covered in my blood. It was already seeping through the cracks as I stared. I cried out when my brain slowly came to the conclusion of what was happening. I wasn't dying. The pain was terrible and the blood was copious, but I wasn't dying. I was just incapable of producing the very opposite of death.

Thomas found me, hearing my cry. He saw the blood and immediately rushed to my side, gripping onto my shoulders as he held me, shushing me as I cried. I'd failed him just as much as I'd failed the babe and for so long, I couldn't excuse myself for that. I couldn't come to terms with the fact I was useless as a wife. Because what good is a wife if she cannot give her husband children?

After the doctor left, prescribing nothing but rest, Thomas sat by my bed, holding my hand.

'I'm sorry,' I said, voice clogged by tears.

He stared at me. 'What? What do you have to be sorry for, darling Blair?'

I closed my eyes, unable to bear the look of utter sorrow on his face. 'We were going to be so happy.'

'We *are* happy.' He leaned forward and pressed his forehead against my temple, kissing my cheek. 'This is nothing but a hurdle. We'll get through it together.'

He never told me how truly affected he was by the miscarriage. Perhaps he went into another room and cried to himself in private and only put on a brave face around me, thinking that was what I needed. I didn't know what I needed. I didn't know anything after that day.

⊷⊙⊶

I slam the glass down on the table, shaking my head to rid the thoughts.

No. Not that one. You're not allowed to remember that one.

My life has been filled with nothing but death. My parents, the babe, Thomas... I've come to know it like an old friend and just like the monsters that continue to ride on my shoulders, death rides there too. For so long I've bore it and I will continue to, or at least continue to try. All I know is, for once in my life, I wish to give death to someone else. Someone that deserves it. Not Mam or Da or the babe or Thomas. But someone that has earned the right to die because they themselves have taken a life. I cannot help but feel this is the only thing that will help me get through. And perhaps it's the only thing that will appease this dark and bloodthirsty grim reaper.

The room is at a lull and for a couple of seconds there's a silence that stills the air. There aren't many patrons in at this time and the stillness sends a shiver down my spine. And then a glass chinks and someone utters a comment under their breath and my breathing starts again. I move in my chair, unable to get comfortable. The drinks I've had have made me dizzy and the room spins. I feel the sudden urge to cry and I blame the thoughts that barged into my brain without my permission. My heart aches in my chest. I try to ignore it. I want to get up and leave and go get fresh air, but the room is suddenly tumbling around me and I can barely stay in my seat. I'm thrown off guard by it. I know it's the drink and the sway of the ship combined that's affecting me. I catch someone's eye — a man wearing a smart suit with a pencil moustache, smoking a cigar. He's looking at me peculiarly, as if wondering why a woman is in the bar, getting drunk to boot. Before he can say anything to me, I force myself out of my seat and quickly finish my drink, making my way out of the room. I'm stumbling and crashing into the walls in the hallway towards the deck. I lean against one to gain my bearings, closing my eyes to see if that will help the swaying, but it only makes it worse. It's as if my whole body has been thrown off its axis and the ship has been left behind.

I make it outside and the fresh night air hits me like a slap to the face. The sea is calm, yet the ship bobs up and down as if it's made of cork. Sucking in a deep breath so my lungs are filled to the brim with cold sea air, I let it out and make it to the railing. The water is dark and I can scarcely make it out from my vantage point. All I can see is blackness — the horizon invisible. But the stars above us are breathtaking. A galaxy of lights, glinting with yellows and blues and purples. This sky is the same as the one in Ireland and even so it still stuns me and I'm left gazing up at it with an open mouth, baffled by its beauty. The lights from inside hardly spill out onto the deck and the darkness envelopes me. The stars above are a welcome sight, gazing down upon me with approval or disdain, I cannot tell. My hands are holding onto the rail so tightly the cold metal is digging into my skin. Looking upwards, I lose my balance as the ship goes over a wave and nearly fall. I keep my grip tight, steadying myself as the ship evens once more.

'Excuse me, miss?' someone asks, startling me out of my trance.

I turn to the voice and see a crew member peering at me through the dark, a concerned look on his face. He's only young, or from what I can tell in the dim light and through my drunkenness.

'Yes?' My voice slurs. I fail to steady it.

'Are you alright?'

I almost laugh at him. 'Of course.'

'Shall I escort you back to your rooms? It's very late and we're expecting to be docked by late morning. You'll want to be up and ready for that.'

'No, I'm fine.'

He hesitates. I see him turn to leave and then he looks back at me and says, 'Is there anyone I can fetch for you, miss?'

This time I do laugh and it's a bitter sound, akin to a cackle one would hear only from an old crone. 'No.'

The crew member nods at me and leaves as I turn my attention back to the sky. I let out a long breath through my open mouth. What a hateful person I must appear to be.

After close to an hour, I decide to head back inside. When I turn to the door that will lead me down a hallway and eventually to the room, I see the glow of a cigarette in my peripherals. I glance over to see Mr McCarthy leaning against a wall further along the ship, but not too far away as to be out of sight. I know he's watching me, as if keeping an eye on me out of concern that I might throw myself overboard. I want to do it right then and there, just to spite him. My stride has faltered when I've seen him and I try to keep walking, pretending to not notice. I know he knows I have. He doesn't move — just keeps smoking his cigarette, eyes intent on me. Fury boils in my gut, but I'm too tired to go over there and slap the cigarette from his mouth. So I head inside to sleep, banishing the man from my thoughts altogether.

6

The ship's bellowing horn wakes me. I sit up in the bunk with a start, heart hammering and I hear cries of joy coming from outside. I glance around. The room is empty. The bags are gone. I curse and get up. I'm in the dress I wore yesterday, so I leave it on and brush my hair back with my fingers to make myself look more presentable. My stomach is rolling and I have a nagging ache in my temple — a little pulse point playing a drum beat under my skin there — but I ignore it. I leave the room to use the latrine and on my way back notice Mr McCarthy is waiting by the door. He raises his brows a little when I meet his gaze.

'Good, you're awake. The ship is coming into harbour.'

'I heard,' I bite. The ache in my head seems to have grown worse as soon as I've laid eyes on him.

I open the door to our room to fetch my suitcases.

'Need a hand with your bags?' he asks from the hall.

'No, I'll manage.'

I pick them up and follow him down the hallway. It's a sunny day outside and the deck is packed with people, peering out over the edge of the railing towards the harbour we're sailing into. I see the tops of buildings in the distance over their heads and my heart stutters. Mr McCarthy leads me to a part of the railing that hasn't been taken and I see the Howells there, their bags on the boards at their feet. Mr McCarthy's one leather bag is there too.

He picks it up, holds it and lets me into the space where a part of the rail is free beside Mrs Howell. They laugh with joy when they see me and Mr Howell points out a huge structure on an island in the middle of the bay. It's the image of a woman standing tall, a crown upon her head. She bears a torch and lifts it up high, as if protecting the bay with her enormity.

'That must be the Statue of Liberty!' he yells over the sounds of people cheering. 'Apparently, it was given to the city by a Frenchman. Imagine that! A Frenchman!'

I glance at Mr McCarthy and see he's staring at the deck, expression stony. The look on his face almost prompts me to ask what's wrong, but the crowd is too loud and I'm being jostled against the railing.

As we sail past the statue, Mr Howell points out Ellis Island. The harbour is so huge and the buildings of the city loom over it. It's nothing like I've ever seen. A building that resembles a palace sits on the island and Mr Howell explains it's the immigration processing building. He proudly tells me his daughter told him about it in a letter of hers. I'm too busy gazing out at the city to hear him properly, lost for words. From this view, America is nothing like I imagined it to be. Thomas had told me about it in letters, describing it as best he could, but even then, I had never expected it to look like this. So large and full of life and technical wonders.

The processing is lengthy. The passengers are split up and taken down into the large building of the immigration complex. We wait in line for hours to be seen by officers and doctors after our baggage is checked. People huddle together in the large hall and all around me I hear people coughing and gagging, still trying to get over their seasickness. We were split up from the Howells before we were taken off the ship and Mr McCarthy stands beside me quietly, as he has been for the hours we've been waiting. I don't say anything to him. We have our papers out ready and I'm clutching onto the questionnaire as if my life depends on it, not wanting to lose it amongst the hundreds of feet around us.

When we're next in line, I'm taken further down the huge room to a place sectioned off by screens. A doctor is behind it and nods in greeting. The officer takes my questionnaire to look over it and the doctor beckons me forward. I put my bags down and he listens to my breathing, checks my tongue, the back of my throat and looks into my eyes closely. After several moments, he nods his head and I'm given new papers and guided by the officer to the back of the large hall. There's another line there, where people are going through a door. I look around for Mr McCarthy and can't see him. There are too many unfamiliar faces. My heart does a little stutter.

It's fine. It's going to be fine.

The line moves and we're escorted through the door. Once we're outside, I see a ferry has been docked by the island and people are already walking up a gangplank to board it. I glance behind my shoulder, my attempts at finding Mr McCarthy in the crowd fruitless. My hands clutch my bags tightly. I don't know whether to stay in line or go and look for him. An officer walks past and I call out to him.

'Sir, I've lost the man I was with, I don't—'

'Just board the ferry when you reach it, ma'am. Your friend will eventually get one and you can meet them at the terminal.'

'What if he gets denied entrance to the country?' I blurt out, expressing the worries that have been nagging at me.

The officer looks at me disapprovingly. 'Then he'll get sent back to where he came. Board the ferry, please.'

Before I can reply, he walks away and I have no choice but to follow the line up the gangplank. The ferry is only small and we all crowd about on the deck, shoulder to shoulder, until they can no longer fit any more of us on. The ride over to New York is choppy and uncomfortable. I struggle to keep upright while holding onto my bags and with nothing to hold on to as the boat rocks over waves. All I can do is lean against the people surrounding me in each direction the boat tips us, as they lean against me, too. We're carted over like cattle, cramped and confused.

I have no idea where Mr McCarthy is or whether he even got in and I'm trying not to panic. The constriction of being surrounded by so many people isn't helping and I try to lift my head above the countless bodies encircling me, suddenly unable to breathe. Dots flash before my eyes. I rock into people and they rock into me and the motion makes me feel sick. Panic grips onto my chest like a vice and it won't let go and it *hurts*. I nearly scream. I swallow the noises before they can come out. The ferry blows its whistle and I look up over the heads around me and notice we're pulling up to a dock. There's a large, red brick building, a bell tower and spire looming above us. Any breath I might have left leaves my body.

The gangplank is lowered and people file off the ferry frantically. I can hear officers telling them to calm down, to come off at a leisurely pace and to be considerate of others' wellbeing. I hear someone cry out in pain and a curse. The more people that leave, the easier it is to breathe. When it's my turn to move for the exit, I go as quickly as I can and when I'm on solid land, I almost trip and fall. I hear the words *train* and *terminal* and am able to make out that the large building is a train station. Officers stand about, assisting anyone who doesn't know what to do. I see a patch of grass close to the paved area leading up to the building where people are milling about. Some people embrace, others head straight for the terminal. I stand on the grass and look about. There's no sight of Mr McCarthy. Not even the Howells. I know I must wait. I know he will most likely come on the next ferry or the one after that.

It's two hours until I see him. I'm sitting on the grass, the sun beating down on the back of my neck, my suitcases sitting either side of me. The whistles of trains and the bursts of steam have been filling my brain with noise for so long. I've seen so many people come through on so many ferries. Most of them have gone straight into the train terminal as I've waited, my stomach feeling sick. I don't know what I feel when I see him. I'd call it relief, only if I can say that it's for myself and not him. He comes down the gangplank with a load of other people. He looks irritable under the brim of his hat and I can see he's undone some of the buttons of his shirt. Or perhaps the doctor had and he didn't bother to do it back up properly. I see his eyes scan across the terminal and I stand up. He sees me and nods once, coming over.

'You took your time,' is all I can think of saying. Because I don't want him to know I was worried, lest he assume that worry was for him.

'Doctors said I was fine. Officers gave me a good look over, though.'

My mouth twists. 'So they suspect you of being the man all those idiots in St Brigid's claimed you to be? That's just what I need.'

He shakes his head. 'I'm here, aren't I?'

'I guess you are.' I look over to the terminal building. 'Come on.'

I pick up my bags and he follows me towards it. We head into the terminal. It's huge, holding countless platforms and walkways that run over the tracks. People crowd the place and it's so loud I'm deafened by the noise. There's a ticket box along the first platform we walk down and outside it is a newspaper boy, yelling out the headlines.

'Jersey City. I don't remember it being this loud.'

'We're not even in the city yet.'

Mr McCarthy looks at me. 'And we won't be. We'll catch a train straight to Washington.'

'Where will we go from Washington?' I ask him.

'Chicago. And then to Cheyenne.'

We've joined the line at the ticket office. My stomach is rumbling with hunger and I'm still swaying from being on a ship for so long. The clock tower chimes — two in the afternoon. I look up and notice the red metal beams in the roof of the huge train shed. The architecture of the building is impressive, like a vast castle and not a train station at all. We reach the ticket seller in his box and we both buy ourselves tickets for the Washington train at three, which include the tickets to Chicago. I'm so tired and hungry I don't even care when Mr McCarthy picks up one of my bags to help me carry it and tells me to follow him to the platform we'll be leaving from. There's the suffocating smell of coal steam and metal about this place that's clouding my brain. I feel so ill, I think I might pass out when Mr McCarthy stops me. We're on the platform, having walked several minutes to reach it and he guides me to a bench to sit on, putting my bags beside my feet.

'I'll be back,' he mutters, leaving his bag with me as well, as if to prove he isn't going anywhere. I feel too ill to care and rest my head back on the bench, closing my eyes.

It feels like only seconds go by when I hear my name being called and the shrill blow of a whistle. I open my eyes and sit up straight. Mr McCarthy is standing in front of me, holding a box of assorted biscuits. In his other hand is a canteen of fresh water. I take them from him, surprised by his kindness. I forget to say thank you, I'm so surprised and start to eat, ravenous. He doesn't look at me expectantly or curse me for being so rude and instead lights a cigarette and leans against the back of the bench I'm sitting on, smoking it.

The train we'll be riding to Washington pulls up soon after I finish my meal. Mr McCarthy and I watch people board it for a little while before getting up ourselves when the crowds slow down. I feel so much better now I've eaten and Mr McCarthy follows me onto the train, which is painted blue and decorated elaborately. The inside of it is even more elaborate — carpeted, with luxurious curtains that are drawn away from the windows, the aisle moving past separate cabins. I've been on a tram before but never a train and this is much more comfortable. We find a cabin and open the door to it, sitting down. Mr McCarthy sits down opposite me and we both lean against the window, looking out of it in silence. Eventually, he pulls his hat down over his eyes and rests back against his seat. When the train begins to move, I get comfortable and close my eyes as well.

<hr />

It's just past eight o'clock at night when we reach the station in Washington. I slept for most of the train ride there and now I'm sore from the awkward position my body has been in for five hours straight. When I woke, Mr McCarthy wasn't in the cabin and only his bag sat on the seat where he had been when I'd fallen asleep. It took him only several minutes to come back and he was silent when he did and has been silent since. We both watch out the window as people begin to file out onto the platform with their bags. It's lit up by lights and I can see other trains arriving and leaving on other platforms.

'Better get a move on. The connecting train won't wait long, I don't think,' Mr McCarthy says suddenly. His voice surprises me. I've spent five hours sleeping and in total silence, I'm now jumpy.

'Another bloody train,' I say exasperatedly.

'There'll be comfortable cabins in this one. A place to sleep.'

I look at him as I'm stretching my tired limbs. 'How do you know that?'

'Saw it on a pamphlet in the bar.'

'Of course you did.'

He looks at me and I can't figure out what the expression on his face is telling me. And then he picks up his bag and goes to grab one of mine, but I take it, shaking my head.

'C'mon,' he says quietly and leaves the cabin.

It only takes Mr McCarthy to ask a conductor where the platform to Chicago is. We're guided to the right place and walk through the crowds towards it. I'm still so tired and hungry from travelling all day and lag behind Mr McCarthy as we walk, my legs wobbling underneath me. I'm struggling with the weight of my suitcases when a hand gently takes one from me, lessening the weight. I meet Mr McCarthy's eye. He doesn't say anything and keeps walking towards the platform. I follow him slowly, feeling a burning in my cheeks.

There are sleeping cars at the back of the train and we're taken to one when another conductor sees our tickets. The train is like the one we were just on, only it contains more cars. The sleeping car we enter contains a thin walkway on one side and on the other are compartments, numbered on the doors. We walk into the fourth one and find there are two beds on either side of the small compartment. There's a shelf for our bags and curtains to pull across all the windows.

Mr McCarthy starts to put his things down. He takes off his waistcoat and hat and runs his hands through his hair, smoothing it back. I do the same, trying to get comfortable. It feels like I haven't changed my clothes in so long and all I want to do is bathe. When I sit on the edge of the bed, I'm happy to find that it's comfortable and there's even a thin pillow at the top of it.

'How long until we reach Chicago?' I ask him quietly.

'About a day, I think.' He sits down on his bed, ducking his head under the shelf above him. His eyes meet mine and then he glances out the window when the train blows its whistle. 'There should be a dining carriage further along... if you're hungry?'

I'm too tired to think. It's getting late and all I want to do is sleep. Mr McCarthy gets up and tells me he'll go find something for us to eat, but I tell him I'm going to sleep. He nods once and leaves. I take off my boots and lie down on the bed, covering myself with the coverlet. The train lurches forward after a moment and we begin to move. I barely feel it, already on the verge of unconsciousness.

My stomach is groaning when I wake up. Light filters in through the gaps of the curtains at the window above my head and I blink up at it. The sound of the train chugging along is a gentle noise and the feeling of it swaying back and forth every so often on the tracks reminds me of *The Sovereign*. I look out the window, peeking through the curtain and see rain dotted along the glass. Outside is foggy and I see trees and fields amongst the mist. Mr McCarthy is asleep on his bed opposite mine and I'm careful not to wake him as I put on my boots and straighten up my dress. I find my pins in one of my suitcases and pin up my hair as it's itching my face, annoying me. And then I move out of the compartment and down the aisle.

It takes a few crossings between the cars to finally find the dining cart. Some people are already sitting down at the booths, eating and sipping coffee. There's a man wheeling a trolley laden with food between tables. The carriage is surrounded by windows that face out to the dreary weather yet the people inside the carriage speak quietly, nonetheless content. I find an empty booth and sit down and when the man reaches me, he offers me sausages, eggs and toasted bread. I take it all with a cup of coffee. There's a pamphlet on the table, boasting of what the train has to offer during the trip. I read it while I eat and look about the carriage again when I'm done, sipping my coffee.

The ladies are wearing fine dresses made of lace and silk. Some wear hats with feathers and others have ribbons weaved into their hair. The men smoke cigars and are dressed in their suits — suits that I'd only see on a man in Galway City if he was getting married. They hold themselves with pride and speak with accents similar to Mr McCarthy's but more pronounced, less lazy. I hear some English accents but no Irish. The train we've boarded seems to be a little too rich and the only reason I could afford it was because of the business money. Thomas left me with a decent sum and I aim to use it by finding these men. I can't tell if Mr McCarthy's money is honest money. He would have won a lot fighting at St Brigid's the way he did and yet I still can't trust that all the money he has is clean. Even being able to afford it, I feel out of place in this carriage, sitting alone in my creased linen dress, my hair messily pinned up out of my face, more for practicality than fashion. I imagine myself as one of these ladies, dressed in silk and laughing merrily, my arm tucked around Thomas' as we walk along the streets of Cheyenne. I shake my head. Doing such things is foolish, even for me.

'Morning,' a familiar voice says.

I look up and notice Mr McCarthy has woken up. He eases himself down in the booth opposite me and I sip on my coffee, ignoring him. The man with the trolley comes along and Mr McCarthy takes his breakfast and a cup of coffee. He goes about rolling up a cigarette before he starts eating and I lift my eyes as he seals it with his tongue. He flicks a match across his boot under the table and cups his hand around it as he lights the cigarette. Puffs of smoke rise above his head. Mr McCarthy takes a sip of coffee and meets my curious gaze. His brows rise a little and I look away.

'How did you sleep, Mr McCarthy?' I ask him, wanting to draw the attention away from the fact that I'd just been staring at him.

'Fine.' He starts to eat. After a while he asks, 'You?'

'Fine.' I mimic him, feeling haughty.

'Good to hear. You were dead on your feet yesterday.'

'Mm.' I sip my coffee. It's bitter and similar to the coffee I drink at home.

I see Mr McCarthy's eyes glance across to the people I was studying before he came. It's like he's only just noticed them and he ducks his head a little while he eats, eyes wary. For a moment I'm able to relate to him, having only just felt as out of place as he must be feeling now. The thought makes my stomach clench.

'Ace high people make me uneasy,' he explains when he sees me watching him.

Ace high.

'Your vocabulary is quite strange, Mr McCarthy.'

He shrugs a shoulder. 'It would be to you.'

'Does every American talk the way you do, or is your speech your own?'

'Someone's vocabulary is always their own, ma'am,' he tells me.

My eyes narrow. 'You know what I meant.'

'Is that your way of asking me where I'm from? If so, probably not. I moved around too much as a kid to get any sort of vocabulary from any one place.'

'Don't make the mistake of assuming my questions stem from curiosity.'

'Then what do they stem from? 'Cause if you ain't curious, then you're just condescending me.' He drops his knife and fork and wipes his mouth with a napkin. I hear it rasp against his whiskers.

I take a sip of coffee, as if the liquid is going to fuel any words I haven't got in mind yet. I know I asked the question to tease his choice of words, but the way he's going about it almost makes me feel bad for ever saying anything.

'I already know you're from Missouri,' I say finally, disgruntled.

'You were listening then?'

I look away from him. 'I could hardly *not* hear. You were speaking to Mrs Howell right next to me.'

'Where are you from, Ms Ryan?' he asks me. There's a gentle tone to his voice, as if he's talking to sooth a frightened animal and it makes me even angrier.

'Ireland.' I say it as if he's stupid. I know he's not stupid.

He blinks at me. 'Where in Ireland? Have you always lived in Galway City?'

'Why are you asking me this?' I ask him angrily.

'Why not? You know where I'm from.'

'So?'

He lifts his hands. 'I won't press you, ma'am. Sorry if I've caused any offence.'

'I'm going to go wash up,' I say, standing.

I make my way back to the compartment and just before I reach it, I request a wash bowl. An attendant brings a bowl and cloth to the room and I thank him, taking it inside. I undress and wash the grime off my skin with the cloth, scrubbing hard. I rub at my arms and face until my skin is red raw and stinging. When I'm clean, I change into a clean dress. It's the colour of cornflowers — one of Thomas' favourites. When I'm done, I sit down on my bed, looking out the window as the train rushes by a large lake. I close my eyes. Mr McCarthy is a confusing man. He takes my every attack with a finesse I never would have expected from a man like him and he still treats me as a gentleman would, even after I'm rude to him. I have no choice but to hate him for the man that he is, the man I *think* he is. And that's what gives me confusion because perhaps he isn't that man at all and yet I cannot stand to try and find out. It would feel odd for me to make friends with this man when I'm using him to gain peace within myself. I'd much rather loathe him while I use him to acquire my needs than care for him as a dear friend, knowing full well I'm exploiting him as I do.

I find a lounge compartment when I leave the room and sit down in one of the many cane chairs. It's comfortable and has a thick cushion on the seat. There are a few people sitting around, reading newspapers and smoking. I pick one up off a table near my chair and begin to read. I don't wish to see Mr McCarthy again any time soon. I feel too conflicted about the man and I also know I should apologise to him for my behaviour.

So I spend the day reading the newspapers in the carriage and anything else with words that I can find. When it grows close to dinner time, I head back to the dining carriage and find there isn't a free booth. As I'm walking down the aisle, a young woman sees me and waves me over.

'You can sit here with us, if you like?' she offers.

I look at the gentleman with her. They're dressed in fine clothes and appear to be Americans. But they're smiling at me kindly and there isn't any judgement in their gazes.

'That's kind of you,' I say quietly, sitting down beside her.

The woman frowns. 'What's that accent I hear?'

'Irish,' I tell her.

'Irish?' the man repeats. He looks at the woman. 'I didn't think many Irish people could afford to ride—' He stops talking when the woman throws him a mean look.

'I apologise for my husband. What he means to say is, we don't often see Irish people riding the trains we ride... English people, yes, but not Irish.'

'It's alright. A lot of us are poor. The famine didn't help that.' I shrug a shoulder.

'I'm Melanie,' the woman says with a smile. She's very pretty and her dark hair is pulled high on her head, a small hat with a feather weaved into the style. The dress she wears is grey, high-necked and frilled with lace. 'My husband is John.'

'Nice to meet you both. Ms Ryan. Um, Blair.'

'Blair.' Melanie rolls my name along her tongue, smiling to herself. 'That's a nice name.'

'What do you do with yourself, Ms Ryan?' John asks me.

'I own a distillery in Galway City.'

Both of their eyes sparkle.

'That's a decent title to hold as a woman,' Melanie says.

'It was my husband's.'

'Was?'

'He died.'

'Oh... I'm sorry.' Melanie lays her hand upon mine on the table. It's cool and soft.

The trolley comes along then. We're given a choice between three meals: fried spring chicken, steak or lamb. I choose the lamb with a side of artichokes in butter and fried sweet potatoes. I'm glad we all begin to eat and the subject of Thomas' death is lost between us.

'What brings you to America?' John asks me after a moment.

'I have a ranch here,' I say quietly. 'I wish to see it, as I haven't yet.'

'Oh, in Cheyenne?'

I nod. 'Near Cheyenne, yes.'

'It's a lovely city!' Melanie exclaims. 'We've lived there for years and it never grows old on you!'

'Mm, and they've just started having an annual rodeo that's very enjoyable to watch,' John adds.

I frown. 'Rodeo?'

Melanie nods, excited. 'Men ride bucking broncos for sport. It can be quite brutal, but there are other things to watch, such as cattle mustering. The cattle and sheep boom has been huge for the city. Cowboys litter the joint and they may be... dirty creatures, but most of them are quite respectable men. You might even find yourself a new husband!'

I swallow my food thickly and say nothing. I know the woman means well and has treated me kindly by offering her table up to a complete stranger, but I can't help but want to slap her for that comment. I stay silent and the couple talk amongst themselves, perhaps realising I'm offended. When I finish, I thank them both for their hospitality and get up.

'Oh, join us in the bar for after-dinner drinks?' Melanie asks me.

I wouldn't mind a drink but I wish to be alone. So I shake my head and smile at her. 'No, thank you. I must go to bed.'

She leans forward in the booth and grasps my hand. 'Try to find us again... when we stop in Cheyenne. We live on Millionaire's Row and throw extravagant parties. I would love to have you over sometime. Mr and Mrs Benson.'

I nod and she lets go of my hand. 'I'll think about it. Thank you, Mrs Benson.'

I buy one drink at the bar when I reach the carriage and I down it easily. When I've had one more, I make my way back to the compartment to sleep. I know it should be soon and we'll be on our connecting train from Chicago to Cheyenne. And in another day or so, I'll finally be seeing the ranch Thomas built for me. My heart aches at the thought. I'm glad to see Mr McCarthy isn't in our quarters when I reach them and lie down, dimming the lantern as I close my eyes to sleep.

7

Cheyenne is extravagant. As soon as I step out of the train station in the middle of town, I can see that. The streets are paved and they are lined with electric lanterns. It's early morning, the sun not having risen above the horizon yet, but I can already see the grandeur of the buildings as Mr McCarthy and I make our way down the street. They're like silent, pale leviathans, gazing upon our quiet and exhausted journey with keen interest. We amble along on foot and I carry one of my bags with two hands, fatigued. Mr McCarthy carries my other bag, having picked it up before I could say anything back at the station. I can smell baking bread coming out of a nearby shop and the quiet snorts and whinnies of horses echo across the town while it still sleeps. The further we travel into Cheyenne, I begin to see the drunks and start to hear the hollers. Mr McCarthy is silent by my side. We're both tired and uncomfortable from our trip. All I want to do is run to the sheriff's office and knock his door down, but I know I need rest.

We find a hotel, having passed a couple of saloons that looked and sounded questionable. This one is quiet and most of the windows are darkened and shuttered. We head up the steps, nonetheless. Mr McCarthy opens the door and holds it open for me and I step through. A man is sleeping in a chair behind the desk in the front room. A set of stairs run up the wall behind him.

I step forward and clear my throat. He lets out a snort as he continues to snore and lifts a hand to rub his face, murmuring something in his sleep. The hotel owner is a portly young man, his hair not yet greying. I go to clear my throat again, but before I can, Mr McCarthy steps past the desk. He nudges the man in the leg with his boot.

'C'mon,' he says, 'geddup. You got customers.'

The man wakes with a start and looks at us. For a moment we all stare at each other and then he shakes his head and murmurs something incomprehensible again.

'Sorry,' he finally mumbles, standing.

Mr McCarthy backs up until he's in front of the desk again, standing beside me.

'Two rooms, please,' I tell the man.

'One night?'

'Yes.'

'Dollar twenty-five.'

'Jesus,' Mr McCarthy swears. 'You lot understand you're nothing but a glorified cow and sheep station, right?'

The man stares at him for a really long time. His eyes are bloodshot and half closed. I spot a bit of drool on his chin, caught in his goatee. I go to tell Mr McCarthy that it's fine, I'll pay the money, but the hotel owner straightens himself up, as if trying to meet Mr McCarthy's height and grunts.

'I'll have you not use the Lord's name in vain in my establishment, sir.'

Mr McCarthy scoffs, waving a hand. 'Sure, mister.'

'I'll pay,' I say to both of them. 'It's fine. I just want a proper bed to sleep in. I don't care how much it costs.' I shoot Mr McCarthy a look. There's no point causing trouble when we're both dead on our feet. Even if he won't admit it.

I take out my purse and pull out a few coins. It's strange money. I barely looked at it when I exchanged it for my Irish pounds at the train station and now, I'm seeing it properly and I don't know what to do with it. But then Mr McCarthy reaches over and takes the coins I need out of my hand and flicks them onto the desktop. The hotel owner grunts and hands us both our keys.

'Don't do food here,' he says. 'You'll have to get it at one of the saloons in town. Baths, however, can be arranged.'

I thank him quietly and Mr McCarthy and I head up the stairs. There's a wooden tag on my key that has '3' on it – my room number – and when I reach the hallway upstairs, I head down until I find it. Mr McCarthy has the room beside mine. He hands me my other bag and I thank him quietly, not meeting his gaze.

'Sleep well,' he says quietly after a moment's hesitation.

I nod and head into my room.

* * *

I sleep like I'm dead and when I wake up, the sun is well on its way through its course in the sky. I get out of bed and brush out my hair, stretching my tired and aching muscles. I want to bathe, feeling too dirty after so long not washing properly, so I head downstairs and arrange a bath with the hotel owner. Half an hour later, I'm back in my room, wearing a green dress, cinched with a leather belt. My stomach begins to rumble with hunger as I'm packing my suitcase back up. I've pinned half my hair up, as it's still wet and I want it to dry, and it's flowing down my arms as I sort the bags. There's a knock at my door soon after and when I open it, Mr McCarthy is wearing his hat. I see a gun-belt at his waist this time. Two revolvers sit on either hip and I lift my gaze back up to him.

'Morning.'

'It's not morning... it's well past noon.' I don't know why I say it.

He blinks at me. 'Did you...?'

'Let's go eat. And then find the sheriff's office.'

He nods to my suitcases, sitting on the bed further in the room. 'Gotta take those. Only bought the rooms for one day.'

'It hasn't been twenty-four hours yet.'

I see him smile slightly at that and then we head downstairs together and back onto the street. There's a cool breeze coming through town, but the sun is a warm welcome, beaming down on top of our heads as we walk, trying to find a place to eat.

'I did some digging,' Mr McCarthy says when we're sitting down at a table in a quiet-enough saloon. We're waiting for our food to be brought to us and I am impatient as I'm so hungry.

'Digging?' I ask, looking at him.

'Mm.' He takes a sip of the coffee we've already been served. 'I know where the sheriff's office is.'

'How'd you manage that?'

'I got up much earlier than you did.' He looks at me and I see an amused sparkle in his eyes that catches me off-guard. I didn't know those sad eyes could sparkle.

'Did you even sleep at all?' I grumble. 'You know it won't do to have you as a guide around this awful country if you're sleep-deprived. Or drunk… Or being untrustworthy.'

The sparkle dies and he looks away from me, mouth turning into a grim line. The food is brought to us then and we start to eat. I don't like the feeling a normal and friendly conversation with Mr McCarthy gives me. It feels wrong. Despising him and treating him like the dirt I think him to be is easier for me. Perhaps it's a part of my own self-destruction — this blocking out of anybody who may grow attached or who may make a difference in my life. A form of punishment, not towards them at all but towards myself.

'Where is it, then?' I ask him irritably. I don't wish to dawdle on my own thoughts about him, lest I start to feel sorry for the man.

'Near the courthouse,' he says, as if I'm supposed to know where the courthouse is.

I glare at him over the table. 'You better not be spinning tales, Mr McCarthy.'

'Why would I bother with a woman with your smarts, ma'am? You'd catch on immediately and I'd be hanging by my neck from the hotel's balcony come sundown.'

I ignore the dry tinge to his voice and say, 'Damn right.'

And then I stab at a piece of bacon with my fork, accentuating the fact that I mean what I say. But he's ignoring me, looking about the saloon's main room with interest. There's a balustrade that runs along the top half of it and people hang over the railings, smoking and speaking to one another. There are already working girls milling about, laughing at the jokes of men still drunk from the night before. I've noticed some of the patrons have cast judging eyes our ways. The girls have looked Mr McCarthy up and down as if he were a treat — young as he is compared to the men they're used to. I suppose he would be. They stare at me with wicked grins and winks. They must see me as nothing but a fair maiden, unknowing to the happenings of what goes on in a man's bed. How surprised they would be to hear the truth.

'I didn't go in and speak to anyone for you, if that's what you're worried 'bout,' Mr McCarthy says suddenly, breaking me from my thoughts.

'As if you would,' I say, 'especially if you do have a reason to leave this country for Ireland.'

He looks up at a man leaning over the railing above my head and for a split second, I think he's rolling his eyes at me and I want to slap him. And then I wonder whether he just used the man as an excuse to do so.

'When did you leave, anyway?' I ask when he doesn't say anything after a few moments.

He's still eating his meal. 'Leave where?'

'You know where. Here. This country.'

'1893.'

I'm surprised by this. 'You were in Salthill for five years?'

He shrugs a shoulder. 'I moved 'round when I first sailed into Galway. Went all over Ireland.'

I harrumph quietly. His answer isn't what I was expecting. 'What made you stay in Salthill?'

'The fighting. It was good money.' He meets my gaze. There's a crease between his brows. 'Why you so interested all a sudden?'

I ignore his question. 'How were you so good at fighting?'

'I've been fighting all my life, ma'am.'

It's my turn to roll my eyes. I shake my head and get up.

'Come on, take me to the sheriff's office.'

He looks down at his plate for a moment and then he sighs and throws his napkin aside, standing. He finishes off his cup of coffee and then he follows me out onto the street. We move through the crowd. There are people walking along the road and alongside shops and saloons and grand buildings. Wagons and horses ride through, their hooves clopping along the cobblestones. I can hear shouts from workmen somewhere in the distance and then I smell the sudden sweet aroma of burning tobacco as Mr McCarthy lights a cigarette beside me. I go to keep walking and he stops me.

'This way.'

I begrudgingly follow him down another side street. Everywhere I look in this city, there are buildings with Romanesque arches at their windows and doorways and iron fences that cordon off little green squares of gardens and trees. This place is fancy. Fancier than anything else I've seen in my short amount of time in this country. We only had quick stops in Jersey City, Washington and Chicago, but nothing ever really caught my eye as this place has. I can tell why Thomas chose it. He always had an eye for the exquisite. I could appreciate it, but it was never really a necessity for me. It makes me wonder how he went about building our ranch and whether the buildings in this place played a part in the inspiration for our ranch house. Thinking about it makes me want to see it even more and I hurry along to catch up with Mr McCarthy's long strides. We seem like such a disjointed couple juxtaposed beside the locals of Cheyenne. Mr McCarthy with his plain clothing and cowboy's hat and me with my dress and messy hair.

'You must hate this place... to be around such "ace high" people wherever you turn,' I say, panting as we walk briskly along.

'There's people like us here too,' he says quietly, nodding his head to a couple of workmen across the road from us. They're loading a wagon full of sacks from a grocer. Ranchers. Not workmen. Ranchers that live out of town, coming in to gather their monthly supplies. My heart aches and I turn my gaze away.

'I don't think there are many people like us, Mr McCarthy...'

He stays silent. I see his eyes glance my way as we walk, but he doesn't seem to want to acknowledge what I just said. I don't know whether it's because he disagrees or whether the statement is so obvious, he thinks there isn't any point in replying.

When we come across the courthouse, I stop and stare up at it for a moment. It's an imposing building, as imposing as any place emanating the law needs to be, I suppose. Trees line the outside of it, softening the hard edges of the square leviathan. It makes me wonder how long it must take to construct such a building. The courthouse in Galway is nothing like this one — the stonework completely foreign.

Mr McCarthy clears his throat and I break from my thoughts. He's pointing across the street to a much smaller building. Hanging from the roof of the porch, there's a sign that reads one word. *Sheriff.* My heart stutters in my chest. I glance at Mr McCarthy and find he's watching me quietly, mouth pressed in a firm line behind his beard.

'Come on, then,' I say, waving my hands about.

He falls into stride with me across the road and we move

around wagons and horses to get to the sheriff's office. When I reach the steps, Mr McCarthy stops and I turn and look at him.

'I'll wait out here for you,' he says.

Frustration bubbles in my gut. 'Why?'

'It ain't my business to be in there with you, ma'am.'

'What if I think it is?'

He looks at me for a long time. His eyes are so dark under the brim of his hat that I can't really tell what look they hold. All I know is he's gazing at me so intensely that I have the sudden urge to look away.

'I'll wait out here for you,' he tells me again.

'Fine.' I scoff at him. 'Have it your way.'

Such a child.

I head up the wooden steps and go inside. The door creaks when I open it. There's a man sitting at a desk near the doorway, his feet propped up on it as he lazes back in his chair. A jail cell sits at the back of the room, across the length of the back wall and there's a man inside one of the cells. He lets out a jeer when he sees me and wraps his dirty hands around the bars. Another man near the cell yells at him, smoking a cigar. I see the shining metal star on his chest, attached to his waistcoat, and I notice another one on the man at the desk. He doesn't stand when he notices me. He looks at me up and down, eyes narrowed.

'What can I do for you, ma'am?' he asks me.

The man at the back of the room continues to smoke his cigar, now reading a newspaper. He pays me no mind.

'I'm Ms Ryan. Thomas Ryan's wife.'

The sheriff nearly falls off his chair as he struggles to get to his feet. When he's standing, he straightens out his clothing, clearing his throat. He's not very old and his moustache is thick and hangs around the shape of his thin mouth. He wears a hat different to the classier men in town and different to Mr McCarthy's too. I didn't expect my husband's name to get a rouse out of him, but I'm glad that it has. I immediately don't like this man. He looks as useless as I know him to be.

'Thomas Ryan?' he stutters. 'The Englishman killed by the Gaitwood gang?'

'The very same.' There's a hard bite in my words and I see the man with the newspaper lower it, peering over the top of it to watch on.

The sheriff holds out his hand. 'Ms Ryan, I am very sorry for your loss.'

I look at his hand, his fingertips stained by tobacco. 'Where's the man who wrote me the letter? The marshal?'

'He's out of town at the moment, ma'am.'

'Well, would you please send word to him that I'm here? Bring him back.'

The sheriff's back stiffens and he puts his hands on his hips. 'He won't be able to tell you anything I can't tell you, ma'am.'

'And what's that? That you all are spineless little men who have no idea what you're doing and that's why the men who killed Thomas are still out there, breathing air they don't deserve to breathe?'

He looks at the man at the back of the room. The prisoner lets out a laugh.

'Ma'am,' the other man says, lowering the newspaper. 'I don't think the words you say are rightly true... and we'd both appreciate—'

'*I'd* appreciate you sending word to this marshal so that I may speak with him. If you don't like the insults I throw at you, you'll do as I say, as they're meant for that bastard as well.'

The men look at each other again and the prisoner continues his loud chuckling.

'Deputy Lowe,' the sheriff says. 'Shut that rat up. I can't think with his incessant laughter.'

The deputy heads for the cell and opens it up. I look away when he begins to beat the prisoner. My eyes go to the sheriff.

He opens a small tin from his pocket and begins to chew on a bit of tobacco. My nose crinkles at the sight. These men are nothing but pigs, snorting and snuffling about in the filth they live in, without a care to the outside world.

'Ma'am,' the sheriff begins, 'I can tell you all about the murder. I can tell you where your husband is buried. But what I can't tell you is where these Gaitwood boys are. They haven't done much since your husband died to give me a good enough location.'

'Even if they did, sheriff,' I growl, 'it'd be out of your jurisdiction and far beyond your competence.'

He shrugs a shoulder. 'The marshal is a busy man. I ain't getting him back in town just for the wishes of a widow of a man who died years ago.'

Fury boils inside me. I feel tears prickle at my eyes.

'The marshal?' I say pointedly through clenched teeth. 'Where is he?'

He doesn't answer. He's looking at me like I'm the biggest nuisance in the world to him.

'I've come all the way from Ireland,' I hiss after a few moment's silence.

'That ain't my problem,' he says slowly.

'Just tell her, sheriff,' the deputy buts in, locking the cell back up again. The prisoner lies unconscious behind the door, face beaten badly. 'It's not like she'll be let in anyway.'

'What?' I growl. 'What is it?'

'You need to calm down, ma'am,' the sheriff tells me. 'Being hysterical ain't gonna get you nowhere but behind those bars.' He jerks his thumb to be back of the room and I want to rush forward and grab him by the neck. Rattle him until he finally has some sense and compassion. 'He'll be at a party on Millionaire's Row in three nights' time. Dunno where he is now, though.' He gives me a smile, but it isn't one of pity. He's telling me he doesn't care about my concerns. He doesn't care because Thomas' death is history and there's nothing either of us can do about it. 'Just go settle down in that ranch your husband built you. Make a new life for yourself and forget this ever happened, ma'am. That's the best you can do... for the sake of yourself and this town.'

I feel my nostrils flare. I'm about to spit my venom when the deputy sighs and steps forward.

'I'll even mark your ranch on a map for ya. You can borrow a horse to go out there,' he says.

The sheriff opens the desk he's at and they go about marking Thomas' ranch on the map they pull out. I'm standing there, shaking, not knowing what to say. I'm so distraught.

'Here.' The deputy shoves the map in my hands. 'There's a livery 'round back on the adjacent street. Tell the owner there, Deputy Lowe sent ya.'

I turn around and burst through the front doors, seeing nothing but a blinding whiteness in my eyes. My feet are pounding the ground and I'm so close to collapsing and sobbing when I hear my name. I blink and my sight comes back. I'm on the side of the busy street and Mr McCarthy is walking briskly to catch up with me, frowning.

'What happened?' he asks me.

'Those men... *bastards*! Useless!' I throw up my hand and the map flutters to the ground.

He picks it up and looks at it, still smoking the cigarette he must have lit while waiting for me. He hums deep inside his chest and raises his eyes to my face.

'You okay?'

I snatch the map from him. 'Everyone from this bloody country are useless, horrible people.'

'A big lot of 'em are from your country...' he murmurs quietly as he begins to follow me to the livery.

I ignore him. I'm so furious I can hardly think straight. My heart is still pounding in my chest and I want to do nothing but weep over what just happened. How can those lawmen be so callous?

'Ms Ryan, where are we going?'

'To the ranch my husband built me. This map,' I give it back to him, 'do you know how to read it?'

''Course.'

'Then take me there.'

I'm walking so fast to where those men told me to go, my feet are aching inside my boots.

'We need horses,' he tells me.

'I'm working on it!'

'Ms Ryan.' I continue to walk, looking for the livery frantically. 'Ms Ryan!'

A hand grabs my shoulder and I immediately throw myself around, shoving Mr McCarthy away from me. He holds up his hands, letting out a little "whoa" as if I'm a spooked horse. My hands are still up in front of me, protecting me and I see they're shaking violently.

'You need to sit down,' he tells me gently. 'C'mon, we don't have to go to the ranch right now. We can head out there tomorrow, first thing.'

'No...' I lower my hands, wringing them in front of me. The street spins. There are so many sounds, so many sights and smells. I feel dizzy. I feel like I'm going to be sick. I want to cry.

'Ms Ryan,' Mr McCarthy says again. 'C'mon, if you can't wait 'til tomorrow we'll go later then. Just sit down for me first.'

He offers me his hand, giving me support if I need it. I know I can walk, so I shake my head and shove it away. I walk slowly with him back to the hotel we're staying at, rubbing my face. My mind feels like it's about to explode. My chest is tight and my throat is constricted by held back tears. I still can't believe how those men treated me. Remembering their behaviour makes me want to go back there and shake them until they're nothing but rattling bones and teeth. We reach the hotel and I climb up the stairs until I'm at the door to my room. Mr McCarthy stays silent as he follows me. He stops in the hallway, watching me as I place my hand against the handle. I look at him.

'Just lemme know when you wanna go,' he says, voice quiet. 'I'll be ready for ya.'

I say nothing and head inside.

<hr/>

I don't know I've been asleep until I'm waking up. I sit up in bed and rub my eyes. The window is still letting bright sunlight stream in. I get up and go through my suitcases. There's a pair of trousers and a linen shirt I sometimes wore to the distillery when I didn't feel like wearing a dress. I put them on now and tighten my belt, my fingers still slightly shaky. I put my boots back on and plait my hair all the way down my back. It's so long and so thick that my neck has been sweating under the weight of it. It's good to have it tied back and away from my face. I grab my suitcases and head downstairs with them. The hotel owner is reading a book in his chair and doesn't look at me as I leave. I stop when I reach the porch, seeing Mr McCarthy is outside with two horses, tightening a girth on a tall chestnut with a thick white blaze.

I don't know what to say when I see him. I want to reprimand him for getting horses without my permission but I can't. It's helped me immensely and saved me a lot of trouble.

'How'd you get them?' I ask him from the porch.

He looks up, only just noticing I'm there, as if deep in thought before I spoke.

'I didn't steal 'em if that's what you were thinking.'

It wasn't but I say it anyway. 'Can you blame me, Mr McCarthy?'

'I dunno.' He nods his head to the chestnut. 'That's yours.'

'How much do I owe you?'

'Five dollars. But don't worry yourself 'bout it.'

I'm already getting the money out of my coin purse. I go down the steps and hand it to him. He takes two of the five notes and calls it even. I don't have the energy to argue, so I put my money away and he starts to help me strap my bags to the saddle. When we're ready, I'm about to mount up when he stops me.

'Here.'

I turn around and see him standing beside his black horse, offering me a wide-brimmed hat. It's similar to his, just more feminine and without the cowboy look. I look at his face, not taking it.

'What's this?'

He looks at the hat in his hand and frowns. 'A hat?'

'What for?'

'For you.'

'Why?'

He looks at the sky. The sun is shining hotly down on our heads.

'This ain't Irish sun, ma'am,' he says. 'You'll need it. Trust me.'

'No.'

I see his expression fall, so I take the hat and shove it on my head, annoyed.

'I'm not going to thank you, so you can stop expecting me to,' I tell him, getting on the horse.

He doesn't say anything and mounts up as well. And then we begin to ride down the street as he follows the map to Thomas' ranch.

The southern part of Wyoming is nothing but vast green plains surrounded by hills and mountains that sit on the horizon. It's a beautiful, picturesque landscape that takes my breath away as we ride. There are rivers and creeks that run through the grassland, providing water to purple flowers that blossom amongst the hills, nestled at their base. When I see a peculiar-looking hill, I pull up my horse and stare at it, trying to take it in.

'Bison skulls,' Mr McCarthy says, stopping by me. 'Don't think you'll ever see the real thing, ma'am. Poor bastards been over-hunted for 'bout twenty years now.'

'Why?'

'*Manifest destiny*,' he murmurs bitterly. 'Men thinking they own everything, thinking they can starve an entire nation of people simply 'cause they see 'em as pests and not real human beings. I'll never understand it.'

'What people?' I ask, confused.

'The natives.'

I look at him. 'My husband told me they're being kept in encampments.'

He nods. 'Poor souls… Army's got their grip tight.'

'There's no sense to their cruelty, is there?'

'No, ma'am.'

We stand in silence for a while longer.

'What will happen with the skulls?' I ask. There's a lot of them, forming a mountain several feet high. 'There must be over a hundred poor beasts in this pile.'

'They'll break 'em down and make glue or porcelain.'

'This place… it's evil.' My voice is tiny, defeated. I feel great sadness to see such devastation.

He shakes his head. 'C'mon. Not far now. Your husband picked a real nice spot for you both.'

The place is beautiful indeed and yet all I can see is blood in the rivers and dotted across the leaves of trees. Even the animals experience pain and loss here. It just doesn't seem right, in a landscape that looks like heaven itself, the wind gentle and the sun bringing a warmth like the arms of a loving mother.

Man seems to have brought death to its doorstep just for the mere point of it and it's as if Thomas didn't see this to begin with, already bewitched by the beauty. He never saw the bad in people. He always looked to the bright side and gave people a benefit of the doubt. And that's most likely the reason why he's dead. Because a country like this doesn't look kindly upon people like him. I now know why Mr McCarthy is the man he is. This country has shaped him, just as it has shaped all the other people I've come across here. There's nothing nice about them because they're all wanting to kill each other and own what the other has; greedy monsters with no compassion, no consideration of the suffering of others.

8

The ride from the city of Cheyenne to Thomas' ranch is three hours. The sun is well on its way to setting by the time we reach the homestead. We stand on a hill looking down upon what my husband built for a little while and I gaze upon it with bated breath, my heart aching behind the cage of my ribs. The house is large and wooden. There's a porch that wraps all the way around its circumference. A barn sits a few yards away from the house and is surrounded by a corral. There's fencing all around the property, meticulously built by Thomas and the men he hired. It must have taken so much love and energy to build such a wonderful home. The grass is overgrown with no livestock to feed off it and the garden at the back of the house is void of everything but dry soil. There's a chimney built at the side of the house, made of different coloured stones, and my heart freezes when I see smoke rising out of the top of it. Mr McCarthy's hand goes to his gun.

'Careful,' he says, knowing I've seen it and want to immediately react. 'We can't just storm in there. We gotta be smart 'bout this.'

'Who would dare use this place?' I growl, pushing my horse forward down the hill.

'Squatters. They're usually harmless.' He rides up alongside me. 'Hang on, ma'am, you gotta have a straight head 'fore you go in there.'

I'm furious. I don't want to see the sense in this. Of all the people I've come across, all the people who are nothing but ghouls, only concerned for themselves, whoever these people inside are, they will face the brunt of my fury. I jump the horse easily over the fence and Mr McCarthy follows. He doesn't say anything anymore. He's either given up or he understands my anger enough to not stop me. Either way, I ignore him and ride down to the front of the house and dismount.

'Come outside!' I yell, voice loud and ragged. 'You bastards, come out here right now!'

The front door opens and three men come out. One is holding a rifle, the others have their hands on their hips, looking at me like I'm a spectacle.

'What d'you want?' the man with the rifle asks. He's not aiming it at us yet. It doesn't matter; it's there and it's the first thing I see.

'You're on my property,' I say. 'I want you gone right now before I string you all up by your toes!'

There's a collective laugh between them.

'Oh yeah? That so, missy?'

'I'd do as she says, boys,' Mr McCarthy says, almost lazily, coming up from behind me to stand close.

They all look dirty and malnourished. Their clothes are practically falling off their backs. There's a crazed look in their eyes, as if they've witnessed hell and can't seem to rid themselves of the memory.

'And who are you?' one of the others calls out. 'Her valiant knight?'

More laughter.

I reach over and grab the gun off Mr McCarthy's side. It's heavier than I expected, but I aim it up at them and pull back the hammer. I've used a gun before. I know how to shoot if need be.

'Get the hell off my property!'

The man with the rifle immediately aims it at us. Mr McCarthy swears under his breath and gets his other gun out as quick as a flash.

'Hey now,' Mr McCarthy says, 'we don't wanna have to kill ya. All you need to do is leave.'

'Tell your whore that!' the man swears.

'Get!' I fire the gun up in the air, the blast scaring the horses, and aim it back down at them, pulling back the hammer once more. 'Out!'

A hand falls on my arm and I flinch, almost pulling the trigger. Mr McCarthy's hand is large and heavy, but he grips my arm gently. I look at him. He's still aiming his gun at them, glancing at me every so often.

'C'mon, Ms Ryan,' he says quietly. 'We don't have to shoot 'em.'

'Yes we do,' I growl.

'Please,' he murmurs. 'You don't want that on your conscience.'

'You know nothing about me.'

I can see sense in his words, but there's a side to me that's dark and full of rage, so hot and vicious that it's hard to ignore. I want to tear things apart and wreak havoc on people just so that they can understand how I've felt since the day I heard Thomas had been killed. Mr McCarthy's hand is still on my arm. He's still murmuring things to me, quietly telling me to stand down and for a moment I nearly don't. I almost listen to the rage inside me and pull the trigger. But then I lower my gun and he slowly lowers his. The man with the rifle laughs.

'Irish women are feisty,' he calls out. 'What she like in bed, oh valiant knight?'

'Get the hell outta here,' Mr McCarthy replies. 'Right now.'

'Or what?'

Mr McCarthy steps forward so that he's in front of me, his broad back blocking my view except for the men's faces. And I see the look on those faces change as Mr McCarthy's hand goes back to his gun.

'You won't be alive to find out what, that's what.' The sound of his voice sends a chill down my spine.

The squatters look at each other. And then they begin to move, scrambling down the porch steps and running past us to leave. I'm shaking when they've gone. I want to collapse to my knees and block out the world. I almost regret not listening to the dark fury inside me and just killing them. And then Mr McCarthy turns around and looks at me. The sun is setting and it's casting an orange-red light across us. He squints his eyes, mouth downturned.

'You okay?'

I hold up a hand. I don't want to hear him, not right now. 'Don't.'

I head towards the porch and go up the steps. Stopping in the doorway, I look into the dim room. It's all wood and smells of it, musty. There's a faded, ripped rug near the fireplace. Tables and chairs have been upturned. There are a couple next to the fire, where the squatters must have been sitting before we arrived. Some of their things sit about the place. Empty cans of food and waste litter the floor. There are bedrolls in some of the rooms as I walk through the house. When I see the bed where Thomas must have slept, turned on its side, the legs broken off for fuel for the fire, I finally do fall to my knees and begin to weep.

<hr />

'Ms Ryan?'

Mr McCarthy's voice comes to me through the numbness. I'm sitting in a chair beside where the fire crackles and he's beside me, offering me a cup of hot coffee. There's a pot on the fire, cooking something. I don't recall how I got in the chair. There's a vague memory of Mr McCarthy coming in after fixing up the horses and telling me I needed to rest and eat, but I can scarcely remember the specifics. I sip at the coffee he's made me, hoping it might clear my head. It's bitter and the warmth and taste are comforting.

'I was going to shoot them,' I finally say out loud, remembering the rage inside me over those men. 'If you hadn't have stopped me, I would've.'

'I know.'

I wipe away a tear that rolls down my cheek and sigh. 'What's it like? To kill a man?'

Mr McCarthy gets up and stirs the contents of the pot over the fire. He's quiet for a long while and then he says, with a sadness in his voice, 'You don't wanna know that, Ms Ryan.'

'I do,' I grate, annoyed at him for being so cryptic. 'That's why I asked.'

'Well, you were stupid to ask.' He looks over at me from the fire. His hat is off now and I can see his face clearly, glowing from the firelight. He doesn't look sad anymore, only as frustrated as I feel. 'And if I can help it, you ain't ever gonna know.'

'Well, you can't,' I bite back. 'And you shouldn't have stopped me before. What I feel and how I go about things is none of your damned business!'

'It is if you want me to ride with you,' he counters. 'I ain't letting a woman like you, overreacting from grief, go about killing folk just 'cause she's angry at the world. Those men were fools, but all they were doing was squatting in your house. That ain't much of a crime to be killed over.'

'No,' I tell him, still angry. 'I say what goes. If I want to kill someone, I want to kill someone!'

'Don't be stupid.'

'Don't call me stupid!'

'I wasn't calling you stupid, I was telling you not to be.' He shakes his head and throws down the spoon, pulling the pot off the fire. 'Now you're gonna eat and then you're gonna sleep. And you ain't gonna tell me more of what you think of anything until the morning.'

'You're a bastard, Mr McCarthy.'

'That ain't even the half of it, Ms Ryan.'

I don't even know how he's bought the supplies to make a stew. I don't rightly care. It's delicious and I eat it hungrily. When we're finished, Mr McCarthy lights a cigarette and pulls out a bottle of whiskey from his bag. I look at it. He drinks from it, resting it on his knee as he gazes at the fire with his cigarette hanging from his bottom lip. When he notices me watching him, he hands the bottle over and I take it. Mr McCarthy has taste in whiskey, I'll give him that. It's smooth and honeyed and it glides down my throat, warming my chest and insides. I want to hug the bottle to my breast and drink it until I feel nothing but warmth. He takes the bottle off me again.

'Go and sleep,' he tells me through his cigarette. 'There's no point staying awake when you're as tired as you are.'

I hesitate.

'Don't worry,' he adds. 'I won't drink all of it.'

I glare at him and get up. 'I'm not a drunk, Mr McCarthy. I don't care what you do with your whiskey bottle.'

'I'm sure you don't,' he says dryly.

'I don't. But I'll tell you what you *can* do with it. Shove it up—'

'Goodnight, Ms Ryan.' He looks at me, blinking tiredly.

I turn around and head into one of the rooms, slamming the door closed behind me. Mr McCarthy must have lit a candle as there's a soft light emanating from one on the walls and the bedroll has been shaken out and aired. I lie down and close my eyes. My body and mind are so weary that I don't know how tired I am until I'm in the bedroll. And then I'm sinking off to sleep almost immediately.

Thomas chose a place for us where the rising sun comes through the leaves like a kaleidoscope of reds, oranges and yellows. Where the wind whispers across the hills and through the grasses. Where birds roost and call out the sun's name once it begins to peek out over the mountains on the horizon. This place is magical, the land special and growing around the house, almost to its doorstep like a leafy welcome mat. Even with Thomas' footprint, it's still so wild, so untamed and unfamiliar. And I know that's why my husband chose this place. He knew I'd love it and accept it with open arms.

I stand on the quietest hill on the property and watch the sun rise. There are tears at the back of my throat, but I don't let them fall. I've been crying in my sleep, crying at the thought of Thomas dying here alone and I know I need to be strong for him. There's so much anger inside me, wanting to be let out and as much as I want to and free myself of its darkness, I know I cannot. The only way is to weep and have it bleed out through my tears, inch by inch as they stream down my face. But it seems the more I cry, the more I no longer want to continue on and it's this vicious cycle I can't relieve myself of.

I slowly make my way back to the house. The day is beginning to look like a clear one and the sun is already warm on my back as I walk. I notice Mr McCarthy is out on the porch, leaning against the wall as he smokes a cigarette. He's been watching me, pretending not to. It reminds me of when I saw him on the ship, keeping an eye on me. At the time I thought it was because he was worried I'd do something foolish, but now I'm not so sure. The man seems too conscious of my wellbeing and not just for his sake and that thought makes me uncomfortable. As if I need to meet expectations I don't wish to meet.

'Morning,' he says to me when I reach the porch.

'How did you sleep, Mr McCarthy?'

I'd noticed him gone from the main room when I left the house earlier, so I assume he slept in another room.

'Fine.' He finishes his cigarette and flicks it off the side of the porch. I turn my nose up at it when he says, 'You?'

'*Fine,*' I mimic.

There's a silence between us and I turn and look over at the sun. The breeze catches at my clothing, gently pulling and pushing. My bones ache and my muscles are tight and yet feeling the motions of the wind is relaxing.

'There's a party on Millionaire's Row in two nights' time,' I say suddenly, turning to look at Mr McCarthy. He's watching me quietly, leaning on the railing of the porch. 'The marshal is going to be there. I'm going to go and talk to him.'

His brows rise slightly, as if he didn't expect me to say that. 'You got that information from the sheriff?'

I nod. 'He didn't think I'd be able to get in anyway, the smug bastard.'

'What makes you think you will?'

'I met a couple on the train, Mr and Mrs Benson. They live on Millionaire's Row and if I can find them, I'm sure I can get access to that party.'

'And what then?'

I cross my arms, annoyed with him. 'I'll question the marshal about these Gaitwood men. And then we'll ride out and find them all.'

'Seems mighty romantic,' he mutters. 'You really think it'll all work out and you'll come outta this a happier woman?'

I screw my face up. 'I can only try, can't I? You can leave now if you like, Mr McCarthy. I thought I might need a tough and heartless man like you to do this but maybe I don't. Especially if he's going to doubt me every step of the way.'

'It ain't you I doubt,' he says, pushing himself off the railing. He shoves his thumbs in his belt, glancing behind me at the hills and mountains. 'It's this damned world.'

'You and I have something in common then.' I shake my head, heading up the porch steps. 'Come on.'

'We're leaving?'

'I don't want to be here any longer. I'm sure you can understand why, Mr McCarthy.'

He's quiet as he follows me inside and begins to help me pack up.

'What are you gonna do with this place?' he asks, breaking the silence that's been between us for several minutes.

We're outside, readying the horses. I tighten my horse's girth and sniff.

'I don't know just yet,' I say quietly. 'I can't really bear the thought of selling it but neither can I imagine I'll want to live here after everything is over with.'

'There ain't no rush.' He pauses. 'I can boarder it up for you? Make sure no one else squats inside?'

'There's nothing stopping them from ripping those boards off, Mr McCarthy.'

'It might deter some away.' He looks at me over the shoulder of his horse. 'I know how upset it made you to see those men squatting here. I won't mind doing it if you want me to.'

I look over at the house. An ache clutches at my chest. I didn't expect Mr McCarthy to offer and I don't know what to think of it. It seems awfully kind of him to and I want to know the reason behind it. I don't want Thomas' legacy being used and abused by bastards thinking they have the right to use someone else's property as their own, so I nod my head mutely. Mr McCarthy loosens his horse's girth again and I watch him as he walks back over to the house. He's inside for a few minutes, but when he comes out, he has a toolbox that had been sitting in one of the rooms and a few pieces of wood under his arm. I watch him as he closes the door once more and seals it with boards, keeping inside whatever horrors Thomas experienced when the Gaitwood gang came with their wave of destruction. Keeping inside whatever memories my husband and I might have made together if he hadn't been killed. Mr McCarthy seals the windows and whatever openings someone might use to get inside. It doesn't take him long. I stand there quietly, watching him as he works, sleeves rolled up, sweating in the sun and yet all I can picture is Thomas, building the house from the ground up with a smile on his face.

⊷•⊶

Our wedding had been a quiet and yet lovely affair. Thomas and I used our local church in Clifden, the church where I had been christened as a babe. My parents were there and his mother and only a few of our friends. We drank wine and whiskey in the pub down the street and sang songs of old and danced to a man playing the fiddle, arm in arm, faces so sore from the constant smiling. My parents sat in the corner of the bar, clapping along. I was twenty and the feeling of being in love and being loved was the most exhilarating thing I'd ever felt. After dancing with my husband, I went over to talk to my parents. They smiled at me and kissed my cheeks and forehead, holding my hands with praise.

'Are you happy, Mam?' I asked her, watching her tired eyes.

She smiled at me and it was the warm smile I remembered from my childhood, over the kitchen bench as we made pies together, our hands stark white with flour. 'Of course, Blair.'

'And you, Da?' I turned to him and held his large, scarred hands in my own. Hands that had picked me up and held on, sometimes too tightly, when I was a child. Hands that had taught me how to bring in a fishing net and to use a filleting knife.

'As happy as I was on your mam and my's wedding day.'

Mam coughed and Da got her a glass of wine to help soothe her throat. I put a hand on her shoulder as she drank.

'It's not going away, is it?' I asked her, worry setting a cold feeling in my heart.

'Go and dance, Blair,' Da told me. 'Your husband needs you.'

I looked over at Thomas. He was talking with his friends and family, laughing with them, and as if sensing my gaze, his eyes travelled across the room and met mine. I couldn't help but smile and made my way to him. He kissed me hard on the mouth as soon as I reached him and the people in the pub, the people we loved and had known all our lives, cheered and laughed. The worries for my mother's sickness disappeared and I instead was just a young woman, fiercely in love with the man I'd known only a year. He held me tight as we began to dance again, laughing with one another, as carefree as we could be.

'You look beautiful. Have I told you that already?'

'Twice at the altar, three times when we left the church and just now,' I said with a laugh.

He grinned and stopped spinning me so he could hold me close and kiss me. I kissed him back, my arms wrapped around his shoulders. The dress I wore was my mother's. A soft silk with laced sleeves. It was the fanciest thing I'd ever worn.

'Are your parents worried for you?' he asked in my ear. 'That you'll soon be taken away from them?'

'They love you, Thomas,' I replied. 'They couldn't be happier.'

My eyes went across the room to them again. Mam and Da were sitting together still, but their eyes weren't on me. They looked so tired, Da's arm around Mam's shoulders. They were talking quietly with one another, as if discussing something of great importance. I felt this odd sense of dread in my heart at the looks on their faces, but being in my husband's arms and kissed by him made me forget that feeling almost immediately. I didn't know then, so young and foolish in love, that I wasn't going to be happy for long after the happiest day of my life.

'Ms Ryan?'

I blink and look up at Mr McCarthy. We're still on our way back to Cheyenne and the swaying movements of my horse under me have sent my thoughts far away. I bring myself back to the present and realise I'm playing with my wedding ring, turning it in circles on my finger with my thumb.

Mr McCarthy's eyes are still on me. 'You good, Ms Ryan?'

I shoot a look at him. 'Of course, why wouldn't I be?'

He doesn't answer, just looks back at where he's riding. It's like he knows I'm lying, making my feelings seem smaller than what they are, as that's the only way I know how to cope. We left soon after he finished boarding up the house and I don't know how long we've been riding for. We must be getting close to Cheyenne.

My thoughts go back to my parents and I feel my heart seize inside my chest. How foolish I'd been on my wedding day not to notice their pain? It's like their deaths were my punishment for not being more conscious of them and for being too selfish. My mother had died from influenza not long after, too rattled by change to pick herself back up. Death had held its grip tight on my life well after she left, as father had followed a year after her, falling from a great height at work. I'd become numb to it, giving up on questioning why it was happening and instead accepting it, expecting it. Then it was the babe. And then Thomas...

I tear myself away from my thoughts. They seem to be plaguing me more and more and I don't know how to stop them. All I can feel is this ache in my heart that won't go away and a heaviness on my being that is terrible and suffocating. I want to break free of it. And the only way I know is down the road of revenge. That whatever darkness is inside me, whatever demons are sitting on my shoulders, claws dug in deep, are the only ones I can listen to, to be free of it all. I feel so alone. There's no one in my life anymore, no one I love or is worth loving.

We come along a crest that gives us the vantage point to look over the city of Cheyenne in all its glory. I slowly make my way alongside Mr McCarthy, tired and upset. He stays silent and I can see he's been glancing at me, frowning. We're coming through a side of the city we haven't been in before and when I see the graveyard beside the church, sitting on a small hill near the outskirts, my heart stops. Without thinking, I jump off the horse and leave Mr McCarthy behind, running up the hill to it. There's an opening in the fence to the graveyard and I make my way through it, panting. There are rows of graves, sitting under the shadow of trees and the spire of the church. I frantically walk between them, reading each grave. And then I find him.

He sits close to the edge of the graveyard, near where a nook of brush and trees grow. He lies in peace far under the earth, beside a place that many people deem holy. I fall to my knees over his grave, my hand resting against the cool stone, moving my fingers across the words etched into its surface.

Here lies Thomas Ryan. Born in England, killed in The United States. Mourned by his wife.

There are sobs racking at my chest, so hard and vicious that I can't keep them at bay. My hands dig into the earth before me, the earth where he lies and all I want is to have him back. To stand atop the highest mountain and scream out at the world for its cruelty. To beg for its forgiveness or whatever I may need from it in order to have my Thomas with me again.

I don't know how long I kneel in the grass. Everything from the outside world is blocked out. All I feel is the savage pain of grief. Those feelings that I haven't allowed myself to feel for so long, they're with me now, clambering up my chest and back, suffocating me. I must endure them now. I must because they won't leave, not now. Now that I've seen his grave, read the words inscribed in his stone, it's real. There's no hiding from the fact, no hoping or wishing that whatever might have happened, might be a different story to what I was told. No. Thomas was murdered by the Gaitwood gang and he lies dead underneath my weeping body. Seeing his grave, feeling it under my hands, has solidified the need to see these men hang. They have left a woman, a wife, alone in the world with nothing but her pain and her demons. They must now know how that feels.

———◇———

The sun is well on its way through the sky when I finally stand up, wiping my face. I'm exhausted. I'm filthy, covered in dirt and grass, my pants stained by it. There's sweat in my hair and on my forehead under my hat and it makes me itch. My eyes are puffy from crying, itchy and sore. I make my way through the graves, back out where I left Mr McCarthy and the horses. He's dismounted, standing across the street from the church with the horses hitched at a post. His eyes are on me as I cross the road, smoking a cigarette under the curved brim of his hat. I know he sees I've been crying. I know he must have watched me kneeling at my husband's grave for however long I was there. Perhaps he looked away out of respect for my privacy. Or he didn't. I don't care. I don't look at him and instead grab the horse's reins and get back in the saddle. He says nothing and follows suit.

I find a hotel close to Millionaire's Row and dismount, taking my suitcases off the saddle. Mr McCarthy takes the horses to a nearby livery as I go inside to pay for our rooms. The hotel owner gives me a look when I walk in, accepts my money and gives me two keys. He mentions there's a bath downstairs for whenever we might need one for an extra fifty cents. I nod my head at him and wait for Mr McCarthy to come back. All I want to do is go to sleep and forget the world for a little while. It's nearing afternoon and I've barely eaten, but I'm not hungry. I give Mr McCarthy his key when he comes back and we make our way upstairs. This place is fancier than the last hotel we were at, being closer to the more extravagant side of town. There are paintings on the walls and the carpet is plush under my boots. When I reach my room, Mr McCarthy tips his hat at me.

'I'm just going to sleep,' I tell him, voice weak.

'Do what you must, ma'am,' he says. 'I'll be here when you're ready.'

I swallow, feeling close to tears again. 'Thank you, Mr McCarthy...' I don't know why I say it. Maybe it's because I know he deserves my thanks after what he did. 'For boarding up my husband's house.'

'You don't need to thank me for that, Ms Ryan,' he murmurs, looking at the ground.

I nod my head and open the door to my room. He still stands at the threshold when I turn to close it and I see the look on his face and it does something inside me, breaking loose the dam that I've slowly tried to build back up since the graveyard. I go to sleep crying once more, my head close to bursting.

9

I sleep and stay in my room until the day of the party. My stomach is groaning with hunger, so when I go to a saloon down the street with Mr McCarthy that morning, I eat the lamb's fry with vegetables and accept the chunk of fried bread Mr McCarthy offers. I drink two cups of coffee and sit back in my chair and Mr McCarthy looks at my empty plate.

'Want some more?' he asks me.

I shake my head. There's some silence between us as he continues to eat, reading a newspaper that sits beside his plate on the table. I watch him as he reads, eats, and then reads again. His beard has grown since I first saw him at St Brigid's and his hair hangs about his shoulders now. Any bruising or cuts that were on his face from his fights have cleared and his skin is weathered and slightly sun-kissed.

'What have you been doing these past two days, Mr McCarthy?' I ask him suddenly, knowing I've been watching him for a while, taking in his presence with more openness than I ever have since we met.

'Not much,' he says, glancing at my face.

'Made any friends?'

'Y'know this place ain't for me, ma'am.'

I shrug my shoulders. 'I don't claim to know you at all, Mr McCarthy.'

'You hardly wanna.'

I don't know whether he says that knowing my choice not to like him, or as a warning that if I ever wanted to, he wouldn't let me. But I ignore his comment and cross my arms.

'I need to meet up with Mr and Mrs Benson and try to get an invitation to the party tonight,' I tell him. 'And then we'll be needing to buy a suit for you and a dress for me.'

Mr McCarthy freezes, looking at me. 'I ain't going...'

'Yes, you are.'

'No, I don't need to. It'd be better for you to speak to the marshal on your own.'

I slam my hands on the table, furious at his stubbornness. 'You're damned well coming with me, Mr McCarthy. I cannot go there alone! What'll that look like? And do you really think I *want* you to come with me? This is my only choice. I need an escort or I'll be the talk of the town. I'll be that "strange Irish widow who goes to parties by herself, seeking attention at every corner".'

'You really care what those fools think 'bout you?' he asks, voice matching mine.

I stare at him. 'Of course not. I just need the marshal to be willing to speak with me.'

'When he knows who you are, I'm sure he will.'

'I was taken advantage of by the sheriff because you had concerns only for yourself and decided to wait outside. I'm not letting that happen again with the marshal!' I sigh, realising that we've caught a few gazes from the patrons inside the saloon, so I lower my voice. 'As sick as it makes me to say it, I need you, Mr McCarthy. This bloody state might acknowledge women more than the others in this damned country, but there are still men that uphold their grossly wrong and judgemental opinions about us. If the marshal is anything like the sheriff and his deputy, I need you to be standing beside me when I go in there seeking information or I'll be ridiculed and laughed at once more. It's not about what they think of me — they can think whatever they like — it's about finding out where these Gaitwood bastards are, so I can see them all pay for what they did.'

Mr McCarthy is silent for a long while. He presses his lips in a firm line and then he nods. 'Alright,' he says quietly. 'I see your sense in it now. I'll come with ya.'

I don't thank him this time. I just nod and get up, expecting him to follow me, and he does.

It doesn't take me long to find Mr and Mrs Benson's mansion. I ask around the street when we reach Millionaire's Row and people point towards it. It's a large house, set at the back of a wide block of land along the street. It's nestled in amongst trees and a beautiful, flowering garden. There's a fountain out the front and a pathway that winds its way around it up to the front doors. The house is similar to the others in the street and it's grand in every way. A three-storey mammoth of a building, with wide windows and buttresses that must be inspired by those from England.

My heart jitters in my chest as I make my way up to the door. Mr McCarthy casually strolls after me and we stand side by side as I lift my hand and tap the door knocker. Not long after, a coloured woman opens the door and looks out at us. She smiles warmly, her eyes bright.

'Can I help you, miss?' she asks me politely.

'Ms Ryan,' I tell her. 'I'm looking for Mrs Benson. I was wondering if I could speak with her?'

'I will see if she's available. Please, come inside.'

She opens the door wider for us to come inside and I enter the foyer with Mr McCarthy. It's beautiful, embraced by a grand stairwell. There's a table in the centre of the foyer, holding an expensive-looking vase filled with a bunch of sunflowers. They stand tall and proud, the colour of sunlight. Mr McCarthy clears his throat when the maid leaves the room and I look at him.

'You met these people on the train?' he asks me, eyes going about the grandeur of the place.

'They were nice enough to let me sit with them when the dining carriage was full.'

'Ace high people are never nice…'

'That's a generalisation, Mr McCarthy.'

'One made up from countless interactions with the fools,' he mutters. 'They're all the same. Empty and shallow—'

'Mrs Benson will see you in the drawing room, Ms Ryan.' The woman has entered the room again as silently as she left it, surprising us. Her eyes cross over Mr McCarthy, as if she heard every word he said and I see him hang his head as he follows me towards the drawing room.

This room is large and filled with lounges, tapestries and carpets. There's a fireplace, its mantelpiece beautifully carved. The lounge that sits beside it is where Melanie sits. She stands up when she sees me, smiling and reaches out so I take her hand as I sit down.

'Oh, it's so good to see you again, Blair!' she says happily. 'I knew you'd come and visit!' Her eyes go to Mr McCarthy, who's awkwardly standing in the centre of the room. 'Sir, come sit,' she tells him.

'Melanie, this is Mr McCarthy,' I tell her. 'I'm sorry for barging in on you without warning.'

She waves a hand. 'Don't be silly, I am want for company. Especially if it is yours.' Melanie smiles and tells her maid to bring tea and biscuits. The maid nods and leaves. 'Have you settled into your ranch?' she asks me.

'Yes,' I lie. 'My husband had good taste. The house is sound and on a beautiful spot outside the city.'

'Oh good!' Her eyes go to Mr McCarthy. I can see the gossip she might share with friends later on. Melanie is a nice woman but I now know what Mr McCarthy means. They're all the same, they all talk and want to hear talk, thriving off it. 'Were you one of her husband's friends, Mr McCarthy?'

'No, ma'am.'

I shoot him a look. If we're going to get anywhere, we need to make up a story for ourselves.

'What Mr McCarthy means to say is he was a workman on my husband's ranch before he was killed. He might not consider Thomas his friend, as he was his boss, but they were close.' I see Mr McCarthy look at me and his mouth tightens. I ignore him. 'He has been looking after the ranch and helped me settle in when I got here.'

'Oh...' Melanie's eyes go to Mr McCarthy and I see them travel up his broad frame. She smiles slightly.

Tea comes then and I'm glad for it. The maid hands out cups and plates of biscuits.

'And look at you, Blair,' Melanie says with a laugh, motioning to my filthy outfit. 'Dressed in trousers and a shirt as if you're a man! You'll be the talk of the town if you're not careful.'

Mr McCarthy's face screws up and I shoot him another look before he thinks to say anything to that.

'It's more comfortable working on the farm as I am,' I explain with a little laugh.

My heart is hammering. Maybe it wasn't a good idea to come here. I don't know how to ask Melanie about the party tonight without seeming like I have ulterior motives.

'You need a fine dress!' Her eyes widen. 'Oh! And I have just the one for you! And just the place for you to wear it!' She puts her teacup down on the small table in front of the lounge. 'You're about my size, surely? Perhaps a little smaller in the bust...' She clicks her tongue. 'Not to worry, I can have my seamstress over here in a jiffy and we can get a dress sized for you for tonight!'

'Tonight?' I look at Mr McCarthy. He's sitting in his chair, jaw tight.

'There's a party the mayor is throwing down the street. Everyone will be there!' Her eyes go to Mr McCarthy. 'You're such a sad-looking man, sir,' she tells him. 'Perhaps a little fun and drink will do you good, too?'

'Only if Ms Ryan allows it,' he says gruffly.

I nod my head. He looks so uncomfortable and I feel suddenly awful for him. I put my teacup down as Melanie goes about telling her maid to send for her seamstress. She instructs Mr McCarthy to go get sized for a suit, writing the tailor a letter for him to give them.

'You can pop it on John's tab. I'm sure he won't mind at all. Go sir! It will take them until the end of the day to make it and we must be ready by then!'

When Mr McCarthy's gone, Melanie sits me back down and grasps my hands.

'I think you need a little culture, Blair,' she says. 'Some good folk to help you get back in the groove of things. This party will be just that for you!'

I don't tell her why I want to go to the party. I don't tell her I'd rather be doing other things than going to a party with people I don't know and have nothing in common with. The thought of it makes me feel ill and yet I know it's the only way to get to the marshal. As soon as I have word of where these men might be, Cheyenne will be behind us and I can finally stop pretending I'm not falling apart.

<hr />

The dress I borrow is all silks and ribbons made of gold and champagnes. A large ribbon cinches my waist and ties at the back and the sleeves fall in lace petals down to my elbows. The neckline accentuates my chest in a soft circle of lace and the skirts hang around my legs, a curtain of silk with a lace overlay. It's beautiful and extravagant. Melanie's seamstress tells me it's French-inspired, as if that means something to everyone else. It's a dress I never saw myself wearing, fancier than even my wedding dress. Melanie's maid puts my hair up, tying ribbons the same colour gold as my dress through it. The gold almost blends into the strawberry blonde locks, but it compliments them nonetheless. When I look in the mirror, I don't recognise myself. I don't really want to recognise myself.

When Melanie's husband arrives home, dressed in a suit and top hat, holding a cane, she lets out a shrill cry of glee, dressed in her finery as well. John kisses my hand and comments on how we both look beautiful and I feel myself switch off. I turn into a woman full of fake smiles and empty comments, if only to cope. Being around these two makes me realise how normal Mr McCarthy is in comparison; as human as I am, as sad and empty as I am, and I feel myself missing that. We leave the house for a stroll up to the mayor's house, John and Melanie arm-in-arm, me beside them.

When I see Mr McCarthy on the street, hair pomaded back, beard trimmed so it's not as bushy as it was before, I feel my heart lift a little at his familiarity. He's smoking a cigarette, dressed in a fine coat and tails that accentuates how broad his shoulders are. Just a shadow in the street, he waits under the halo of an electric lamp for us. All he gives me is a nod of acknowledgement when I reach him, crushing his cigarette on the floor with his leather shoe, and we walk with the Bensons towards the mayor's house. The house is lit up with light and I can hear the sounds of people and music from the street. It's large, larger than any other house in the street, and the front of it holds a grand garden like the Benson's. Melanie looks at me excitedly and I feel myself give her another one of those fake smiles.

'Come! Let us go have some fun!'

We go around the house to where there are crowds of people milling about, drinking in the garden. There's a fountain where water dances in arcs and lights hang up in the trees. A lot of the garden is paved and tables have been set out near the shelter of the mansion, holding food that smells delicious. Waiters walk around with trays of drinks and Mr McCarthy snatches one and gives it to me. I look at him questioningly, but he says nothing. He looks as uncomfortable as I feel. I drink half of it and give the rest to him and we share a look of understanding. He downs the rest, his eyes still on mine, and puts the empty glass on a nearby table. We're both outcasts here, surrounded by strange people with even stranger outlooks on life. We don't belong and we know that.

When I look around, Mr and Mrs Benson have wandered off to talk to a group of men and women. I sigh and look around.

'How are we supposed to know what the marshal looks like?' I ask Mr McCarthy.

'We'll ask.'

I look up at him. The drink he gave me has slightly calmed my nerves. I need more. I take another drink off a tray that passes by and drink it in one go. Brandy. Fine brandy that doesn't give me the type of burn I'm used to, the burn I need.

'Take it easy,' Mr McCarthy says, standing close. 'Surely you don't wanna be a drunken mess when talking to this fool?'

I let out an annoyed growl and slam the glass down on a table. 'I need to calm my nerves.'

'That's why I gave you a drink. One drink should be enough.'

'You know that's not true; it takes more than that for me.'

He shakes his head and I see a slightly amused look in his eye. 'C'mon. Stop feeling sorry for yourself and start looking for him. The sooner we find him, the sooner we can leave.'

'If you're so uncomfortable here, Mr McCarthy, I might just have to keep you here as long as possible. Give you what you deserve.'

'You're just as uncomfortable, ma'am,' he grunts.

I look up at his face. He looks different with his hair brushed back and with his grand necktie. It's a pale blue colour that matches the dark blue of his eyes. This look doesn't suit him. The rolled-up sleeves, the scruffiness of his overgrowing beard and messy hair, his hat with the bullet hole in its brim. That's the look of this outlaw I've come to know. This man that's both no-nonsense and awfully glum and yet gentleman-like and kind. It makes me want to know why he's like this. What's shaped and formed him into the man he is? I shake myself from the thought. There are more important things to focus on and I can't be stupid about it.

'Let's ask around, then,' I say. 'Should we split up?'

'I ain't talking to these fools without support.'

I can't stop myself from letting out a laugh. 'Fine. But be nice. I don't want these people thinking I allow such behaviour.'

'What behaviour is that, Ms Ryan?'

I don't answer him. Melanie soon waves us over when she sees we're keeping to ourselves and she introduces us to the group she and John are standing with. Rich folk who live on Millionaire's Row as well, making their money from cattle and sheep trades. I introduce myself as politely as I can and make conversation with them. Even Mr McCarthy makes some comments that make them chortle, like the fluffed-up birds they're dressed as.

'You sound quite cultured for a man of your stature, Mr McCarthy,' one lady, Miss Clark, says to him. I see her eyes take him in, half closed from the smoke of the men's cigars and the drink in her hand. She smiles at him languidly when he looks at her.

'Guess I've been 'round enough, Miss Clark,' he replies.

'More than any of the men here, surely,' Melanie buts in with a laugh. 'They're all content to spend the rest of their lives making money while doing not much at all.'

'It's the life of privilege, darling,' John tells her softly. 'That's how it works.'

'I'd much rather get my hands dirty to know my money's worth it,' I say before I can help myself.

Everyone looks at me. I see Miss Clark jut her chin out.

'That's mighty revolutionary of you to say, Ms Ryan,' she says.

'You must have, working at your distillery,' Melanie chimes. 'Ms Ryan here owns her late husband's distillery back in Ireland, so her statement was said from experience — she actually does work hard for her money.'

I don't correct her and say I never really worked there. I did the books and ordered the men when Thomas wasn't around. Sometimes I helped them down where the batches were made, but after Thomas died, I hated the place and tried to keep well away.

I can tell Mr McCarthy is watching me, smoking one of the cigars that John gave him. He drinks his glass of brandy and I take a sip of mine, not knowing what else to say as the group begins to discuss other matters. Melanie is suddenly beside me, murmuring in my ear.

'There's the mayor and his wife,' she says, nodding her head to a tall man with greying hair. There's a woman on his arm, about the same age, and she looks as if she's tasted something sour. I see he's talking to another man with silver hair and thick moustache.

'Who's that man he's talking to?' I ask her.

'That's the marshal, I think,' she says. 'His wife is ill, so she couldn't come tonight. It was nice of him to come... I hear he's a very busy man and doesn't really like these sorts of events.'

I nod, trying to keep calm. *Good.* Now I have a picture of him. My eyes go over to Mr McCarthy. Miss Clark seems to have backed him in a corner, talking to him about something. He's nodding and smiling as politely as he can. Melanie chuckles, looking at where my eyes have gone to.

'Miss Clark has your ranch hand in her sights. He's a fine man for someone of his class,' she says to me quietly, a wicked tone in her voice. 'And she's desperate enough to grab onto any man at this point.'

My stomach revolts. I swallow thickly. 'Mr McCarthy is of the same class as me, Melanie,' I tell her.

'Of course he isn't,' she replies with a shake of her head. Her dark curls move about her forehead as she does. Her eyes meet mine. 'Not if he is what you say he is.'

'What do you mean by that?'

She sips at her drink, mouth crooked up in a smile. A sneer. Not a smile. 'I saw him on the train with you, Blair. No one could forget such a forlorn-looking individual.'

'He picked me up from Jersey City. Met me there so I wouldn't have to travel alone.' The lie comes so easily, I almost believe it myself.

'Whatever you say.' I realise Melanie has no proof Mr McCarthy is anything but my ranch hand and she's only amusing herself. 'What would be more of a scandal? You taking up with your late husband's ranch hand or you travelling around with a man you don't even know?'

I tense my jaw, staring at her. 'A scandal is a scandal to you people, isn't it? Doesn't matter what the context is, it's all the same beast. And you'll still lynch me if you believe you must.'

Mr McCarthy is right. I know that now and I want to go to him and have him beside me so I can at least have some familiar thing to hold on to in this pit of snakes.

Melanie lets out a laugh. 'You know I'm only teasing you, dear,' she says. Her eyes go back to where Miss Clark is still talking to Mr McCarthy. 'All I'm saying is if you two stay around here long enough and don't make any plans together, Miss Clark will snatch him away from you.'

'Mr McCarthy is a man of his own mind, Melanie. I'm sure the last thing he wants to do at the moment is settle down with some ace high lady almost half his age.'

I can't believe what I've just said and I see the amusement on Melanie's face at my words. Saying that makes me realise I don't know Mr McCarthy at all and I've never cared to. And yet I've defended him from this woman's assumptions as if he were a friend or someone I cared about.

'Enjoy yourself tonight, Blair,' she tells me, stepping away. 'If you'll allow yourself that.'

When she's gone, I finish my drink and grab another, shaking. I look around and see the marshal has moved on from the mayor and is standing with a group of men, smoking a cigar. He looks like a serious man, but I see him smile at some of the things his companions say. My eyes go back to Mr McCarthy. Miss Clark is trying to get him to go for a walk with her around the garden. I move over and clear my throat.

'Mr McCarthy, if you don't mind,' I say. I look at Miss Clark. 'Can I take him from you for just a moment?'

She rests a hand on his arm. 'As long as you bring him back.'

Mr McCarthy nods to her and then he comes towards me. He puts the cigar in his mouth and I see the corners turn downwards when he notices I'm laughing at him. I hide my smile and walk with him until the marshal is in our line of sight.

'Over there,' I murmur. 'The man with the silver hair and thick moustache. That's the marshal.'

Mr McCarthy hums. 'Well... let's go over there then.'

I stop him before he leaves. 'Wait... I don't know if I can do this.'

'What do you mean?'

'I... The men in the sheriff's office. If I'm laughed at again, I might attack someone.'

He smiles slightly at that. 'I'll stop you before that can happen, ma'am. You have my word.' Sticking the cigar in his mouth, he offers me his arm. 'Here,' he mutters through it. 'C'mon.'

I stare at his arm for a little while. And then I slowly lift my hand and put it there. I can feel how powerful it is and it makes me remember watching him fight in St Brigid's for a week and how relentless and terrifying he was. We make our way over to where the marshal stands and Mr McCarthy pulls me with him into the group without saying anything.

'It was quite a pandemic but we all must agree the world is becoming much more civilised. Even within this past decade, with the advancements in technology and our industry, we're improving as mankind. There's no reason to pillage and kill and steal anymore. Not when a man can make an honest wage working for such folk as us,' one of the men is saying.

A few of them make noises of agreement out from behind their cigars and I see the marshal nod with approval. He's a stout man and he holds himself as tall as he can, even though his back is slightly stooped. His eyes go to me and when he sees me watching him, he nods.

'I'm sure a woman such as yourself can agree with what these men are saying, too, Ms—?'

'Ms Ryan,' I say, nodding. 'Of course I can. We are no longer in the dark ages, where we must fight for everything we own. We're more civilised now, curious and open to ideas. The world will continue to evolve with us.'

'Hear! Hear!' He raises his glass with the other men.

'Hah, I didn't think an Irishwoman could have such insight,' one man says.

'Is that because I'm Irish or a woman, sir?'

'A bit of both,' he says with a grin.

I feel Mr McCarthy tighten up beside me. Before he can say anything, the marshal lifts a hand.

'Please ignore Mr Grant,' the marshal says. 'He's had a little too much to drink.'

Mr Grant shakes his head and stays silent. As the conversation turns to another topic, I clear my throat and let go of Mr McCarthy's arm to move closer to the marshal.

'Sir?' He bends over to put his ear closer to my mouth so that he can hear. 'Can I speak with you alone?'

He looks at me, frowning. 'I suppose...'

'I won't take too much of your time, I promise.'

When he's following me towards the house, I see Mr McCarthy step in line behind us. I take us up to the back of the house and through one of the open doors. We walk into a large sitting room, warm from a fire on the far wall. It's so grand I hardly know where to stand without fear of knocking something expensive over. I turn around and look at the marshal. Mr McCarthy closes the door behind him and the sounds of talk and laughter immediately drown out. The marshal looks back and his face pales when he sees Mr McCarthy.

'What's this about?' he asks, agitated.

'I'm not trying to intimidate you, sir,' I tell him. 'I just need to speak with you... get some answers.'

'Out with it,' he demands, waving his hand.

'I'm Blair Ryan. Thomas Ryan's wife,' I say, voice shaking. 'The man that was murdered out at his ranch three years ago, just outside of town. You sent me a letter all the way to Ireland to tell me the news.'

I see his expression fall and he nods his head slowly. 'I remember.'

'Those Gaitwood men. Why haven't they been caught?'

'I-It's much harder than just going out there and catching them, Ms Ryan,' he explains. 'They disappeared soon after and, trust me, we had men searching for a little while. There's even a bounty on their heads... there might not be posters up anymore, but if a bounty hunter were to bring them in, they'd be rewarded handsomely.'

I feel sick. I shake my head and the room spins. 'That's not an excuse. Those men *murdered* my husband and nothing has been done about it!'

He holds up his hands, trying to calm me. 'I've heard some things... they're about a year old, but I know that the two younger Gaitwood brothers might be distinguished members of society now. Someone out in Memphis was cheated in a deal and reported them. I don't believe it, personally, so I never investigated it. Men like these don't have the capability to be within society. There's word of another one up in Montana... Harry Oswald. He's a lot wilder than the others, not one of the brothers by blood, but they consider him as such.'

'So you know where they are, but you've done nothing?' I feel the anger bubbling up inside me. I want to throw things. I want to lurch forward and strangle the man.

Mr McCarthy comes forward.

'Where in Montana?' he asks him.

'Great Falls. The information was vague. Reports of a "wild man" attacking anyone who got too close.' He looks at me, trying to reason. 'Either way, it would take a lot of money and work to get men up there, especially in winter through the snow.'

'It's not winter now!' I retort.

'What about the leader?' Mr McCarthy asks calmly.

'Russ Gaitwood?' The marshal shakes his head. 'I don't know. Disappeared. Probably in another country. Maybe if his men are questioned, they'll tell you where he is. I do doubt it, however. They're as loyal as anything.'

I let out a noise of frustration. 'There's no excuse for what you have or haven't done. You're useless, just like the sheriff and his deputy!' Before he can answer, I say, 'I'm going out there to kill these men. If you think it costs too much in *resources* to bring them back and hang them, I'll kill them myself!'

I see his face blanch. 'I don't advise that at all, ma'am.'

'It's fine,' Mr McCarthy says. How can he sound so calm? 'I'm going with her.'

'And who are you?' The marshal looks at him closely then and my heart lurches. 'You... you look familiar.'

I see Mr McCarthy's jaw tense below his beard. 'Do I?'

He's staring the marshal in the eye, facing possible conviction if the man realises who he is. What he is.

'Yeah...' The marshal's frowning at him.

'Must have an unfortunate face. We ain't never met before, mister.'

'Come on,' I say quickly. 'We've got the information we came for.'

I move through the room and he goes for the door. We leave the marshal behind and rush through the garden. I'm no longer in the mood for prancing around the place with these people. I want to saddle my horse and ride out right away. Mr McCarthy catches up to me on the street and he falls into step beside me. I glance at him and he meets my gaze under the soft haze of the electric streetlights.

'He recognised you,' I say, voice shaking.

'He might've.'

'Your face has been on a wanted poster before, hasn't it?' I accuse. 'Or worse, you *have* met him and you've even had a shootout with the man.'

'Nothing that memorable, I can tell ya.'

I shake my head. 'Mr McCarthy, if he actually figured out you've got a price on your head, he would've taken you away. And I'd be... alone.'

He nods. 'I know. That's the main reason why I didn't wanna go. It's even why I didn't go into the sheriff's office.'

I stop walking and put my face in my hands, trying to collect my thoughts. 'I didn't want to have to believe it all... do I have to worry about this getting in the way of what I want?'

'Not when we're out in the wilderness. The sooner we get out there, the better.' He points back at the party. 'Those men who were talking 'bout the world becoming more "civilised" have no idea. Out there... out where the wolves and bears will attack you on sight — that ain't civilised. And the men who live out there might as well be those wolves and bears.'

'The only reason why I brought you along is because I was half mad by grief... and I knew you'd know how to use a gun and you'd know what these men are like and how they think, because you are one.'

'Was one,' he corrects quietly. 'Or maybe I will always be one and that's my punishment.'

I swallow, not knowing what to say. 'You were right,' I say quietly after a moment of thought. 'When you said we'll have to get to know one another at some point. There's no stopping it, I can see that now.'

'C'mon,' he says after a tense silence. 'Let's get out of these damned clothes and some real damned food.'

I smile grimly and follow him to the nearest saloon.

'So what do we do?' I ask once we're seated at a table.

The saloon is crowded at this time of night and there's music being played on a pianola in the corner. There are working girls and men alike, drinking and laughing raucously as they dance to the pianola's rhythm. We're eating a beef stew that's thick and gluggy but flavoured nicely with herbs, the beef seared and melting in the mouth. There's a bottle of whiskey between us and we share it between our glasses. I'm still in the fancy dress and it's cinched tightly at my waist, making it hard to breathe while I sit down.

'Montana,' Mr McCarthy starts, pouring himself some more whiskey. He fills my glass for me and sets the bottle back down, starting to break apart his piece of bread. 'Great Falls. I know of the place, just never been.'

'What's there?'

'Not much. It's just as it sounds — mountains and waterfalls.' He starts to eat more of his stew and I sit back in my chair, worrying my bottom lip with my teeth. 'We'll go there first. Find out where this Harry Oswald is.'

'So he's hiding?'

He shrugs. 'The marshal called him "wilder" than the others, so perhaps he's taken up living in the wilderness 'cause city life don't much suit him. It happens. All that killing, all that stealing and causing harm... some men can't adapt back into normal society after all that. They get paranoid... nervous around others they don't know, they don't trust. It's worse if there's a price on their head.' He looks at me and meets my eye. 'He'll be dangerous, this one.'

'Aren't they all going to be?'

'Probably.'

I shake my head. 'It makes me sick some of these men — the younger Gaitwood brothers — can be distinguished members of society.'

'It's just an act, Ms Ryan. They'll do anything to make them seem like they're someone else.' He scoffs, shaking his head as he picks up his glass. 'Never did see one try to act like a gentleman, though. Didn't really think any outlaw was *capable* of acting like a gentleman, especially not a Gaitwood.'

'So you've heard of them?'

He looks at me. 'Yeah, I know of 'em.'

'What stories have you heard?' There's a morbid curiosity within me that makes me ask the question.

'They're like any other gang, stealing, killing... They lost a few men in a failed bank heist down near the Mexican border. Didn't hear much about them after that. Not 'til...' He looks at me.

Shaking my head, I finish off my bowl of stew with the last piece of bread and then wash it down with some whiskey, filling the glass back up. I fill Mr McCarthy's glass when he hands it over the table and we drink in unison. Then he goes about rolling up a cigarette and I look about the room.

'We're going to have to arm ourselves to the teeth,' I tell him. 'Your two revolvers aren't going to do.'

His brows rise. 'Y'know how to shoot a gun?'

'You saw me shoot one the other day, Mr McCarthy.'

He shrugs. 'So you figured out how to shoot it, but d'you know how to shoot *at* something?'

Rolling my eyes, I say, 'I know how. My father took me hunting when I was younger. He had a rifle, but I got the gist of your revolver pretty quickly.'

He nods. 'Okay. You really wanna do this? 'Cause this'll be your last chance to pull out. You can settle down at that ranch of yours and forget—'

'*No.*' I stare at him. 'How dare you? You've seen how torn up I am about this. You've seen how useless the marshal and his men are! I have no other choice!'

He holds up his hands, nodding. 'I'm sorry. Was just asking... I thought maybe—' He stops and sighs. 'I was just asking. I'm sorry, ma'am.'

'Do you doubt me, Mr McCarthy? Do you think the moment I'm in danger, I'll curl up into a ball and become a damsel in distress? Is that what it is?'

'No, ma'am. Although, no one knows how they'll react when in danger... and there ain't no shame in it for listening to your body's instincts and running away from a fight you know you can't win.'

'Do you speak from experience?'

His mouth twists. 'Maybe. Either way, I know what it's like. You were right to bring me along with you.'

My eyes go to the dancers and I feel my foot tapping to the music under the table. I chew on my lip.

'We'll go to the gunsmith tomorrow morning. Maybe the morning after that we can set off to Montana?'

Mr McCarthy nods. 'It's gonna take a week or more to get up there on horseback.'

'That's fine. I'm looking forward to some quiet.'

He lets out a quiet laugh, surprising me. 'You and me both.'

I feel my stomach sink at the thought that this is finally it. I finally have some information on where some of the men that killed Thomas are. And I'll be going ahead with finding them in only a matter of weeks. It's both terrifying and comforting to have that knowledge. Knowing Mr McCarthy is coming with me is a comfort. My opinion of the man has slowly changed over the past few days. I've tried to ignore the fact he's a much more decent man than I expected him to be, but it's hard not to. He's helped in so many ways and seems open to continuing to do so. I can't help but wonder if there's an ulterior motive for him as well. Perhaps he too, is on a road to salvation, for his own reasons. And perhaps the only reason why he's helping me is because he isn't only sorry for me, but because he sees the benefit in giving justice to these murderers. When I asked him what his reasons for changing his mind were back in Galway City, he basically told me it was none of my business. And he was right to, it isn't. But it's impossible to not wonder why a man would risk his life for a woman he doesn't know, to go out and kill men he doesn't know. There isn't value to my life. I know if I die trying to kill these men, at least I'll die trying to give Thomas' life meaning. I can't see why Mr McCarthy would want to risk dying simply just to help me.

'Do you think we'll be able to find all these men?' I ask him after a while. He's been sitting across from me smoking, looking about the room, his eyes mainly focused on the dancers, as mine have been.

He turns his head to watch me. 'You have my word we'll find the ones the marshal knows 'bout. And if those sonbitches know anything 'bout their brothers' whereabouts, I'll get it outta them.'

I stare at him for a long time, heartbeat drumming rhythmically with the music in the room. And then I nod at his words. 'Let's go and get this done, then.'

10

The sun is harsh as we head out of Cheyenne and up towards Montana. It doesn't take long for me to see Mr McCarthy was speaking the truth about the American sun being different to the Irish sun and I find myself being grateful for the hat he gave me, its wide brim giving my face and shoulders welcoming shade. But I sweat under my linen shirt as we ride and the breeze from off the mountains isn't enough to cool me, as there's no escape from the heat as we continue to ride amongst the open plains. The revolver and belt I bought before we left sits at my waist and the added weight of it continues to prod me in the side from the movements of my horse that I haven't gotten used to yet. Mr McCarthy rides slightly ahead of me, leading the way and I see sweat has gathered at his back, making his shirt cling to his skin there. He doesn't complain and keeps quiet as he rides, giving his horse little words of encouragement and subtle movements of his legs whenever it falters. I notice how natural he looks on top of a horse, especially since it has been a while since I've ridden and I'm only just getting the hang of it once more. He rides the horse as if he was born within the saddle and perhaps he was.

It doesn't take long for me to grow sore and tired. We've been riding for a couple of hours; Cheyenne no longer a speck in the distance and only a recent memory. My thighs ache and my back craves a stretch. I continue on for a little longer as it looks like

Mr McCarthy hasn't tired at all, but when my horse begins to slow down and grow stubborn, I direct her towards the river we've been riding along for the past hour and let out a yell to Mr McCarthy. He turns around and follows me and I dismount by the water to let my horse drink. My legs feel like jelly and can barely hold my weight, so I lean against the saddle, panting. The sun is still relentlessly shining down upon us.

'Tired?'

'It's been at least six hours, surely?'

''Bout that, yeah.'

He gets off his horse and takes off its saddle. Foam has gathered around the sides of the gelding's dark back. I take off my horse's saddle as well and set it on the ground close by. I go about unpacking some things to eat and sit down on the ground with a sigh. Mr McCarthy fixes up the horses and then comes over, sitting down beside me. He takes the salted beef I hand him and we eat in silence.

'The sun is relentless,' I murmur, squinting from under my hat. My forearms feel singed by it already.

Mr McCarthy glances up at the clear sky where my nemesis hangs proudly. 'Summer sun. Don't worry, it'll get colder the further north we go... and it won't stay summer much longer.' He lowers his head to look at me and I see amusement play across his scruffy features. 'You gotta be careful with that fair skin of yours.'

'So do you,' I mumble, but I know I'm more susceptible than him with my pale, freckly skin and strawberry blonde hair.

He rolls up a cigarette and lights it. The fizzing noise of the match when he flicks it across his boot is a comfort to me and I don't know why. And then the sweet smell of the charred tobacco fills my senses and I rest back in the grass on my elbows, watching the horses eat by the water. We sit in silence, surrounded by nature's beauty and I start to see this cruel country in a new light.

The resentment I had for it for so long after Thomas' death begins to slowly lift. With my sad and quiet companion beside me, I start to find my purpose and become more confident in the fact that what I'm doing for Thomas is the best thing I can do.

It takes us a little under a day to reach a small town called Sweeney. Because we've hardly been in the wilderness, we opt to get any last-minute things and continue on. I go to a general store and buy a coat for when the weather gets colder — although right now that is unimaginable. I also take a spare shirt and another pair of pants, trading two of my dresses for them. When I'm packed down to one bag, with extra clothes and provisions, I tie it to my horse and wait for Mr McCarthy outside on the street.

Sweeney is smaller than any town I've seen, mainly just a long strip of buildings, with a few houses on the outskirts and a small, white building that poses as a church. It's busier than I expected, riding in with Mr McCarthy, and people pass by on the road on foot and in little wagons, going about their daily life. They pay me no mind and I'm slightly grateful for it, wary of these Americans just as they're wary of us Irish. Mr McCarthy comes out with a rifle on his shoulder and I frown at him, glancing at the two repeaters already strapped to his saddle. When he walks up to me and swings it off his shoulder to give it to me, I stare at him.

'You're used to rifles, yeah?' he asks.

I nod my head slowly. 'So you're taking those two repeaters for yourself?'

His mouth twists in an almost-smile. 'One's a shotgun, ma'am.'

I look back at the saddle. I can barely tell the difference. I don't know guns well enough. 'Right...'

'Here.' I take the gun from him when he holds it towards me. It's heavy, but lighter than my father's old rifle and I can't tell whether it's because the gun is made differently or because my childish arms were weaker when I last held one. 'I'll teach ya how to use it again in case you're rusty.' His eyes glance around the town, squinting in the midday sun. 'We'll just get outta earshot of here lest we scare some folk for no reason. Let's get a drink before we go.'

Mr McCarthy shows me how to sit the rifle in the holster on my saddle so that it's secure and then we leave the horses and head to the only saloon in the street. It's quiet when we enter and whatever patrons drinking inside, lift their heads up from their glasses to watch us walk to the back of the room where the bar is. Mr McCarthy rests his forearms on the bar and pays for two drinks, one for me and one for him. I try to slide the coins for my drink to him, but he pushes them back towards me without a word and I give up, putting them back in my purse. I drink the whiskey when it's served and let out a sigh. Whatever reliance I might have with drink has been gnawing at my stomach for days. Finally, drinking again makes me crave the numbness it brings, the burn and the feeling of nothing at all but everything at the same time. I know the emotions inside me are dangerous, especially if I keep pushing them down and locking them up in dark recesses. I just can't seem to quit the habit. Mr McCarthy might be my only companion, but he's not my friend and neither is he a person I care for, or someone I wish to connect with. I'm still alone in this foreign country and I feel like it'll always be that way now that Thomas is gone. I'll always be alone in Ireland, just as I'll always be alone in America.

After three rounds, I stand back from the bar and rub my forehead. I'm about to tell Mr McCarthy we should go, that being in civilisation again is making me feel nauseous, when a few men enter the saloon. The doors swing open abruptly, creaking as they do and a few people shuffle about to get out of their way. I look up. They look mean — guns at their sides and rifles on their backs. Spurs jingle every time they step and the one leading the small group has a savage gash across his mouth, only just healing. He comes to the bar and sets himself down close to where Mr McCarthy stands, having still not looked up, too intent on his drink. I'm about to get his attention, to tell him that we should go, when the man with the scar looks up and meets my eye. A cruel smile curls up the scar across his lips, making it look even more grotesque and deformed. My heart skitters.

'The hell is a woman doing in here?' he asks. A couple of his cronies laugh and the bartender serves him and his fellas drinks, keeping his head down. 'What you doing, sweetheart? You a new whore for us, huh?' He leans past Mr McCarthy to get a good look at me. 'Not sure your whole getup is going to get a paying man's attention, but I'll still take ya for free.'

'Shut your mouth, you ugly bastard,' I growl across at him.

I see shock register on his face as his men let out a hoot and then he scowls at me. He finishes his whiskey in one go and steps forward. Mr McCarthy has done nothing until this point. I want to tell him to leave with me and I'm confused as to why he's still looking down at his drink, keeping his head lowered.

'What you say?' the man asks, getting closer.

I stick up my chin, but my heart is racing. 'I said shut your mouth. You've got no business talking to a lady like that.'

His brows rise. He's ugly, missing teeth and straggly, oily hair hangs about his ears under his floppy hat. 'Do I not?' He looks back at his boys. 'Fellas, apparently this here is a *lady* and we got no business talking to her.'

The men all laugh. I'm looking at Mr McCarthy, jaw tight. I don't want to leave because I don't want this man to think he has it over me. I know he's not going to listen to a woman and if Mr McCarthy could just stand up and tell him to leave... I feel that dark anger start to bubble in my gut, brought up by the frustration of it all and my hand goes to my gun. The man sees and he lets out an ugly snort.

'Gonna shoot me, girly, huh? That it?'

He's coming closer and closer and I'm about to pull out my revolver when Mr McCarthy suddenly jerks into action. He leans over the bar and grabs a bottle. Turning around, he lifts it up and smashes it hard over the man's head. Glass and liquor spray everywhere and the man's eyes roll back as blood and his hat go flying. He falls to the ground like a dead weight and I jump, startled. The saloon is quiet for a moment, everyone frozen while they try to register what just happened. And then Mr McCarthy is pushing me out towards the door and I can hear the other men yelling after us. We're at our horses when the first gunshot fires out towards us. There's a *thwang* as the bullet lodges into the porch above the hitching post. My horse scatters underneath me as I'm mounting and I grab the reins, trying to pull her up. But then Mr McCarthy is pushing me forward, yelling at me to ride, so I let her run and sit in the saddle with tight legs.

I think we're safe, as we've been riding for several minutes, when I hear hoofbeats and a shout come out from behind us. I look back and see a rider coming at us on a grey horse. Mr McCarthy grunts and I see him pull his revolver out of his belt. There's another gunshot and I duck down, yelling. My hand goes to my gun and I pull it out, firing wildly behind me in the hopes that it'll scare the rider away, but he keeps shooting. I see a burst of red mist at the corner of my eye and look towards Mr McCarthy as we ride. As the horses run up the dirt track alongside a crop of trees, I see Mr McCarthy outlined around them, grimacing in pain as he clutches his shoulder. I let out a curse. Stupidity makes me pull my horse up and she skids to a stop. I turn her around with my legs and lift my gun. My hands are shaking. The sights wobble in front of my aiming eye. The rider gets closer and closer up the slope where the track leads to where we're standing. I don't know whether Mr McCarthy is still riding or whether he's stopped too, because all I can hear is the sound of my breath. And then when the rider enters my sights, I pull the trigger and the revolver throws itself back in my hand. I grit my teeth. Missed. He continues to ride towards us. There's no time to turn back around and run. I'm stupid to have stopped. There's a short moment and then I see him lift his gun and aim it right at me. A gunshot sounds out and my horse panics underneath me so I'm nearly thrown as she rears. I manage to clutch onto her neck as she lifts herself up off the ground, but not before the back of her head connects with my face. I feel my teeth sink into my tongue and blood floods my mouth. I cry out.

When I look up, there's a horse standing on the track behind us, its rider lying on the ground, dead. I look around, panting and spitting blood. Mr McCarthy puts his revolver back in its holster at his belt and lets out a groan of pain. There's blood all over his shirt. I curse and settle my horse enough to ride towards him.

'What the hell was that?' I yell, panic making me foolish and mad.

He looks at me, wincing. 'What the hell you talking 'bout?' he grates at me. 'We just had our first gunfight, that's what that was.'

'I had him! The ugly one back at the bar! Why the hell did you smash a bottle over his head?'

'You *had* him?' He almost laughs at me. 'Him and his boys were gonna eat you alive, Ms Ryan.'

'You don't know that,' I growl, 'I could've talked him down.'

'Yeah... right.'

He's bleeding so much. My mind is in a panic at the sight of it and yet I can't seem to form articulate thoughts in order to act accordingly. A man is dead and my mouth feels like it's on fire.

'You're bleeding,' he tells me, voice gravelly.

'So are you, you big buffoon,' I spit.

He grunts again. His hand is pressed tightly to his shoulder and I hear it squelch against the amount of blood that's gathered in his shirt. He uses one hand to direct his horse up the road and I follow him, livid.

'It didn't have to come to this, you know!' I yell after him. 'Do you think it necessary to smash bottles over the heads of every man that might throw an insult our way?'

'Ms Ryan, if you don't stop right now, I might have to—'

'Might have to what, Mr McCarthy?' I shout. 'Hit me like that man would have? Show me that being an outspoken woman such as myself will get me nothing but a bloody nose?'

'You already got one of those,' he hisses.

'Shut up!'

He rides up into the trees and we find a rocky outcrop there that's covered in fallen leaves. It's well sheltered from the road and out of the sun. He slides out of his saddle and staggers to the ground. I get off the mare and tie her to a tree, loosening her girth. I take my rifle off the saddle and sling it over my shoulder, just in case any of the other men decide to come snooping about. When I reach Mr McCarthy, he's sitting with his back against the trunk of a tree, panting. His face is white. There's blood in his beard from where it's sprayed upwards from the wound on his shoulder. He has a small kit in his lap and I watch him struggling to take off his shirt so that he can get to the bullet hole. I'm so angry with him, firstly for smashing the bottle over the idiot's head and secondly for being mad at me for getting mad at him. Blood is still dribbling down my lips and onto my chin. I wipe it away with the back of my hand and spit on the ground beside me. My face hurts and I can feel an intense headache coming on, tightening up my jaw.

'This is exactly what I was worried about,' I tell him once I've gathered my thoughts, shaking my head. 'You thinking you can attack anyone for any damned reason and blowing things up in our faces. I thought you were a stupid man to begin with, Mr McCarthy, but not *this* stupid. They should have called you the Dangerously Impulsive American Outlaw at St Brigid's.'

'Doesn't have much ring to it,' he says and his voice is quiet and deadly. I look at him. He's still struggling to get his shirt off.

'You need to agree with me, Mr McCarthy, or we're going to have a problem.'

He doesn't look at me, having gone to putting his shirt between his teeth and pulling to try and get it off.

'I make the rules,' I continue. It hurts to talk but I have to say it. I'm so heated by what's just happened. 'Because obviously you're not in the right state of mind.'

He drops the bit of shirt from his mouth to say, 'You nearly killed some squatters in your husband's ranch, Ms Ryan. I don't think either of us is fit for the position of making decisions.'

I kick at his foot and he glares at me. 'That's not fair,' I hiss. 'I had reason to be upset with those men!'

'Maybe I had reason to be upset with these men,' he mutters.

I sniff. 'Did you? Did you know them, perhaps? Were they once *your* fellas?'

He doesn't say anything and finally tears at his shirt enough to get it off his ruined shoulder. The wound is a gaping hole and is pulsing blood down his chest. I nearly swoon at the sight of it and look away.

'I know you're angry with me right now, ma'am,' he says, voice quiet, 'but I might need your help.'

Pride makes me want to refuse. I look back at him, struggling to stem the bleeding, and sigh. I walk over and set my rifle down. Kneeling down beside him, I pick up a piece of cloth from the kit in his lap, pressing it firmly against his wound. He bares his teeth in pain and gasps.

'Is there an exit wound?' I ask him.

'Yeah, you've got your hands against it.'

'That's good at least.'

'Stitching it ain't gonna work. I'll have to cauterise it.'

I pull him forward to look at the other wound at the back of his shoulder. 'You've got matching shoulders now, Mr McCarthy,' I say, seeing the other scars on his left shoulder that I first saw at St Brigid's.

'Nice of you to show me the bright side of things, ma'am.'

My hands are already covered in his blood. I pull away from him and start to build a small fire. He gives me his matches and I light it. When the flames are going, I take his knife off his belt and rest the blade in the flames. I think of the whiskey in his bag and get up to fetch it, knowing both of us will need some to get this done. He takes the bottle from me with shaking hands when I hand it over and he drinks a lot of it. Some of it dribbles in his beard as he winces, pouring a little over his shoulder. A growl emanates from his chest and I take the bottle from him. The whiskey burns the cuts on my tongue when I drink, but I feel better after a few mouthfuls. When I'm done, I set the bottle down and pick up the knife. It glows red hot and I take it over to him.

'You want to do it, or shall I?' I ask.

He grimaces. 'I don't have a good enough angle.'

I get down beside him. 'What do I do?'

'Hold it against the wound and sear it until it stops bleeding. Just keep checking until the blood's gone. Don't hold it on there too long 'cause you don't wanna burn healthy skin.'

'You've done this before...' I laugh nervously, unable to help myself.

'Dozens of times.' He picks up the cloth I used against his wound and screws it up in a ball, shoving it in his mouth.

I lick my lips and slowly press the knife to his skin. It sizzles immediately and I see his eyes close tightly as he cries out against the cloth in his mouth. I pull away on instinct and he lifts a bloodied hand and wraps it around mine, forcing the knife back onto the wound. I'm startled, letting him hold it there until he pulls my hand and the knife away. When I see a little bit of blood still weeping from the bullet hole, I push my hand forward again and he lets me, still holding tightly. His fingertips dig in tight to my skin, bruising me, but I hold it steady and pull away again. The smell of burnt flesh is making my stomach roll and I feel a wave of giddiness sweep over me. I ignore it as best as I can. When I'm satisfied, I put the blade back on the fire to heat up and he takes the cloth out of his mouth, gagging. I look back at him as he picks up the bottle of whiskey, drinking some more. He's pale and sweating heavily.

'You ready for the next one?' I ask, surprised by the shakiness in my voice.

He nods, eyes closed, the back of his head pressed against the tree. I get up, holding the knife and I can feel the heat coming off it. When I reach him, I help him lean forward. He puts the cloth back in his mouth and I cauterise the second wound. He doesn't grab my hand this time and the sounds of his groans of pain make me dizzy. When I'm done, he falls back and spits out the cloth. I put the knife down and my legs collapse underneath me. I'm dizzy and my stomach feels tight and sick. Mr McCarthy weakly picks up the bottle of whiskey and drinks some, pouring some on the wounds again for good measure. And then he reaches over, handing it to me, and I take it from him and drink deep.

'Thank... you...'

I glance at him. I don't know what to say. The dumb bastard got himself into this mess, but I can't help but feel like he did the right thing back there and we'd be in an even worse position if he hadn't knocked that man out. I don't say that. I say nothing and give him back his bottle of whiskey so he can finish it off and collapse into a fitful sleep. When he's unconscious, I go about unsaddling the horses and getting out our bedrolls. The rocky ledge we're on is a decent enough campsite and I don't see us moving on any time soon. I try to eat some salted beef but my stomach is still revolting at what just occurred. I grab the rifle and lie it across my lap as I rest by the fire.

———○———

It's past nightfall when Mr McCarthy wakes up. The crop of trees we're in blocks out all light from the sky and it's dark, apart from the small fire I have going. It's grown cold and I've thrown on my duster coat to keep warm, sipping at another bottle of whiskey I found in my bag. I hear his grunt first and look over my shoulder at him. He gets to his feet and his ruined shirt falls to the ground. I've already packed up the kit we used and the knife lies on the ground beside me. Mr McCarthy gets another shirt out of his bag, his braces hanging loose around his hips. I get up and go to him, pulling the kit back out to take out the bandages I saw in there.

'We'll need to cover that shoulder of yours up,' I murmur.

He looks at me, as if only just remembering I'm here and it makes me wonder how much pain he's in. He nods and lets me wind the bandages around his shoulder until they're tight and secure. He takes off his hat to put his shirt on and sighs.

'That was a mess.'

'You don't say,' I reply dryly.

'Those men were sonbitches,' he growls. 'See how everyone in that saloon ducked down and grew quiet 'round them? Was doing the world a favour putting them in their place.'

'*I* was putting them in their place,' I bite back. 'You hit one over the head with a bloody bottle. What good is that going to do?'

'What good is telling them they're being naughty boys gonna do, ma'am?'

'Oh, shut up.' I wave my hands at him, turning away. 'You got yourself shot, you buffoon and you could've been killed. What good are you to me, dead? You're just as bad as they are, Mr McCarthy. And I think that's why you attacked them, because you hate those bastards just as much as you hate yourself.'

He's silent for a while and I feel like I've hit a nerve, but I don't apologise and neither do I look at him. I get my rifle and sling it over my shoulder. There's no point staying here. I don't want to be near Sweeney anymore and we're only half an hour out of town, not even. I kick dirt and wet leaves over the fire to extinguish it and go over to my horse to saddle it up.

'We're moving on,' I tell Mr McCarthy.

He says nothing still, but I see him go about gathering his things as best he can out of the corner of my eye. I want to help him as he struggles with his horse's saddle and yet there's a part of me that relishes the sight. It's only when he takes too long do I go over and tighten his horse's girth for him and strap his bag back to the saddle. He grunts a small thanks. I don't reply and mount up. He gets on his horse and follows me as we ride back out. When we get out of the trees and back onto the track, the moon and brilliant stars light our way. It's a beautiful sight, only I'm too tired and on edge to appreciate it.

Just when I started to see Mr McCarthy in a different light, he's proved himself to be the man I pinned him as. Uncontrollable, impulsive, rude, dangerous and stupid. Like any other man in this damned country, he's nothing compared to the man Thomas was and has no hope of being. He's driven only by instinct and is as brutish as he looks. The life he's led has taught him that way and that way only and he's stuck in a loop. There's no saving him and neither is there any chance of befriending such a man. It's as if he knows it, too, angry at himself and saddened by what he's seen and the blood he's spilled. But there's no pity in me for him, not when it's his own fault. He makes me sick. He makes me furious and if he wasn't helping me kill the men that killed Thomas, I'd probably kill him, too.

⊷•⊶

Great Falls is wild and vast. There are so many rivers, creeks and lakes that are connected to one another. I soon start to see, amongst the hills and mountains and forests, why the place got its name, as there are waterfalls, big and small, everywhere we go. The place echoes with the sound of rushing and raging water. The roar of it vibrates the ground and shakes the leaves in trees that sit close enough to the rapids. The sound of it reminds me of the River Corrib and when I close my eyes, I can picture myself standing on the Salmon Weir Bridge and the thought brings a lump to my throat.

We've been here two days, searching for any signs of life. It took us over a week to get here from Sweeney, slowed down by Mr McCarthy's injury. In these nine days, we've rarely spoken to one another. I've preferred it, sick of the arguing and sick of him talking back to me when he has no right to. I've tried to embrace the days riding in silence, left with my thoughts. But I've been plagued by them, more so than ever and it's getting hard to ignore the dark fury inside me. So many nights I've dreamed of Thomas with a bullet hole in his head. I've put it down to witnessing Mr McCarthy's wounds and my mind trying to sort through the memories, yet I can't avoid the feeling of unrelenting pain those dreams give me. The anger towards the Gaitwoods and specifically to the man who pulled the trigger. It makes me eager to find Harry Oswald, tracking him down, my eyes sharp on any movement as we travel through the wilderness of Great Falls. I'm too focused on finding this wild outlaw that I can't fully admire the beauty of this place. I don't know what I'm going to do when we find him. All I know is, I want him to feel the pain he's made me feel.

It's early morning when we're riding along the road and hear the beats of hooves coming towards us. I see Mr McCarthy tense in his saddle in front of me and he holds out an arm, signaling me to pull up my horse. I tug the reins gently and she stops, nodding and pawing. We both listen intently towards the direction of the sound and I can hear it coming closer, my pulse beginning to quicken. And then two riders appear around the bend in the road. The first thing I notice is the blood stains on their clothes and my stomach turns. Mr McCarthy moves his horse backwards until he's closer to me, his arm still out wide, protective.

My eyes haven't left the riders and when they see us staring at them, they too pull up. Two men, both middle-aged. There are dead rabbits tied to the sides of their saddles, bobbing against their horses' flanks as they slow down. My fingers begin to tingle and I feel a spike of anxiety pierce my chest.

'Howdy,' Mr McCarthy starts, keeping his voice light. 'You fellas okay?'

'We ain't looking for a fight, if that's what you're asking,' one of them, the one with a bloodied bandage on his head, says. 'Already had one of those.'

'What happened?'

'We were attacked,' the other one says, voice shaking. 'Big, wild man with an axe. Told us we weren't allowed to be hunting on his land.'

This piques my interest.

'Mr McCarthy,' I murmur.

He nods, not taking his eyes off the two men. 'What he look like?'

'I just said,' the man replies, voice heightening with frustration and fear, 'big and wild.'

'He hurt you?' Mr McCarthy nods to the bloodstains.

'Gave me a bit of a clobbering, yeah. Came out of the bush like a bear, didn't see him 'til he was on me.' He shakes his head and I can feel the fear radiating off him, even from the distance between us.

'Said something about us stealing food out of his belly. Belittled our manhoods and threatened us,' the other adds. He shakes his head. 'Now, if you don't mind, we're getting out of here and I implore you to do the same.' He finally meets my gaze and his eyes widen when he realises I'm a woman. 'Especially you, ma'am. This ain't no place for a woman.'

'Where'd this happen?' Mr McCarthy asks before they can leave.

'About half a day's ride down yonder. Where the river grows wide with rapids.'

Mr McCarthy doesn't have a chance to say anything else before they're kicking their horses into a gallop past us. The mare skids sideways underneath me and I squeeze my legs, shushing her and urge her forwards.

'Where you going?' Mr McCarthy asks, not following.

'To where those men said Harry Oswald was,' I reply.

'You don't know it's him, Ms Ryan.'

'*Who else* could it be?'

He's following me now, his horse moving in tandem with mine.

'This is a big country.'

'Harry Oswald is depicted as a big, wild-looking man. The marshal told us he'd be here in Great Falls. It's him.'

The men's story, the sightings. Everything is falling into place and I'm convinced. It doesn't matter what Mr McCarthy thinks, it's up to me. This is what I want, what I *need*; he has no say.

'So what?' he asks, voice growing more exasperated. 'You find this man who attacked those boys back there and expect me to shoot him? I won't do it, not if I don't know it's Harry.'

'I'll do it, then.'

He grunts. 'You content in killing a man who might not even be the man who deserves it?'

'He attacked those men, didn't he? Probably would have killed them if they didn't get away. If it's not Harry Oswald, his actions are still abhorrent enough to justify us killing him, aren't they?'

'I don't think it is, no. Starving men are dangerous, but that don't make them deserving of death.'

I look heavenward, frustrated. 'It's Harry, Mr McCarthy.'

'You don't know that.'

'I don't care.'

Perhaps it's this anger within me that's driving me to be unreasonable. I can't explain to Mr McCarthy why I'm so sure this man is Harry Oswald. I just know it is. There's logic within me, questioning that side, arching a brow at my brashness, but I ignore it. I need this. Whether it's Harry or not, I need to *believe* it's him to do this.

We ride in silence the rest of the way. My heart is hammering and won't seem to settle. I feel fatigued from the ride, but I keep going, urging the mare with gentle words. She seems to sense my discomfort, flighty towards birds that spring from branches or puddles in the road. Mr McCarthy follows on. I don't know what he's thinking and I don't care. I didn't ask him to come to America with me for his opinion.

A few hours pass until Mr McCarthy calls for me to stop and rest the horses. I don't want to. I want to keep going and find this wild man, but I listen and dismount off the side of the road. I loosen my mare's saddle and let her graze on a patch of grass. Mr McCarthy settles down beside his horse, drinking water from a canteen. I sit down a few paces from him, relieved to be sitting on something that isn't a saddle. I pick up a piece of grass and twirl it between my fingers, lost in thought.

'So what's your plan?' Mr McCarthy asks suddenly, making me jump.

'What?'

'If you're gonna go through with this, what's your plan when we find this man?'

'Question him?' I want to seem certain, confident, but I can't muster the energy to appear that way. 'I'll decide at the time.'

Mr McCarthy makes a face. 'You gotta be prepared for things like this, Ms Ryan.'

'That's why I brought you,' I counter. 'You're the one versed in killing.'

He shakes his head, not saying anything else. We sit in silence and I'm consumed by my thoughts once more. I don't even notice when Mr McCarthy stands back up, tightening the girth on his saddle.

'You coming?'

I blink and quickly stand. We move on and I take the lead again, eager to continue.

<hr>

Several hours later, I see the rapids the men described. I glance behind me, to where Mr McCarthy is catching up and I see his eyes moving along the trees on the opposite bank. There's a mountain rising up above the treetops and I lift my eyes, squinting against the sunshine. Smoke is billowing above the trees on the other side of the river, just under where the base of the mountain begins. My heart jumps in my chest and I immediately pull my horse towards it, directing her to the edge where the river flows. It's not so wide, not anymore and there's a small waterfall where rocks rise above the surface, making it shallow enough to pass. I hear Mr McCarthy swear behind me and tell me to stop, but I push my horse through the water. I'm thankful for the beast when she does, lifting her head up a little with fright.

'Ms Ryan!'

I'm not thinking. I get over the other side, my legs slightly wet from crossing and I kick her into a canter towards the trees.

She springs into action under me. Over the past week, I've gotten to know this horse well and she's gotten to know me, too. We're just as stubborn as the other and I'm grateful for her bravery and her trust. My eyes are wide, focusing in on the trees ahead of me, looking for any sign of the source of the smoke. I can hear Mr McCarthy riding after me. When I get closer to the base of the mountain, I pull her up and dismount, taking the rifle off her saddle. Mr McCarthy jumps off his horse and I hear him marching towards me in the fallen leaves. When I turn around, he's glowering at me, breathing hard.

'Don't be stupid 'bout this,' he hisses. 'You'll get yourself killed and then what?'

'I'll die trying to avenge my husband, that's what!' I bite back.

'You don't even know if it's *him*!'

'I don't care!'

It's the first time we've spoken to each other in hours. Our words are so heated I can already feel the fury inside me clawing its way up, begging to be let out. If Mr McCarthy doesn't stop, it'll be let out on him and I'm not sure I'll be able to stop myself doing something rash and wild. I feel like a lioness, backed in a corner, ready to maul and rip apart anything that may pose as a threat. I turn away from him and tie my horse to a tree. I start to move forward through the leaves on foot and I hear Mr McCarthy hitch his horse and follow me. He comes up beside me, expression unreadable, shotgun in his hands.

'So you're really gonna do this?' he asks.

I stare at his face, considering it. 'Yes,' I say after a moment. 'I have to. It has to be him. It can't be anyone else, Mr McCarthy.'

'You really believe that?'

'I have to,' I say again.

I turn back around and keep going. My thoughts are running. I'm so close to what could be the first man that's connected to my husband's death that I don't know what to do, what to think.

All I can do is let instinct take over and that forces me to react like a wild animal, attacking anything in sight. My heart is hammering so hard it hurts and I'm so on edge that I'm jumping at anything that moves in the forest, any sound.

'Easy...' Mr McCarthy's voice is quiet and husky.

I see what he's already seen. A small, wooden hut sits in a clearing close to the mountain. There's a fire crackling outside and furs hang up around the hut on makeshift racks. A dead deer has been strung out across a table near the fire, its entrails hanging out of a bucket at its base. And then I see him. He comes out of the hut, dressed in his undershirt and a pair of dirty trousers. His beard is long, sitting across his broad chest and his hair falls down his back. If this is Harry Oswald, he looks like an untamed creature more than a man. He's big and tall, large with both muscle and fat. He moves like a predator and his eyes, even from this distance, are a stark green against his grubby face. It has to be him and I hate him. I hate everything that he is, everything he represents. He's nothing but an animal that needs to be exterminated, a pest, a cockroach. Fury blinds me. I march through the leaves, pushing Mr McCarthy away from me when he tries to stop me, and aim my rifle at Harry Oswald's head.

'Hey!' I growl as I enter the clearing.

Oswald looks up and he bares his teeth when he sees me. They're like fangs, half rotten inside his skull.

'You Harry Oswald?' I ask.

'Who the hell are you?' he spits.

'The wife of Thomas Ryan. You and your Gaitwood boys murdered him on his ranch three years ago.'

He lets out a laugh and my gut twists. 'Murdered a lot of men. What makes yours so special?'

'He's special because his wife won't let the men who killed him breathe air they no longer deserve to breathe.'

Mr McCarthy steps beside me. His shotgun is pointed at Oswald's chest. The man snorts with a shake of his head and spits on the ground beside his feet.

'What if I'm not Oswald, huh?' he asks. 'You'll be killing me for nothing.'

'Don't you dare,' I hiss. I don't need reminding that this man might not even be him. It's too late for that. The fury within me wants a victim and it's found him.

He starts to move and Mr McCarthy yells, 'I wouldn't if I were you. Listen to the lady and maybe she'll let your death be not as painful as she was planning.'

'No way in hell!' I step forward, keeping my rifle on him. 'Tell me where Russ Gaitwood is.'

Oswald laughs again. 'You think I'm gonna tell you that when you're killing me either way?'

'Tell me, you bastard!'

Oswald stares at me, his eyes unnerving. He's grinning like a maniac, as if amused by my pain and it makes me feel ill. I'm so furious I'm shaking. I don't know how to control myself. I feel like crying and tearing him to shreds. It's hard to focus. I can feel Mr McCarthy has stepped beside me again. I step away from him. I don't want him interrupting me. I circle Oswald, watching for an opening. He turns his body towards me, still grinning. I know he won't go down without a fight.

'Mr McCarthy,' I say. 'Tie him up like the pig he is.'

Mr McCarthy glances at me, hesitating. I hear breath leave his lungs when he lowers his shotgun and removes his lasso from his belt. Oswald snorts and I growl, jerking my rifle at him to accentuate the fact that if he tries anything, I'm pulling the trigger.

'You really gonna let a woman tell you what to do? You got any kind of manhood about you, boy?'

'Shut your mouth or you're eating bullets,' I hiss.

Mr McCarthy reaches him and forces the butt of his shotgun against his face. I flinch, not expecting it and Oswald crumples. Mr McCarthy begins to hogtie him, hands rough, as the man groans. I can feel myself shaking as I watch on, so close to a precipice of something I'm uncertain of what exactly it is.

When Oswald is tied, Mr McCarthy hoists him up by his shoulders until he's kneeling in front of him. I move forward, fuelled by anger. I grab Oswald by the hair, lifting his face up so he's forced to look me in the eyes.

'You killed my husband. You owe me more than your pathetic, little life,' I spit at him. 'Tell me where that coward Russ Gaitwood is hiding.'

Oswald laughs again. I tighten my fist in his hair and he still keeps laughing. I can't handle it. Mr McCarthy comes forward.

'Ms Ryan...' he says quietly. I look at him, but I'm not listening. His eyes are tensed. I can see he's worried I'm going to do something drastic — that I need to calm down and think logically. But all logic has left my body.

'Yeah... I think I remember now...' Oswald starts. I look back at him, breathing hard. 'Your husband... he was on that ranch just outside Cheyenne, yeah? Little yellow-belly begged for mercy like a girl. We did you a favour getting rid of him. He wasn't a man at all. Surely you knew that being his wife and sharing his bed?'

I know there's a knife at Mr McCarthy's belt. I know it has a wooden handle with the carving of a doe inlaid in the wood. I know because I've used it before and yet it feels heavier than the last time I held it in my hands. That's the only thing I can think about as my mind turns off and my body lurches forward, filled with nothing but primal energy. Primal rage. Something inside me snaps, similar to the feeling I first got in the Salmon Leap all that time ago. It snaps and my mind goes blank. There's a dark colour in front of my eyes and at first, I think it's blackness and

I've somehow lost consciousness but then I see the knife in both my hands and I see the blood, so red and so thick that it's black and it's covering me. It's on my hands, it's on my face. I can taste it as I scream. It's hot, almost burning my skin and it's sticky and I'm wondering why there's so much of it until someone is grabbing my shoulders, pulling me away. I can hear them telling me something. I don't know what they're saying. I can't hear anything over the sound of my own cries and my heartbeat. I think my heart is going to explode inside the cavity of my chest. All I can see is the colour red. All I can smell and taste is blood and I know it's not my own.

And then I'm trembling. My whole body is shaking and I can't stop it. The arms that hold me tightly try to steady me but the shaking is deeply set inside my bones. My teeth chatter. I feel hot and cold at the same time.

Eventually, I'm aware that Mr McCarthy is the one holding onto me. He's somehow dragged me back out to the river and we're sitting on the rocks beside where the water flows. He doesn't let me go, his arms tightly holding my back to his chest. I'm staring blankly into the trees across the river and at the blue sky above their canopy. The sun is a blanket over the both of us and with the heat of Mr McCarthy's body against mine, I'm shrouded by warmth. But it doesn't take away the cold I feel inside me or the shuddering and shaking my bones continue to do. However, the weight of him and the feeling of his powerful arms is almost a comfort. I feel if he lets me go, I'll float away or sink down into the depths of hell. I know my mind is trying to process what just happened. I know it needs to, so I'm not driven mad. After a little longer, I recognise what I've done and I recognise that I'm covered in the blood of the man I've just brutally murdered.

11

I don't know how long it is until my mind clears enough to think straight and the shaking inside me subsides. The sun is close to setting when I lift my head and I feel Mr McCarthy's hold on me loosen. I'm still clutching his arm, where it's wrapped around the front of my shoulders, and I slowly let it go, my hands sticky with dried blood. Mr McCarthy pulls away from me. I don't know what to say to him. He's held onto me for so long that it feels odd to not have his weight and heat against my back. I quietly go to the water's edge and kneel down in the sand. My hands shake as I start to carefully wash the blood off them, all the way up to my arms. The water clouds with red and I try to ignore it as I clean myself. Congealed globs are stuck on the hairs of my arms and they hurt as I scratch at them with my nails. I want to scratch all the way down to my flesh, to rid myself of this man's blood. The smell is in my nostrils, as if burned there. As if only fully aware of it now, I feel my stomach revolt. I lean forward and vomit onto the sand beside where I kneel. I retch and cough until there's nothing left inside my stomach, equal to the emptiness I feel in my heart.

'Here,' a gentle voice says.

Mr McCarthy stands above me and he offers me a water canteen. I take it from him and drink deep, washing the taste of bile out of my mouth. When I'm handing it back, I see blood has transferred onto him as well, across his chest and arms when he grabbed me. His brown shirt is now black. I look down at my own clothes. They're hanging onto my skin, soaked.

'I'll get you your bag,' he murmurs. 'You'll feel better in fresh clothes.'

I nod silently and when he comes back with my bag, I go about taking off my ruined clothes. My hat, my shirt, my belt, my trousers, my boots. My undershirt is ruined as well and I take that off too. I'm too unfocused and in shock to care about modesty. I don't know whether Mr McCarthy looks and neither do I care. All I do is take off my clothes and walk into the depths of the river until my head is submerged. As soon as the water is in my ears, rushing and gurgling around me, I use it to drown out all my thoughts, holding my breath for as long as I can while the current pushes and pulls me. The silt at the bottom of the river is soft on my bare feet and I dig my heels into it to steady me. I lift my head up for air and take my hair out of its plait. It's covered in blood too and I slowly wash it out, finding a rock to help scrub it and my skin. When I feel cleansed, I move back to the shore where my clothes are and get dressed into fresh trousers and a shirt. My clothes stick to my damp body, but they're not bloodied and I can no longer smell it and that's all that matters.

My teeth still chatter. I hold my arms around myself and find Mr McCarthy has brought the horses down where they graze on a patch of grass a little further along the river. I pick up my hat and leave my ruined clothes behind, heading down towards him. He looks up at me from where he sits on a rock, smoking a cigarette while he keeps an eye on the horses. He's washed the blood off his arms and changed his shirt already. I sit down beside him because I don't think my legs can carry the weight of my body any longer. After a little while, he offers me the cigarette he's been smoking and I take it, lifting it to my lips. The taste of tobacco and the burn of it in my lungs is a reminder I'm still alive, still breathing. The smell, the taste, the feeling of smoke passing through my airways, reminds me of home, of being with Thomas so much that I begin to weep, my body shaking with sobs as they grip like a vice around my chest.

I don't know what to say to Mr McCarthy. I don't have any words for the feelings inside me because I don't think I know what these feelings are just yet. I don't want to believe that I lost control of myself and killed a man because I believed he deserved to die. I don't want to acknowledge I've taken a life for the first time and for the first time, after death has ruled my life, it's finally been under my terms. I don't want to consider the fact that I didn't expect it to feel like this — so empty and so incredibly lonely. I've killed the first man belonging to the gang that killed Thomas in the hopes to avenge his death and bring light back into my life, a purpose, but after today I don't know what to think. I don't feel like I've gained a step further towards salvation and contentment. Neither do I feel like I've been damned, and yet this feeling of loneliness is so familiar and such a deep-set ache that I think I was wrong to believe I could rid myself of it so easily. If easy is even the word for it. I feel utterly shaken to the core. I'm no longer just afraid of not giving meaning to Thomas' life. I'm afraid of much, much more. I'm afraid of myself.

Our way back to Cheyenne is slow. I feel myself fading, stuck inside my thoughts and unable to express them aloud to Mr McCarthy. He's gentle with me. I think he might be afraid for me or afraid of me. Perhaps it's both. I can barely function like a normal person. He cooks me my meals and handles my horse when I'm not riding. He doesn't say anything, doesn't conjure up conversation. Perhaps he wishes to give me time to process.

Or perhaps he doesn't care enough to bother to speak. Either way, I'm glad he's a man of few words. I'm glad because I don't want questions I don't know how to answer. I don't want accusations when I know exactly what I've done and when my own mind is consistently cursing me for my actions.

I take each day as it comes. I wake up screaming every night from the memories representing themselves in my dreams. I feel the claws of those monsters and demons on my back, deeper than ever. After several days, I can't help but feel like I've done this to myself. This is the hand I've allowed to be dealt to me. I'm playing a game of cards with the devil and those monsters prowling amongst the shadow I cast. I'm in too deep and there's no pulling out now, not after what I've done. In order to give Thomas peace, I must sacrifice my own.

〰

The city Billings is surrounded by rocky outcrops and mountains on all sides. Wild horses roam amongst the hills and birds flock near the forests that lie at the base of the mountains and along the Yellowstone River. Mr McCarthy gently tells me about the mountain ranges surrounding the city as we make our way down to it, pointing out the Bighorn mountain range and a towering peak called Black Tooth Mountain. I listen to his quiet, gruff voice as we ride and I take in the scenery as best I can, but my heart is bleeding inside my chest. It's like Mr McCarthy knows this, as he's gently trying to distract me with names and sights.

When we're in the city, he finds a hotel for us and I don't complain when he pays for our room. We go upstairs with our bags after leaving the horses in the stable down the street and enter the room we share. There are two beds on either side of the room and a fireplace at the back beside the only window. Mr McCarthy puts my bag on one of the beds for me. I nod silently when he suggests getting something to eat and we go downstairs again. The hotel serves food and supplies hot baths. There are tables and chairs in the main room and even a bar off to the side. People mill about and the smell of food and alcohol makes me feel sick. We sit down at a vacant table and I sit there with my head down until food is in front of me. Braised chicken and grilled vegetables. I eat as much as I can until my stomach tells me no more and I rub at my face.

'Maybe you should get some sleep?' Mr McCarthy offers.

'I don't know what I need,' I whisper, feeling painful tears scratch at my throat. 'I need to be stronger... I thought I was, but obviously—' I rub my temples. I can't gather my thoughts, they're still so scattered.

'You need to talk about it,' he says.

A part of me agrees with him. But I don't want to talk about it. I don't want him to know how I feel.

'With you?' I grate.

'Well... anyone...'

'I don't want to talk about it. What good is that when I can hardly understand it myself?'

'Talking helps, I've—'

'What would you know? You're a heartless killer. You shot that man down on that track outside Sweeney like he was nothing! You've done it that many times that you're used to it, familiar with how it feels. It means nothing to you. How could you possibly sympathise with what I'm going through when you don't have any clue how I feel?'

I get up from the table abruptly, ignoring the attention I've gained by raising my voice. I leave the hotel and walk out onto the street, not thinking, just letting my body run. I'm shaking again. I'm sick of this damned shaking. I find a garden a few streets away and sit down on a bench under a large tree. The day is clear and hot. I try to find beauty in it, but my thoughts are so addled and so full of darkness that I can't. All I can do is sit on the bench seat and try not to cry, dropping my head down as people walk past so they don't notice and ask me what's wrong. I want to be left alone. I want to be held so I can stop falling apart. I want Thomas.

⊢•⊶-◦-⊷•⊣

I was nine years old when I killed my first rabbit. Da gave me his rifle and after days of teaching me breathing techniques and patience, I was finally allowed to have my first kill. It took a lot for me to pull the trigger. I remember being nervous about it and feeling the heavy weight of guilt sink to the bottom of my stomach like a cold stone. My father's pride and encouragement quickly took that away, however, and I picked up my prize as if it was nothing. As if the corpse in my hands never breathed life to begin with. After, he showed me how to skin it and chop it up so we could cook it. While doing so, he sang ancient songs and I sang with him, knowing the words as I was practically born with the lyrics already on my tongue.

Rabbit was nothing like eating fish. It was a delicacy my father and I shared, like an oily secret that would remain on our lips and the tips of our fingers when we returned home to Mam. It went best with rosemary, cooked over an open fire. After the first, I never felt bad killing the wild rabbits that roamed around outside Clifden. My father taught me to thank the earth for its gift and to never kill more than what I needed, so I respected that and never did. I killed so we could eat, just like he fished in the oceans so we could get money to sustain us. It wasn't a luxury; it was a duty and that duty made me completely disregard the fact that what I was doing was killing harmless animals. I was young and whatever childish worries I might have had about that were wiped away by my father's words.

Kill when you have to.

q

It's dark when I make my way back to the hotel. Inside, it's rowdy and I move my way through the crowds of people and upstairs to the room. I smell tobacco when I close the door and glance up to see Mr McCarthy drinking and smoking on his bed. He glances up at me and lifts the half-empty bottle my way. I go over to him and take it, drinking deeply. My body is weary, so I sit down on the bed beside him. The cigarette he smokes crackles in the silence around us and the whiskey swishes inside the bottle as I take another sip. I let out a breath, not knowing what to say. And then words are spilling out of my mouth and I can't stop them, too upset and too tired.

'I'm a killer. I'm no better than the men that killed Thomas.'

Mr McCarthy's silent beside me for a little while and then he murmurs, 'I think you're a real strong woman, Ms Ryan. And I think you've been backed to a corner for so long that you finally lashed out. You ain't anything like those Gaitwood fellas. They're predators. All you are is a wild horse that's learned how to fight back.'

When I feel the tears I've been holding back start to slide down my cheeks, I turn and take the cigarette from him and smoke it, breath shaking as I breathe out. I sniff and I can tell he's watching me. My hands are trembling and I can't seem to stop them.

'It ain't easy...' Mr McCarthy continues. 'If it's easy, then you're damned heartless and there's something wrong with ya. Lotta these gangs out there are just like that... killing folk that don't need to be killed, taking advantage of the weak and the poor, making widows outta women and orphans outta children... That's why I—'

He stops and I look up at him.

'That's why you what, Mr McCarthy?'

His fingers gently take the cigarette from me again and I watch him as he smokes it, breathing out a plume of smoke from his nostrils.

His eyes are on the floor and they hold a faraway look to them. He meets my gaze after a little while.

'I'm already tainted, Ms Ryan,' he says quietly. 'Lemme kill the rest of 'em for ya. You don't need to be having their lives on your conscience.'

His words go against everything inside me — the side of me that doesn't care I just murdered a man, the side that still wants to see them all dead, that I haven't come all the way over here for nothing. I don't know which one to listen to. I know I can do it — I can keep going on if I just tough it out and tell myself this is for the best. *Kill when you have to.*

'Just don't let me near your knife next time,' I murmur. 'Teach me how to shoot properly on the way back to Cheyenne.'

'Alright,' he says after a moment's silence, 'as you wish.'

'I think I need to accept the fact that there's nothing in this world for me without my husband and my old life with him,' I continue, not really knowing why I'm telling him. 'You say you're tainted, but I'm just as tainted, Mr McCarthy. My life has no meaning — what we've been doing here for the past few months has given me a purpose I haven't felt in three years. It's been hard.'

I've started to cry again and I can't stop the sobs racking at my chest. I turn my face away from him, my shaking hands holding the bottle of whiskey weakly between my legs. But then I feel his hand fall across my arm and my gaze meets his once more.

'We'll get it done, Ms Ryan,' he says, voice gruff and quiet. 'You got my word on that.'

'I'm afraid of myself... of the anger inside me.'

We've sat sharing the bottle of whiskey on his bed for several minutes in silence and as soon as I've spoken, I can see Mr McCarthy has blinked, having almost been on the verge of sleep.

'I get that,' he murmurs, shifting his weight on the bed. 'And you ain't gonna find yourself getting any happier if you keep going down this road. I don't think killing these men will give you any satisfaction.'

'I don't want to do it for satisfaction. I know I'll have no inner peace after this except for the fact that I'll have gotten justice for Thomas' death. Other than that, I'll be a scarred woman and no one will want me. I must accept that's the way my life is going to be.'

'I'm not telling ya to stop. Only to listen to your needs. If you get sick of the killing, if you can't stomach it, tell me. There ain't no shame in backing down. You can give these men justice in other ways. And I'm happy to oblige.'

I look at his face. His head is bent down where he sits beside me, our shoulders almost touching. He doesn't look at me, his eyes focused on his boots. He must see me looking at him because after a while, he turns his head and meets my gaze. His eyes are tired and sadder than I've ever seen them. The question I've always wanted an answer to comes to my lips again.

'Why, Mr McCarthy? Why help me?'

'Ain't nobody want me neither, Ms Ryan,' he says. 'It may disgust you to know this, but we got that in common. I had my chance years ago to have a better life and didn't take it.'

'Why not?'

'Blind loyalty... stupidity.' He smirks. 'You do dumb things when you're young and righteous.'

'You do dumb things when you're old and heartbroken,' I murmur with a sad smile.

He lets out a short laugh. 'Ain't that right?' His eyes meet mine again. 'But you ain't old, Ms Ryan. You're in your prime.'

I look away from him. 'I don't feel it.'

'Wait 'til you get to my age. I look in the mirror and hate the old, ugly bastard I see.'

A laugh erupts out of me and I'm surprised by it. I take a look at his brown hair and the skin on his face. 'You might be slightly wrinkled, but at least you're not grey.'

He shrugs a shoulder. 'A lot can happen in less than ten years, Ms Ryan. A lotta growing, a lotta horrible shit you don't really wanna live through but hafta 'cause life is strange and wonderful and forces you to experience things you never thought were possible. But all those things age you. They weigh down on your back 'til you're nothing but a hunched fool, hating the world and everyone in it, living in the mountains somewhere, mistrusting of anything and anyone.'

'That sounds like a choice, Mr McCarthy.'

'It is... to an extent.'

I press my lips. 'Am I making the right choice? Going around and killing these men because I want vengeance for my husband's murder?'

Mr McCarthy lets out a long sigh. 'I honestly don't know, ma'am. All you can do is try 'cause you ain't ever gonna know the outcome of an action until you've done it.'

Closing my eyes, I hang my head. My heart is sore and I'm so weary. 'All I know is that I don't think these men deserve to be out in this world, living as if they've done nothing wrong and ignorant to my pain. I can't continue to live until I've done something about it.'

'Then there's your choice,' he replies gently. 'You're already on that road.'

'What if... after everything is over and all these Gaitwood boys are dead, I don't feel as if I've done anything? What if I don't find the contentment I seek, but only more pain?'

'I ain't a man of God, Ms Ryan and that sounds like a question only he can answer.'

I wave my hand. 'God has forsaken me...' I look at him as he sits back with a small grunt, stretching. 'I didn't enjoy doing what I did... killing Harry Oswald. I don't want this to turn me into a monster, yet at the same time, if I must become one to give Thomas' spirit rest, then it's what I have to do.'

'I can't speak for your husband, Ms Ryan... but maybe he wouldn't want you to do this?'

At his words, I feel my heart squeeze in my chest and fresh tears fall down my face. I turn away from him and take another sip of whiskey. It makes me wonder whether I'm doing all of this out of a selfishness inside me that grew after Thomas' death within my own depressive thoughts. I can no longer distinguish between what is best for me and what is best for Thomas. I know he's dead. I accepted his death years ago. I feel as if I would be doing him a disservice sitting around being miserable. There's a strong sense of justice inside me I have to listen to, that I'm urged to listen to. I must give these men what they deserve and disregard any sort of repercussion that comes from their deaths until the very end. Until it's over, only then can I face how I feel and how I wish to live after.

'Let's continue,' I tell him, voice hard. 'If I start to show you weakness like this again, Mr McCarthy, I implore you to snap me out of it.' I turn back and meet his gaze. He looks at me as if he doesn't agree with what I'm saying and wishes to speak up and dispute my every word. I speak again before he can. 'I want these men dead and I tell you this now, while my mind is clear. You must agree with me... having known men like these? Any man that makes a widow out of a woman or orphans out of children — as you stated — must pay the price, yes?'

He takes his time to answer. His eyes have gone dark and hard. ''Bout the gist of it, yeah.'

'Then let us go to Memphis. We'll find Joseph and Edwin there and ask them where their big brother is.'

12

Before we leave for Cheyenne the next morning, I tell Mr McCarthy to go to the doctor so he can have his shoulder looked at. After a few grumbles and a number of "I'm fine"s, he eventually agrees with me and I take him down the street to where the doctor's office is. It's a small building, painted white with a sign out the front that holds a red cross. Another one hanging above the door says *doctor*. There's a small group of women standing near the front window, talking amongst themselves and grinning. We go inside and stand around the waiting room until two men walk out from a room at the back. One is limping, leaning his weight on a makeshift cane.

'Now, you stay away from those bulls until that leg heals completely, Mr Hennesy,' a young man with blonde hair and wearing spectacles says to the older one. He sees me and Mr McCarthy standing in the room and gives us a quick nod of acknowledgement before he wishes Mr Hennesy goodbye. 'Come back if the pain doesn't go away.'

'Yes, Dr Reading.' The old man waves his hand and leaves.

'Hello,' Dr Reading says, looking back at us. He's younger than I expected a doctor to be, with kind eyes and a gentle mouth. He's clean shaven and quite striking to the eye. I realise now why the women are milling about outside, staring in through the window. He sees my attention go there and clears his throat.

'What can I do for you?'

'Uh...' Mr McCarthy stops when we hear laughter from outside and Dr Reading grunts, waving us into his room out the back and closing the door behind us.

'Sorry. I've been here less than a month and apparently all the women in town think it necessary to see me every day. I've had to get someone else to help me — a woman, mind you — just to draw them away.' He sighs. 'But enough about myself. What can I do for you?'

'I got shot... over a week ago. Cauterised the wound, but Ms Ryan here wanted a doctor to take a look at it.'

I'm surprised by Mr McCarthy stating outright that he was shot and feel my heart clench in my chest with anxiety.

'Oh. Of course.' Dr Reading directs him to a chair with a long back and Mr McCarthy sits down. He shrugs off his shirt and the doctor takes a look at the scars once he unwinds the bandages I fitted. Clicking his tongue, he looks up at me. 'Did you sterilise the wounds before cauterising them?'

'I did,' Mr McCarthy says, eyes on my face. I look away. 'Just poured some whiskey on it.'

'Whiskey,' Dr Reading laughs.

'All I had.'

'Well, it's good you did. The front wound is infected, but not anything to worry about. I'll give you some medicine for the pain and put a salve on the wound that will help fight the infection.' He gets up and fishes through a few cupboards on the wall behind the chair where Mr McCarthy sits. I meet Mr McCarthy's gaze, chewing on my lip. I'm worried the doctor is going to say something to the sheriff as soon as we leave.

As if sensing my worries, Mr McCarthy clears his throat.

'You ain't gonna ask why I have a bullet wound in my shoulder, doc?'

'Hm?' Dr Reading looks up from the cupboard. 'Oh, no... Why would I? I have that many people come in with gunshot wounds around here that there's no point in asking why or who or where. I'd go out of business if the locals didn't think they could trust me. Plus, I'm bound by patient confidentiality.' He grins with a sort of pride and continues, 'You can count on the fact that nothing we have spoken about leaves this room once you walk out today.'

Mr McCarthy looks at me and I feel the tension in my shoulders fade. Dr Reading comes back and puts some salve on the wound after he cleans it with salted water.

'Did a good job,' he tells me. 'Your first time?'

I think about how I hardly did anything, with Mr McCarthy's hand over my own, forcing the hot knife against his skin. I remember the look on his face and the bearing of his teeth, the groan of agony. Feeling a little faint, I nod and look away, sucking in a deep breath. I can feel Mr McCarthy's eyes on me, but I don't meet his gaze again.

'Well, I'll put some fresh bandages on this and you should be good to go. How's the arm working for you?'

'Fine.'

'The pain?'

'Bearable. It's gotten better since it happened.'

'I can imagine. You're quite fortunate — I've had patients with injuries in the same spot where they've lost use of their arm.' He pauses and starts to put his things away as Mr McCarthy shrugs his shirt back on. 'If you do start to lose feeling in your hand or arm, friend, please see a doctor immediately.'

'I'll do that.' Mr McCarthy gets up and I step towards the door. 'How much do I owe ya?'

'A dollar twenty-five.'

When Mr McCarthy pays, Dr Reading sees us out. I hear the ladies at the window audibly gasp when they see him and some of them make comments about how handsome he is. Mr McCarthy and I head back down the street.

'You okay?' he asks me after a while.

'Yes, of course.' I blink. 'I'm glad you saw a doctor. You would have been in a terrible spot if the infection got worse.'

'Ahhh,' he grunts dismissively, 'I've had worse.'

I go to my horse and make sure everything is fitted and strapped onto the saddle. I can feel Mr McCarthy's eyes are still on me and I get a little annoyed at his worry for me.

'Thanks,' he says, surprising me. 'For getting me to go there. I can be a fool and not care so much 'bout my wellbeing when I probably should.'

I glance at him over my shoulder. 'It's fine, Mr McCarthy. Come now, we should get back to Cheyenne.'

⊷⊶

The ride back to Cheyenne is slow and torturous. It rains, a torrential, drenching rain that soaks us to the bone. For once I'm actually cold in this unforgiving heatwave we've been experiencing and I huddle under my duster coat as I ride, keeping my head bent down so the water drips in front of my face off the rim of my hat. Mr McCarthy protects his wound as much as he can. He wears layers of clothing and his long coat and hat, but I can see him struggling, worried about getting the wound wet when it needs to stay dry in order to heal and take in the salve that has been applied. I feel a sort of worry about it myself, nagging inside my stomach and after a little while of riding and seeing how the rain isn't going to relent any time soon, I direct Mr McCarthy down into the trees we're passing. There's an inlet that leads us to a wooded area, thick with brush and holding a canopy that keeps back most of the water like a large, bushy dam. It's close to a cliff face where a trail leads up to higher ground. I want to stay down low, as far away from the wet as possible. I lead my horse in further towards the trees, my eyes scanning the cliff wall as best I can in the dim light and through the large drops of rain escaping through the dam above our heads. I hear Mr McCarthy grumble something, like a complaint over my sudden need for shelter, but I ignore him and continue on.

And then, as if a gift from a higher power that neither of us really deserves, I see the cliff face juts out over a rocky area beside where the trees clear. Underneath is dirt and rock, sheltered by the cliff's overhang and large enough to fit us and the horses. I get off my horse and lead her under and she shakes herself out, dotting the rocky walls with droplets of water. I take off her drenched saddle and let her rest as I start to prepare a little camp for us. We're most likely half a day's ride out of Cheyenne, still too far to forget all this and wander down, especially in this rain. I'm tired of being wet and cold. I shrug off my coat and get a fire started with broken branches and twigs that have collected under the shelter. I hear Mr McCarthy slide out of his saddle and go about making his horse comfortable. He's holding his shoulder with one of his hands, as if protecting it.

'Is it hurting you?' I ask him.

'I'm fine.' He waves dismissively at me as he puts his saddle down and organises his things.

'You don't have to be rude to me,' I spit.

'We didn't need to stop here just for me. I can handle this wound. I've had one before.'

'I didn't stop here for you, so you can stop flattering yourself on that account,' I say icily. 'I was tired of getting wet and hardly being able to ride at a trot without fear of tripping over and breaking the horse's neck, mine or both.' I pause as I finish building the fire and welcome the warmth and crackle it brings. 'Your wound didn't come to mind,' I continue and I see him look at me over his shoulder, as if sensing my lie even from the distance between us.

Frustrated, I pull out a can of beans and place the can by the fire to warm. Mr McCarthy scuffs his way over and sits down on the ground opposite me at the fire. He shrugs off his coat, as I've done and unbuttons his waistcoat. When the waistcoat is off, I see the wound on the front of his shoulder has wept through his bandages and shirt, leaving a dark stain on the pale material. I clench my jaw and look away, shaking my head.

'It's just 'cause he put ointment on it. It's drawing out the infection,' he says, as if to reassure any worries I might have.

'Oh,' I say and smile across the fire at him tightly, 'I'm not worried about your wound, Mr McCarthy. You've made it known on many occasions that you're more than capable with it.'

He grunts under his breath and looks into the flames. 'Don't have to give me sass 'bout it, ma'am.'

I ignore him and take the can of beans, serving him and myself a plate of them. I pass him his plate and spoon and we start to eat in silence. We're both tired and frustrated by the inevitable delay the weather has given us. I'm so uncomfortable in these wet clothes, with my damp hair hanging limply around my face and my shirt stuck to my back. I want to strip them all off and climb into fresh clothes, dry and warm, but I don't have any spare clothes that are clean and, despite undressing in front of Mr McCarthy before, I'm in the right mind now to never be doing that again. It feels as if the wet weather and the thought of a long journey to Memphis has taken us back a step. I don't know why I'm so up and down with Mr McCarthy, yet I do know I owe him nothing.

I spread my bedroll out after I eat and I keep close to the fire, relying on it to dry me off and keep me warm. When I lie down, I have a view of the fire, Mr McCarthy and the rain continuing to plummet down outside. The sun has set and there's nothing else I can do but sleep. There's nothing else I want to do.

The rain has eased when I wake up. The fire is beginning to die beside me and I get up to tend to it so the flames grow a little higher again, providing more warmth for us. I can hear the horses munching on some grass Mr McCarthy has picked for them and look around to see him brushing his black steed, murmuring quiet words to it as it eats. Seeing him in such a relaxed state, so calm and smooth, gentle with an innocent animal, paints him in a picture I've never allowed for him to be painted in. It goes against everything inside me that has resisted this man — pushed him away and hated him for what he is. There are two sides of me: one wants to become this man's friend and know him better and get to know why he is who he is and how he's lasted this long, living a life of such sadness. And the other wants to take advantage of him; keep him at arm's length and use him for whatever I might not be able to do. And I can't help but hate both of those sides, which adds to the conflict inside me. I don't want this man as my friend, but neither do I want to callously use him for my own good. I know the past few days, even weeks, have brought us closer together — given us both understanding of who we are as people and where we stand. I don't like the feeling that gives me, the room it provides to build a relationship with this man. I have this urgency inside me which identifies itself as a need to protect myself from him, or anyone else. The only way to do so is to continue to fight myself over thoughts of him until I no longer have to — until we've parted ways and he's only a distant memory.

I'm glad to see I'm mostly dry and I stand up to stretch my tired limbs. The sun's only just rising and there are birds up in the trees, calling out to it with all their might, in case it may disappear again and the rain comes back. Mr McCarthy nods to me when he sees that I'm up, but we don't speak and instead go about packing up our little camp in silence until we're ready to set off again. And when we're back in the saddle, on the road back to Cheyenne, it feels good. There are rivulets on either side of the road and puddles in the holes from the deluge. I'm glad the rain itself is gone. There's a freshness to the world around us — a newness about it that makes the air easier to breathe, a cool relief on my lungs after being close to the fire all night. We've got half a day's ride ahead of us, so I sit deep in the saddle and get as comfortable as I can, letting the mare underneath me do what she needs to manoeuvre down the wet and slippery track. Mr McCarthy is once again my silent companion, his face like stone.

<hr />

We stop to rest the horses a couple of hours out from Cheyenne beside a river that sits inside a valley. I get off and take off her saddle so she can drink and graze without the weight of it. And then I wash my face at the water's edge, scrubbing the road dust from the back of my neck. Mr McCarthy leans against a tree up off the bank of the river, smoking a cigarette and I climb the bank to join him when I'm done. He offers me the cigarette and I shake my head, watching the horses as they eat at the grass growing along the bank. Clouds have gathered above our heads and I'm worried it's going to rain again, not wanting to get wet. It's close to nightfall, the blue hue of dusk settling down around us and I can hear insects buzzing about the water, joining the chorus of frogs and roosting birds. It adds to a continuous whine in my ears that hurts my head. It's such an unfamiliar sound — the song of this wild and untamed country — an uncontrollable whirring that builds into a never-ending crescendo of noise.

Mr McCarthy stirs and I look at him. He's got his thumbs hooked in his braces and he's looking out at the river with a frown on his face, the cigarette hanging out of his mouth.

'I guess we're going to have to plan our trip to Memphis as soon as we get back to Cheyenne,' I say quietly.

'Mm...'

'What should we do? Catch a train or just ride out?'

He looks at me then. 'Up to you. It'll only take 'bout a week if we ride. No mucking 'round or spending money on trains if we do and we'll have the horses with us if we need 'em in the city.'

'Okay, good.' I nod my head quickly. 'We'll ride then. But let me sleep in a bed in Cheyenne first. My back is aching like nothing else.'

I see him smile slightly at that. 'Fine by me.'

I find a rock close to the tree he leans against and sit down on it, sighing. Mr McCarthy steps out from under the tree after a while, standing close to the rock where I sit and we're both watching the horses, saying nothing. The noise is still around us, drowning out any clear thought I might have had in my mind.

After a while longer, he lets out a breath and says, 'Let's do some shooting.'

I look up at him, startled. 'Now?'

His eyes narrow slightly. 'You did want me to teach you, yeah?'

'I've already been *taught*, I just need fine tuning.'

Those eyes shine slightly with amusement and he nods, 'Right. Well... get your gun, I'll see if I can *fine tune* ya.'

I roll my eyes at him but do as he says, heading to my saddle to take my rifle from it. I come back up the slope and he stands me several metres from the rock I've been sitting on. He's propped up some of the empty whiskey bottles we've accumulated in the past few days on the rocks and points to them.

'See if you can get those there. We're not too far off. You can use the revolver if you want, but rifle is fine too.'

'I used to shoot rabbits in Clifden as a kid. I'm sure I can do it.' There's a short silence after my words and I realise I've just shared something about my life with him I haven't really shared with anyone else.

'Then you should be a natural.' He's watching me closely, but he doesn't comment any further and I let out a breath.

'Good,' he says and I look at him, confused. 'You wanna always squeeze the trigger after letting out all the air in your lungs.'

He nods to me to continue and I lift the rifle up, aiming it towards a bottle. I close one eye and he clicks his tongue, stopping me. He steps close, voice low.

'Keep both eyes open, Ms Ryan. I know that sounds strange, but you gotta have your peripherals so you can see everything that's happening 'round ya.'

I look down the sights of the rifle with both eyes open and start to see double, shaking my head. 'I can't.'

'It'll feel odd at first. You get used to it with practice, trust me.'

There's two rifles in front of my eyes, swaying over the bottle I wish to shoot. I grit my teeth and steady myself. I feel Mr McCarthy step close and his hands fall across my arms, fixing my position.

'Remember,' he says softly, 'breathe out and squeeze the trigger when your lungs are empty.'

I do as I'm told and shoot. There's a puff of smoke as the rifle jumps in my hands. I hold tight and look up, seeing that I've missed. The smell of gunpowder washes over me and I see my father in my mind's eye, his rough hands blackened by work, handing me his gun.

'Good try,' Mr McCarthy murmurs, breaking me from the memory. 'Give it another go, you got this.'

It takes two more tries before I finally hit a bottle, seeing it burst upwards in a spray of glass. I pull the gun down and look at Mr McCarthy.

'Good,' I say. 'That was good.'

He nods. 'Try the revolver. Same sorta thing, it'll jump about a little more though.'

I remember shooting at the man outside of Sweeney and how I missed, the revolver odd and unnatural in my hands. I pull it from my belt and aim it. I keep shooting until I finally hit a bottle and sigh.

'Keep at it. On the way to Memphis, you should keep practicing. You'll get there.' He nods his head to my guns. 'Remember to clean 'em and look after 'em. It's life or death out here and without a reliable gun, you'll surely die.'

His words remind me of my father again. Of killing rabbits for dinner out in the wilderness of Clifden, surrounded by the bogs of the Connemara, close to the smell of peat and salt water. Crouching low amongst the grasses, my father lifting a thick, calloused finger to his mouth to remind me to be quiet, a silent hunter. I feel a sudden rush of emotion overtake me and I turn away from him before he can see my tears, taking in a breath that shakes inside my chest.

'Ms Ryan...' His voice is gentle, wary. I can hear the worry inside it — the same worry I heard in his words after seeing Dr Reading — and I feel anger towards it. 'You wanna go? We can head to Cheyenne now—?'

'Don't,' I say, voice harsh. I turn and look at him, glaring at him through my tears. I don't want him to think he can get away with treating me like I'm a friend of his. Someone he needs to worry about. 'Stop showing me this pity, Mr McCarthy. Stop showing me the only reason why you're helping me is because you feel sorry for me, because I know there's more to it. I'm not your friend and I'm barely your companion. Any kind of emotion I might feel about all this is *my* business and not yours; I don't care if you think you might know what I'm going through. *I* don't believe you do. How could you?'

I see his jaw tighten and a small frown creases the space between his brows. He puts his hands on his hips and takes in my every word with a tight-lipped mouth. I head over to the horses and saddle up the mare once again. I don't wish to hear what he thinks. I don't want his compassion or his companionship. I don't want to know whether he can relate with me or whether he feels as if he can help me in some way. Mr McCarthy isn't here to be my mentor, my friend or a source of advice towards the feelings I've been experiencing. He's here to help me kill the men that murdered Thomas and that's it. That's all I'll ever want from him.

—•—

We leave for Memphis two days later. Cheyenne, early in the morning, is an accumulation of tall, silent buildings sitting amongst a dense fog encasing the sounds and smells of the city that's slowly waking up. They watch us like mute giants as we walk the horses along the cobblestones, our paths lit up by streetlights still flickering in the dark. Mr McCarthy and I are well out of the city by the time the sun has fully risen and I feel better having slept in a bed and eaten a proper meal. With the prospect of being in Memphis in a week, tracking down the next two Gaitwood men, I feel as good as I can. We've stocked up on food, ammo and supplies. I've bought another pair of trousers and a shirt, since my others were ruined and left behind beside that river in Great Falls. We're ready and wide awake and the horses are content beneath us after spending the night in a warm stable with oats and hay. And yet the tension between Mr McCarthy and me still hangs in the air and I cannot settle it, as much as I would like to.

We ride all day with minimal breaks and when night falls, we rest out on an open plain with the stars above our heads and a fire at our side. The stars are brilliant and I lay back in my bedroll watching them, imagining far-away lands and eyes of loved ones amongst those shining lights, smiling down at me, wishing me well. Perhaps it's the exhaustion from travelling so much the past few weeks, but I'm incredibly emotional. I think about the man I killed — Harry Oswald — and how after his death I still haven't felt like myself. I'm a mess. More of a mess than I was when I first arrived here. I don't know what to do. That familiar loneliness is as prevalent as ever.

Mr McCarthy gets up and stokes the fire, breaking me from my thoughts. We've scarcely spoken a word to one another. He looks up from the fire and meets my gaze. After a while, he gets a bottle of whiskey from his bag and opens it, starting to drink. I immediately crave it, my stomach clenching. I stay in my bedroll, trying not to look at him.

'You should sleep,' he murmurs suddenly.

'Don't tell me what to do.'

'I ain't. I'm *suggesting.*'

I look at him, angry. 'Well, don't suggest.'

He's silent for a little longer and then he asks, 'Have I done something wrong, ma'am? Is that why you're so cold again?'

'Of course you have,' I say, my voice cracking. 'I've had the same view of you ever since I met you, Mr McCarthy. You're just like the men who killed Thomas — an outlaw, selfish and without feeling.'

I know the words I say are scarcely true as soon as they come out. I try to stand by them, pride making me stubborn.

Mr McCarthy is silent again for a moment. 'I've killed men,' he suddenly starts, 'plenty of 'em. But I ain't one of the men who killed your husband. You can despise me all you like, Ms Ryan, just make sure you have a good reason to first. Putting me in the same view as the Gaitwoods is unfair. Don't get me wrong, I'll be the first to admit I'm a bad man — I've done terrible things to decent folk — and I'm a damn fool. But that's got nothing to do with you and your husband. You don't need to judge me for what I've done 'cause I'm already serving my sentence for that and I repent, I can tell you.'

I sit up in my bedroll and look at him across the fire. My heart is bleeding inside my chest. Not for him, not entirely. I know what he says is true. There's so many things inside me, both agreeing with him and lashing out at his words, scorning him for even daring to say such things. I let out a breath, not knowing what to say. He gets up without a word and comes to me, passing me the bottle of whiskey.

'Why don't,' he grunts, getting down beside me as I sip at the golden liquid, 'we agree that we're both damned fools? That we'll hate one another's guts some days if we must. But let's have an understanding... whether it's as simple as going out to avenge your husband's death together or something deeper, I don't care. Let's just agree that we're too very imperfect people out doing what we need to do.'

I sniff, taking another mouthful of whiskey so I don't have to answer right away. His offer sounds appealing. It brings a warmth in my chest towards the man that I immediately disregard as the whiskey and nothing else. After a moment of thought, I nod and look at him.

'Fine,' I say.

He smiles slightly, grimly. 'I don't like fighting with you, Ms Ryan. We're both doing our best out here and that's all we can do. Unfortunately we gotta stick together if we wanna do that.'

'I know.' I rub my face and he takes the bottle from me to drink. I feel woozy already. 'I'm so conflicted, Mr McCarthy.'

'You got every reason to be.'

'I don't know how to properly feel these emotions that are inside me.' I wipe away the tears that slide down my face. I don't try to hide them this time, unashamed. 'It's like I'm incapable of processing them — feeling them how they're supposed to be felt. Sometimes I have this belief in me that I'm not normal... like there's something wrong with me.'

'You ain't alone in that. Life's all about questioning our actions and how we feel. We're emotional beings.'

I take the bottle from him. 'How are you so wise, yet so bloody foolish?'

He laughs and I laugh with him, unable to help myself. He meets my gaze, eyes soft under the light of the fire and stars. 'I knew a real wise man when I was younger. Taught me a lot 'bout the world and how unfair it is, kept me on track, even when we were robbing and killing. He was just as damaged as the both of us.' He pauses and sighs, looking up at the stars. 'Damn fool blew his brains out.'

'My God.'

'Wisdom can be a burden, ma'am,' he murmurs, looking back at me. 'They say education is important and I agree... but only to an extent. I think a lot of us can't handle knowledge. It eats away at us and drives us... mad.'

'I don't care about wisdom,' I say, shaking my head. 'I just want contentment.'

'Not a strange thing to want in life.'

The bottle is getting closer and closer to emptying as we take turns drinking from it. I can feel it already affecting my head, making me tell him things I wouldn't tell him while sober. I feel the dam I've built, keeping all my emotions and thoughts at bay, break loose now that whiskey is in my blood. I feel bold. I feel like anything I tell him he'll understand and won't judge.

'Do you ever wonder *why*?' I ask. '*Why* do these bad things happen? Why is my life ruled by death where others in this world live happily and love wholly and never experience the sharp pang of loss?'

'All the time,' he drawls, amused. 'I don't think we'll ever get an answer to those sorts of questions. And it's when we're asking those questions we lose sight of the things we should be focusing on.'

I look at him. 'What's that?'

He shrugs a shoulder and his gaze meets mine. His eyes are heavy-lidded by drink and exhaustion. I know I must look just as tired and unkempt as he does. I don't care, the drink helps with that. For the first time in a while, I feel like letting go and drowning in gold once more.

'Could be anything. Friends, family, people you care 'bout that are still 'round. Your horse, a prized possession. Some sort of anchor to stop you from floating away to places you have no business going to.'

I laugh at the image and yet I agree with him. 'Home,' I say quietly. 'The only thing I can think of is Ireland.'

His eyes soften on my face. 'You'll go back again one day, Ms Ryan,' he tells me, voice gentle and hoarse. 'And you can leave all this behind you.'

'That's the plan,' I murmur, 'but who knows?'

'Ain't no shame in taking things day by day,' he says. He hands me the last bit of whiskey and I finish it off.

I'm so tired I can hardly stay in an upright position. Before I know it, I'm leaning my temple against the edge of Mr McCarthy's shoulder, staring into the flames before us.

'Sometimes it seems easier to just end it all, like your friend,' I say quietly.

'Yeah,' he says, voice gruff. 'But that ain't the way to do it. He was a sad man... and not a day goes by do I wish I could've done something. Feel like I owed him that much.'

'I don't think there's much you could have done, Mr McCarthy.' I feel tears welling in my eyes again and sniff. 'I'm sorry for your friend.'

'I'm sorry for your husband.'

I let out a sob and I feel him wrap his arm around my shoulder, his hand holding the side of my head. I turn my face against his arm and he draws me closer as I weep. He shushes me quietly, like I'm a small, upset child in his arms and I feel him gently rocking us back and forth, his hands gentle on me. I feel so fragile against him, against the power of those hands. I feel like I'm about to break open — the cracks that have formed since Thomas' death are splitting further and further apart and I don't think I can hold myself together anymore. I've always wanted to be strong, to continue on, to push the emotions too painful to deal with aside. It's been a coping mechanism for me most of my life, with my parents' deaths and now with Thomas'. The exhaustion inside me and the grieving my body has done has finally taken its toll. Killing Harry Oswald has opened a Pandora's Box and unleashed a maelstrom of feeling. Mr McCarthy is the only one with me to take the brunt of its force. I've drunk too much and as a result, I've opened up to him more than I wanted to. But the way he holds me, the way he gently murmurs things, gives me a comfort I haven't felt in a long time. Being in someone else's arms is something that brings relief to anyone. That connection it brings, that foundation and solidarity; when it all gets too much, you know you can rely on someone else to help you bear the weight. I can't avoid feeling this when Mr McCarthy holds me, even amongst my angst and the numbness the whiskey has given me. I *like* the way he holds me. I *want* him to hold me, to continue whispering sweet nothings near my ear, his breath tickling the hairs against my neck. I haven't been held like this in years and I don't want it to stop.

'C'mon, Ms Ryan,' he tells me after a while, once my tears have dried on my cheeks, leaving them sticky and red. 'You should get some sleep. We'll be in Memphis soon enough and you can get more answers.'

He helps me down into my bedroll and pulls the cover up over me. My hair is stuck to my face and my eyes are bleary. I'm drunk, the world spinning around me, the fire too bright against my aching eyes. I feel his fingers move the hair that's stuck to my face and feel it crackle on my skin by my ears and neck as he pushes it back and out of the way. And then they softly trail along the line of my jaw and I can't tell whether it was intentional or not because he gets up soon after, a deep frown between his brows and I'm already drifting off into an exhausted sleep.

13

I wake with a headache. Mr McCarthy is already boiling coffee
in a pot on the fire when I sit up, bleary eyed and feeling as if I
didn't sleep at all. He gives me a small smile over the blaze of the
fire and I hold a hand to the ache in my forehead.

'Why did we drink that whole bottle?' I moan.

'Think we both needed it.'

'You're feeding my bad habits, Mr McCarthy and I don't agree
with it.'

'Sorry, ma'am.' There's amusement laced through his voice,
just as delicate and soft as his smile.

He's kneeling beside the fire and he gets up after pouring two
cups of coffee and passes one to me. I take one from him gratefully
and blow at the steam until it's easy to drink without scalding the
inside of my mouth. The field we're in is peaceful this morning
and the sun is slowly rising over hills in the distance. The horses
graze close to us, snorting amongst the dust and grasses, content
as their ears twitch against the strain of a bird's shrill morning
call.

I think about last night and the feelings that all came at once. It
makes me remember Mr McCarthy's arms around me, the heat
from his skin through his shirt against mine. I clench the cup
tightly in my hands and take another drink. It's obvious we're
two broken people, stuck together in this cruel and wild country.

I know I shouldn't feel ashamed enjoying a comforting embrace from a man who I've come to know has similarities with me and who understands the things I'm feeling like no one else has in the past three years. But I can't help but feel a flush creeping up my neck at the thought of how I wanted him to keep holding me, even when he pulled away. I put it down to wanting comfort in these trying times — to not having that in so long, that my body craves it and doesn't care who it's from, as long as I get it. There's no other way I'm comfortable interpreting those feelings.

'You ready to head out soon?' he asks me, breaking me from my chain of thought.

'Oh...' I choke a little on the coffee and swallow hard. 'Yes.'

'You alright?' He's looking at me across the fire peculiarly.

'Yes.' I cough and clear my throat. 'Of course.'

It's like he can see the flush on my face, even across the fire and I curse myself inwardly, quickly getting up and packing things away so he can't see the redness.

You're a fool, Blair Ryan.

Memphis is at our feet in just over a week. The weather has been clear, the horses happy. Even my body has gotten used to the feeling of sitting in the saddle all day and the aches and pains have minimised. I'm dirty and sweaty and in great need of a bath when we stand upon a rise that gives us the view of the city sitting along the great and mighty river Mr McCarthy calls The Mississippi. The air hangs around us, wet and clinging and bugs buzz amongst the grasses, as if letting out their own complaints — or joys — over the heat. The city is large and I see smokestacks rising from factory chimneys and a network of roads. Steam-powered paddle boats move along the river and there are large docks down on the water. Memphis looks like a thriving city, a mass of brick and steam, a creature in itself.

I glance at Mr McCarthy, unable to keep back a smile. It's good to know he isn't the monster I made him out to be. I'm glad we had the talk we did the other night; drunken ramblings or no, he showed me a kindness I hadn't seen from another person in years. There's a side to this man I haven't been aware of — too selfish in my own thoughts, too uncaring about who or what he is, as long as he did his job. He warned me we'd have to get to know one another, uncomfortably close as we would be on the road, and I'd not heeded those words. I'd laughed at him, taunted him, called him things that he isn't. My anger and pain had made me cruel. And that very same anger and pain had driven me to plunge Mr McCarthy's knife into Harry Oswald again and again until he was dead. Since that moment, I've broken into little pieces once again. And those pieces are so small, so delicate, I've seen a different perspective. I've seen Mr McCarthy *can* be a friend if I only let him in. I know I need it. I know I need to be understood and supported. I can't let what happened with Harry Oswald happen again and I know Mr McCarthy has known that from the start. Perhaps he underestimated me and didn't think I'd do something so drastic. He'd tried to warn me, to put sense in me, but he'd failed. And who could blame him? I'd been possessed, a demon myself, unleashing a torrent of fury and rage upon a man. Harry Oswald may or may not have deserved the death I gave him, but I cannot think about those sorts of things. I must, somehow, accept the things I've done. I must, if I have to, push that aside until this is all over. I can't let guilt get in the way. Not when grief and pain and fury are already barging down my door. It hurts me to think it, but I know Mr McCarthy is capable of being that solid, iron bar that goes across the door to keep those things at bay. All I have to do is allow him.

'You ready?' he asks me, giving me a lopsided smile under the shade of his hat.

'Damn right I am.'

We stable the horses at a livery around the corner from the saloon we choose to stay at. There's music being played loudly inside, even with the afternoon being early and people look up at the building as they pass by on the street and I see a lot of them smile at the sound. The music is interesting, a mixture of beats and melodies I haven't really heard before.

'Dark folk have started playing their music here in Memphis and it's getting 'round,' Mr McCarthy says. 'You'll like it, c'mon.'

We head inside with our bags and get a key to a room. The front entrance is just a desk with a man standing behind it, stairs behind him leading up to the next floor. There's an archway on the right wall that opens into the saloon and I glimpse through a cloud of smoke tables, the bar and a band playing close to the far wall as we walk to the stairs. Mr McCarthy has asked for baths to be organised for us and the man tells us there's two rooms across from ours that will be ready in a few minutes. We get to our room to put away our bags — a decent size with two beds on either wall, a window that looks onto the street and a dresser to put our clothes in if we wish. I take out a dress and take off my hat, resting it on my bed beside my bag. My hair is messy and in great need of a wash, falling from my plait. There's a knock on our door soon after and a woman shows us to the bathing rooms. I take one and Mr McCarthy takes the other and I wash myself red raw, making sure my hair is clean before I plait it. It's getting too long — the plait reaches my waist easily. But it's good to wash with soap and feel refreshed again, with the hot water bringing the aches out of my neck and back. I sit in the water for a while longer, closing my eyes as I relax against its warmth, my skin tingling.

When I hear the door to Mr McCarthy's bath close, I get up and dry myself down before getting into the cornflower blue dress and stockings from Ireland. I slip back into my boots and head into our room. Mr McCarthy has a cloth around his shoulders and is scrubbing his head dry with it. His beard has grown again and it's just as wild as his hair is. I realise I'm staring when he looks at me and I quickly look away.

'Good to be clean,' I mutter awkwardly.

'Yeah. Damn hungry. You wanna get food?' He looks out the window. 'Close to supper anyway.'

'Sure.'

The saloon is louder than before and more people have come in, laughing and drinking. I see some of them eating meals at the tables as the band continues to play — a few dark-skinned men on a piano, double bass and drums. There's a man singing, his voice thick and smooth like honey and I'm hypnotised by the emotion behind his words. Mr McCarthy orders our meals and we head to a table that gives us a good view of where the band is performing. He sees me watching them while I eat and smiles slightly.

'Like it?'

I nod. 'It's so full of emotion. I haven't heard anything like it.'

'Always used to like coming down to Memphis...'

I look at him. 'You've been here before?'

'Few times.'

I frown. 'Where did you say you were from, Mr McCarthy? Missouri?'

He nods, sliding a glass of whiskey he got from the bar to my side of the table.

'Is that close to here?'

''Bout a day or so's ride to reach the state line. Few more to get to my county.'

'That's not far at all.'

'No, it's not.' He meets my gaze across the table. 'I was based here for a while with the... people I rode with. We came into the city when we thought it was safe — back in those days our faces weren't on wanted posters in these parts.'

I feel a breath escape me. He's never talked about his past as an outlaw until now and I wonder if being back in this city is bringing up new memories — so many that he has no choice but to tell me. He opens his mouth to say more, to tell me more about his past and what it was like, and I find myself leaning closer so I can hear him over the beautiful music, when someone comes up behind his chair.

'Colin?'

I look up at the woman standing over him. A dark-haired lady in a lavender silk dress with frills at the neck and cuffs. She's beautiful, her hair up out of her face with a small curl touching her forehead. Her eyes are inky and mysterious and her mouth is full, curving into a smile when Mr McCarthy looks up at her. As soon as he sees her, I feel like I'm imposing, as if I'm not supposed to be there.

'What in the world are you doing here?' she asks him when he doesn't speak for a moment, as if too stunned to say anything.

He quickly stands, facing her. 'Caroline...'

Caroline beams and reaches out, placing a hand on his arm. 'It's good to see you, Colin.' Her eyes go over his beard and hair. 'You look different...'

'Older,' he laughs.

'No. You look well...' Her eyes go to me and I awkwardly nod at her.

'Hello,' I say.

Caroline stares at me for a little while and then her eyes go back to Mr McCarthy.

'What are you doing here, Colin?' Her voice is strange now, holding a hard edge.

'I...' He pauses and looks at me. 'There's so much to tell you.'

A man calls for Caroline across the room, looking as if he's about to leave. He's dressed as smartly as she is, clean-shaven and handsome. She looks at Mr McCarthy again and I see his expression fall.

'I'm sorry, I can't stay. It was nice to see you again, Colin. I'm glad you're alive.' Her eyes go to me again and her mouth tightens. 'All I ever wanted was for you to be happy.'

'Oh, I—' I start, but she grasps Mr McCarthy's hand briefly. As she does, I see a wedding band on her finger and I notice Mr McCarthy sees it too. She turns to leave with the man without another word.

Mr McCarthy stays standing, watching after her for a moment. I don't know what to say. I feel as if I've already seen too much. His face is pale. I can see his jaw is tense under his beard, eyes dull. He slowly sits back down and I slide the glass of whiskey I haven't drunk back at him. He picks it up and empties it in one go.

'Let's get some more, hey?' I say, not sure what else to tell him.

I don't know who this Caroline is to Mr McCarthy, but the way he's acting now shows me she must have been quite important to him. And perhaps she still is. I get up and get several drinks of beer and whiskey from the bar, bringing them over to our table on a tray. Mr McCarthy is staring into space. I slide a drink under his nose and he looks down at it, emptying it again in one go. The place is louder now and the music has picked up. People are piling around tables and at the bar, laughing and chatting. The place is so lively and the music is forcing my foot to tap to the rhythm under the table. My eyes go back to Mr McCarthy. I start drinking one of the beers and he takes one as well. I don't like the look on his face — the change in his disposition as soon as Caroline had come and gone. He looks... defeated. I don't know what to say and I don't know whether to take his mind off it or ask him if he's alright.

'Do you want to talk about it?' I ask him over the noise.

'No.' He looks at me and tries to smile. It comes across more like a grimace. 'There's nothing to talk 'bout.'

I know that's a blatant lie. I don't say anything.

We sit drinking for an hour. The place becomes livelier as that hour grows and the band begins to play tunes that the crowd dances to, across a floor clear from tables and chairs. I find myself sitting in my seat, itching for a dance as I watch men and women twirl across the floor as they laugh. I've drunk enough to have a buzz and I'm enjoying myself, my heart filled with warmth at the looks of joy on the dancers' faces. They remind me of when Thomas and I used to dance. He'd dance with me anywhere, even if there was no music playing. He'd hum a tune and make me laugh as he spun me under his arm. I feel my eyes filling with tears and look away, finishing my drink. Mr McCarthy hasn't spoken, barely looked up from his beer and cigarette. I glance back at him. He's smoking, his eyes on the bottle in his hands that he slowly spins in his fingers like it's his own dance partner. I get the sudden urge to make him feel better, not able to stand the look of sorrow on his face, deep in his eyes. It's always been there, but it's worse now since he saw Caroline, whoever she was.

'Come on, Mr McCarthy,' I say loudly, boldly. The drink helps. 'You're the only man in this room that hasn't asked a woman to dance with him.'

He regards me for a moment and I see the look in his eyes change. A slight shift of light in them that's so small I hardly know if it happened at all or if it was just a trick. His gaze passes over the dancers and the band.

'You wanna dance?' He's drunk as much as I have and his voice slurs when he asks the question.

I get up and offer him my hand. 'I'll have you know dancing is a favourite pastime of mine.'

He smiles slightly and takes my hand, his grip sure, his skin calloused but warm. I take him over to the floor and turn around, pulling him closer to me. He comes in and I feel his hand rest against the small of my back and we start to dance with one another. The music moves us and we move with the rhythm the other dancers form. People laugh and twirl around us. I start to laugh myself as we pick up speed and I realise quite quickly that Mr McCarthy is a surprisingly good dancer.

'How did you learn how to dance like this?' I ask him as we spin through the crowd.

'I was brought up by a gentleman, 'course I was taught.'

I see his eyes have brightened and his mood has slowly shifted back to what it was. We keep dancing and when we tire, we get more drinks, only to go back and dance some more. I'm stumbling with the steps the later the night goes on and Mr McCarthy and I fumble with one another, laughing at ourselves as we struggle. I hear him laugh properly for the first time and, through my drunken haze, I realise it's just as gruff and husky as his voice. But it's a sound that lifts my heart, like hearing the song of a bird after a long, dark night. We move with one another, just as sloppy and clumsy as the other and I find myself having the most fun I've had in years. We drink more than we should. I see him let go of his worries and let himself succumb to his drunkenness. He enjoys himself more the further he gets and so do I. The singer and band keep us occupied, as the saloon fills so much with people it's hard to move from the bar back to the dance floor. Mr McCarthy pulls me close again when we reach it and we join arms with other dancers and spin amongst ourselves. I see him smiling and clapping to the beat, stomping his feet here, stepping side to side there. When we draw back together, his hand fits into mine easily and my drunken thoughts drift to the memory of being in his arms while I cried, of feeling his nose against my hair, of…

'I need air!' I yell at him over the sounds of the saloon.

'Wha..?'

'Air!'

I grasp his hand and pull him with me and we stumble and push through the crowd until I'm at a door at the back of the room. It brings us to the rear of the saloon, into a little garden between the buildings on the street. I suck in a deep breath of fresh air. It's cool on my sweating skin. Mr McCarthy crashes into me and I nearly fall over until he catches me and I let out a laugh. We almost collapse to the ground together, laughing, and yet we manage to lean against the railings of the little porch the door has opened onto. I'm out of breath, laughing hoarsely and Mr McCarthy's weight is still against me, his sweating skin on mine.

'Sorry,' he mumbles and moves off onto the railing. 'Jesus I'm drunk.'

I laugh until I snort and we both start laughing again until there's tears on my face and I don't know whether I'm full of glee or grief. I wipe my face and breathe deeply. We stand in silence for a little while and I look up at the sky between the tops of the buildings. It's a clear night and the stars are as beautiful as always.

'Who was that woman?' I ask him quietly, suddenly bold and unthinking.

He's quiet for a second. 'Caroline?'

'Mm.'

'I knew her years ago.' His voice is distant, not really his.

I look at him as he stares out into the garden. 'You were lovers?' I know I shouldn't be prying. I'm drunk. I feel entitled to know without really knowing why. Perhaps it's because I was subjected to their awkward reunion.

'Yeah.'

'What happened? It looks like she's married now.'

Damn it, Blair.

He pushes himself up from the railing, shaking his head. 'I'm drunk,' he says again, as if that's his answer.

I can see he's gloomy again and all this dancing, all this drinking has done nothing. I don't know why, but I'm annoyed. I'm annoyed at him. I'm annoyed at Caroline.

'Let's go back inside,' I tell him, putting my hand on his arm, just as she had done. 'Come on.'

'No, ma'am.' He shakes his head. 'I think I need to go to bed.'

'But we're having fun, Mr McCarthy,' I say, as if I'm a child, upset because my mother is forcing me to go home early from a play date. 'Why are you so bloody gloomy all of a sudden?'

'Are only you allowed to be upset 'bout things, ma'am, that it?' he asks me angrily.

I glare at him, feeling shame turn my cheeks red. 'No.' I push away from him. 'You're such a bastard.'

'Yeah, well, you ain't that great of a companion either.'

His words cut through me like a knife. I don't think. I just lift up a hand and slap him across the face.

'Get the hell out of my sight!'

'Gladly!'

He stalks back inside and slams the door behind him, making me jump. I'm filled with so much anger, too drunk to feel it properly. I go out into the garden and sit down on the wall that lines it, shaking. I'm trying not to cry. The sobs are clawing so much at my chest, begging to be released until one slips past my teeth. I feel so stupid. So childish. For the first time, we were enjoying each other's company and I knew he was starting to trust me, just as much as I was starting to trust him. I know I shouldn't be angry at Caroline — a woman I don't even know — for ruining that, but I can't help but put the blame onto someone else.

<hr/>

'It's easier that way, isn't it? Blaming other people so that you don't have to deal with it?' he asked heatedly.

'*Don't* you dare put this all on me, Thomas!'

The fire on the hearth was blazing beside us and, as if personified by our anger towards one another, it seemed to grow bigger and bigger as we fought.

'You can't just admit it, Blair? That you're wrong? You know it's okay to admit defeat every once in a while? You don't always have to be right. That seems mighty exhausting.'

'Oh shut up.' I turned my back on him to continue slicing the onions I had been cutting. The knife shook in my hand. I hated fighting with Thomas. He was such a sweet and reserved man and I loved him dearly. Fighting with him hurt and yet I could never back down when riled up. 'Martin O'Hughe is a snake and he should be held accountable alongside me. And I know he calls me "Blair the Banshee" behind my back.'

He ignored that. 'Do you realise how much money we lost with this mistake, Blair?'

'Of course I do!'

'Why are you blaming just Martin, then? You know the mistake you made, just admit it!'

I turned back on him, knife still in my hand. 'Why?' I cried. 'We both know I did it! Why must I admit it? Do you really wish to see me so backed into a corner, Thomas?'

His shoulders fell then. 'No,' he said, voice softer now. 'Of course not. But I just...' He put his hands on his hips and looked at the fire, sighing. 'Blair, I can't stand this side of you. I love you so much, but you're a pain in my bloody arse sometimes.'

'I'm aware of it, if that helps.'

He laughed. As soon as he did, I knew the fight was over. I put the knife down and went to him. He immediately drew me into his arms and kissed me. I pressed my face into his neck, holding him tightly, kissing his skin there.

'I'm sorry, dear one.'

He kissed my cheek. 'I know, my darling. It's just money. I'm sorry for yelling at you.'

'Yell at Martin too,' I murmured, 'he deserves it.'

He laughed again and squeezed me tighter.

———

I push myself from the memory and wipe my face. I've been sitting on the wall in the garden so long that my back is aching. I get up and go inside. The place is noisy. I move to the bar and drink some more. I see Mr McCarthy nowhere. I don't know what to do when I go back up to our room. I don't know what to say and whether I should apologise. I know I shouldn't have been so harsh. I know his reunion with Caroline doesn't sit well with me and a part of me pushes away any reasons why. Reasons that are dangerous, things I don't wish to think about right now.

After a few more drinks, I summon up the courage to go upstairs and I push my way from the bar and slowly make it back upstairs. My head is buzzing. My limbs are heavy and my eyes are bleary. I almost fall into the room when I open the door. When I see Mr McCarthy half naked on the floor, I'm suddenly awake and more sober. I close the door and rush to him.

'Mr McCarthy?'

He's awake, struggling. I put my hand on his bare back and my other against his bearded cheek, turning his face up towards mine so I can see him, see what's afflicting him.

'What's wrong?'

He mumbles something. There's a bottle of whiskey on the floor beside him, on its side, the liquid resting level. He's drunk out of his wits. I push the bottle away and try to lift him up, to get him into his bed. He moans and shakes his head and I swear at him, pulling him. But he's a dead weight and he crashes into me, his knees striking the boards as I fall down onto the side of the bed. I get back up and try to lift him again, growling at him, but we fall once more. He ends up half sprawled across my lap, his feet hanging over the side of the bed. I'm about to get up and try and push him onto the bed properly so he can sleep it off, but he grabs my hand and turns on his back, gazing up at me from where he lies across my thighs.

'You bloody drunk fool,' I tell him, shaking my head.

'I'm… Ms… Blair.' I see his eyes cloud with tears and my heart bleeds, my annoyance towards him evaporating almost completely.

I cradle his head in my arms as he lets out a sound of remorse and shush him quietly. It's my turn to comfort him now, cooing to him just as he did to me mere nights ago. I stroke back his hair with my hands and smooth his beard with my fingers, wiping away the wetness that gathers there from his tears. He clutches onto me, hands shaking and I tell him that it's alright to cry, that he doesn't have to hold it back, that I'll never think him weak for doing so. We're both drunken idiots sprawled across the bed, comforting one another again, or at least trying to. I see myself in him now, broken down by love, by loss. I want nothing but to protect him from it. To tell him that it will be alright, even though right now it feels as if it won't. I don't know how badly Caroline hurt him. I don't know how badly he hurt her. I just know heartbreak when I see it. I know he once yearned for this woman, once loved her wholly and truly. Whether he does now or not does not diminish the pain he feels. I lost Thomas from the clutches of death. Mr McCarthy lost Caroline from something else, something sometimes much more painful — a change of heart. Thomas is gone, out of sight, but Caroline is here, alive and a constant reminder of what they once had.

'It's alright, Colin,' I tell him quietly, pressing him against my breast. 'It will be alright.'

'Damn fool,' he mumbles through his tears. 'You're a damn fool, McCarthy.'

I close my eyes and press my cheek against his forehead, stroking my fingers through his hair. It's surprisingly soft, his beard a rough contrast.

'Hush now.'

We're there for so long. I hold onto him, not letting go, even when my back tires and I start to blink heavily. When Mr McCarthy stirs, he doesn't lift himself off my lap, only looks up at me, eyes clearer.

'My mother was of Welsh descent,' he says quietly, voice slurred and thick. 'She lived in Missouri during the war. It came on her doorstep one day and she was assaulted by a Confederate soldier. I was the result of it.' My breath stops and I stare at him. 'I was told for many years my father was her husband, Mr Colin McCarthy, and I took his name. He went to war, fighting for the Union, and never returned. She was full of shame, full of regret and grief. I don't think she could love me as much as she wanted. I was always a stark reminder of what happened to her and I think that hit her hard. She died... a year later. I was brought up in an orphanage 'til I was sixteen. When I got out, I made friends with some men, older than me, but they became brothers, fathers, comrades. They were outlaws. Bad men, killing anyone who got in their way and stealing from decent folk. Folk like my mother. I don't think I knew any better. I was pushed towards violence because I was born from it, a product of it.'

He stops and catches his breath, his eyes holding a faraway look, as if stuck within memories he wishes to get out of.

'I was twenty-three when I met Caroline. We came to Memphis to lie low after causing havoc in the east — a robbery gone wrong. She was the light of my life. When we got ready to leave again, she asked me to stay. She knew what I was and couldn't stand the thought of me running 'round America with a gang that was killing and thieving.' He sighs and it's a heavy sound. 'I was blinded by loyalty. I didn't stay.'

I hold his cheek with my hand, my thumb stroking the patch of skin above his beard. 'But you left the gang... you were in Ireland when I found you?'

He nods slowly. 'I was thirty when I realised I didn't wanna be the type of man my mother would've been afraid of. I fled and they didn't like it... shot at me coupla times. Got me in my shoulder.' His hand falls across his shoulder, where my hand is already holding him secure. His fingers rest across mine and then slowly curl around until they're holding on. 'I'm a bad man, Blair. I've been a fool. I haven't done nice things. I've killed more men than I can count. I pushed away the only chance of happiness in my life 'cause, deep down, I knew I didn't deserve it.'

'Don't speak such words,' I tell him quietly, close to tears myself.

He turns on his side again, head still in my lap and I softly stroke his hair as he holds my other hand. He's nothing like I expected. His story is full of loss and grief, just as much as mine is. I can't imagine how he feels, knowing who his father is and how he came to be in this world. I want to hold him tightly until he understands how important he is.

'It doesn't matter what you've done, Colin,' I tell him quietly. 'What matters is what you do now. Who you make yourself to be, with all that collected pain and suffering at your back. Some people become terrible monsters because of the pain they've experienced. But others...' I lean down and press my lips to his cheek, feeling an impulse to, through my drunkenness. 'Others use those emotions to their advantage. They grow... flourish.'

His eyes are closed and I know he's fallen asleep to the sound of my voice, so I slowly get out from under him and rest him down on his bed. I go to my side of the room and take off my dress and boots. In my undergarments, I climb under the covers of the bed. My head is whirling. Not just from drink but from the words Mr McCarthy has told me and the emotions they've brought up. My heart bleeds for him. I turn on my side and gaze at his sleeping face across the room. When my eyes fall closed, the image of him remains behind my eyelids.

14

Mr McCarthy isn't in the room when I wake. The sun is streaming in through the window behind my head, raining down on my bed. It's warm and high in the sky. Midday. I sit up and look around. There's a pounding in the side of my head I try to ignore and rise out of bed, getting dressed into my trousers and shirt. I tie on my boots and leave my hair down, pinning half of it up so that it's out of my face. When I head downstairs, I turn into the bar. There are a few people milling about, talking quietly. Some play poker at a table in the corner, already drinking whiskey and smoking.

I get a cup of coffee from the barman and glance around. I can't see Mr McCarthy anywhere and try not to panic, sitting down to drink my coffee. I don't order food. My stomach is cramping from how much I drank last night and the headache is adding to that nausea. My thoughts go to the night before, a little hazy. I know Mr McCarthy was upset. I know we fought. I know I slapped him. I know I found him drunk in our room and felt things for him I hadn't ever felt for him after hearing his story. Pride makes me want to block those feelings out, pin them down as drunken ramblings my mind conjured up for the sake of it, accentuated by the loneliness I've been feeling. But now, wondering where he is, waiting for him in this saloon, I can't help but picture him going out to see where Caroline is and the thought makes my stomach tighten. I hate myself for it. I don't want it.

After an hour, I get up and leave. The sun is warm on my back as I walk through the street. I don't know where I'm going. The air is hazy from steamships when I make it down to the Mississippi. The water is calm, however a few boats stir it up as they chug along. I see men and women enjoying the sun out on deck as they sail past and some lift their hands to wave at the people along the docks. I stand close to where people are boarding a boat and watch men in suits and ladies in fine dresses going out to enjoy their afternoon sailing and drinking. There's someone close to the docks playing a trumpet. I can hear a newspaper boy competing with the noise the musician is making, yelling out headlines as loud as he can. I glance around. The road near the docks is busy with carriages, horses and people. Further along there are boats bringing in exports from places far away and I wonder where the boxes and crates they carry, being unloaded by men on the docks, come from.

After a little while, I push myself away from the railing overlooking the river and turn down the street. I walk slowly, feeling a calm that my surroundings have embedded in me. My headache has faded. The sun is warm on my cheeks. There's a cool breeze coming off the water. I see through the city muck, steam and crowds, Memphis is a pretty city. There seems to be music on every corner, as I find another busker playing a harmonica down the next street I turn into. Some people stop to listen, forming a semi-circle around the performer beside the building he leans against.

There are shops and stalls and some lanes hold markets where people sell fresh meat, handmade clothes and pelts. I'm trapped amongst a flow of smells and sounds and sights. Everything seems alive and flowing in a deep and resonating rhythm the city itself seems to be emitting from the ground it sits upon. I find myself enjoying what I see and hear, loving the sticky heat the day has brought, sweating within the smoke and crowds.

And then I step into a prettier side of town where trees line the streets and great, grand houses like those on Millionaire's Row run along the edges of the road. Women are dressed in fine silk and men wear top hats and smoke cigars as they walk arm in arm. They walk through gardens and parks that hold ponds filled with ducks, where women sit on seats that are planted under weeping willows, the leaves kissing the tops of their feathered heads. Children fly kites and run about, laughing as dogs bark alongside them. The lives they have are so far from my own that for a moment I'm disorientated. I don't know where I am or what foreign place, unfamiliar world, I've stepped into. And as I walk past, I notice they look at me, dishevelled and sweating and so full of remorse that it plainly shows on my face. And they turn away, they lift their noses up in disgust and make nasty comments under their breath. They are content in their own ignorance. Beautiful to look at and admire from afar, but uncultured and judgemental up close. I'm separate from them. I can never act like they do, mingle amongst them and pretend I understand who they are. I am not just a foreigner to this country, I am a foreigner to their way of life — everything to do with them. I am alien and they see that, plain as day and they hate me without knowing me at all. But they do not need to. Fear drives them to that conclusion, to that repulsion.

And then I see a familiar woman on the street with a man, smiling as he speaks to her, her beautiful hair and gown shaded by the parasol she holds. An idea suddenly takes hold of me and before I can think it through properly, I'm crossing the street to greet her and as soon as she sees me, her smile disappears and her chin lifts a little. The man she's with regards me with concern, his eyes taking in my masculine attire.

'Ms Caroline,' I say quietly, not really knowing what I'm saying. 'I need to speak with you. I'm Ms Ryan, I—'

'I know who you are,' she tells me. 'We met last night.'

'We hardly met. You didn't even get my name.'

'I've got it now.' She's looking at me as if she would do anything to make me go away. I can't, I need to speak with her.

I look at the man she's with — her handsome husband, who looks nothing like Mr McCarthy.

'Can you leave us for a moment?' I look back at Caroline. 'Let's go speak in the park. We'll find a seat in the shade — I won't take too much of your time.'

'Please,' I say when neither of them answers me.

She finally nods, stiffly, and we cross the road and enter the park. When we find a seat and sit down, her husband says he'll take a walk and steps away from us hesitantly. I notice him watching us from a distance as he strolls and turn to Caroline. She's put her parasol down now that she's shaded and she's watching me, expression guarded.

'I'm looking for two men,' I tell her.

She blinks. She didn't expect for me to say this, I can tell.

'Apparently they're distinguished members of society here,' I continue. 'Because of your... status, I was wondering if you might know them? Or know of them? Their names are Joseph and Edwin Gaitwood, but they'll be known by different names now.'

'Mr Van de Berg is the one with status in this city,' she tells me, and I assume she's talking about her husband. 'Perhaps he'll know.'

I look over to where her husband is pacing close by, far enough away to not overhear. I'm about to get up and go and ask him when Caroline reaches out and puts her hand on my arm. I look at her.

'Is he happy?' she asks me.

I stare at her. 'Mr McCarthy?'

She nods.

'I... I don't know. I don't think he's as happy as he can be, but who is?'

Her mouth tightens. 'Make sure he is.'

'Mrs Van de Berg, I'm not involved with Mr McCarthy. He's only helping me find—'

'He shouldn't be here,' she interrupts, shaking her head. 'He needs to leave here and go back to wherever he came from, wherever he's been safe for all these years.'

'Ireland,' I say, nodding. 'But why can't he be here?'

'They know him.' She's staring at me as if I'm stupid. 'They're the reason why he escaped in the first place.'

My heart drops. 'They? Who's they?'

'The marshals. Members of his old gang. If either one finds him, he's a dead man. Surely you know this?'

I blink. My mind can't seem to comprehend what she's saying. 'Why would he come back here if he's at such a great risk of being recognised?'

'I think you know the answer to that better than I do, Ms Ryan.'

'Darling?' Mr Van de Berg is back. He's looking at us, impatient.

'Sorry,' I tell him. 'I... I should go.'

'Ask my husband about these men, Ms Ryan,' Caroline tells me.

'I... er.' I look at the man. He doesn't hide the dislike for me in his face at all. 'Joseph and Edwin Gaitwood? They're brothers. They will go by different names these days.'

'Why are you after these men?' he asks, voice stiff.

'Old friends,' I say dryly.

'Haven't heard of them.'

I nod, biting back a rude remark. I don't like this man just as much as he doesn't like me. I turn back to Caroline.

'Thank you for taking the time to talk to me.'

And then I escape that part of the city and when I find the docks again, I buy hot bread from a vendor on the street and eat it. I'm shaky and my breathing is uneven. Caroline's husband put me on edge and I'm thinking about what she told me — about Mr McCarthy being a dead man if he's recognised by marshals or his old gang members. Dread fills me. I quickly finish my meal and rush back down the streets until I'm back at the saloon. I'm panting, hurrying through the bar. When I don't see Mr McCarthy there, I run upstairs, pushing through a group of men as I do. They yell after me drunkenly. I take no notice of them, taking the stairs two at a time. I barge into our room and Mr McCarthy looks up at me with surprise.

'There you are,' he says. 'Where've you been?'

Relief floods through me. I almost embrace him. I'm so happy to see him, so glad that he's safe and alright.

Damn Caroline. The woman put unnecessary worry in my mind.

'Nowhere,' I say quickly. 'Out and about. Trying to find information about these Gaitwood bastards.'

He nods, face solemn. 'Me too.'

There's a short silence between us and I see he's acting a little strange, not really looking at me.

'I'm sorry... 'bout last night.'

'I'm the one that got violent,' I say, shaking my head. 'I shouldn't have slapped you.'

'It's fine,' he murmurs. 'It got a little outta hand. I shouldn't've let seeing Caroline again get to me like that.' He pauses, shaking his head. And then he says, almost under his breath, 'Fool...'

'She obviously means a lot to you.'

He blinks and looks at me then. 'Uh, yeah. Not much I can do 'bout that now.'

I don't tell him I've just come from seeing her again. I don't tell him about what she said, about the seed of worry she's planted inside my mind. I want to tell him to leave, that I no longer want his help finding the Gaitwoods, just to protect him from any chance of being noticed. But I don't. Out of selfishness, I don't tell him. I want his help. And, with a feeling of shame, I want his company.

'Did you find anything out?' I ask him.

'Nah. Maybe something small… 'bout the docks and river, but I dunno if it was 'bout them getting cargo from there or owning a business 'round there or what. Could be anything.'

I sit down on my bed, feeling dizzy and tired.

'We need to find information about two brothers who arrived in town only recently, within the past two years. It shouldn't be that hard. How many brothers show up and become distinguished members of society so quickly?'

'Not many, you'd think. But this here's a big city, Ms Ryan.'

I remember him calling me Blair last night and his hand wrapped around mine and shake my head to escape the thought.

'We'll spend as much time here as we need until we find them,' I say, voice weak. 'I have all the time in the world.'

He smiles slightly at that and sits down opposite me on his bed, watching my face quietly. 'It won't take long,' he tells me. 'I'll make sure of that.'

'Thank you.' I meet his eye. 'Really, Mr McCarthy, you've been a great help and I know I haven't been as accommodating as you deserve.'

'I don't deserve nothing from you,' he says with a shake of his head.

I know he's right, only to an extent. He isn't the man I thought he was and never once deserved the harsh judgement I cast upon him.

'Besides,' he says with a small smile, 'I know damn well you could've done this all without me.'

I laugh, not believing him. I would have lost my wits long ago without his guidance. I think of Harry Oswald and how brutally

I took his life and shudder, my laugh dying in my throat.

'Ms Ryan...' Mr McCarthy says gently. 'Don't think 'bout the things you've done to get here or to try and make yourself feel better 'bout all this. You ain't a bad person.'

I look up at him, feeling tears itch the back of my throat. It strains so hard it hurts.

'Let's just find these brothers,' I say, ignoring everything else.

I want him to comfort me again. I don't want the maelstrom of emotions inside me to be this wild, this uncontrollable. But if I start to cry, if I start to think about what I did again, I won't be able to stop. I don't have the energy to deal with those thoughts right now and I have to continue on. I have to hold fast, for Thomas' sake. I can feel his memory slipping away from me day by day and it scares me. I don't want to let go of him just yet.

<hr />

We go out every day for a week, searching for any information about Joseph and Edwin. We stay close to the docks and the Mississippi, following the small rumour of two brothers having a business to do with the river somehow. It takes us days, even when we split up and search separately and at different times of the day. I start to grow worried, my stomach twisting in knots, thinking we'll never find them. Mr McCarthy keeps me level-headed. He's my companion those nights where I'm irritable and frustrated when we've spent a full day and come up with nothing. We don't know names; we don't know faces. They're needles in this giant haystack of a city. Mr McCarthy murmurs words of encouragement over glasses of whiskey. He keeps me from going to the next person we question and shaking them for answers.

A week later, we hear about two rich brothers who own a riverboat down by the docks. They deal in running shipments of meat and pelts to other states and have made a name for themselves with the efficiency of their business. On weekends they cruise along the river and bring other rich folk with them, drinking, dancing and playing cards, a number of butlers and maids at their stead. Living a languish life. My blood boils when I hear the information, seeing the advertisement for their business in the newspaper, the man at the post office hands me. Mr McCarthy puts a hand on my shoulder to steady me and thanks the man. I'm stuck staring at the words on the page.

Watson and Co. Fresh meat delivery state to state.

'C'mon, Ms Ryan.'

Mr McCarthy takes me out of the post office and onto the street. The wind is gusty today but warm and damp and it clings to my face and clothes. I'm still looking at the advertisement until he takes the newspaper out of my hands gently.

'We got 'em,' he assures me. 'There's an address here.'

I nod.

His hands are suddenly on my shoulders, his face in front of mine. 'Hey.'

I look at him, blinking.

'You alright?'

I nod again. I don't know what to feel. I'm numbed by the fact we've finally found them, after all those long days of searching. It pains me to know how successful they are. How rich and ignorant they are to my pain. The feeling I had right before I murdered Harry Oswald is slowly rising from the dark depths and it scares me. I'm afraid if I open my mouth to speak, I'll only shriek like the banshee Martin has always claimed me to be and wreak havoc on the street until those two men are in my grasp, begging for mercy.

'Ms Ryan, why don't we go back to the saloon? You can have a well-earned rest there.'

His hands are still on my shoulders and they gently squeeze me there, his thumbs rubbing the groove of my collarbones. I press my lips and look away. He lifts one hand to brush my cheek with the back of his knuckles and the other falls down my arm until his hand is around mine, guiding me along the street. I don't say anything. I follow him, my heart beating heavily in my chest.

When we're back in our room, he puts me on my bed and I gingerly lie down on my side, my arms cradling my head. He sits down on his bed opposite mine and watches me quietly for a moment, elbows on his thighs, back bent down almost lazily.

'How do we go about this?' I finally ask. 'I-I don't want what happened last time to happen again.'

'It won't,' he tells me quietly.

I close my eyes. 'Mr McCarthy, I don't know if I can control it. The anger. I want them dead, I do and I want to see it be done so I can find peace knowing they no longer breathe air, but I don't know if I can do—' I swallow back a sob.

'I've already told ya, I'll kill 'em for you if it comes to it. If you want me to.'

I nod and open my eyes to gaze at him across the room. 'It hurts to know they're so happy.'

'You don't know that,' he murmurs. 'They might be as sad as the both of us.'

I don't smile at that. How can these men be sad when they don't know what it's like to lose someone they love? When they have no hearts in their chests, no souls caged between their bones?

'Sleep,' he tells me quietly. 'I'll go out and see what I can find out 'bout those cruises they do on the river.'

He gets up and straightens his gun-belt, putting his hat back on. Before he can leave, I reach out and he takes my hand, bending down beside my bed so that our faces are level.

'Be careful,' I tell him, remembering the words Caroline said. 'Please.'

His hand squeezes mine. 'You got nothing to worry yourself 'bout, ma'am. Now rest up, I know you ain't been sleeping much this past week.'

He's right, I'm exhausted. Before I can say anything, he lets my hand go and leaves the room. I lay there for not much longer until I'm falling asleep.

I wake up late the next day. Mr McCarthy is nowhere in sight and I can hear the bumbling of activity downstairs. I fix myself up and then I head down towards the saloon. My stomach is grumbling with hunger and I still feel incredibly tired, as if I haven't slept at all. I'm craving a coffee and some beans and lamb, so I turn into the saloon and make my way to the bar. Once I've ordered, I take a look around the tables. I freeze when I see Mr McCarthy is seated at one of them, talking quietly to a woman whose back is turned to me. She's dark-haired and wearing a fine gown. I don't need to see her face. I know who she is. Seeing her leaning forward over the table towards him does something inside me that I don't like, that I feel ashamed of. I turn my face away and wait for my food to be served, keeping by the bar. My heart is beating quickly. I don't know whether Mr McCarthy has noticed me or not and perhaps he doesn't care either way. Ignoring the conflicted feelings bubbling up inside my empty gut, I take my plate and cup of coffee when the barman hands them over and head to a table as far from Mr McCarthy and Caroline as I can.

I sit down and eat, ravenous and try to keep my mind off the couple. After a few minutes, I can't help but look up curiously when I've finished eating, sipping at my coffee. Caroline has put her arm across the table, taking a hold of his hand. Now I can see her face, I see a worried crease between her brows and she's talking to him, voice low but obviously animated. I think back on what she told me and can only imagine she's begging him to leave Memphis, to get back to Ireland, where he's safe. I feel guilt clutch at the food in my belly for not telling him. I don't want him to go back to Ireland just yet and I wonder whether he'll listen to her. He's stroking his thumb across her knuckles. I see it in his face that he feels just as conflicted as I do. My stomach sinks at their closeness and I hate myself for it. I force myself to look away and continue to drink my coffee and when I'm done, I get up and leave the saloon.

It's warm outside, the air humid and sticky, the sky a murky grey, threatening rain. I walk along the noisy street and up to where factories blow smoke into the sky so much that it's hard to tell what's cloud and what's steam. There are workmen milling about and horses stand with their wagons at the side of the road, pawing their iron-shod hooves across the cobblestones as men load them. I continue on, taking in deep breaths and trying to rid myself of the thoughts that are twirling inside my head. I don't want to think about Mr McCarthy. I don't want to have to feel guilty about the things I've thought about him and Caroline lately, as it shouldn't be my concern whatsoever about what he does. If he decides to leave me on my own, to fend for myself in getting these last Gaitwood men, so be it. It's his choice and I can't force him to help me. Whether or not I enjoy his company now doesn't matter either. I can't be selfish about this, not when his welfare is at stake.

After a while, I decide to find the address of the Watson and Co warehouse that was in the newspaper. It doesn't take me long to find it on the other side of the city, next to where the docks hold cargo ships and not passenger steamboats. It's in an area where the swamp trees mingle along the shoreline and where insects and frogs are so loud it's as if they're competing against the sounds of the city. The warehouse is a large, brick building with the Watson and Co sign out the front. The doors are huge and one of them is open. Men mill about outside, some carrying cargo in and out. I find a wall to lean against across the street and watch on for a little while, waiting to see anyone that may be Edwin or Joseph.

It doesn't take long until a man in an expensive suit comes down a set of stairs at the side of the building from the top floor, where I assume the offices are held. He straightens his jacket when he reaches the street and waltzes off along the sidewalk. I immediately get up from off the wall and follow. Keeping back amongst the crowds, I track him along several streets, winding and twisting until we reach the upper part of the city, where Caroline and her husband were walking the week before. It's hard to follow him discreetly through these streets as there are less people and when he takes a shortcut through the park, I use the trees and shrubs to keep me out of sight. The man turns out onto a street on the other side of the park and up a lane that runs along the backs of the large houses. There's barely anyone here now and I stop at the start of the lane, hoping he'll turn off into a garden at the back of a house somewhere, but he continues along. I have no choice but to step into the lane when I lose sight of him and hurry down along to where he last was.

I'm getting close to where I last saw him when someone steps out from behind me and grabs my arm harshly. I spin around, startled and the man in the suit holds up his other hand to his mouth. He looks as surprised as I do and we stare at each other for a moment in an awkward silence.

'You're a woman,' he says, voice quiet.

'I-I—'

He quickly lets go of my wrist. I can already feel his fingers have left a bruise. 'Are you following me, ma'am?'

'Mr Watson?' I ask, not sure what else to say.

'Yeah?' He's staring at me peculiarly. 'Sorry for startling you… I only saw you at the corner of my eye and you're—' He gestures to my trousers and shirt. 'I didn't realise you were a woman until I saw your face.'

I don't know what to say. He seems genuinely kind, not at all a man that would be a part of the gang that murdered my husband.

Maybe I'm mistaken. Maybe Mr McCarthy got the wrong information. I don't know how else to ask him that won't make him close up and run away. He's not old at all, perhaps Mr McCarthy's age and he's dressed smartly, his dark hair smoothed back like Thomas used to wear. His face is clean shaven and he gives me a little smile, as if finding this whole awkward scenario slightly amusing.

'I apologise,' he says when I don't say anything, staring at him like an idiot. 'Why don't we go to my house? It's just up the lane here and you've obviously been so startled by me that you look as if you need to sit down.'

All I can do is nod numbly. Not because I want to go, but because I need to be around this man as long as I can until I know for certain that he's either Joseph or Edwin. I don't know what else to do. Mr McCarthy has no idea where I am and all I have is the revolver at my belt. Mr Watson takes me down the lane a little further and then he turns into a gated garden, letting me through first before closing the gate behind us. He leads me along the garden path and to the back steps of a porch. The garden is beautiful, filled with fragrant flowers and humming with life. The house is massive, yet quaint, and he guides me in through the back door.

'Bessie!' he calls out when we enter a long hallway. 'Can you put the kettle on for two, please?'

'Yes, Mr Watson! Right away, sir!' comes a reply from down the hall.

He guides me through and we turn into the first room, one that is lined with books on the walls and a comfortable-looking leather lounge on the floor by a cold fireplace. He takes me inside and we sit down. Soon after, a heavy-set coloured woman comes into the room, carrying a tray laden with cups, a kettle and a plate of biscuits. She smiles warmly at me and sets about pouring coffee and serving us. Mr Watson stays standing by the fireplace while she does this, having lit a cigarette that he's now smoking. His eyes are on me, clear and yet intent. The woman goes to leave and I thank her quietly.

'Anything else, Mr Watson?' she asks him in the doorway.

'That will be all, thank you, Bessie,' Mr Watson says, eyes still on me.

She nods and leaves.

I take a biscuit and start to eat, nerves niggling at my throat. There's an open letter on the table between us and I see his eyes move to it, flicking back up to me nervously. I put the biscuit back down on the plate, my attention now on the letter.

'What's your name?' he asks me, trying to catch my attention.

'Ms Ryan.' There's no point in lying and I play his game, pretending to not notice the piece of paper between us.

He moves to sit down in an armchair across from me, still smoking his cigarette, and picks up his cup. His hand wavers a little too long, close to where the letter sits. 'What can I do for you, Ms Ryan?'

'Do you own Watson and Co?'

'My brother and I are the main partners of the business, yes,' he replies. 'We've had a tumultuous year, however, and have grown enough to have other shareholders.'

Brother.

I let out a breath. It has to be. I set my cup down on the table in front of me and sit up straight, looking Mr Watson right in the eye.

You can do this, Blair. Do it for Thomas.

'Are you Edwin or are you Joseph?'

Mr Watson's expression changes. He slowly puts his cup down, just as I've done and puts his cigarette in his mouth, puffing on it. He never once loses eye contact. His eyes have gone hard, his jaw jutted. The smoke floating around his head isn't thick enough to conceal the change in his manner.

'I don't know any Edwins or Josephs,' he says slowly.

I press my lips. 'What's your Christian name then, Mr Watson?'

'James.'

We gaze at each other across the little table between us. I can feel the weight of the revolver hanging beside my hip, resting against the lounge I'm sitting on. My hands are in my lap — it wouldn't take too long to draw and fire if I needed to.

'Are you sure?' I ask him.

'Quite.' He watches me for a very long time. My heart is beating in my chest, banging hard against my ribcage. I feel slightly dizzy and try to ignore it. 'But... say I was a Joseph or an Edwin,' he murmurs after. 'What would that mean to you?'

'I just need to speak with them,' I lie.

'What for?'

'A man was killed on his ranch just outside of Cheyenne, Wyoming in 1895. I'm looking for the men who might know what happened and who killed him.'

He's good at keeping his expression neutral. But I see the shift in his eyes. I see the slight stiffness at the corner of his mouth, the little shake his hand does when he lifts it to remove the cigarette from his lips.

'That's unfortunate, Ms Ryan. Who was this man? That was killed?'

'Thomas Ryan. My late husband.'

'Why was he killed?'

'His cattle were taken and he had some valuables inside his home at the time. It's suspected the men knew this and robbed him. Perhaps he wasn't meant to die and he got in the way? I wish to know... for peace of mind.'

I see his eyes go to the revolver at my hip. He nods his head, movements careful.

'I can understand that. And if it means anything, I'm sorry for your loss.'

'It would mean more if you could tell me who did it.'

'You're a resilient woman, Ms Ryan.' His voice has dropped to barely a whisper. 'A lot of women wouldn't go to the trouble to do what you're doing, even if it was their husband that was killed.'

'You don't know women at all if you think that.' My hands are tingling, every muscle in my body tense and ready for action.

He smiles. 'Perhaps I don't.' He finishes his cigarette and slowly leans forward to put it out in an ashtray beside our coffee and biscuits. And the letter. His eyes stay on me. He knows I'm ready to shoot him and he's not taking any chances. 'I like to think I know people, though,' he continues. 'And there is one thing in this world that everyone wants... everyone needs.'

'What's that?'

'Money.' He rubs his fingers together to emphasise his words.

I laugh, unable to help myself. 'When you've lost everything like I have, Mr Watson, that is the last thing you want.'

'It helps. You can't disagree with that.'

'Are you trying to buy your life? Is that it?' My stomach feels sick.

He shakes his head. 'If you think it best to kill me, you'll kill me. I don't think I have much control over that. I'm merely telling you, I have a lot of money. My brother does too. We could provide for you... to apologise for taking your husband.'

'Which one are you?' I spit.

He stares at me for a long time and then he says quietly, 'Joseph.'

'You don't want to die, is that it, Joseph?'

'Not particularly.'

'Do you think that's how my husband felt before you shot him in the head?' My voice is wavering. That anger inside me is climbing back up the inside of my throat and I'm starting to lose control again.

His jaw hardens. 'If it helps, Ms Ryan, I wasn't the one who pulled the trigger?'

'Who was?'

And then I see it. As quick as a flash, his eyes go back to the letter and I know who it's from. I know what he's protecting.

'Russ...' He sighs, careful at keeping up his act. 'We struck your husband around a bit. He fought back and we held him down while the cattle were being driven out. We weren't gonna kill him, just knock him about until he was unconscious for long enough until the job was done. But he insulted Russ and—' He's shaking his head. 'You don't insult Russ, you never insult him. It was too quick. He turned to walk away and for a moment I didn't think he was gonna do anything about it but then he...' He holds out his hands in a hopeless gesture, shrugging.

I push back the tears that are threatening to spill. The images his words have painted are new and raw, devastating. 'Where's Russ Gaitwood now, then?'

'I-I—'

'*Tell* me,' I hiss. I finally draw the revolver and pull back the hammer.

Joseph Gaitwood stares at me. 'He's my big brother, Ms Ryan. I *won't*—'

'If you won't, then you *die*.'

He stares at me. 'Won't you kill me, anyway?'

I don't answer, I just say, 'Tell me where your brother is.'

He holds up his hands, shaking his head. I stand up and move towards the letter on the table. He sees me go for it and lunges forward. We struggle for a moment, snatching at the paper until it tears. Using the revolver in my hand, I swing it around until it catches the side of his face and he slumps back in his chair. Shaking, I keep the revolver pointed towards him and read what's written on my half of the note. Words like *ranch* and *men* catch my eye.

'This is from him, isn't it?' I grate.

'He's my *brother*,' is all he says. There's a wound above his brow and blood is dripping into his eye. He squints at me, breathing hard.

I move towards him, uncaring and hit him again. The anger inside me has taken over and I'm hardly inside my body as I do. I just react to it as it consumes me. I'll do anything to get what I want. All I can see is a bullet flying through Thomas's head, again and again and I know the only way to push away that thought is when I know the man is dead.

'I'm a good man now, Ms Ryan,' Joseph pleads. He's still clutching the other piece of the letter in his fist. 'I'm betrothed, I've got a good business, I—'

'My husband was a good man, too. He never once struck someone out of anger, let alone killed. I've found out you don't have to be a bad person to have bad things happen to you. But it damned well helps to know a piece of *filth* like you and your brothers have gotten their comeuppance.'

'Your husband will still be gone...' He doesn't look me in the eye. He's protecting his head in case I hit him again.

I let out a growl. 'Give me the letter and I will consider not shooting you.'

He lets out a breath. 'How can I take your word?'

'You can't,' I admit. 'But I'll shoot you and take it from your corpse if you don't. Either way, your brother is a dead man.'

Joseph swallows — I hear the air trapped in his throat, trapped by fear. 'I can't give up my brother.'

'What of your other brother, Edwin? Where is he?'

'He's sick... In bed upstairs as we speak.'

'How do I know you're not lying?'

'Go and check if you wish!' he cries.

I feel a wave of resentment and anxiety wash over me. It makes me hit him again, acting out. Tears are suddenly on my cheeks and my voice is thick, full of them.

'Do you know what it's like to lose someone? To not have the chance to say goodbye?' I hit him once more and he cowers, crying out. 'Do you? You have no idea! You and your men kill mercilessly and you go from town to town, stealing and making widows of us all! You need to know how it feels! You can't get away with this!'

'I'm sorry!'

'No, it's too late! It's too late to be sorry, my husband is gone and you don't *deserve* to live! You need to die because you can't live a life of killing and expect to be forgiven as soon as you're a man of leisure!'

'I don't—' he stammers. 'I regret it. I do, please, I'm sorry, Ms Ryan. Let me do whatever I can. I'll help you.'

I'm numb. The rage within me has surged upwards and has grown like a shadow across the ceiling, towering over the both of us. His pleas fall on deaf ears. All I can see is the anguish in his eyes and the feel of the cool metal of the trigger against my finger.

'Give me the letter and I'll spare you.' My voice sounds far away.

'He doesn't deserve death,' he whispers.

A woman's scream pierces the air. We both jump at the sound, snapped out of the confrontation. I turn and see Joseph's maid in the doorway. She's looking at me as if I'm a demon, the most frightening thing she's ever seen. I see her gaze travel to her employer, to the blood on his face. And then a hand grabs mine and I'm thrown sideways as someone tries to yank the gun off me. We collapse. The side of the table catches my hip as we fall and pain blasts all the way down my leg. Joseph is on top of me, grappling for the revolver, the look on his face wild. His smoothed hair is now unkempt, falling across his forehead. There's a madness in his eyes, a madness that seems to have come from within; the man he once was rising to the surface. I can't let him overpower me. If he wins, I'm dead and all my effort to get here will be for nothing. I have to do something. Through my panic, I can see the barrel of the revolver is still pointed towards him. His hands are against mine, fingers bruising, as he tries to take the gun. When he can't break my hold, he hits me across the face in an attempt to stun me and my teeth clash against my tongue at the force. I fight back, keeping the gun pointed towards him as much as I can, and I can feel my grip hasn't slipped from the trigger. With all my strength, I hold the angle, close my eyes, grit my teeth and pull.

'No—!'

An explosion sounds out. I'm splattered with heat and the smell of gunpowder and metal makes me retch. Joseph's weight collapses against me. He's no longer moving, no longer fighting. There's wetness in my hair, seeping into my ears, which are ringing and I'm coughing, tasting bile. I know I need to get out, to get the body off me and escape as fast as I can. I can't be caught. I have to run.

I can hear the woman Bessie screaming. There's blood and chunky bits of bone and brain on my face, my hands. With all my strength, I move the body off me and crawl out from under it. Bessie is still in the doorway, collapsed to her knees, face contorted in horror. Her wails send a shudder through me. I step backwards, shock taking a hold like a cold vice. My revolver is still on the ground and beside it is the other scrap of paper, covered in blood. I stoop to pick it up, stumbling.

'You killed him! You monster!'

I look back at Bessie, startled by the force of her words.

'He attacked me...' I say dumbly.

'Bessie?' a weak voice comes from up the stairs.

'Help me! Mr Watson, please!'

Something within me breaks the spell I'm in and I realise I've been here too long. I need to leave, to get out. Bessie is starting to get back up, still calling for help, voice now ragged from her screams. I shove the pieces of paper into my pocket, backing out the door Joseph led me through. There's the sound of footsteps coming down the stairs. And then I'm running. I run and I don't look back. I'm out in the garden again, the flowers and serenity of it now shocking to my senses, the air too thick with fragrance, the colours too alarming to the eye. I rush through the gate, the gun still in my hand, blood and bits on my face, on my arms. My breath is wheezing through my throat. I'm about to choke. I'm about to throw up.

I see an alley off the street I'm on. I have no idea how long I've run for. I have no idea where I am. I just rush into the alley and into an alcove, panting, shaking. I look down at my shirt. It's splattered with blood and there are bits of Joseph Gaitwood's head stuck to the material. I quickly take it off and wipe my face and arms down. I don't think, I *can't* think. My mind is whirling. I'm listening only to instinct. When I hear whistles blowing, I throw the shirt into the corner of the alcove and run down the alley in my undershirt. There's still blood all over me, I have no time to get it all off. I press my hat further on my head and keep it down as I cross the street. I go south, towards where I know the water is. If I can find the water, I can find my way back to the saloon, back to Mr McCarthy.

15

It takes me almost an hour to reach the docks again. Every time I hear whistles blowing or see the blue uniforms of policemen, I duck into a wall or hide behind a wagon. When I'm at the docks, I rush through the crowds. Scarcely anyone looks at me and I'm grateful for it, hurrying along. It's getting close to sunset, the air still thick with humidity. I struggle to breathe amongst the smells of the city and the people I pass, Joseph's blood up my nose. There's such a strong smell of death that I'm dizzy. The food I ate earlier today keeps wanting to come back up and I keep forcing it back down, stumbling through the streets, aware some people do look at me and frown.

I'm close to where the Watson and Co warehouse is, where everything started earlier today, where I wish to be back in time so I can do things differently, when someone comes out of nowhere, swearing gruffly under their breath. Mr McCarthy has a waistcoat around my shoulders in seconds and he's standing in front of me, buttoning it up to cover my undershirt before I can even realise he's there. He's muttering things and I hear something else in the dizziness, the nausea.

'We can take her to mine. They won't look for her there,' a woman says.

I stumble. Mr McCarthy grabs a hold of me, his fingers like an iron brand against my skin. I let out a little, involuntary noise and he shushes me gently. I'm not functioning properly. I'm barely conscious. He grabs a hold of me and doesn't let go, taking me further along the street. We only walk a few paces when I feel a horrible wave of nausea crash over me. I retch. Mr McCarthy pulls me to the side of the street and I vomit until my stomach is empty, until it's cramping so painfully, I only want to vomit more. And then my vision flickers. My limbs feel suddenly heavy, a dead weight and I lose consciousness.

'Colin, why did you ever agree to this? Do you really think this *isn't* going to draw attention to you? Why would you put yourself at so much risk just for an Irish widow?'

'I ain't gonna talk 'bout it now, Caroline. What's done is done.'

'Fine... I won't ever claim to know you, Colin McCarthy, just as I never have.'

There's a soft click of a door closing and I open my eyes. I'm in a comfortable bed and the ceiling above me is a myriad of carvings depicting flowers and insects and trees. I stare up at it for a long while, at the plaster so beautifully crafted and gilded. For a moment, I don't know where I am and I don't have the energy to care. And then the memories of what happened slowly start to sink in and I feel the tension seep back into my muscles and I sit upright quickly.

'Hey, hey,' a gruff voice says. 'You're alright, you're safe.'

Mr McCarthy is sitting in a chair beside the bed I'm in. He's holding out his hands to me and I stare at him for a moment, panting.

'Mr McCarthy...' I feel tears cloud my eyes.

'What the hell happened back there?'

'God...' I swallow thickly. 'Mr McCarthy, we need to get out of here.'

I go to swing my legs over the side of the bed, but he stops me, grasping my hand. He's staring at me.

'Ms Ryan, tell me what happened.'

'Joseph Gaitwood...' I swallow again. My throat is so tight and there's no clearing it. 'He's dead.'

'Did you kill him?'

The tears come out of nowhere. I'm shaking, my muscles seizing up.

'It was an accident,' I whisper and he squeezes my hand. 'I-I didn't think I was going to, I just wanted the letter he had and then he attacked me.'

'Did anyone see?'

I nod.

'Jesus...' He shakes his head. 'Alright. We'll get outta here as soon as we can, but for the time being, we're fine. We're at Caroline's.'

Caroline's.

'She doesn't want me here...'

'She was kind enough to offer her place to shelter you,' he says, shaking his head. 'She does want you here.'

I'm panicked. 'We need to get out... We need—'

'Hey.' He squeezes my hand and I look at him. 'I want you to go get cleaned up first. I'm gonna go get our bags for us and the horses. We'll leave as soon as you're no longer in shock. You don't gotta tell me anything 'bout what happened with Joseph Gaitwood 'til then, you hear?'

I nod again, his words sinking in. His hand is warm and his grip is sure. I'm shaking violently, but his hold is steadying me and he's watching me quietly. He gets up from his chair when the door opens and Caroline comes in. She looks at me.

'Come, Ms Ryan,' she tells me. 'I have a bath for you.'

I get up and Mr McCarthy puts a hand on my back, dropping it when I reach Caroline. She looks at him.

'I'm gonna go get our things,' he murmurs.

She nods. 'I'll look after her.'

'Wait,' I say before he goes. He stops and looks at me. I pull the two torn pieces of paper from my pocket. Caroline makes a noise at the sight of them, bloodied and crumpled. Mr McCarthy frowns, not yet taking them from me. 'Keep them safe.'

He lifts a hand and takes the letter from my grasp, putting it in his pocket. With Caroline there, he asks no questions and instead leaves the room without another word. I know for now they'll be safe with him.

Caroline takes me out of the room and down a long hallway adorned with paintings on the walls, a beautiful long rug and hall tables that hold fresh flowers in china vases. She opens a door at the opposite end of the hall and we enter a room with a bath and a fireplace where the fire is crackling gently. A maid has fixed up the bath and she nods her head to Caroline when she sees us. I can hardly think, incredibly numb, and I'm thankful for Caroline and the maid as they help me out of my ruined clothes and into the hot water. The maid helps me clean the blood from my skin as Caroline washes my hair. The feel of the hot water on my skin and the smell of soap in my senses makes me emotional again and I silently sob as I bathe, continuing to shake.

'Hush now, Ms Ryan,' Caroline says gently. 'It's alright, you're safe…'

She plaits my hair when I'm out and dry and the maid puts me in a plain linen dress, tightening the ties at the back for me as Caroline goes about burning my old clothes. When I'm freshly washed and feeling a little more relaxed, the two women take me downstairs. The house we're in is grand and every room holds paintings and flowers. I'm sat down in a comfortable chair across from a fireplace and a cup of tea is pressed between my palms.

'Try to drink and relax,' Caroline tells me. 'Colin will be back soon.'

The tea is sweet and comforting. I sit back in the chair, the tremors in my body slowly easing. When I look up, Caroline is sitting across from me, a tea cup and saucer in her hands. She's watching me quietly, a look I can't quite define in her eyes.

'Why did you think it necessary to kill a man without Colin there with you?' she asks quietly.

I frown at her. 'W-What?'

'You do remember what I said to you the other day? If this doesn't draw attention to him, I don't know what will.' She frowns at me, shaking her head. 'I suppose you don't very much care about what happens to him once you've finished your little vendetta.'

I don't know what to say. I feel like I'm a child, being reprimanded by her mother.

'He has no connection to the killing...'

'He has a connection to you,' her voice is bitter when she says the words. 'And if there is a witness, then they know to look for a woman with your stature and your hair colour. It won't take too long for them to connect the dots when they've arrested you to know Colin is a wanted man as well.'

'I won't get arrested.'

Her mouth tightens. 'Don't you think it's absurd that you're after these outlaws for the sake of your husband and yet you yourself are now an outlaw because of it?'

I stare at her. I can hear Bessie screaming at me again, calling me a monster. 'You believe I should be arrested?'

'You killed a man in cold blood. There's already talk all over the city. James Watson was a well-known and well-loved man here in Memphis.'

My heart clenches painfully in my chest. '*Cold blood*? He attacked me!'

Caroline shrugs. 'You've put everyone at risk when you could have gone about this very differently. That's all I'm saying. Even I am at risk now for harbouring a fugitive.'

'*Two* fugitives,' I bite. 'Your precious Colin is one, too.'

Caroline sighs, putting her cup and saucer down. My stomach revolts. I get up and leave the room. Caroline lets out a noise of complaint as I leave the house, sucking in a deep lungful of fresh air once I'm out on her porch. She comes up behind me.

'Come inside, Ms Ryan.'

My eyes are on the street. When I see Mr McCarthy riding up it, leading my horse alongside his, I grip tightly onto the railing and watch him. Caroline comes up beside me and we wait for Mr McCarthy together.

'I know how hard this must be for you,' she says quietly.

'Do you?' I ask, looking at her. 'Do you really?'

She stares at me for a moment, face tight. 'Ms Ryan, I don't dislike you as much as you might think I do. I only care for Colin and it's my worry for him that makes me snap at you. I just don't think you have his best interests at heart.'

'You're right, I don't. I have *my* best interests at heart.'

She frowns at that. 'So you're using him?'

My stomach twists. 'He's aware of it.'

'Mm...'

We both watch as he comes up to the house. He dismounts and ties the horses to a post at the foot of the porch stairs. He looks up at us and his eyes meet mine.

'You look a lot better. Needed some air?'

I nod. 'We should go, Mr McCarthy.'

He hesitates. Caroline puts her hand on my arm, surprising me.

'She's right, Colin,' she says. 'Mr Van de Berg will be home soon. And you two should put some distance between you and the city...' Her grip loosens on my arm and she looks away. 'This is greatly reminding me of all those years ago.' She clears her throat and steps away. 'Excuse me.'

Mr McCarthy comes up the stairs. 'Caroline...'

My heart tightens. I look away when he goes to her.

'I can't do this again, Colin,' she tells him quietly.

'I'm sorry.'

'Please, just go. You shouldn't be here.'

There's a short silence and then I hear Mr McCarthy sigh.

'Caroline, thank you. For everything.'

'Just go, Colin. Don't make me live through all of this again.'

'I'm so—'

'Please.'

Mr McCarthy slowly moves off the porch and back to the horses. I look back at Caroline. There are tears on her cheeks and I don't know what to say to her. My heart feels heavy for her. I know she still loves Mr McCarthy and I can imagine how hard it's been for her seeing him again. She meets my gaze.

'Thank you, Caroline,' I tell her, meaning it.

'Make sure I don't regret helping you,' she says to me, voice hard. 'Look after him.'

I nod and head down the steps. I get on my horse, tucking the dress around the saddle, and then Mr McCarthy leads us out onto the street and as far away from Memphis as possible.

I know Mr McCarthy wants to go back to Caroline. I see it in the stiffness of his back as he rides. In the emptiness in his eyes. The tension in his mouth. His fingers are tight around his reins, knuckles white, and he's quiet, deep in thought. I know he wants to set things straight with her. I know he's still in love with her. I know it because I can see it plain as day. And I hate myself for it. I hate myself for feeling defensive over him. I hate myself for being selfish, for thinking I have the right to Mr McCarthy's company over another woman. For thinking I have the right to take the life of a man just because he was a part of the gang that killed my husband.

You're a monster.

We stop to rest several hours outside of Memphis. The weather is already clearer. The night is cold and I shrug my coat on once the horses are sorted and the fire is burning. The sky is clear and gives us a good view of our surroundings, the tops of trees and the surface of the lake we're beside, coated in a silvery film from the moon's light. Mr McCarthy is by the fire, cooking up a can of beans. We left in a hurry and I know we don't have much food left, but he cooks the can up anyway, his grim face peering into the flames.

'The letter I gave you,' I start, chewing on my food as we start to eat. 'Do you have it?'

''Course,' he mumbles.

'Did you read it?'

'No.'

'Good.' I get up and take it from him when he draws it from his pocket, sitting back down in my place by the fire.

'What is it?' he asks, curiously, looking through the flames at it.

I hold it to the light and piece the two broken parts together on the ground by my bowl. The envelope is crumpled and covered in dried blood, but I can make out the words on the front of it, addressed to Mr and Mr Watson. Carefully flipping it over, there are only a few words that are decipherable amongst the bloodstains on the back, where the return address should be.

Fargo, North Dakota. Parker.

'I think I know where Russ Gaitwood is.'

Mr McCarthy doesn't say anything and when I lift my head, he's staring at me incredulously.

'You did it...' is all he says and I hear the sadness in his voice and it breaks my heart.

I lower my gaze. A silence falls over us again and I don't know what to say to him. I hadn't even thought of the letter since leaving Memphis because my mind had been too focused on him, on my own selfishness, on Caroline. It makes me wonder how important it is to me now, in comparison to my life, my sanity... Mr McCarthy. I shake my head. I can't do this. I can't keep thinking like this.

'I'm sorry,' I say after we've eaten. I know I owe him it.

Mr McCarthy lifts his eyes to my face. It's as if he's expected me to say it and has been waiting. Instead of feeling angry over that thought, I'm even more resentful towards myself.

'I was stupid,' I continue.

'We were there too long anyway,' he murmurs. 'It was getting dangerous for us both. All that asking 'round... they would've gotten us soon enough if you hadn't've gotten him. Only thing that matters is that you got what you came for.' He pauses, frowning. 'What 'bout the other brother?'

'Sick,' I say. 'I heard a man's voice from upstairs. Sounded weak and I assumed it was him.'

He harrumphs.

'Mr McCarthy, I know you're angry at me,' I say. 'I know you want to go about taking these men out differently and I keep letting my anger get the best of me. But I— I don't think I actually wanted to kill him.' I can feel tears in my throat again and it makes me frustrated. 'I don't think I was going to. I just wanted the other part of the letter, but his maid walked in on us. He attacked me and I— I pulled the trigger.'

He watches me silently for a while. And then he says, 'You want these men dead, ma'am, not me.'

My stomach twists. 'That's not what you told me in the past.'

He looks away, jaw stiff. 'I just don't know anymore... you say you're afraid of yourself yet you keep going against everything *right*. I won't lie, I am angry at you. You risked a hell of a lot killing that Gaitwood boy back there. Not just you or me, but Caroline—'

I throw up my hands. '*Caroline* didn't have to help us!'

'Well, she did!'

'My business is none of her business!' I growl at him over the fire. 'She didn't have to get involved! I didn't *want* her to get involved and yet you took that upon yourself.'

'We wouldn't be here if she hadn't! I felt like a damn fool having to ask her.'

I stand up. I've had enough. I don't want to hear it. I want to run away and drown out his words.

'Ms Ryan!' he yells at my back as I try to storm off.

I turn back to him. He's stood up, about to chase after me.

'Why don't you figure out whether you're doing this for me or for yourself, Mr McCarthy? You'll get yourself nowhere if you can't distinguish that fact. And I couldn't care less which one it is, but if you want to go back there to Caroline, by all means, go. I'll be fine without you. I've already done what I came here to do twice without your help. I don't think I need you after all.'

'Without my help?' he asks, voice tight. 'That so?'

I clench my teeth. 'You don't know what you feel just as much as I don't. I at least have got a purpose and I'm on the road to it. You're lost, Mr McCarthy. But I saw you with her. You looked like you had finally found what you were after. Maybe you shouldn't push that away for a second time? She's in love with you.'

He's shaking his head, staring at me, arms slack at his sides. 'You telling me all this 'cause you want me gone or 'cause you think you know what's best for me?'

'Would it matter?' I ask, unable to control the tremble in my voice. 'You should do what you think is best for you, Mr McCarthy, not me.'

'I said I'd help you. Months ago, back in Ireland, I *promised*.'

I feel my heart bleed. 'I won't take it personally if you break that promise.'

'I ain't going back to her. It didn't work between us for a reason. I left her and she'll never forgive me for that, whether she still loves me or not, that don't matter.'

We stand in silence for a moment. The horses are snorting as they graze several feet from us. The fire shifts as a log falls and there's a crackle and hiss as embers float up into the sky.

'But if you want me to go, I'll go,' he continues. 'I'll leave ya alone, if that's what you wish.'

I can feel my hands trembling. I try to steady my voice, to clear my throat so I don't stumble on what I'm going to say. My body fights me. I don't want to speak the words. My heart aches.

'You can leave as soon as we reach the next town,' I tell him, jutting up my chin. 'I know where Russ Gaitwood is now. As soon as I'm in Fargo, I'll find him and kill him and then I'll head home. There's no need for you anymore.'

He nods. His face is like stone again, guarded and he turns his head away as he steps back to the fire.

'As you wish, ma'am.'

It's just over a week's ride when we reach Kansas City. I know it's in Missouri. I know we're in Mr McCarthy's home state as we ride in through the hills. I see the pain on his face as we go and it hurts me to see it. I stay quiet, not wanting to intrude. The city is large and filled with people. Streets hold massive billboards on buildings and trams shuttle along lines on the roads, a jostling sound with an incessant ringing of a bell, and there's a bustle and life to it that reminds me of Memphis, the air only cooler, cleaner. We find a hotel near the centre of town and I tie up my horse once I've dismounted. Mr McCarthy gets off and I turn to him, jaw hard.

'Well, Mr McCarthy,' I say. My back is aching from the ride. We've ridden hard to get to Kansas City quickly and I'm exhausted, having not gotten much sleep this past week. 'Thank you for all your help.'

I hold out my hand to him to shake and he looks at it. He doesn't make a move at first and for a moment, I think he doesn't want to touch me. And then he pulls one of his revolvers from his belt and I feel the cool grip enter my palm when he passes it to me.

''Cause you lost yours,' he explains softly.

I try to thank him, but my words catch in my throat.

He picks up my other hand and squeezes it between his.

'Ma'am.'

I lift my chin, finally able to find my words.

'I hope you find what you're after,' I tell him.

'You too...'

And then I grab my bag from my horse, stuff the revolver in it and head inside the hotel, forcing back the tears that are clawing at my throat. I pay for a room and head upstairs. I'm able to keep the tears at bay until the door to my room is closed behind me and then I'm weeping uncontrollably. I fall to the bed, hiccuping, exhausted.

The next morning, I get on my boots, gun-belt and hat and make my way downstairs. I have breakfast and then I head out with my things. My horse is still tied up outside the hotel and I tighten up her girth again, strapping my bag to her saddle. I take her reins off the post and lead her along the bustling street. A numbness has come across me. I know why I let Mr McCarthy go. I could no longer use him like I was.

I walk through the city in a sort of spell, not really knowing how I'm going to go about getting to Fargo. My horse ambles alongside me and I twist the reins in my hands worriedly. When I come across a sheriff's office, I hesitate for a moment and then eventually tie her up outside and go in.

'He was drunk. Just handed himself in.'

'Didn't he have a horse?'

'Yeah, I put it in the livery out back. Had guns, too. They've been confiscated.'

I stop in the doorway when I overhear the conversation, my heart jamming painfully against my ribs.

'Didn't think there was any of 'em left. Thought any of the ones we didn't catch all went to different countries.'

'Would've been the smart thing to do, yeah.'

'Gotta be a sad individual to hand yourself in knowing full well you'll be hanging from the gallows come sundown.'

'Sirs,' I walk into the room, panicking. 'That man you're talking about—?'

The two men look over at me and one stands up from his desk, his eyes raking over my dirty, crinkled shirt and the mess my hair is under my hat.

'Ma'am, can we help you?'

'That man that handed himself in?'

'The McCarthy boy?' the other laughs. 'You know how long he's had a price on his head? Not as much as the others, yet still enough to set a bounty hunter up for a few years. Too bad no one gets it, as he's handed himself in instead.'

My stomach drops. I catch myself on the wall before I fall over completely and the men step forward out of concern.

'You alright, ma'am?'

'Yes,' I say, shaking them off. 'I-I... Where is he? The McCarthy boy?'

The two men glance at each other.

'Er...'

'Please.' I look at them. 'He killed someone close to me. I wish to see him hang.' The lie comes easily, even in my panicked state.

'Of course,' the sheriff says. 'You from 'round here?' When I shake my head, he sighs. 'The courthouse. It's not far. I can take you to it?'

'Please, sir.'

He takes me outside onto the street. My thoughts are scrambling.

Colin, you fool.

Why would he hand himself in? Drunk? I'm losing control, not sure what to do. I can't let them hang him. I can't let him die. I leave my horse outside the sheriff's office and follow him along the road, trying to stay calm. I collect my thoughts as much as I can, remembering the conversation I walked in on. Colin's horse is in the sheriff's livery out the back of the office. I keep that in mind as I continue to follow the man.

We reach the courthouse in a matter of five minutes. It's a large building, larger than Cheyenne's courthouse and a lot more foreboding. Gallows have been set up outside it — a platform along a strip of grass beside the trees that line the building's steps. It presents itself as a threat. I know Colin will be hanging from those gallows within a matter of hours if I don't do something.

'He'll be in there, rotting in a cell, ma'am,' the sheriff tells me quietly.

I hardly listen to him, staring at the courthouse, my heart hammering.

'It'll be alright. He'll be swaying on a noose by this evening and your heart will be at rest.'

His words do something to me. I stare at him. He's telling me Colin's death will put my heart at ease, just as I think the Gaitwood gang's deaths will. I feel dizzy. I thank the sheriff when he leaves, my voice hollow and not my own. I stand on the path, staring at the building for a long time. And then, when I have a plan, I head back to the sheriff's office.

When I reach it, I leave my horse tied out the front and head around to the livery. It's a small stable, holding six horses. There are saddles on each stall and I see Colin's dark gelding as soon as I step inside. A man comes along through the back door and walks along the stalls and I quickly duck behind the door as he passes through. When he's gone, I rush forward and enter the gelding's stall. It approaches me, familiar with my scent and I pat its dark head, kissing its large cheek. I murmur comforting words to it, just as Colin always has, and then I start to put its bridle and saddle on. When the horse is ready, I look out and around, keeping an eye out for the man. I don't see him, so I pull the horse along with me. My heart is thundering. There's sweat on my palms, the reins slipping in my grip, but I hold fast and quickly lead the gelding around the front of the office to where my mare is waiting. When I reach her, I quickly mount up and kick her into a trot, pulling the gelding along.

I let out a breath of relief when I'm on another street. I click my tongue and lead the horses back to the courthouse. There's a saloon on the street opposite, fittingly called *The Gallows*, and I shudder as I tie the horses up at a post. I take my revolver out of its holster and instead put it in the band of my belt, concealing it with my shirt. I leave my hat on my saddle and take my hair out, letting it fall freely across my back. And then I rush across the busy road towards the large building.

I don't know what I'm doing. I don't know how I'm going to find Colin, let alone get him out of there. I'm not even thinking. My body is taking over again and I'm only a background witness to what it does. I come in through the doors and into a large hall of marble and staircases and balustrades. There are two guards at the door and they look at me questioningly, but they don't say anything as I hurry along, looking for a set of stairs leading down or a door on this level. I don't expect Colin to be on ground level and neither do I expect him to be upstairs. There must be holding cells in the basement. I go off that intuition and when I find a stairwell that leads down; I follow them, my footsteps too loud, echoing off the empty walls.

I'm breathing hard, panicking. I need to keep my mind as clear as possible and when I reach the lower level, I enter a long hall with heavy doors either side. I hurry down one side. I can't tell whether it's my footsteps that are too loud or my heartbeat. My breathing is in my ears, consuming my brain and I try to steady it as much as I can, rounding a corner.

The basement is cold and the walls are stone, the doors iron and thick. I start to see differences in the doors on this side of the hallway. There are holes built into them, little squares with slats that can be slid across to look inside. I start to go through them, looking into dimly lit cells. There are prisoners in some of them, older men and younger men alike, even some women look up when they hear the door, eyes wide and distrusting. I grit my teeth and keep going. I find Colin behind the ninth door I peer into and gasp when I see him, laying on a hard bed in the corner of his cell, half in shadow. I try the door. Locked.

'Colin,' I whisper.

He doesn't stir and I look down the hall, frightened a guard will show up any minute and catch me. I take the gun out of my belt and hold it down close to my hip, keeping it concealed as I continue to walk through the hallway. It loops around the whole base of the building, holding cells and other rooms. I quickly slip into an alcove when I hear footsteps rounding the next corner and press myself against a door as a guard comes past. When I see he's alone, I step out and follow him until my gun is pressed up against his back and I have a hand on his arm, gripping tight.

'Don't you dare make a sound,' I threaten.

The man holds up his arms slowly and I take the gun off his belt and stuff it in my holster. And then I prod him forward, hearing keys jingle as he does and almost letting out a crazed laugh of relief. He lets me lead him back the way I've come, towards Colin's cell door. When we reach it, I order him to get his keys and open the door. When he does, I close the door behind us, in case someone comes. I then tell the guard to face the wall. He does, saying nothing and I keep my gun pointed at him as I walk over to Colin, who's still lying unconscious on the bed. I bend down beside where he lies, breathing hard.

'Colin?' I say.

I lift my other hand and shake his shoulder. He stirs and his face enters the patch of light on his bed and I let out a gasp of horror. They've beaten him, parts of his face bruised and bloodied.

'Bastards,' I hiss.

When his eyes open, he stares up at me as if he can't believe I'm there and I hold my finger against his mouth, silencing any noise he might make. He blinks up at me and behind the blood on his face, I can tell he's surprised to see me. That breaks my heart and I can't help but gently stroke his beard. I tell him to get up and he does, swaying. And then I turn to the guard and put all the force I can muster into my hit as I strike him across the back of the head with the gun I hold. He falls to the ground like a dead weight and I quickly take his keys off him. I look back at Colin as he struggles to stand and I swear.

'Come on, can you walk?'

He tries to stand and grunts.

'Are you drunk or are you injured?'

'Bit of both,' he mumbles.

I try not to panic. I let out a shaking breath through my mouth and look around. There's nothing for him to lean against. I'm going to have to support him in order to get him out. I don't know how we're going to rush out of the building if he can barely stand. I look back at the guard. My hands fumble across his belt and all I find are handcuffs. A thought strikes me like a blow across the face. I shed my clothes quickly. I take off the guard's uniform, struggling with his unconscious body and heavy limbs. His clothes are too big for me and I know I must look strange, but it's the only way. I push my hair under my collar and shove the guard's hat on my head. I go to Colin and put the cuffs around his wrists, closing them but not locking them. He doesn't say anything. His breath is wheezing in his chest. I can hear it as I bend down to help him up, supporting his back as we walk.

'Come on,' I tell him gently. 'Let's get out of here.'

It's a slow journey back to the stairs. My senses are on fire, my muscles tense. I'm on high alert, listening for any shouts, any footsteps. Colin struggles on the stairs. I support his weight as we climb them one by one and the slow progress frustrates me. I know it's not his fault and I'm patient with him as he goes as fast as he can, breath wheezing through broken ribs. He holds onto me tightly, as if I'm his lifeline, and I vaguely think on our ascension that I am. I'm the only one standing between him and a noose. That clarification is what pushes me forward, coaxing him gently, keeping my arms strong and tight around him, my shoulder up against his back as we move. And when we reach the landing, I press my lips to his cheek and whisper to him.

'You're doing so well,' I say against his skin. 'Just a little further. I need you to stand straighter for me, okay? Shuffle your feet if you need to.'

He nods. All he can do is nod. His eyes are half closed and I don't know if he's putting on an act for me or if his injuries and drunkenness have sent him stupid. We continue on and he does stand straighter, he does shuffle his feet and I stand beside him, walking as fast as I can with him under my grip. I hold my breath as we round the corner where I saw the guards at the front entrance. They're still there. They're talking to one another, not paying attention. My eyes cross over the exit. So close. They're standing only several feet from it, backs turned at the moment. I keep walking, holding tightly onto Colin's arm. His hands are still bound by handcuffs in front of him. I look like a guard taking a prisoner out.

Where? To the gallows? There isn't going to be hanging until close to sundown.

The sheriff's office.

I press my lips. It'll have to do. If they don't believe me, I've got a gun. I can take two men down if need be. I keep walking.

Colin continues to shuffle beside me, head bent down. I can hear him groaning every so often in pain and my heart clenches every time he does. The exit is getting closer and closer. My heart is skittering inside my chest. I feel dizzy. I don't know if I'll be able to get out of here without passing out. But I hold fast. The door is so close. The guards' backs are still turned. My grip on Colin is sure to be hurting him, I'm holding on so tightly.

And then we reach the door and I'm through the threshold, the afternoon sun warm on my face, the breeze cool and catching the baggy uniform I wear—

'Hey!'

I almost skid to a stop. And then I force myself to keep walking and pull Colin after me.

'Hey!' comes the yell again.

My heart is beating so fast inside my chest I think I'm going to be sick.

'You! With the prisoner!'

16

I hear footsteps. I grab the revolver on my belt, holding it but not drawing it just yet. I keep walking. I can see *The Gallows* across the street. I can see the horses tied up outside. Someone grabs me. I almost shriek it surprises me so much. One of the guards has rushed down to us and he's glaring at me, wrinkled and grey, but furious.

'What do you think you're doing?' he demands. And then he sees my face. Sees the bagginess of the uniform I wear.

My revolver is up against his chin before he can do anything and he stares at me, eyes wide.

'Don't you dare do a thing,' I hiss. 'Let us leave peacefully or I'll pull the trigger.'

He swallows and the point of the revolver bobs against his throat.

There's a loud crack and for a moment, I think I've done it again. I think I've accidentally pulled the trigger out of fright and I've killed another man. But the guard continues to stare at me, eyes wide and I start to feel a horrible, burning pain in my back. I stumble forward. Shock grips my body and I fall to my knees. Colin staggers. I look up at him as he lets out a yell.

'Go!' I barely have a voice. My demand comes out like a breath of air with no form. 'Colin, go!'

The pain is blinding. I try to get back up. The guard next to us is suddenly forced to the floor and Colin is on top of him, slamming his fists down against the guard's face, hands now free from the handcuffs. He gets back up and I look up the stairs to the door where the gunshot has come from. The gunman is coming down towards us, yelling. Things happen in slow motion. I'm struggling to comprehend. My brain is sluggish and the pain isn't helping. Someone suddenly has a hold of me, pulling me down the rest of the way, and then it's like I'm awake again and I realise I'm crying out with how much pain I'm in, sobbing as we run. Colin is beside me, urging me, holding onto my arm with both his hands, his fingers screwed up inside the uniform I wear. My body doesn't want to work. The pain is so great I want to throw up.

We're on the street when another gunshot sounds out and people scream. They're all looking at us, trying to figure out what's happening. I point in the direction of *The Gallows*, unable to form the words to tell Colin that's where the horses are, but he sees it and we keep going. We're so close. There's shouts and I can hear thundering hoofbeats in the distance and the sound is so ominous it sends shivers down my spine. We have to go. We have to get on the horses and ride as fast as we can until the city is on the horizon.

And then I'm up against the warmth of my mare's coat and she's making nervous noises in her throat, pawing at the ground. Colin forces me into the saddle, throwing me up with all his strength, and he lets out a groan of pain as he does. I pull her around as he mounts his gelding and then we're riding and I'm screaming at people to get out of the way, off the road and there are riders behind us, yelling and shooting their guns in the air to force people and horses to scatter. And they do. It's mayhem, a mass of bodies and panic. Within the chaos, I see Colin beside me, slumped against his horse. His mouth is moving, words drowned out by the noise, and I know he trusts his gelding enough to get him out. My back is hurting so much I see my vision flicker, but

I hold tight and squeeze my legs in the saddle. We make our way through the city as fast as we can until the outskirts of Kansas City are nearly upon us.

I can hear a ringing bell, like a harbinger of doom. I'm so out of my wits I think it's in my head, a warning summoned up by my own subconscious. But then I see the tram coming down the street to our right. We're at a crossroads and it's so close I can clearly see the driver frantically waving his arms at us, telling us to stop. I look at Colin. There's no time to think. Before I can ask, before I can even pull on the reins in hesitation, he lets out a yell and throws his hand forward, telling me to go onward. And I realise why, as our horses fly across the tram tracks just before it reaches us. I look behind me, seeing the lawmen pull up abruptly. Some are thrown from their mounts in the confusion, close to being hit. The tram keeps ringing its bell and a manic laugh escapes my throat at the sight. We keep riding, using this advantage to gain as much ground as possible.

Colin has led me through twists and turns, going up side alleys and dirt tracks in order to lose the lawmen. I can still hear their shouts in the distance, but now we're on the outskirts of the city, we have coverage from buildings and a large cornfield. He must see an opening because I notice him kick his legs and his gelding surges forward. The mare follows suit and we lunge straight into the rows of corn. I'm whipped by the stalks as we're enveloped by them, feeling the bristles against my legs and arms. Colin suddenly slows.

'Good,' he murmurs quietly. He's talking to his gelding, running a bloodied hand over its neck. He turns to me and lifts a finger to his lips.

I can feel my blood pulsing in my ears and it's so loud for a moment I don't hear the lawmen shouting close by.

'You see them?'

'No.'

'You go that way, I'll circle 'round.'

It won't be long until one of them thinks to look inside the cornfield. Panic starts to grip me. I look at Colin. He nods once to me and we slowly begin to move forward. We duck down low in our saddles and allow the horses to find their way through. Every so often, Colin stops and we listen out for voices. It feels like an age until we're out the other side. There's a slope that leads into a copse of trees and Colin leads me down it. I'm struggling to stay conscious and I can see he's struggling, too. We have no choice but to keep going.

We're a few hours out from Kansas City when I'm certain we've lost the lawmen. The sun has set and the moon is slowly rising up over the hills. Colin leads me into a clearing in the forest we're in and I'm grateful we're finally getting a chance to rest and attend to our wounds. The pain is on a constant level and it's at the point where I'm now numb to it. I ease myself out of the saddle when we're in the middle of the trees and I see Colin do the same, stumbling as he gets to his feet. I tie my horse up and take off her saddle, dropping it immediately as I try to lift it, a hot fire flowing down my back as I do. I cry out and Colin comes over, gingerly lifting my saddle for me and taking it to the small clearing where we both collapse, out of breath.

'I gotta get that bullet outta you,' he pants.

'Bullet?'

'You were shot back there, don't you remember?'

'I didn't want to accept that I had,' I say, voice trembling.

He lets out a gruff sound, as close to a laugh as he can get. I hear him get up as I lay trembling on my side in the leaves. When he comes back, he gets me on a bedroll and is carrying his saddlebags.

'Glad you got my saddle back,' he murmurs as he gets down beside me. 'Wouldn't be able to do this if you hadn't.'

He builds a fire to give him light and I feel the heat of it across my back as he lifts up the shirt of the uniform I'm still wearing.

The wound feels sticky. I numbly feel my belly, looking for an exit wound.

'It's stuck in your back,' he says quietly. 'Gonna have to dig it out.'

I close my eyes, gripping the bedroll underneath me. I feel his hand on my shoulder and it slides up to my neck, where he pulls the hair off my sticky face.

'Just do it,' I tell him.

'Breathe deep when I tell ya to,' he instructs. 'And out when I tell ya, okay?'

'Mm.'

'In.'

I suck in a breath of air and I feel something enter the wound. I grit my teeth. Something catches against my flesh and there's a sharp pain.

'Out.'

I let out my breath and it shakes through my chest as I feel the bullet being pulled from my back.

'Good girl.'

He rolls me onto my stomach and I hold my head in my arms, trembling. I hear him going through his bag and then there's a bottle of whiskey under my nose. I drink as much as I can, feeling the burn all the way down my chest. I hear the liquid slosh and know he's just drunk some too. And then he gives me something else: a bundled up piece of cloth. I lift my head and look at him.

'Put it between your teeth.'

'Oh Jesus...'

His mouth twists. 'It ain't pretty, I won't lie to ya. But I'll get it done as quick as I can.'

I shove the cloth between my teeth and press my forehead on my arms, squeezing my eyes closed. It doesn't take Colin long to heat the knife up. I hear the slosh of the whiskey bottle again, but then a burning sensation is against the wound and I let out a small moan.

'Let out a big breath and bite down in three... two... one...'

The pain is blinding. There's a sizzling sound and a strong smell of burning flesh. The sickening aroma of whiskey and blood. The pain is like nothing I've ever felt before. I scream through the cloth in my mouth, biting down so hard I think my jaw will break. It seems to go on forever and when I do realise Colin's finished, I can still feel the burning and I sob and I moan, begging him to make it stop. He shushes me quietly and wraps the wound up. And then he gently lifts me up and takes the cloth from my mouth and gives me more whiskey and I drink most of it, coughing and spluttering through my tears. He pulls me close and I feel his lips against my hair, his gentle murmurs at my ear.

'Good girl,' he says, 'you did real good.'

'Your— your wounds,' I say quietly.

I need something to take my mind off the horrible burning, the pulling and the twisting. I know his wounds still need attention and they can't go left untreated. There are cuts on his face and I know his ribs are most likely cracked. He lets me clean the wounds he can't see and we sit beside the fire, nursing one another, sharing gentle touches and gentle looks. I see the way he looks at me and leans his face closer to my fingers as I clean the wounds there. I feel his hands softly stroking the tension from my shoulders and arms, his fingers slipping along the line of my jaw and down the column of my throat. We're close, closer than we have ever been, and that closeness takes the attention from the pain. His eyes are bruised from the treatment he received from Kansas City's lawmen and they see me clearly now, bloodshot but clear. And I see the look in them. The utter awe in the way he regards me. We're both delirious with pain and drink and utter shock over what's just transpired. I'm practically in his lap, trying my best to ignore my own pain as I finish cleaning his wounds, but when I go to pull away, he lifts his hands up and keeps mine there against his face. My fingers are against the softness of his beard, the hardness of his jaw underneath. When I lift my eyes to his, he's watching me quietly and I realise what he wants, just as quickly as I realise it's what I want too.

I lean forward and kiss him and he draws me in close, lips soft under mine as he lets out a small noise in his chest. My thoughts are whirling. I don't realise I'm kissing him until it's happening and his hands are against me and I can feel my blood is on fire, a heat blooming down low in my belly. I make my own noises as I open myself up to him and he accepts me, opening in unison, until we're just fumbling hands and clashing tongues and heavy breaths. The pleasure that's flooding through me is something I haven't felt in years, something my body has sorely missed, that I haven't even recognised until this moment. Colin's hands are in my shirt. His hands are pushing up against my breasts, his thumbs rubbing their tender areas, and I'm keening, lifting my head up towards the trees for air, his mouth hot and wanting against my open throat.

'You're such a bloody bastard,' I find myself saying, breathless, clinging to his hair with shaking fingers.

'I'm sorry.' His voice is gruff, heady. 'You're a damned marvel, woman.'

'What were you thinking?' I kiss him again and bite at his bottom lip hard and he moans.

'I wasn't thinking.'

He's at my throat again, his tongue against my skin, pushing against my pulse point, and I'm out of breath, gasping up above our heads, trying to drink down air that doesn't seem to exist.

'Colin.'

I'm starting to come to my senses. His hands are still against me and as wonderful as it feels, I can't let it get any further. We're wounded, drunk from pain and not ourselves. I can't let us act out of pure want when we are hardly thinking straight enough to make good judgements. I want this. I know I want him more than anything, but I still need to come to terms with that and doing so by making love to him right now is not the way, I know that. And I don't want to be his bandage, covering a wound that Caroline has caused. I don't want him to be mine, either. My feelings for him are coming up now, screaming at me in a deafening roar as thunderous as my heartbeat, but amongst those emotions are the feelings of fear and even shame. He kisses me again and even though I want to stop him, to tell him we can't do this, I let him kiss me and I kiss him back just as fervently, holding his cheeks between my palms. My body is hurting so much and I can tell he's still hurting too, his hands shaking against my sides, still trapped underneath my shirt.

I'm about to get carried away again, I'm about to let him draw me closer until there's no going back, until I can do nothing but fall to the bedroll with him and give him all of me. But then I hear one of the horses nicker worriedly in their throat and I pull my mouth from Colin's. His mouth moves along my cheek and my jaw and he's breathing heavily against me. I hear hoofbeats in the distance and I pull away from him, looking out into the dark trees. Colin lifts his head, finally hearing it too.

We quickly stand up, drawing away from one another immediately, and stand there by the fire as we listen. It sounds like there are riders out on the road by the trees we're hiding in. Colin quickly kicks dirt and leaves over the flames, extinguishing it, but smoke plumes upwards like a signal and I grit my teeth.

We've been stupid. I feel like a fool, letting myself get carried away with him, allowing my body's urges to take control and completely block out any logic. I curse myself under my breath, feeling a flush rise up to my cheeks. We're quick to pack things up and get the horses. Colin helps me saddle the mare, as my back is aching still and we quickly mount up and ride through the trees, further away from the sounds of riders. When we hear shouts, we kick our horses into a fast gallop out of there and burst through the trees out the other side, into an open plain. We ride under the moon and stars, across the plain and up along hills to cover our tracks. It takes us a few more hours until we know we're safe again and we dismount at the foot of a hill. We don't light a fire this time, too worried about getting noticed, and instead we roll out our bedrolls and I collapse into mine, exhausted.

Colin wakes me up at dawn and as soon as I'm conscious, I feel the pain flooding back. I let him help me up in a sitting position and grit my teeth. He's made coffee on a small fire and gives me a cup as well as a plate of beans.

'That's the last of the food,' he mutters. 'Gonna have to do some hunting if we wanna eat in the next week or so.'

I feel sick. I don't want to eat, but I force myself to because I know my body needs it. I'm in so much pain and I can hardly believe what's happened the past few days. Colin wasn't supposed to stay with me. He wasn't supposed to get himself arrested and I wasn't supposed to go in and save his life. We weren't supposed to kiss, to express feelings for one another that we aren't supposed to have. I can't meet his eye as he goes about sorting what we have and don't have in our packs, jaw hard. I press my lips when I think about how his mouth had felt under mine; his hands against my skin.

'How you feeling?' he asks when he starts eating across from me, sipping at his coffee.

'Horrible.'

He gives me a grim smile. 'I'm sorry, Blair.'

I shake my head. 'Don't worry about it.'

'This weren't supposed to happen.'

I press my lips. The thought has been nagging at me, at why he thought it was a good idea to go hand himself in, to take his own life through the hands of the law. It makes me feel sick to the stomach at how he could reach such a low point to even consider it, let alone act it out.

'Why did you do it?'

When I lift my head and look at him, he's paused, spoon halfway to his mouth. His eyes are focused on his bowl and he doesn't look up to meet my gaze, even though I desperately want him to. He takes so much time to answer for a moment I don't think he's going to, as if trying to pretend he didn't hear me.

'I'm an outlaw...' He says it so matter-of-factly that I feel silly for even asking. He finally lifts his gaze to mine. 'I went to Ireland to escape the law and found myself fighting in a mud pit, just as I'd fought here in America. It was all the same — dirt, blood, pain... loneliness. I didn't see much point in living any other way until you asked for my help. And when that was taken away, I didn't see much point in living at all.'

In a way, I know exactly how he feels. Finding and killing these men for Thomas has finally given my life purpose after three years of anguish. Even I'd considered ending things but had never gone through with it because there was always *something* worth living that extra day, just to see if things got better.

'I hope you're a little more clear-headed now and know that there's more to life than fighting... or helping me. And you can talk to me... if you feel you need to. I want to help you too.'

'I know.' There's a short silence and then he says, ''Bout last night...'

My heart clenches in my chest and I swallow thickly, looking at him. 'Can we not talk about that right now?'

He nods quickly. 'Alright.'

'We were delirious and in shock. And if we kept on going, we would have been found by those riders and shot on the spot. It's a bloody good thing I came to my senses when I did.'

''Course.' His gaze drops from mine and my heart aches at the look on his face.

I get up and go through my bag until I find a spare set of trousers and a shirt. I take off the uniform I stole from the guard and put on my new clothes, coat and hat. The bindings Colin put around my wound are still tight, so I leave them and gingerly lower my shirt down. As I change, I think about the expression on Colin's face, how hurt and confused he looks. He must be feeling the same emotions as I am. He must know how I feel and yet I can't bring myself to talk to him about them.

The past week has been a whirlwind and I don't think my mind and emotions have caught up yet. I'm a wreck. I don't know what to think and I can't help but blame all of that on the way I acted last night. It wasn't supposed to happen, kissing him and almost letting him take all of me, wantonly and with utter eagerness. The loneliness and self-annihilation I've been experiencing since Thomas died has finally caught up to me and it's making me act like a madwoman, not myself. I can't trust that I have deep and wonderful feelings for Colin. I feel them, almost so viciously that I'm scared of them, but how am I to know they're real? All I know is I'm glad he's not dead. I'm glad he's with me again and I don't want to be so proud as to tell him to leave ever again.

'Let's just get to Fargo and find Russ Gaitwood. Neither of us belong in this godforsaken country.'

'Yes, ma'am.'

We reach a city called Sioux Falls in a little over five days. The constant riding has exhausted me to the point of delirium and the pain in my back hasn't lessened. My stomach is growling and cramping, having only eaten half a rabbit Colin shot and a handful of berries we foraged a few days ago. I see a train moving along the horizon towards the city, its smoke billowing in the air behind it and a small sob escapes my chest. I don't know why

I start to weep. I'm so sick of being in the saddle and sleeping on hard ground, uncomfortable and in agony, that the thought of a cramped, yet comfortable train carriage is torturous. We're riding along the large river and falls that flow down towards the city when I can't take it anymore and collapse from my saddle, hitting the hard earth below so forcefully that the breath rushes from my lungs. I black out for a half a second and then Colin is above me, murmuring something as he picks me up. Instead of putting me back on the mare, he puts me in his saddle and mounts up behind me. I slump across the gelding's neck and I feel Colin wrap his arms around my waist as he gathers the reins, clicking his tongue as he leads the mare onwards. My eyes close. The motion of the gelding walking beneath me lulls me to sleep. The precipice of consciousness, of discomfort and exhaustion and then the pit of freedom, of comfort and unconsciousness, linger. It doesn't take long for me to slip from that edge and plunge into the dark depths.

<hr />

I'm in a doctor's clinic when I wake up. There's a window to my right and the first thing I see is an opaque sky and what looks like sleet falling from it, splattering the glass with frosted water. I turn my head and see there's a man in the corner of the room, his back to me, rummaging through a shelf of glass jars. Colin is in a seat beside the bed I'm on, his head tilted to the side, eyes closed in sleep. I ease myself up and the man at the shelf turns around. He's old and wears spectacles and a simple shirt and jacket. When he sees I'm awake, he smiles a warm smile and steps up to the bed.

'Ms Ryan,' he says in a gentle voice. 'I'm Dr Boyd. Your friend here brought you in a few hours ago. Don't worry, you're safe, and I've already given you something for the pain. How are you feeling?'

'Fine…' I look at Colin, who's still sleeping beside us.

'He's quite exhausted. I thought I might leave you two here until you were ready to go.'

'How long have we been here?'

'Only a few hours,' the doctor says. 'Not so busy today.' He looks out the window at the weather. 'Doubt anyone will want to go outside in this lest they have to.'

I frown, blinking. 'Where are we again?'

'Sioux Falls.' The doctor smiles at me. 'You were unconscious when Mr McCarthy brought you in.'

'M-My back.' I reach around to touch the bullet wound and feel thick bandages under my shirt. The pain is much less than what it was.

'Mm, yes. It's healing well enough. You'll need to take off the bandages in a few days to let the wound breathe and I wouldn't recommend getting it wet if you can help it. I've given you some morphine, so you'll be feeling a little strange, but I'm sure you'd rather that than the pain, yes?'

I nod numbly.

Colin stirs and we both look at him. When his eyes open, I see them search for me immediately. He sits up quickly, leaning towards me.

'You right?' he asks, voice clumsy with sleep.

'Yes.'

'You're doing alright yourself, Mr McCarthy. I'd suggest finding a proper bed to sleep in.' Dr Boyd meets my gaze over his spectacles. 'No more travelling for the time being. Your body needs proper rest and food. There's a hotel just down the street. Stay there a couple of days and see me again.'

My mind is numb and wavering. All I can do is nod. Colin gets up and helps me out of the bed. When he pays the doctor, he lets me lean against him as we leave the surgery. We find the hotel the doctor told us about and Colin helps me upstairs after we've paid for a room. He sets me down on the bed when we enter and helps me out of my coat and boots. I lay down on my stomach, the world spinning around me. My hair's wet from the sleet outside and I'm shivering, not sure if I'm cold or ill.

'Rest up,' he tells me gently and I feel his weight sink down on the bed beside me as he sits down. His hand pushes my hair away from my face and I turn my face towards the warmth of his skin.

'You need to as well,' I mumble, voice slurred.

'I'll find a chair, don't worry 'bout me.'

I glance around the room. There's only one bed, pushed up against the far wall under a window. There's nothing else but a mirror and a dresser. The room is tiny, but warm and the bed is comfortable. I move across it so I'm closer to the wall and reach out, patting the mattress.

'There's room for two. You need a proper bed.'

I'm so tired. I see Colin hesitate. I'm already falling.

⊷⊶

Someone is in my arms when I wake up. My face is pressed into warm skin and there's a slow, strong heartbeat somewhere close to my ear. A profound feeling of emotion comes over me when I finally come out of the vagueness of sleep and for a moment, I think I'm back home, in bed with Thomas, his arms wrapped around me, his skin up against mine. It's so powerful I'm overcome, weeping, drawing my arms tighter around the body I'm next to; needing the warmth, the familiar smell, the touch of strong hands around my shoulders. I know the man I hold isn't Thomas and it makes it so much worse as I feel like I'm betraying someone and I don't know whether it's him, Colin or myself. Yet when I hear Colin shushing me, when I feel his lips press against my brow and the softness of his beard on my skin, I take comfort from him. He's offering it to me, openly and with no judgement, and I know I don't have to reject it in order to feel better about the way I'm handling this. And I can't help myself.

I kiss whatever skin of his I can reach. I'm so thankful for him and his comfort, in a time I need it so incredibly much that I have no other urge but to pull him as close to me as I can and kiss his skin and whisper my thanks. His hold, his touch and his comfort is something I've been craving for years — something no one has ever offered me, something I've never allowed myself to feel alright about accepting. In that little bed, with the rain falling down outside the window, the town of Sioux Falls quiet in the early hours of the morning, I let myself be comforted by this man. I let myself because I know it's alright. It's okay to feel this way. It's okay for me to be confused, just as much as it's okay to let him comfort me if he wishes to. And he does. I can feel it in his touch, in the way he kisses my cheeks and my jaw, his mouth nudging close to the edges of mine, his hands cupping my face as gently as they would cup a rose.

'I'm sorry.' I try to explain myself to him through my tears. He shakes his head and presses his lips against my forehead again.

'You don't gotta be sorry, Blair. It's alright. You're alright.'

I know that Colin and I are two broken people. I know that we're both damaged by the horrible hand life has dealt us. I know that we're taking comfort from each other because the trust built between us throughout our journey is enough for us to know there's understanding and no judging. I don't want to hurt him with my own foolishness or out of the disorder that's in my mind and yet I don't want to push him away just because I'm scared of that, either. All I can do is let him hold me and hold him just as tightly. I don't want to think about the bad things I've done to get here. I don't want to think about the lives I've taken in return for the life I lost. All I want to do is numb myself to the pain inside me and use Colin as an accessory to do so. And I don't know if that's just as cruel of me.

We lay beside each other for a long while. The light slowly

begins to strengthen outside, but it's still a dreary day, cold and grey. It's so much colder now and I find relief being under the blanket, up against the warmth of Colin's skin. He rests beside me, his mouth softly pressed against my forehead, his fingers in my hair. We lay quietly, not speaking, just feeling. I drift in and out of sleep, still exhausted and in pain from my wound.

Colin is drawing away from me when I next open my eyes. He picks up my hand and kisses my palm when I try to reach for him and gives me a soft smile.

'Gonna go get some food for us,' he murmurs. 'Won't be long.'

I nod, grateful. My stomach is empty and it's been cramping with hunger for hours. When he leaves the room, I slowly lift myself out of the bed and tie my hair back in a plait. I rub my eyes and face, trying to rid the exhaustion that seems to be clinging to my skin. When Colin comes back, he's holding a tray laden with plates of beans, cornbread and cups of coffee. I get up and help him in and then we sit down beside each other on the bed and eat, shoulders touching. I'm ravenous and I finish my meal quickly, hungry for more. Colin gives me half of his piece of cornbread and I take it from him with small thanks, scoffing that down too. He laughs at me, eyes crinkling at the sides and I get the urge to kiss him again, feeling my heart flutter in my chest. I shove the feeling down as far as I can and turn away.

'We should get to Fargo soon,' I say after a while.

I see him glance at me out of the corner of my eye, his jaw hardening.

'You need to recover first,' he murmurs. 'I ain't taking you out there 'til you're all better.'

'I'm fine, Colin,' I tell him, shaking my head.

'If you're planning on shooting up the town as soon as you find Russ Gaitwood, you're better off waiting 'til you're completely healed.' He puts the plates back on the tray and gets up. Before he reaches the door, he looks back at me. 'I won't hear nothing more 'bout it 'til you're better, alright?'

I grit my teeth. I know he's right, and yet why should we waste time in Sioux Falls when we could be in Fargo in a few days, handle Russ Gaitwood and head back to Ireland?

'Maybe I don't want to listen to you,' I say, knowing I sound like a spoiled brat.

Colin shakes his head and leaves without another word. I let out a long breath when he's gone.

17

'I don't think we should be talking 'bout Russ Gaitwood right now,' he says when he comes back in, surprising me.

'What do you mean?' I'm still sitting on the bed, having mulled over my thoughts.

He looks at me, eyes honest. 'I mean, I don't think he's your main priority right now.'

'What do you know?' I mean for my words to sting, to have a barb to them. Instead, they come out like a small, weak breath and I hang my head.

He moves forward and then he's kneeling down beside where I sit so his face is level with mine. I meet his gaze. His eyes are dark, still slightly crinkled at the sides. It's not from laughter anymore, it's from something else. I feel my gut turn over and almost look away from him, but I manage to hold my gaze steady.

'Maybe I don't know much at all. I ain't an educated man. I know how to read some words, but that's 'bout it. But I'd like to think I know a little bit 'bout life and how trialling it can be. And with that knowledge, I think I might be able to hear from you if you were to ever try and reach out to me. If you ever wanted to talk.'

I know he knows I'm struggling. But the thing is, I've been struggling for three years, not just lately. Not just in America. I've had demons haunting me for longer than I've known him.

I'm not even ashamed of it anymore. It's just the way I am now, what my life has driven me to become. I've regarded the horrible feelings killing Harry Oswald and Joseph Gaitwood gave me. I know it's made me feel worse, not better. I know I am the monster Bessie claimed me to be. *Blair the Banshee.* But to take all of that on and accept it would destroy me, so instead I'm pushing back those feelings. I'm continuing on, in the foolish hope that killing Russ Gaitwood as well will tie it all together. It might not — that's the most likely outcome. I just can't give up now.

'I don't know whether I'm doing this for Thomas anymore or for myself. I honestly don't know much anymore.' I sniff, close to tears. 'I'm afraid that killing Russ Gaitwood is going to be the tipping point — that I'll finally be driven mad by it all.'

Colin rests his hand against mine and I feel his fingers squeeze it gently. 'Y'know you ain't alone, yeah? And you don't gotta kill him if you don't wanna. I've told you this before.'

I look at him, tears in my eyes. That's where he's wrong. I do have to kill Russ Gaitwood. Just as I had to kill the other two. It's not a choice for me, it's a command from something deep within me. Something terrible gnawing at my bones, creating a screaming havoc inside my mind. And I can't tell Colin this. Not if I don't want to scare him away.

'I have to,' is all I tell him tiredly.

He draws me to him, shaking his head as I begin to weep. He holds me tightly, murmuring things in my ear.

'I got ya. You're gonna be alright, Blair.'

It's mid-afternoon when Colin decides going for a walk around town might be good for me. I don't disagree, as I feel a stretch of the legs and some fresh air might make me feel a little better. We've laid in bed, snoozing for hours, and my head feels heavy and clouded when we step outside. I keep my hat down and my coat drawn as the day is cold and even though the rain has stopped, there's still a wetness clinging to the air. Colin walks closely beside me, letting me hold his arm as I use him for support. My back doesn't ache as much today and yet there's still a pulling sensation to the wound that makes me queasy.

The city of Sioux Falls is modest enough. In some of the streets closer to the falls, I can hear the roar of the water, a distant call of home. Our walk is uneventful and it's good to be out, distracting myself with sights and sounds so the turmoil in my mind can be kept at bay. Colin is warm beside me, his arm strong against mine. I start to allow myself to enjoy the peaceful feeling this city holds. Everyone is polite and quiet. There are strange lilts to their voices that is charming and they smile at us as we walk along the streets. We stay close to the hotel, only wandering around streets that are in easy walking distance. I find myself smiling back at the locals and bringing myself closer to Colin's side, pressing my cheek against his arm, his woollen coat scratching at my skin.

A child runs out in front of us from a side street and we stop, startled. It's a small boy, very young and he grins up at us, his cheeks rosy from the cold. His hair is thick and blonde on his head. He reaches up to me and my heart squeezes in my chest.

'Oh, I apologise!' A woman comes forward, wrapping her shawl around her shoulders. She bends and picks the boy up, shaking her head. 'He's always getting away from me, this one.'

I don't know what to say. I'm looking at the little boy, feeling my heart bleeding at the sight of him. Of his clear blue eyes and his smiling, chubby face.

'No trouble, ma'am,' Colin tells her.

'Oh, he really likes you,' she says to me, laughing.

I see the child trying to reach for me again and my heart plummets. I quickly nod and look away and I can feel Colin watching me.

'Have a good day, ma'am,' he tells the woman and we start to move along the street again.

We're getting close to the hotel when he looks at me.

'You alright?' he murmurs.

I nod. 'I'm tired again,' I tell him. 'I just want to rest.'

''Course.'

I'm close to tears as we head back inside. I don't want Colin to see me crying again. I don't want him to ask me questions. Seeing that child has opened up old wounds and has made me think of the what ifs that I'd always thought about after losing the babe. Thoughts I haven't endured in years. Thoughts about a child with hair dark like Thomas, eyes big and blue. And no matter how hard I try to tell myself it's foolish to think such things, that doing so hurts me more than anything, I can't stop.

I take off my coat, hat and boots when we enter the room again and lie down under the blanket on the bed. Colin is silent behind me while he kicks off his boots and stokes the fire on the wall opposite the bed. I lay with my back facing him, keeping quiet as tears stream down my cheeks. I hold myself under the covers, heart aching, throat begging to let out the noises bubbling up there. And then, after a little while, I feel the bed shift as Colin sits down on the edge of it. His hand rests against my shoulder and gently rubs.

'I don't need to know what happened to you in the past to make you so upset now,' he says quietly. 'You don't need to tell me anything 'bout it if you don't wanna or can't. But I ain't gonna pretend not to notice your mood shifted right after seeing that kid. And for whatever reason that is, Blair... I'm sorry. I'm here.'

I let out a small sob and turn over, reaching up for him. He meets me halfway and draws me into his chest and I cry against his shirt. I'm so overcome with emotions I've been ignoring for years. Emotions that I've seen as nothing but lurking shadows, lingering in the corners of my mind, whispering reminders every now and again. Now all of them have come out into the light, showing their ugly faces and rearing their heads, and the only thing I can do is ride the wave and weep and let Colin's comfort in.

⊷⊶

'I wouldn't have made a very good mother.'

We're lying in the bed, listening to the storm outside, when I say the words. I haven't told Colin anything and now my tears have dried, I suddenly feel like speaking.

He shifts his weight on the bed and I feel him press further against me, his arm tightening around my waist. I turn my head and look at his face and see he's watching me intently, eyes sad. I lift my hand and stroke his cheek gently. I'm so thankful for the comfort he's given me, with no questions asked.

'Maybe that's why the babe was taken from me. Or maybe it's because whatever's up there knew it wouldn't have a father for very long and I definitely wasn't going to cope.'

Colin's mouth tightens. 'You can't look at it like that, Blair.'

I smile grimly, close to tears again. 'I can't help but not.'

'I know...' He leans forward and I feel his lips press against my forehead. 'But you can't blame anything or anyone over what happened. Especially not yourself.'

I wipe my face and sigh, shaking my head. 'I don't know what's wrong with me... I think I'm going mad. I've killed two men in cold blood and I was foolish to think it would make me feel better. I know I need to kill Russ Gaitwood. I know I need to because he can't get away with what he did to me. And I... I feel as if my mind can't handle anymore.' I meet his gaze, wanting to scream. 'I just want to sleep and never wake up.'

Colin pulls me close as I begin to weep again. It's too hard. I don't think I can do it anymore. His hold on me is tight.

He's murmuring words by my ear, kissing my hair, but the raging turmoil inside me makes it difficult to listen.

'I got you. And I know you got this, Blair. I know you do. You've done so much already. You're alright. It's okay to feel like this. It's normal, you're only human and you ain't flawed by any of these emotions. You're damn lovely.'

'If I can't pull the trigger,' I say when my tears grow sticky on my cheeks, 'if, somehow, I just can't and it's looking like Russ Gaitwood is about to get away with what he did, I want you to kill him.'

I meet his gaze again and he's staring at me, expression hard, eyes dark. His palm is against my face and I feel his fingers clench against my skin.

''Course,' he says after a moment. 'I've told you before that you don't hafta do this alone if you can't.'

'I want to.' I take the collar of his shirt in my hands, gazing into his dark eyes. His face is shadowed amongst the dim light in the room, his thick beard covering half of his features so that I can barely read his expression, can't guess what he's thinking. 'And if I can get past the way I feel about it, I'm going to.'

He nods. 'Okay.'

'I don't want you trying to protect me, Colin. I know I've told you how I feel about this and that I'm slowly losing my mind, but I don't want you thinking you're the thing that's going to stop me from getting too far. I can't rely on you...'

'You can.' He grasps my wrists, gently pulling my hands from his shirt. 'You just won't.'

'It's dangerous,' I tell him, shaking my head. 'What we're doing... it's stupid and it's dangerous.'

He sighs. 'Blair...'

I pull my hands away from his and put my hands against his throat, my thumbs on his jaw under his beard. I push myself closer to him on the bed and kiss his mouth once. He blinks, surprised and I shake my head when he tries to draw closer, tries to kiss me back.

'We're both idiots, Colin. We're both hurt people and we're going to hurt each other if we're not careful.'

'Ain't no harm gonna come from tryna comfort one another.'

'I agree.' I can't help it. I kiss him again softly, and he draws me close, holding my cheek. And then I pull away, whispering, 'But what we did the other night wasn't right. You... with Caroline and me... with Thomas and all this... bollocks.' I shake my head. I know I'm not making sense and I know he's staring at me, frowning, trying to give reason to what we did.

'You ain't ashamed of it, are you?' he asks me hesitantly.

'I'm not ashamed of the comfort you've given me... of accepting it and letting you in. I just know I'm acting out of my confusion and hurt... I don't know how else I feel. Especially about you.'

'I ain't expecting you to be clearheaded 'bout all this. But I want you to know I ain't confused. I care 'bout Caroline, 'course I do, but I wasn't acting out of confusion the other night.'

'You were drunk.'

He smiles sadly. 'I wasn't.'

'I was...' I swallow. 'I was in pain. We both were.'

'You don't hafta make excuses for what we did, Blair. It happened. If you don't like that it happened, I won't blame ya. And if you want me to apologise to you for letting it get that far, I will.'

'No,' I say, looking away. 'Of course I don't want you to apologise... I just didn't want to give you any ideas... any expectations.'

'I got none.' He brushes his thumb across my cheekbone. 'I'd be a sonbitch if I did.'

My heart warms and I can feel an affection towards him that scares me. I want to put it down to other excuses that don't involve the fact that I am actually falling for this man and yet I struggle to.

'Hey,' he says, seeing the look on my face. He brushes my hair back and traces the line of my bottom lip with his fingers. 'We're gonna get you to Russ Gaitwood so you can sort him out and then we're gonna get you home. That's what matters, right?'

I smile grimly. 'Yeah.'

I can taste the lie on my tongue as soon as that single word leaves my mouth.

<hr />

It's a week until we're leaving Sioux Falls for Fargo. I've listened to Colin and spent most days in bed as he went about town, checking on our horses and buying supplies. We visited the doctor before we left and he cleaned my wound and gave me the all clear, saying there was no sign of infection and it was healing well. It feels good to be back out on the road, supplies packed in our bags, the wind cold on our faces. The horses even seem eager to run, having spent their week in a stable. I look at Colin as we ride and the new feeling of affection for him I've been getting lately comes back up again and I feel my heart squeeze in my chest at the sight of him. He looks larger than life upon his dark horse, wearing his hat and a coat that makes his shoulders much broader than they already are. He trimmed his beard before we left, yet it's still thick upon his face and his hair is hitting his shoulders now. His eyes are dark and watchful under the brim of his hat today and he doesn't seem to notice me watching him as we ride side by side.

I'm glad for the talk we had about what transpired between us that night after Kansas City. I'm glad because he made me realise I don't have to worry about feeling as if I'm using him for comfort. I don't have to feel like I'm betraying anybody. But I do feel as if whatever has changed between us is something that I'm going to have to figure out before we go back to Ireland. I haven't even considered the fact he might not come. I think he would want to, knowing the bounty on his head and now mine. I don't know what will happen after Fargo. All I know is I think I want him to stay with me longer than the boat ride home. I don't want to think I love him because that thought in itself is so incredibly overbearing and frightening that I can't bear to acknowledge it. All I know is, there are feelings for him, deep inside somewhere, too afraid to come out of the shadows. And I know I must face them sooner or later.

The ride to Fargo takes three days. The grasslands and hills we ride through are stunning, but the weather is cold and rain continues to fall, leaving us drenched to the bone and grouchy. Even the horses have lost their eagerness to run and instead trudge through the mud and grass as we ride along. The rain eventually calms down the further north we get and it makes me wonder what season it must be for it to be so cold.

Colin is blowing into his hands as he rides when I look his way and I move my horse closer to his. It's stopped raining for the time being, yet the wet is hanging in the air, making me shiver.

'Have you ever been this far north?' I ask him.

'Yeah.' He looks at me and smiles. 'You alright?'

'Yeah. It's just damn freezing.'

He laughs.

'Is it always this cold?'

'Closer to winter, it is. It ain't even snowing yet.' He looks at me. 'You need another coat?'

'No, I'm fine.'

I reach down and pat the mare's neck. We're treading along through a pasture, which Colin has told me is a part of something called the Red River Valley. It's an expanse of relatively flat land, sparse of many trees. There's a river somewhere in the distance and mountains sit far, far away on the distant horizon. An eagle is soaring above our heads, moving in circles over us. I know it most likely has its eye on a rabbit somewhere in the grasses that

I cannot see, and yet I wonder if it's curiously watching over our journey as well. I think, what it must be like to fly so high above the clouds, the world nothing but an irrelevant mass below. I suddenly envy the eagle and its ability to so easily escape; to fly up into the air, away from everything, not a care in the world.

'We'll arrive in Fargo soon,' Colin tells me, his voice cutting through the still surroundings.

I lower my gaze from my opaque sky back to him and nod. 'We've made good progress, then.'

He reaches across and grasps my hand and it surprises me. I let him squeeze my fingers, his grasp warm and strong.

'You've done real well, Blair,' he says quietly. 'Real well.'

I sniff, emotional. I don't know what to say. We've come so incredibly far and his words have clarified that for me, made the fact so stark, right in front of my eyes so that I'm stunned by it. We continue to ride and for a while we go hand in hand until we reach a slope that carries along the river. I ease the mare down it, going in a diagonal line and squeezing my legs in encouragement as she follows the footfalls of the gelding in front of her.

18

Fargo is a decent-sized city with brick buildings built in a sequence of blocks across the land. There isn't a bustle of people and horses and wagons, but a steady stream. People stroll about the streets, tucked under large coats and hats. Horses snort vapour on the sides of roads and chimneys puff out smoke, smelling of burnt wood and sweet sap. It's a quiet enough city. There are the usual sounds a city has — the clopping of horses, the rattling of wagons, people shouting, men at work and ladies chattering to one another on the threshold of shops. The lilt in their voices is stronger this far north. Their accents are nothing like what I've heard in my travels across the middle of America and it intrigues me.

It's late afternoon when we pull up outside a hotel and dismount. I'm exhausted and I can see Colin is as well as he's grown quiet. We head inside the building once we've sorted out the horses and pay for a room and for dinner to be brought up. The room already has a fire going when we walk in and I'm glad for the warmth as my hands and face are numb from the ride. I take off my coat and wash my face at a washbowl in the corner of the room. After a while, there's a knock at our door and bowls of soup and bread are handed to Colin by a young girl. He thanks her and brings the tray inside, setting it on the small table in the centre of the room. I sit down with him and we eat in silence for a little while. I force myself to eat, as I hardly have an appetite. My stomach is doing somersaults at the prospect of finding Russ Gaitwood tomorrow. I'm terrified of what's going to happen, but at the same time I can't wait to go back home. I miss the green of my homeland. The smell of brine and fish by the ocean. The feel of cold pebbles under my feet on the shore. The haze of peat fires gathering amongst the ancient buildings.

Thinking of home brings a lump to my throat. Thoughts of Galway only make me think of Thomas and what I lost when he died. I try to tell myself it's alright for me to feel this way. That after years of blocking it out, I'm finally doing myself a favour and allowing myself to feel the true emotion of my loss. That perhaps getting rid of Russ *will* indeed fix everything — that his death will be the weight that finally tips the scale — and I'll be able to go home with new hope in my heart and the prospect of a better future.

'How're you going?'

Colin's voice is so quiet, so deep, that it rumbles across the table towards me and I look up, startled.

'Alright,' I lie. I swallow and think for a little longer. 'If I'm honest, I don't really know.'

'That's fine.' He gives me a weak smile. 'You don't gotta know right now.'

'I'm eager to find Russ... The letter Joseph had came with a return address to here. The words are hard to make out, but I can see the last name Parker and can only assume that's the alias Russ has taken to protect himself. We can ask at the post office. Surely they'll know an address?'

'We rode past a sheriff's office before. You sure you don't wanna go there in the morning and let 'em know 'bout all this?'

I shake my head, clenching my teeth. 'No. This is something I need to do by myself. We can't risk dealing with lawmen right now, anyway.'

Colin sighs, looking at the table for a moment. He's hardly touched his soup and bread and I realise he must have less of an appetite than I do. 'You said to me back in Ireland that you wanted to see them hang... two of the brothers we've found so far, you've killed yourself. You let Edwin die of his sickness — that's if he even did — and yet you seemed content with the idea before all of this with letting the law handle it.'

I feel sick to the stomach. 'And then I found out how useless the law is.' I stare at his face but he's not looking at me, jaw tensed. 'You don't agree with how I've gone about this, do you, Colin?'

'I didn't say that.' His eyes lift to mine.

'You might as well have! I've been reckless with my emotions. I've let them get the better of me and murdered these men like it was nothing — that's what you're thinking!' I push myself away from the table, the chair knocking out from under my legs. I'm breathing hard, not sure what to say, what to think. I feel betrayed and I don't know why. A little voice inside me tells me it's because I *know* how reckless I've been, how terrible, how thirsty for blood, and to have someone else say it, makes it true. That I'm just as bad as these men.

You're a monster.

'Blair, calm down.' Colin has his hands lifted towards me. He's stood up, still on his side of the table. 'I ain't saying any of that. I just know how this has affected you and you told me *yourself* you were scared that killing Russ Gaitwood would drive you mad.'

'That doesn't mean I don't have to do it!'

'Alright.' He pauses. 'I'm sorry. You're steadfast on the idea that you'll kill him and that's fine. I won't try to stop you or get the law involved if you don't want 'em.'

I'm shaking. I don't answer him and turn my back. I hear him step closer and lower my head when he comes around and takes me in his arms. He murmurs his apologies to me again and I clutch onto his back, pressing my face against the side of his neck. I know he's concerned about me and I know it's because of how chaotic I've been. I can't control that side of me — the deep, resonating anger over what these men did — and I don't know whether Colin's worry over me is a sign for me to stop or keep going.

'You can do this, whatever way you feel best,' he murmurs to me. 'I'm just making sure you know your options, okay? 'Cause letting the law handle it *is* an option, even if the law ain't real good at what they do or our bounties might be found out, it's still an option. He'll still hang if they know he's out there.'

'I've got to be the one to do it. For Thomas.'

'I get that. I do. You just gotta watch out for the ones that are still alive, too, Blair. And you're one of 'em.'

I pull away and look at his face. 'One more,' I tell him, shaking my head. 'Just one more and then I can go home.'

He nods. Leans in and kisses my forehead. 'Post office should still be open. How 'bout we go ask 'em?'

I agree and we shrug our coats back on and pull on our boots. Colin leads me downstairs and I follow him out of the building and down the street. It doesn't take us long to find it, asking a workman who points the way. There's a line when we reach it, people waiting with letters and packages to send, horse-pulled wagons full of stock out the front. Colin takes me up the steps and we fall in line.

There's only one man behind the counter, so it's a little while until we're served. He seems flustered and yet manages to greet us with a smile.

'I'm just after a name of a man who lives here,' I tell him when he asks how he can help.

'A name, hm?' He bends down behind the counter and lifts a large book up onto it. Pushing his spectacles up his nose, he asks, 'Surname?'

I let out a breath of relief. 'Parker?'

He flips through the pages, lined with names and addresses. 'Parker...' His finger travels down the list of names when he finds the right page and he clicks his tongue. 'Only one Parker in these parts. Jeremy. Lives just outside of town, Parker Ranch.'

I feel Colin's hand brush mine and nod to the postman in thanks.

We've found him. It has to be him.

⊢•⊶•⊙•⊶•⊣

The sky is a rage of storm clouds and lightning when morning comes. I've hardly slept, listening to the rumbling shake the windowpane above the bed, shuddering the glass so it rattles against the wood, vibrating down the wall and across the floorboards. In my daze, exhausted with hardly any sleep, I wonder whether the storm is an omen — a warning to not go out to Russ Gaitwood's ranch and instead turn tail and flee. Or perhaps the weather is merely mirroring the turmoil of emotions inside me — the constant battle that's been raging all night, making me lose sleep, has burst through my chest without my knowledge and manifested itself outside.

I know Colin has hardly slept a wink, either. I've listened to his breathing, on and off during the early hours, at the shallowness of it, the skip of breath every so often as if an anxiety has overtaken him. We don't acknowledge one another. We don't touch, lying on each side of the bed, separated by a heavy blanket to keep us warm. I don't know whether I long for his arms around me, for the comfort of his warm breath against the back of my neck, the groove of his body slipping against the curl of my spine, because he doesn't make a move to touch me or whether it's because I truly do find comfort in his arms, and deep down I know that. I can hardly think straight, within a delirium of thoughts, memories, worries. The storm started before the sun even began to rise and with its presence, I know it will stop the sun completely, stifling it behind a heavy layer of cloud and fury. I see the storm as me and the sun as the lives of the Gaitwood men. Once they were the storm, the heavy layering of cloud and thunder and my Thomas was the sun, his shining rays slowly dying out, suffocated.

I start to shiver for the first time all night, as if the energy the storm is creating is shuddering not just the bones of the hotel but the bones inside me, too. The sound of the rain, of the howling wind and the rumbling thunder do nothing to soothe the trembling. I clutch at myself, roll onto my side and collect my knees with my arms, bringing them to my chest to secure me, in a vain attempt to stop the shaking. The window rattles again. The wind pushes at the building and howls in anguish when it can't knock it down, even with all the force it can muster. I suddenly think of an old song my mother used to sing to me when I was a child. The thought is so profound, so sudden, I feel tears scratch at the back of my throat and burn my eyes.

I'd get scared of the storms on the coast. The sea would be a raging, violent turbulence below the cliffs and the same rage would be above our heads, as if there was no escape. So young, so in love with the water because the water gave us life, it was my father's friend; I'd see it as a betrayal. I'd question why it was so angry, why it was crashing against the cliffs so violently. My mother wouldn't answer my questions, she'd only sing to silence me, to soothe me.

The lark is singing and soaring in the skies,
We brought the summer with us,
The cuckoo and the birds are singing with pleasure,
We brought the summer with us...

Only then I would see that maybe the ocean wasn't angry with us at all. That it was instead furious with the sky and the only reason why it bashed itself against the cliffs was because it was trying to reach it, to tame it and to tell it to leave poor, young Blair alone.

When I feel Colin's hand against my shoulder, I flinch, releasing my knees and turning my head towards him. I can only just see his face in the murky light, the fire dying behind him in the hearth, but the touch of his hand, the warmth of his skin through my shirt, makes me shift myself across the bed towards him and climb into his arms.

'Are you cold?' he asks me and for a moment I don't know why he asks and then I realise he must have felt me shaking.

'A little,' I murmur.

He holds me tighter. He's extremely warm, his chest soft beneath his shirt. He smells like the bed we're lying in, as if we've been lying here for years and have taken on its form.

'Have you slept?'

'No.'

'Neither.'

'I'm sorry.'

He squeezes his hands against me, shushing. 'You got nothing to be sorry for, Blair.'

I can't resist the urge to lift my head and kiss his neck, the corner of his mouth. He moves his nose along my cheek, presses his mouth against my jaw. His hand moves across my hip, along the edge of my thigh. A fluttering happens inside me, different to the trembling I was just experiencing. I clench my eyes closed. I know I've told him that what we did after Kansas City was stupid, wrong and at risk of hurting us. And yet we keep getting drawn to one another, eagerly and foolishly. Each time I start it. Each time I kiss a part of him, touch him and I see him crumple against it, invite it in and reciprocate with a passion that ignites me further. It makes me feel horrible. For denying him by telling him that we're fools, only to come back and push us to the precipice once again.

'I'm cruel to you,' I tell him quietly, lifting my chin as his beard tickles my throat. 'That's what I have to be sorry for.'

He opens his mouth against my skin, making my breath hitch, and he says, 'How are you cruel, Blair?'

'I haven't ever treated you fairly.' It's like I'm trying to make up excuses. To finally gain some clarity and stop us before it gets too far. But we're as mad about the other and it shows and it *hurts*.

'You've had your moments,' he jests, and I laugh, the sound a forlorn call in the dark. 'But you ain't cruel.' He lifts his head, meets my gaze through the drear light. 'We've talked 'bout this already. I'm sorry if I'm pushing boundaries again and if you saying all this stuff is an effort to make me stop.'

My heart squeezes. I feel tears behind my eyes again.

'No,' I say breathlessly, bringing him into my arms, 'no, that's not it. I'm just so muddled, you have to understand, it's not you.'

'I'm here, Blair,' he tells me, voice muffled against my breast as I hold his head in my arms.

'I know.' I lift his head towards mine and kiss his cheeks, his nose, his chin. I kiss his mouth. 'I know.'

He draws me to him. We share a kiss that's just as passionate as the one we shared outside Kansas City. This time there isn't a desperation behind it, replaced only by a need to comfort. Colin gathers me against him, his hands gripping the material of my shirt. I'm grasping his jaw, keeping his mouth against mine as if it's the only thing that will give me air and anchor me down against the battering storm outside. I love him. I know I do and I know it with such a determination that it scares me. That it makes me almost pull away from him, afraid of it, of how it may change things. I can't tell him. I may be doing so with my kiss, with my gentle touches, but I refuse to say the words. Holding him to me, feeling his tongue against mine, his teeth scraping against the shape of my lips, I know that he is *here*, the most tangible thing to me. And my heart swells at the realisation that he's open and willing, that when he says that he's here, he's meaning it as a promise.

As the storm continues to howl outside, I feel the heat of his skin envelope me, rough in some places and soft as petals in others. I feel the scars he's gained being the man he was under my fingertips, and then, gingerly, under my tongue. And he becomes pliable to me, to my touch, letting me do as I wish, returning those gestures in fervour when he can. Naked and open to him, the storm drowns out any noises I make to the rest of the world. Instead, those noises belong to our ears only. And I notice how they encourage him, how they make his touches and kisses surer. The storm is no longer an enemy to me, a threat, but instead a blanket suspended above us, protecting us from judgement, lest it be the judge itself. It rumbles and shakes the building again and again, but we're so lost within one another that neither of us notice. All I can feel are Colin's hands, taste his lips, smell his skin.

And when he takes me, I'm overcome with emotion, with pleasure, with an intense sense of belonging and love for this man. I clutch at him, my legs about his waist, his own noises muffled by the skin of my throat. The woman that I am, that I have become in this country, through the trials and sins that have shaped me, cries out into the early morning. Her lips are covered by her lover's, her thighs and hips stroked gently by powerful hands, loving hands. And then one of those hands goes to the place just above where she and her lover are joined and her back arches, her mouth opens agape.

⊱•—◦—•⊰

I don't realise I've been sleeping until I'm blinking, seeing the room in front of me, lit up by weak sunlight. I'm on my side, near the edge of the bed and no longer beside the wall where I was. And then I feel Colin's arms are around me, his hands pressed against my belly, mouth against the blade of my shoulder. I turn my head and catch a glimpse of his face, eyes closed in sleep, mouth softly parted against my skin, and I'm filled with an affection for him so strong that I roll over, still inside his arms and begin to kiss his face. He's roused slowly, as my kisses are soft and I know he's just as exhausted as I am. But when he's awake, he kisses me back and draws me over his body so that I'm straddling him, gasping as his mouth goes from mine, down my throat and to my breasts. I hold his head, fingers clenched in his hair.

We're like two foolish lovers, oblivious to the world outside, completely and utterly invested in one another instead. And as he kisses my skin, tracing the curves of my breasts with his mouth, I think of how he gathered me against him earlier, breathing heavily, sweating skin against my own. He kissed every inch of me, whispered words to me that brought tears to my eyes, told me that I was strong, lovely, marvellous. I was still within the throes of the pleasure he'd given me, unable to answer him, unable to kiss him back. All I could do was clutch onto him, hold him against me, and stop myself from weeping.

When there's a sudden knock at the door, we both freeze.

'Breakfast orders?' someone says through the door.

Colin gets out from underneath me and puts on his clothes. He answers the door and I watch him from the bed as he makes an order for coffee, eggs and beans. When the hotel worker is gone, he closes the door again and by then I've gotten out of bed and have begun to dress. I see him watching me, perhaps admiring the curve of my spine or the freckles spattered along my chest and back. And yet he doesn't approach me, he doesn't take me in his arms and it's as if our newfound intimacy is strictly secluded to the bed behind me.

I've washed at the washbowl and pinned half of my hair up when breakfast arrives and we sit at the table to eat. Colin's shrugged on a shirt and I can see the hairs on his chest near where the collar hangs down, and I suddenly wish to feel it again, to run my fingers along the power of his chest and back as I did last night.

'When do you wanna leave?' he asks me before taking a sip of his coffee.

I shrug a shoulder. 'It's still raining outside.'

I see his eyes go to the window and he nods. 'Not keen on getting wet?'

I think about how hellish it was travelling here in the rain, cold and soaked to the bone. 'Not really.'

He smiles slightly at that and I feel my heart jitter at it, at the crinkles beside his eyes, the little shine to them, at the dimple in his left cheek, only just visible beneath his beard.

'We can leave today, or wait out this rain. The decision is yours.'

I want to stay in this room for longer. I want to learn the ways of his body better, for him to learn mine, to come to terms with the way I feel about him without guilt and not have the need to finish what I came here for getting in the way.

'Wait it out,' I say and I see his eyes acknowledge that, see them travel down the length of my arm as I lift my fork to eat. 'Even if it means leaving tonight, so be it. I'll ride in the dark. But there's no point riding in the storm.' I lick my lips when I swallow and I do it on purpose because I know he watches me.

After breakfast, we can't help but disrobe again, and he joins me in the bed once more.

⊱──⊰

We ride out the next day, the ground still wet and filled with puddles from the passing storm. Our horses are eager for a run and we're just as eager for fresh air and to finally end this journey we've been on. It's biting cold out on the plains and Colin rides close to my horse, shielding the mare and me from the worst of the wind. I tell him I'm alright, that he doesn't have to take the brunt of it, but he shakes his head and we continue on. From the directions a man in town gave us, we know the ranch isn't far. I know soon the weather will be the least of our problems. I have my rifle strapped to my saddle, close to my leg and my revolver is at my belt under my coat. I'm prepared. The chambers of both guns already filled with bullets with Russ Gaitwood's name on them.

Feeling the frigid cold of the day makes me want to go back to the warmth of the hotel bed, of Colin's body, and it makes me think of the night we shared, before we fell into a deep, exhausted sleep, entangled in one another's limbs. Of the noises we brought out of one another, the incredible feelings we created through touch. We hadn't been able to separate after breakfast. We'd spent most of the day in bed, making love, laughing at one another's stories, dozing, eating a quick dinner of beef stew, only to make love again. The storm passed late at night, but we had hardly noticed, lost within the little world we had created for ourselves.

I shake my head to rid myself of the memory. I need my head straight for when we reach the Gaitwood ranch. I hear a small voice telling me that I'm a fool for letting it all happen, for allowing myself to feel so wholeheartedly for Colin before the journey is even over. I know I'm at risk of being distracted now. I'm also at risk of being incredibly hurt if anything is to happen to one of us. But I also know that I couldn't keep pushing him away from me, selfishly and blindly, for the simple fact of being afraid. I can't regret what transpired between us back at the hotel, simply because I don't. I don't regret it because I love him, so fiery and so wholly that I scarcely know how to express it. All I want is to protect him, to let him protect me, just as he wished to shield me from the wind, because in what other way are we to express our love for one another if we cannot with words?

Colin takes my hand and I look at him, broken out of my thoughts. He's not looking at me. When my eyes raise up towards where a fence line begins, buildings in the distance, I know we've arrived at our destination and my heart stops. Colin's hand squeezes mine and he lifts it to his lips.

'You ready?' he asks me. 'It ain't too late, y'know?'

I stare at him and instead of reproaching him for warning me yet again, even after he knows how I feel, I smile grimly.

I have to be ready.

19

We devise a plan to ride in like lost travellers. We plan to figure out which one of them is Jeremy Parker, instead of going in and shooting up the place. I notice how my admiration for Colin changes the way I listen to him. I'm no longer blinded by my resentment, by my righteousness, or by the fury forever boiling deep in my gut. Instead, I nod along to what he says. He's reasonable, more reasonable than I'll ever be and it makes me want to kiss him, between the trees where we rest the horses, on the edge of Russ Gaitwood's land, so I do.

He kisses me back and when I draw away, I thank him.

'Why you thanking me?' He's genuinely confused, a small furrow between his brows that I reach up and soften with the tips of my fingers.

'I should have listened to you with the others… I should have—' I sniff and duck my head and he kisses my forehead and draws me close, arms around my shoulders.

'You've done nothing wrong, sweetheart. As far as I can see, you're driven by nothing but love and that's something to admire.'

I shake my head against his chest. 'Anger,' I say quietly. 'A fury so terrible it's frightening.'

'Because you loved so deeply. It was tainted by your loss and it turned into the fury you speak of. But it's stemming from that love. It ain't nothing else.'

The sounds of the horses ripping and chewing on the grass soothe me. I close my eyes, cheek against his coat.

'So we go in,' he murmurs after a while of silence. 'If they offer us a bed, we'll accept. We'll take as long as we need to figure out who Russ is. If he ain't there, if he's out hunting, we'll fake an illness that prolongs our stay. I'll offer to help out as payment. We'll take as long as you need.'

'What if they're not as accommodating as we're expecting?'

'I'll ask to speak to the owner. Get his name. If it's Jeremy, we'll know it's Russ and we'll figure it out from there.'

'Okay.' My voice is tiny. I'm afraid and I don't want to say it out loud.

'Darling,' he lifts my chin with his fingers and kisses me, 'you're gonna be alright. Any time you don't wanna do it no more, you just say the word, you hear?'

I nod numbly, mechanically. I see him frown at that and he kisses me again and again and then he buries his face into my neck, tickling me with his beard, nipping my skin with his mouth, so that I laugh and try to push him off.

'Good,' he says with a crooked grin as he pulls away, 'was scared for a second you weren't feeling anymore.'

Back in the bed at the hotel, between the times we made love, the times when the only noises we made were sounds of pleasure, he would murmur to me little stories, ones I couldn't believe happened to him, but that made me laugh, nonetheless. I learned that he was a funny man, a man with a sense of humour and one only had the honour of knowing if they bothered to go deep enough; if they cared enough to get past the sadness and the brusqueness. He made me laugh until my throat and belly hurt and I called him stupid every time, too overcome with love to show it any other way but to scold him between my snorts. And when I recovered, he asked me for my own stories and I told him ones familiar only to those from Ireland. Some of them were so absurd to him that he didn't know what they meant. I watched the confusion manifest in the sparkle in his eyes, in the shape of his mouth as he watched me speak, the corners slowly lifting upwards with puzzled amusement. And when the story came to the punchline, he laughed and it was a sound that ran through my body, kissed at my soul and made me laugh in turn. He was no longer the man I believed him to be when I first met him in St Brigid's pub and perhaps that was because he'd changed since then. The journey we'd gone on together shaping him into the sensitive and emotional man I had come to know. We both were no longer the people who'd sat at that table in Cheyenne, two strangers drinking whiskey together.

Russ Gaitwood's ranch is an expanse of land, rolling hills on either side, his home residing within the valley between them. It's a huge lot, with several outhouses, a large barn, a stable and the main house. As we ride in through the front entrance, hearts pounding, I see several ranch hands going about their days; cows, horses, chickens, pigs, all of them accumulating, giving life to a place I imagined to be desolate and filled with horror. Colin gives me a compassionate glance as we slowly ride in towards the main house and I nod to him, to let him know I'm alright, that I want to keep going. Soon people begin to notice us and we gain a few peculiar looks, arms hanging over fences, eyes peeking out just above them.

A man steps off the porch of the house when we reach it, hands on hips. He has a pipe in his mouth, the end of it pinned between long, cracked teeth.

'Can I help you?' he asks us.

'I'm Mr McCarthy. This is Ms Ryan, my employer. We've gotten ourselves quite lost and sick, due to travelling in the storm. We were wondering if…'

Another man comes out onto the porch through the front door, his hair dark, peppered with grey at his temples. His goatee is trimmed, tidy. And his eyes, shadowed and foreboding, look into me, pin straight through my forehead. I feel a burst of pain behind my eyes and close them on instinct, hanging my head. My heart is slamming in my chest. I know this man is Russ Gaitwood. I know it before he even introduces himself with his alias.

'Mr Klein? What's going on?' Russ Gaitwood asks.

'Oh, Mr Parker, these people just came riding in, I was questioning them—'

'That's alright, Mr Klein.' Russ Gaitwood steps down the porch steps and my legs tighten in the saddle, ready to turn my horse around and flee if I have to. My mare throws her head up, shifting underneath me and I see Colin glance my way, frowning. 'How about you go back to your daily chores and I'll deal with them, hm?'

'Yes, Mr Parker, of course.' Mr Klein rushes off, pipe still between his teeth.

When Russ Gaitwood looks back at us, his eyes meet with Colin's.

'Now, sir, what can I help you with?'

'I was just saying, we got lost and now we've come down with an illness... probably 'cause of the storm last night.'

'What were your names?'

'Mr McCarthy. I'm Ms Ryan's employee.'

'Well, Mr McCarthy, the city of Fargo is only a few hours' ride south from here, but if you two are too ill to ride, I will of course, give you a bed and anything else you need.'

Colin glances at me. I nod numbly, quiet.

'That would be greatly appreciated,' he says to Russ Gaitwood. I can hear it in his voice, the hidden fury over what this man has driven me to do, what he's put me through. 'I can do some work around here as payment, as I'm not doing too poorly, however Ms Ryan here would be grateful for a bed and some hot food.'

Russ Gaitwood's eyes go to me and I feel my heart plummet into my stomach, twisting up with my intestines. And then he smiles and it's surprising because it looks genuine and he nods.

'Of course.' He turns around, towards the house, and lets out a yell, 'Marcia!'

A tanned woman comes out through the front door. Even though her dress is plain and her black hair is tied back, she's beautiful. There are wrinkles around her mouth and brown eyes and they light up when she sees us.

'Yes, *mi alma?*' she asks Russ.

'Are you able to take Ms Ryan here to one of the vacant outhouses? She isn't feeling well. And if you can bring her some food to eat from the kitchen, I'm sure they'd both appreciate it.'

'Of course.' She beams at us and Russ leans to kiss her cheek.

My heart stutters. I barely feel my feet hit the floor when I dismount and Marcia puts her hand on my back and leads me to one of the outhouses. I'm trying not to tremble. I'm afraid that I'll fall into a rage again and destroy everything I see. I'm also terrified I won't be able to do it because Marcia seems so kind and Russ Gaitwood appears to be nowhere near the devil I imagined him to be. My eyes burn. Marcia sees my face when we reach one of the small houses that sit to the side of the property and she tuts.

'You do look ill, you poor *chica*. Come, there is a bed inside and I will get one of the women from the kitchen to bring you something nice and hot.'

The building is small, painted white and cottage-like. There are two steps up to the door and she leads me inside. It's a one room building, a bed at the back, a wash bowl and basin to the side sitting behind a screen. There's a hearth and a table, with empty shelves on the other side. The hearth is cold and Marcia is quick to light it when I've sat down on the bed. She tells me to take off my shoes and coat, assuring me the room will be warm in no time. I take off my coat, swallowing.

'Where's Mr McCarthy?' I ask her.

'I think my husband was talking to him, coming to an agreement,' she says gently, helping me out of my boots.

My mouth goes dry.

Husband?

She takes off my hat and tuts at my hair. 'This won't do at all.'

Finding a brush in the bedside drawer, she sets to tidying it up for me. I thank her when she's done and she helps me into the bed. There's a way about her nursing me that doesn't make me feel ridiculous, even with the fact I'm not at all sick. Although my stomach is twisting in knots and I feel nauseous, close to passing out. Marcia tuts again.

'You look very pale, *chica.*' She puts the back of her hand on my forehead. 'You're not fevering. Perhaps I should call for a doctor from town?'

'No.' I shake my head. 'No, it's not necessary. Thank you, I just need to rest.'

'Of course...' She gets up and smiles at me. 'I'll go get some food for you and Mr McCarthy.'

Five minutes after Marcia's gone, Colin comes inside and I stand up, breathing hard. He catches me, holds me against his chest as I hyperventilate, shushing me gently, stroking my hair.

'He has a wife. Marcia is his wife. Jesus, Colin, I don't think I can do this.'

'It's alright, it's alright.' He kisses my hair. 'Just get some rest and let's take time to think this through.'

The door opens and we pull away from one another immediately. Marcia comes in with a young girl who's carrying a pot and she smiles when she sees Colin.

'Mr McCarthy. We brought some for you too!'

They set the pot, bowls, spoons and a basket of bread down on the table and we go over to eat. Marcia takes the lid off and the smell of the stew instantly makes my mouth water. I've never smelt anything like it. I gaze into the pot, frowning.

'*Pozole!*' Marcia says. 'It's beef, onion, cabbage, garlic, radishes and chilli peppers. My mother's recipe.'

'It smells delicious,' Colin tells her.

'Thank you, enjoy.' The young girl leaves and Marcia says to Colin, 'Oh, you'll be needing another bed, won't you?'

We look at one another. I duck my head and pretend to cough into my shoulder.

'I'll sleep in a bedroll on the floor,' Colin tells her. 'There's one on my saddle. I'll fetch it after.'

'Are you sure?'

He nods. 'I prefer it.'

'Alright.' She smiles again and looks at me. 'Feel better, *chica*. Straight to bed after this, you hear? And I won't mind if you can't finish it all.'

When she's gone, we eat in silence. The stew is delicious, so full of flavour. And the bread she brought in has been pressed flat and fried and it soaks up the sauce. I eat the whole bowl and two slices of the flat bread. Colin eats just as much as me. I get up and wash at the washbowl and afterwards, I sit by the fire in a comfortable chair. Colin washes while I gaze into the flames. Both of us are silent, thinking over what's just occurred, unsure what to make of it.

I keep imagining Russ Gaitwood, with his dark eyes and his tidy beard, putting a bullet through Thomas' head. I force myself to picture it, as gory and horrible as possible, to make myself believe that what I'm planning on doing is right, regardless of whether he has a beautiful wife that loves him and is kind to strangers, welcoming them into their home like they were friends.

'Sweetheart.'

I snap out of my thoughts, seeing Colin has knelt down in front of my chair, his hand on my knee. I blink at him. It's late afternoon outside and there's a howling wind at the window again, but this one doesn't rattle and the loss of that sound, so attached to such an intimate memory, is like a blow to the face.

'Maybe you should get some sleep?'

I nod mutely. He takes me to bed, folding me under the blankets and I press my head into the feather and down pillow. It's so comfortable I almost cry.

'What are you going to do?' I ask him.

'I'm gonna go suss some things out,' he murmurs, stroking back my hair. 'I might get started on any work Mr Parker wants me to do.' I know he says Russ Gaitwood's alias instead of his real name just in case we're being watched, just in case they realise who we are and what we're here to do. 'Just go to sleep, Blair. You're safe and I'll be back later.'

'Wake me when you come in.' He smiles at that, but I clutch his hand, serious. 'Please, Colin.'

'You're exhausted.'

'I'm never too exhausted for you.'

He leans down and kisses me and I kiss him back, clasping the back of his neck. 'We'll figure things out in the morning, alright? Just sleep, damn you.'

He kisses me again and again.

'Stay safe, Mr McCarthy, you silly man.'

'Yes, ma'am.'

***

Colin comes back just past eight. I know because there's a clock on the wall near the entrance, ticking away and chiming once every hour. I sit up in bed as he comes in. The room is lit up only by the fire and I watch him as he goes about lighting a lantern near the door and another closer to the bed. When the second lantern is lit, he sees I'm awake and comes to me. He sits on the side of the bed, kisses my cheek and starts to take off his boots.

'How'd it go?' I ask quietly, leaning on my elbow as I watch him.

He takes off his hat and his profile is illuminated by the lantern as he sets his boots and hat aside. His straight nose, his thick beard and grim, yet soft mouth. He turns to me and his face darkens, away from the light now.

'Just cleaned out the stables and lifted some hay bales with the men. Looks like Mr Parker works alongside them, doesn't just act like a foreman.' He sighs, not sure whether to continue. I sit up and put my hand on his shoulder, wanting him to, and he puts his hand over mine. 'Looks like he's rehabilitating people... young men, mostly. He's opened up his ranch to help 'em with their lives... help 'em get the skills to have outside here, earning some money on the side.'

I can't believe it. I don't want to believe it.

Colin stares at me, forlorn. I lie down, staring at the ceiling. He slowly climbs into bed beside me, slipping under the covers until his body is pressed against mine. His arms wrap around my belly and he presses his forehead against my temple, not saying anything, waiting for me to process the information I've just heard.

'What do you mean?' I ask weakly after a while.

'I mean, it looks like he's made a small business of it. But an honest business. And... he and Marcia have a son. Pablo. He's fifteen.'

I suck in a breath. I almost pull away from him, but then I remember he isn't to blame for any of this. He's not there to taunt me, he's only telling me because I need to know what I've gotten myself into.

'Oh, God...'

'Blair, I'm so sorry.'

'I don't know... I don't know what to do.'

'We'll stay here a while. We'll figure something out, okay?'

This time, I do pull away from him, turning on my side, my back to him.

'Don't try and tell me that it'll be okay, Colin. How in the hell am I supposed to go about this?'

'Hey, my darling.' He's soothing me again, as he's always done, as if I'm still that wild horse he described me as, spooked and dangerous. 'Come here.' He curls up against my back, kisses my shoulder tenderly.

'Just let me sleep.' My voice is small. I'm so afraid of what will happen now. I no longer know what to think, where to go with this.

'Of course, I'm sorry.' He pulls his arms from me and gets up out of the bed.

For a moment I think he's leaving me, but then I hear him going about the room, putting out the lanterns and then I feel his weight shift against the mattress again. He doesn't touch me and I lay on my side, tears wetting the pillow beneath my head. I cry until I'm exhausted, until my head is pounding, until I feel sick to the stomach. And then, after what seems like an eternity, I roll over and tuck myself into Colin's side. He immediately draws his arm around me and I feel his lips in my hair. And I fall asleep to the sound of his heart against my ear.

⊷−◦−⊶

Marcia greets me in the morning, meeting me outside the house as I go out to have a look at the property. We stand at the steps of the porch, looking out at the men as they work the fields. I see Colin amongst them, sweat staining the back of his dark red shirt. He stops a moment to fix his hat, wiping the back of his arm across his mouth, before continuing to shovel.

'They work hard,' she comments lightly. 'That's why I feed them well.'

'Your husband is amongst them,' I observe.

'Yes. He likes the work. Because of the young men he employs, he tries not to be their boss and instead their *amigo*. It helps them stay in line and not retaliate. He of all people, knows how insufferable it can be, to be told what to do every single moment of your life.' She chuckles at that, smoothing back a stray lock of dark hair as the wind takes it. She's not grey like Russ Gaitwood is. She seems younger than him, yet at the same time I see wisdom in her eyes and the laugh lines around her mouth are years in the making. She's a charming woman, not just with her foreign accent but with her positive way of seeing things, of telling me about things as if we've known each other for as long as she can remember.

She takes me around the house to the back garden where they grow vegetables. She shows me her prized chickens that lay her prized eggs. The pigs that eat the scraps, so nothing goes to waste. The rooster that likes to steal beloved items — Mr Parker's switchblade, a ranch hand's beaded necklace, Pablo's favourite wooden toy horse. She talks about her son then, of the young man she's brought up. She sits me down below a shady tree in the garden, smoothing her skirts, her hands weathered, scarred. I stare at them, but she doesn't seem to notice.

'Jeremy was gone for a little while... Almost ten years of Pablo's life, he didn't know his father and Jeremy didn't know his son. He'd come to visit every so often, when he could. It was hard for us all.'

I clench my teeth. I want to tell her that during that time her husband was slaughtering mine and countless others. For what? A few cows and chickens. Perhaps even the cattle that he owns and takes pride over now. I feel sick to the stomach. I want to grab her by the shoulders and shake her. I tell myself to stay calm. This woman has no idea who I am. She probably has barely any idea of the things her husband did before he finally gave up the life of an outlaw and settled down with her and their child, an alias the only thing standing between him and the swinging rope of a noose.

'Where was he?' I ask instead, as if seeing her try to come up with an excuse for him, an elaborate lie, will give me satisfaction.

'He was here, in America. We were in Mexico.' She smiles at me and I feel the spitefulness sink into my stomach and twist my guts. 'My son and I couldn't come here for a long time. Jeremy fought hard to get us and, finally, he did.'

'I'm happy for you.' The words aren't as empty as I thought they'd be. Deep down, I do feel happy for Russ Gaitwood's wife and son. I feel happy they're content in the lie he's created for them, as long as they're together within the sweet bliss of ignorance. Happy and a little jaded, because only if I could live like that, forgetting everything that's happened simply because it's easier.

But nothing is easy. Not when it comes to love, to loss. I imagine Marcia cries herself to sleep most nights, every waking moment terrified a US Marshal will break in the door to their beautiful home and take her husband, to give him the justice he deserves.

Don't! Please spare him! She'd yell, claw and screech.

Spare him? But what of the men he killed? What of the wives that grieve because they no longer have a husband? The children that weep because they no longer have a father? The mothers, fathers that cry out into the night sky because their son is gone? What of them?

I close my eyes, forcing myself to think straight.

'I'm sorry,' I tell Marcia, realising she's said something I haven't heard.

'No, don't be,' she murmurs, placing a hand on my shoulder. 'You're still unwell. How about some coffee and cake before you go back to rest?'

I nod and follow her inside to the kitchen. There are several women working in there, as the room is large and it can fit them all as some wash and cut vegetables, others plucking chickens, a few scrubbing dishes and stacking them away. Marcia sits me down at the table and I see at the end of it sits a boy, close to being a young man. His skin isn't as dark as his mother's but he still has her complexion and her deep, brown eyes. His hair falls into his face as he carves a piece of wood with a small knife, tongue set between his teeth with concentration. My heart squeezes at the sight of him, at the look of pure innocence on his face.

'Pablo,' his mother scolds. 'We have a guest.'

He looks up and sees me. Perhaps he sees the image of Thomas, the man his father killed in cold blood, in my eyes staring back at him. Or perhaps he sees the hatred I hold for a man that he loves more than anything else in the world instead. Whatever it is, he nods his head to me, saying a small greeting and I reply kindly. His mother serves me a cup of coffee and cake and Pablo's eyes go to it.

'Mama?' he asks her expectantly.

'Have you done your chores today, *mi hijo*?' she asks him across from the kitchen.

He grunts, dropping his knife and little wooden carving on the table. It looks as if he's trying to make it into a bird, maybe an eagle, only one wing done so far. I marvel at his skill from a distance.

'Not all of them.'

'Well, when you've done all of them, then you can have a piece of cake.'

His mother comes with her own piece and cup of coffee and sits down to my right.

Pablo stands up, grunting again. 'But it's cold out there today and the cows are agitated.'

'They are?'

'One tried to kick me while I was milking her.'

'You probably pulled her teat too tightly. Do what I taught you, talk to her and respect her and she will respect you.' She beckons him forward and he mumbles, but does as he's told. She kisses his cheeks, laughing as he tries to pull away. When she lets go of him, he immediately runs out of the kitchen as Marcia chuckles to herself. She looks at me. 'Every time I kiss him, he'll run away. I should be sad that he sees it as a torture but at least it gets him to do what I want.'

I smile, heart clenching in my chest. Even though the cake is delicious, I can't finish it. I feel incredibly sorrowful over what I've just seen. Marcia loves her son unconditionally. I can't forgive myself for imagining I could break them by killing her husband. I bite my lip, squeezing my hands on my knees under the table to stop them from shaking.

'How are you feeling, *chica*?'

'Fine.'

'I see Mr McCarthy is feeling better.'

'He is, yes.'

'He's a very nice young man.'

'I enjoy his company, I suppose.'

She's smiling at me when I glance at her and I see the look in her eyes.

'What is it that you employ him for, anyway?'

I can't believe how inappropriate she's being, the smile on her face bold and amused. 'He's guiding me through the country. He was my husband's ranch hand.' I close my mouth before I can say anymore, cursing myself for saying anything at all.

It's already piqued Marcia's interest, as she's raised her brows, watching me.

'I didn't realise you have a husband?'

'Late husband... He's passed.'

'Oh, I'm sorry.'

'Tuberculosis, he couldn't be saved.' I hang my head, gripping my knees tighter until my nails dig in through my trousers.

A tut. 'Terrible sickness.' She sighs and sits back. 'Where are you two headed?'

'Ireland,' I say, because it's not exactly a lie. 'Back to where I'm from.'

'I thought there was something about you that I liked,' she said, 'you're a foreigner like me!'

I smile at her, nodding. 'I guess I am.'

The door at the back of the kitchen opens and several men come in, Colin included. I see him and can't help but smile when he meets my gaze and I see his lips lift at the corners slightly at the sight of me, eating cake and drinking coffee at midday like a real lady. And then I see Russ Gaitwood behind him and the men join us at the table, sweating and shaking their heads.

'It's damn cold out there and yet that work's still hard enough to get us sweating!' Russ says and a few men laugh.

Marcia gets up, as if sitting idly in her husband's presence is a sin in their family and goes about serving drinks and slices of bread and honey for the men. They don't get cake and I see Colin eyeing mine from the other end of the table. Despite the way I feel, I laugh at him under my breath, my heart swelling with fondness. It's amazing how in the company of the man who murdered my late husband, Colin is still able to make me laugh, even without trying. I feel suddenly sad and the smile falls from my face. I drink my coffee in silence as the men talk.

'Your man's a good worker!'

It takes me a moment to realise Russ Gaitwood is talking to me, smiling through a mouthful of bread and honey. I start, looking down the length of the table at him with wide eyes.

'I know,' I say jerkily. 'He's very good.'

Colin's watching me, tense in his chair as if he thinks I'm at risk of diving down the table and stabbing my fork into the soft part of Russ's throat, ready to hold back anyone that wants to stop me if he can.

'How are you feeling now, Ms Ryan?'

'I'm alright. Still a little woozy.'

'Let us hope it passes soon so you can continue on,' he replies. 'Not that we want you gone any time soon, though! We welcome you to stay as long as you like, especially if it means I get a good worker such as Mr McCarthy out of it.'

Everyone laughs and I smile tightly.

'We appreciate your hospitality.'

'Any time,' Marcia says behind my chair, putting her hand on my shoulder. I try not to flinch.

'I'm sure your horses are enjoying a warm stable to sleep in, anyhow. They must be very tired, given the journey you've had.'

'We all are.'

Russ Gaitwood smiles at that. 'Probably why you got sick so easily, you poor dear.'

I grit my teeth. Being called "dear" by him is wrong. Talking down the table to him over coffee makes every fibre of my being recoil. This man, so gentle and kind, so accommodating, can't be the man that led a gang of outlaws who killed for his gain. I'm suddenly convinced that we've got it all wrong. That this man isn't Russ Gaitwood at all — that the letters Joseph received weren't from his older brother but from an old friend. That he fought to keep the letter from me for some other reason and not to protect his brother. A man like Jeremy Parker can't kill people without a single thought, can't execute my husband just for a herd of cows. I try to piece images of him doing awful things in my head, but they don't fit. I stare at Colin, pleading. He sees my expression and clears his throat. He takes up a conversation with Mr Parker, drawing the man's attention from me and I get up after a few moments, telling Marcia I'm going to go rest. She nods, giving me a look of compassion and offers to take me to the house. I tell her I'm well enough to walk myself and take my leave.

When I get in bed, I bite the pillow to block the sounds escaping me, forcing themselves painfully from my throat.

20

I'm standing at the fire when Colin comes in. The clock on the wall has just chimed five and the sun has already set. It's cold. So cold that there'll most likely be a frost fall overnight. After I hear him shrug off his coat, I suddenly feel his arms wrap around my waist. His nose is cool when he presses it against the nape of my neck. I close my eyes and let him rock us back and forth.

'It's not him,' I say quietly, defeated. 'It can't be.'

Colin's silent for a while and then he says, 'I'll find out for ya, if you want?'

I laugh bitterly, but I still feel that fondness for him come back. 'How exactly?'

'I'll find a way.'

'You're a fool.'

He kisses my shoulder. 'I think it is him.'

'Why?'

I feel him shrug against me. 'I just have a feeling. Call it instinct, I guess, I dunno. I've spent more time with him than you have and it seems like he's a man repenting his past... tryna make up for it now while he still has a chance.' I hear him swallow, hear him let out a deep breath through his nose and feel it against the hair sitting against my neck. The fire crackles and a log falls in the silence, causing embers to dance about before they settle back down. 'I can see a sort of fear in his eyes that I can relate to.

He's scared of getting caught.'

I imagine the US Marshal again, this time a real marshal, bursting through the door of the outhouse, here to take Colin from my arms and I suck in a breath, clenching my eyes closed to rid the thought. Colin feels me tense up, feels me shudder at the thought and turns me around, holding my face in his hands. When I open my eyes, he's watching me closely. I see it in his eyes; he knows what I'm thinking and he's shaking his head at me, earnest.

'I ain't going anywhere.'

I grasp his wrists. 'How can I be so hypocritical? Afraid that they will take you from me when I would do the same to Marcia and Pablo?'

Colin doesn't answer me and I know it's because he can't answer that. He doesn't know. Instead, he draws me into his arms and holds me close to him. I clutch at his broad back, fingers gripping his shirt. There's an understanding between us that I can feel is slowly driving a rift straight through the middle of our bodies, separating him from me. It's that, in another scenario, Colin is Russ Gaitwood and I am Marcia. And the wife of any man Colin has killed in the past is here to kill him, to seek vengeance with his blood.

'Can I forgive him?' I sob. Because if I cannot, I must listen to the fury inside me and kill him.

'Can you forgive me?'

Colin holds me in bed that night, but he doesn't make love to me. There's a rift between us now, an understanding of why it's there, yet a confusion over what to do about it. I take comfort in his touch, as I've always done and a part of me wants to straddle him again, to draw groans out of his chest by using only my mouth, to use these conflicted feelings as fuel to our passionate intimacy.

I'm just so tired, so incredibly torn that I can hardly sleep, hardly stay awake. I doze all night until the rooster that steals personal belongings crows, until Colin gets up, puts on his boots, shrugs on his coat and shoves his hat onto his head. Before he leaves, I see him hesitate at the door. And then he turns back around, strides across the room and kisses my outstretched hand gently. His eyes hold a sorrow I haven't seen in a long time. I don't know what to tell him.

Can you forgive me?

For him to compare himself to the likes of Russ Gaitwood hurts. But I know he has reason to, as I know he must have done horrible things in order to become the outlaw I first met in St Brigid's, a bullet hole in the brim of his hat, another in his shoulder. And when I close my eyes, I see Colin holding the gun in Russ Gaitwood's place, executing Thomas with not a care in the world for his widow back in Ireland. And when I try to rid myself of the thought, I see myself instead. Shooting Joseph Gaitwood in our struggle and furiously stabbing Harry Oswald. How can I cast judgement on a man that wishes to repent, when I myself have drawn blood, out of selfishness, out of the desire to destroy something simply out of spite?

I get up and wash before changing into a dress. I put on my coat and boots, leaving my hat on the chair as I head outside. I breathe in the cold morning air, frost crunching under my boots as I walk through the property. Even so early in the morning, the ranch is alive with life, with noise that echoes out across the empty hills. Without the sounds, it would be silent, almost peaceful, a void fit for the likes of me. I know that if hell exists, Russ Gaitwood will be sent to its very depths. The Gaitwood gang — the men I killed — are already there waiting. But, when he goes, Colin McCarthy will follow and me right behind. As I walk, I know we are all the same creature. For whatever reason, we all act on impulse. We all want something we don't need, but think we do. We all are cruel out of our selfish greed — whether it be for a herd of cows, for money, for love, for retribution. I'm no better than any of them and yet I've given myself the title of judge, donned the robe of a grim reaper simply because I saw it fit to, because it suited my narrative. It felt right. And as soon as I felt the hot blood against my skin, felt the blinding loneliness of what I had done, what murder had done to my very being, my very soul, I had become what I hated.

My mare is lying in sawdust when I enter the stable. She snoozes without hearing me enter, head hung low so her soft lips touch the ground, the dust rising and falling with her breath. I hang over the stall door and watch her, admiring her strength, her gentleness. On many occasions I compared her to myself — stubborn and yet holding a perseverance that was admirable, controllable to an extent when given the respect she knew she deserved. I continue to watch her for a long while. The stable is cold, but it's sheltered from the windchill and the mare is comfortable enough, her familiar companion hanging his head over his own stall to watch me. Colin's horse is a great and mighty animal, powerful and sure. I rub his face affectionately, breathe in his scent like I do to his master every time we share a bed.

'Oh, you're up early, Ms Ryan.'

I start and turn around. The stable door has opened and I see Russ Gaitwood standing on the threshold, illuminated by the morning light behind him. His features are in shadow and my heart jitters in my chest. I instantly feel my palms start to sweat, my eyes search for another exit. Russ Gaitwood steps into the lantern light and I'm shocked to see he's smiling at me.

'How are you feeling today?' he asks me when I don't answer.

'Fine.'

'Good, good.' He's carrying a bucket of horse feed. 'Want to help me feed the horses?'

I nod numbly after a moment's hesitation. He hands me the bucket and tells me which stalls to go in, watching me over the door. I go in to a draught horse and it stamps its feet impatiently.

'Watch him. He's feisty when it comes to food,' Russ laughs.

'Aren't we all?'

'Too right.'

I continue to feed the horses he directs me to, heart still stuttering in my chest.

'Mr McCarthy is already out taking bales of hay to the cows,' he comments after a moment's silence. 'Didn't even have to ask him.'

'He's a good worker.'

'He is. He's a good *man.*'

I look up at him, jutting my jaw. 'What do you know of good men, Mr Parker?'

He stares at me and I see the confusion in his eyes at my question. 'I think you have to be aware of yourself as a person to truly be good, however, no one is ever completely good. There's darkness in us all and I'm definitely the one to know that. But helping people every day and working towards who you want to be, learning and being open to learning, gets you there.'

'You think Mr McCarthy does this?'

'I do. Don't you?'

I nod silently. Of course I do.

'What made you do what you do here? Helping young men that have gone down the wrong path?'

'Everyone deserves a second chance,' he says honestly.

I'm patting a tall grey horse and it seems to feel my nerves as it throws its head up and stamps a hoof. I draw away from it and leave its stall.

'Why do you think that?' I don't know why I'm trying to get it out of him, as I did with Joseph Gaitwood. I know it's dangerous, but there's an urge inside me to know that it is him, so I can truly come to a decision, with no doubt in my mind.

'I've lived it.'

'You've lived it?'

He nods. Laughs a little. 'It might surprise you, Ms Ryan, but I'm an old man.'

I grit my teeth and force myself to smile slightly.

'I've lived just over half a century and a lot of the memories I have are filled with regrets.' He shrugs a shoulder. 'I was just like these men... perhaps even worse than most of them. I was not kind. I did not give second chances. When I saw God... when I repented for my sins, I knew He forgave me. But I had to do something in return, so I am doing this. I must protect my wife and son. I must make them proud of the man that I am, forget the man that I was.'

'That sounds very brave,' I murmur, because I don't know what else to say.

The stables seem to be getting smaller and smaller and all I want is air. Luckily, a ranch hand comes in to tell Russ something and I take my leave, sucking in a deep breath once I'm outside. My thoughts are whirling. I'm exhausted again. I head back to the outhouse and go back to bed.

⊶⊙⊷

I wake up to a knock at the door and Marcia is there with a tray of food when I answer it. I let her inside and she fusses over me, sitting me down to eat as she cleans and restocks the fire.

'I spoke to your husband this morning,' I tell her. Looking at the time, I see it's early afternoon.

'Did you?' she asks, spooning more beans onto my plate. 'Eat! Eat!'

'Was he a bad man?'

I don't know why I ask the question. I'm reckless, not sure how else to act.

Marcia's mouth tightens and she lowers her gaze. 'He isn't a bad man at all.'

'No, but was he?'

'I... he made some questionable choices. But Pablo and I didn't experience that side of him. He loves us very much.'

My heart bleeds for her. 'I'm sure he does,' I say earnestly.

'Eat!' she tells me with a small laugh. 'I can't let you waste away in my house!'

'He's doing a good thing, helping these men.'

She nods. 'He feels he needs to, to make up for... his choices.'

'How long have you been together?'

'Seventeen years.'

'That's a long time.'

'It is.' She sets the spoon down, giving up forcing more beans onto my plate for now. But then she reaches across and piles another piece of toast onto it. 'No one knows my dear husband... sometimes I hardly think I know all of who he is. But that's marriage for you... forever learning one another. And I love it. I love him.'

I agree with her words. In the time I knew Thomas, I didn't get to know him for who he truly was. I knew his body, almost every inch of it like the back of my hand. I knew his likes and dislikes. I knew his past, or what he told me of it. But now, looking back at that man, he seems almost a stranger to me and the thought drives a stake through my heart. I'm forgetting the shape of his face, whether it was round or square. I can't quite make it out anymore. I'm forgetting his smell, the sound of his laugh. The memories I was having of him are no longer invading my mind every single day. Maybe the subconscious reason I came to America was to forget Thomas, not to avenge him. Either way, I've almost done both of those.

'You look sad, *chica*.'

'I'm fine, just tired.'

'Is Mr McCarthy being kind to you?'

I glance up at her, frowning. 'Of course he is.'

Marcia doesn't know the weight of Colin's arms. She doesn't know the heat of his skin, the caress of his soft lips, the pressure of his fingers. She'll never know the rumble of his voice against the side of her throat as he whispers comforting words, sweet words, gentle words. She doesn't even know that I know all of those and more. She doesn't know the love I feel for him, the love I try to hide. Or maybe she does and that's why she asks.

A week goes by. I busy myself helping Marcia as much as I can while Colin continues to work tirelessly on the ranch. As each day passes, with each interaction with Mr Parker, I start to build a solid confidence he is indeed Russ Gaitwood. Colin tells me things the man says, every night in bed, his arm around me, telling me gently that it's definitely him, that I don't have to worry. That all I need to be worrying about is the decision on what to do. And yet the rift between us grows and grows. Some nights we seldom speak. Some nights I see Colin succumb to a deep thought, unable to be roused and when I lay in bed beside him, he feels like a stone weighing down the mattress beside me. My worry no longer is about Russ Gaitwood. It slowly starts to be over what I've created with Colin, the mess we've made with one another, foolishly unable to control our feelings for each other. It has gotten in the way of things, as I expected it to. And I can't help but feel anger towards Colin for it, because it's not just my fault but his too.

When he comes in one night, still out of breath from the work he's been doing, snow covering his shoulders and stuck to his boots, I stand and stare at him across the room from the fire. A shawl is wrapped around my shoulders because even with the fire, it's freezing and I'm shaking but it's not just from the cold, it's from the frustration I'm feeling, the confusion, the need for intimacy again because I miss Colin's body. I miss his mouth, I miss his words, I miss *him*.

He greets me quietly after shedding his coat and boots and then he eats the leftover chicken Marcia brought earlier. He drinks whiskey out of a cup, the whiskey I've already been drinking by the fire, stewing in my thoughts.

When he gets up, he comes to the fire and sits down. I stay standing and he sighs heavily. I know he's tired from working. I feel like a lonely wife, cooped up at home while her husband works all day, doing God knows what else.

'You okay?' he asks me suddenly, glancing up at my face.

He's brought the bottle of whiskey over with him and I let him pour some into my cup.

'I don't know if I can do this any longer, Colin,' I tell him.

'Do what?'

'*This.*' I point out there, out to where Russ Gaitwood most likely dines in his kitchen with his beautiful wife doting on him, his son at the other end of the table, carving a magnificent eagle out of a single piece of wood. 'Why can't they be bad people? Why can't this be easier on me?'

He shakes his head. I know he doesn't know what to say. I know he's too tired to try and comfort me, because that's all he's done for the past week and it's done nothing and I feel bad for it.

'Have you thought about the fact that I'm just like him?' he asks me suddenly.

I stare at him. He knows I have. We both know that's what has driven the rift between us. Why we haven't made love in over a week, why he hasn't shown me his usual comfort and support. We're both confused, unsure how to go about things because either way one will betray the other if we act.

'You're not.' I shake my head. I don't want to believe it, even though I know it to be true.

'Blair, I told you ages ago that I'm a bad man. I wasn't lying then. I'm... If you think he deserves death, just like the others, then I deserve it too. You might as well kill me for the sake of all the widows out there that I made.'

'Jesus, Colin, *don't*!' I throw my cup aside and it clatters across the boards. 'Don't you dare!'

He stands up, the chair falling out from under him. 'Why else d'you think I took myself to the sheriff back in Kansas City? I know I deserve what I get 'cause I did some horrible things for the sake of my men! I trusted them. I was a part of a brotherhood that taught me to kill for what we needed. That's how it worked. Russ Gaitwood is the exact same! We're both repenting, but maybe that ain't enough for you, if you really think he still deserves to die. And I won't blame you. No one has the right to take a life and what other punishment is justice enough than death?'

I slap him. I want him to snap out of it. I want him to stop being so damn stupid. He takes my hit and turns his face away from me, pressing his lips.

'*Don't*!' I shriek. 'You're not him! You're a better man than any of those bastards combined!'

'I know I'm better now, Blair, but if we're going off the basis of your belief, then I deserve to die. Harry Oswald deserved what he got. He was still as evil as they come, but Joseph?'

'He attacked me!' I cry.

'I know, to protect his brother,' he says gently. 'But does it really matter?'

'What are you saying?'

'I'm saying that if you kill Russ Gaitwood, I'll support you as much as I can. But I know it's not what you wanna do. It's not. I know it. And if you do, if you force yourself to believe it's the right thing to do, then you might as well kill me too, because it's the same thing.'

'It isn't the same. You didn't kill Thomas — he did!'

'I've killed countless Thomases, they just weren't yours.'

I grab his collar. I shove him so hard he stumbles. 'I hate you!'

He lets me hit at his chest in my rage, silent, face stony.

'Get out!' I point at the door. My voice breaks under the strain of the words. 'Go out and freeze, you bastard!'

He takes his coat and leaves. I fall to the floor as soon as the door closes and sob. I can't control it. I know what he said is true. I know it and I believe it too, but it still goes against everything I've been telling myself since the day I found out Thomas was dead. Why else would I be here? I don't want this to be for nothing. I don't want all this pain, all this anguish, to be in vain. I don't want Thomas to have died alone and afraid only for me to not do anything about it. I first vowed I would see the Gaitwood men hang. And then I vowed I would kill them myself. What I've done has nearly broken the woman I am, but I've done it for Thomas. If I leave now, if I go back home, it would surely mean his priority is no longer my first concern. And that thought scares me.

When the clock chimes another hour, I force myself to breathe properly. To get up off the floor and collect myself. I force myself to stand up, to pick up the cup I threw and place the chair Colin kicked back in its spot. I listen to the sound of the fire to calm me and when I finally relax enough to collect my thoughts, all I want is for Colin to come back. I don't want him to freeze out there alone. I want him here, in my arms. I want to apologise to him. To tell him I love him, that I didn't mean what I said, that he's right.

When the door opens, I turn around and we stare at each other for a moment. And then he closes the door and I meet him in the centre of the room, smacking into him so hard I lose my breath. But it doesn't matter because his arms are around me and he's so cold, his coat covered in snow, his beard almost frozen as I kiss it, heating it with my breath. He kisses me back and I tell him I'm sorry through the kisses and he shakes his head.

'Sweetheart, no, don't be. I was out of line.'

'No, you weren't. You have every right to feel that way, my love. And I'm sorry I forced you to believe that, because it's not true.'

He kisses me hard, his hand clasped against the back of my head. He's holding me so tightly I can only kiss him back, my tears mingling with our breaths.

'I'll be here,' he reminds me when he draws away for air, 'whatever happens, I'll be here.'

'I know, my love, I know.'

We're both so overcome with emotion, breathless with it, that for a while we do nothing but stand in the middle of the room, holding one another. I find myself wishing that time could fast forward to a point in our lives where we are happy — where we no longer have to live with this awful sorrow, this conflict within our hearts. When Colin moves, he breaks me out of my thoughts with a soft kiss against my cheek. Wordlessly, he takes my hand and leads me to the bed. This sanctuary, where all I need to focus on, is him. This place is a welcome relief, after so long and so I take this opportunity with open arms and draw him down to me.

Colin is kissing the puckered flesh of the scar on my back when I wake. I feel his fingertips soften over the edges of the deformed skin, still slightly tender to the touch, but not painful with how gentle he is, cautious not to wake me. I'm on my side, facing away from him. I don't roll over and gather him in my arms and kiss him like I want to. Instead, I marvel at the idea of him marvelling me — gently studying my body with his mouth and his fingers, perhaps imprinting it in his memory, perhaps reminding himself that, yes, I really am here and I'm his as much as he wants me to be. He's found the secret places of my body already, the places that make me sigh when touched. He knows my body well now;

he doesn't need to kiss the bones of my shoulder blades, smell the scent of my skin, trace the lines of my freckles as if they match the constellations he was taught years ago. And yet he does while I sleep and now while I pretend to slumber, he is careful and soft and devoted to his task. In that moment, so profound as it is to me, I'm able to believe this man loves me more than anything. That the sour-faced, feisty Irishwoman he met in St Brigid's all those months ago, that he would never dream of helping, let alone fall for, is everything to him.

And still holding onto that belief, as if I need it for strength, I finally do roll over and gather him in my arms. The skin on his shoulders is cool against my warm arms, having been out from under the blankets. I warm them with my flesh, pressing him close, kissing his cheeks and nuzzling the side of his throat.

'Does it still hurt?' he asks me, face pressed against my hair.

'The bullet wound?'

'Mm.'

'Not really. It's slightly tender.'

He's silent for a while and I kiss his cheek, looking up at his face. Morning light is coming in through the curtain, a dreary grey colour that speaks of snow and cold. I don't want to leave this bed any time soon. I don't want him to leave either. I can see an expression on his face, something hidden deep in his eyes, a slight, down-turned twist at the corner of his mouth.

'You alright, my love?'

He gives me a small smile, eyes crinkling at the sides. ''Course.'

I can see it in his face. The fear he has over what I'll do, what I'll choose to do. I know he's forgiven me. I know he understands my plight, almost more than I understand it myself. He'll stand beside me, no matter what I'll do. I know that more than anything and the thought is a comfort. But what frightens me is the doubt I see. The fear eating at the corners of his eyes. He's afraid it'll be like Harry Oswald all over again. That it'll be a slaughter and he'll be powerless to stop me. The thought makes me feel sick to the stomach. It makes me feel like I'm a feral animal to be feared, a lioness driven wild over the smell of blood.

'I don't think I feel that hatred anymore,' I tell him quietly, unsure of what else to say.

All I know is the deep and primal anger I felt within me when I killed the other men is gone. The act of killing Joseph Gaitwood alone stripped it away from me, knocked me back and almost ruined me. I can't go back there again. If I'm to kill Russ Gaitwood, if I'm to come to that decision, it won't be a slaughter. He'll have the chance to pray.

Colin's hands move up my rump to my hips and he pulls me closer to him. He cradles my face in his hands, but I can't meet his gaze. I'm afraid I'll still see the fear there. I don't want him to be scared of me, even though I know he has every reason to be.

21

I help Marcia with the washing later that day, sitting in the dining room by the fire to stay warm. She talks to me of her homeland Mexico, painting a picture of a land that sounds completely different to my green and rolling country. I'm enthralled by her story-telling and find myself hanging on her every word, grateful for the distraction as my back aches while we work. It feels good to be doing something with my hands and the hot, soapy water, the steam rising in my face and the fire by my hip, keeps me warm and comfortable.

Colin eventually went out to help the men in the stables to fix the roof, as it had partially caved in from a good snowfall the night before. We'd been warm together in bed, dreamy-eyed, but our small place of bliss had been interrupted by a knock at the door.

'I feel bad for having stayed here so long,' I tell Marcia after a while. I don't tell her I feel bad for wanting to end her husband's life when she herself is a wonderful, gentle woman.

'Nonsense!' She smiles at me, hair covered in a colourful scarf, sleeves rolled to her elbows as she scrubs a pair of trousers on the scrubbing rack. 'My husband and I are very grateful for all the help you and Mr McCarthy have given us.' She meets my gaze then. 'Plus, it's been nice to talk to you.'

My heart clenches in my chest and I look away from her, feeling unworthy of her compliment. I quickly nod and mumble something under my breath. Pablo comes in from the back of the house, wearing his boots and coat, ready to go outside. Marcia stares at him and I see her raise her brows in his direction, waiting for him to notice.

'Mama.'

'Have you done your morning reading, *mi hijo*?'

He sighs. 'Yes, Mama.'

'Two chapters?'

'*Yes*, Mama.'

'Alright. Try to stay warm out there. I don't want you catching a cold.'

'I'm helping Papa and the men; I'll be warm in no time.'

'Be careful, please.' The door is closed behind him before she can finish the sentence and she shakes her head, chuckling. 'Maybe I am too hard on him. He acts as if it's the worst thing in the world.'

'He's a teenager,' I murmur, remembering how I was with my parents at Pablo's age. 'You care for him a lot... there's nothing wrong with that, Marcia.'

She smiles at me. 'Do you have children, *chica*?'

'No.' I shake my head. 'I could have... with my late husband... but I lost it.'

'Oh... I'm so sorry.' She nods, her eyes sorrowful. 'We lost one too, about a year after Pablo was born. It is never easy, you poor dear.'

'It's no bother.' I wave a hand, trying to push back the immense emotion I still feel about the baby's loss to this day. It's something I know I'll never really get over. 'I don't think I'd make a great mother, anyway.'

'Mr McCarthy is good with Pablo.' When I lift my gaze to Marcia, she's got an expectant look on her face, as if she thinks I'm supposed to know what she means by that statement. 'I saw him giving whittling tips to him just the other afternoon.'

I can't help but smile. I didn't know Colin whittled.

'And he talks to him like he's on his level... not like he's beneath him.'

I nod, believing it. Colin always talks to me respectfully, even when I was a pain in his backside the first few weeks we arrived in America. He never once ridiculed or called me names.

'He's a good man.'

'Your love for him shows, you know?' I stare at her, but she continues to scrub a shirt, keeping her eyes on her work.

'What do you mean?' My voice is low. I suddenly feel on edge with the words having been said out loud for the first time.

'Your eyes shine. I hear it in your voice when you speak.' She finally meets my gaze and smiles. 'It's not a bad thing, *chica*. All I mean is that you must love him dearly... for me to notice so easily.'

I shake my head at her, not knowing what to say.

We finish our work in silence and we hang the clothes on a rope suspended by the fire to dry. My hands are warm from the water and my fingers have turned into prunes and my nails have blanched. Marcia gives me a cup of coffee as thanks and I take a biscuit from the plate she offers me. My stomach is rolling at the thoughts the woman has put in my head — not just of the obvious love I have for Colin, but the simple fact this woman has become a friend of sorts to me, has welcomed me into her house, into her life and I could easily betray her trust if I do decide on killing Russ Gaitwood.

The snow keeps us at the ranch for another week. It's so heavy, the men can no longer work the fields and instead are set to tasks on repairing things around the house and in the outer buildings. Colin still goes out every day and comes back every evening and I join Marcia in the house to help her with her chores. We feed the chickens — on the only occasion they leave their warm nests to eat before going back in to roost — harvest the vegetables we know won't survive the heavy snow, jar the fruits and organise the larder for their winter stows. My days are filled with work to keep my mind occupied and on several occasions, I'm allowed the solace of forgetting why I'm there, becoming only a woman who works on a ranch, making friends with the lady of the house and her kitchen hands.

But every time I see Russ Gaitwood, everything comes flooding back and a sweat breaks out across my palms, an anxiety gripping tight on my chest. I know I need to come to a decision soon. I can feel the confusion in Colin, can see it in his face and the things he said come to mind every time I see the grimace he can't seem to hide from me. I'm torn between wanting to end this, after everything I've done already, and not wanting to hurt any more people. I know I've become a monster, the thing I hated when I was still in Ireland and there's a part of me that's stubborn in its ignorance at that fact; that wants nothing but blood, nothing but to see the men that killed Thomas suffer. It's a tug-of-war between them, and I'm caught in the middle, tearing at the seams, hopeless.

The emotional turmoil of it soon breaks me down again and I'm unable to leave bed in the mornings when Colin wakes, when he rouses me with soft kisses and his gentle hold. He sees it in me and I see his worry and yet I can't do anything. It's as if I've taken hundreds of steps backwards and I'm once again the lost and angry widow, hopeless on what to do or where to go. All I can do is protect myself by shutting down, by shutting the world out with sleep and the warmth of the bed inside the outhouse, the fire crackling a soft lullaby.

Marcia visits me one day and sits on the side of the bed silently for a while. She's placed a cup of tea on the table beside the bed and smoothed the blankets down around me.

'I know it might not sound consoling, but I know how you feel, *chica*,' she suddenly says. 'When my dear husband was away from me and Pablo, when I couldn't see him and didn't even know if he was alive, I was succumbed by a sadness that ate me alive. A *fragile disposition* is what the doctor called it, yet he didn't take me seriously.' She clears her throat and gets up, beginning to tidy and fold the clothes strewn on the floor around the bed. 'Whatever it is that is ailing you, *chica*, I hope you know you can talk to me about it. Especially if it's something you think you need a woman to talk to about — Mr McCarthy is a gentleman, but he is a man, nonetheless.'

'I don't think I can,' I say, voice strangled with unshed tears, 'but thank you, Marcia.'

'You should go home, back to Ireland,' she tells me. 'Perhaps your own culture will make you feel a lot better. It's so different here. This country is so wild and busy.'

I almost cry at the realisation that Marcia thinks I might be homesick and that's why I'm so upset. That instead, the reason is something she could never imagine, something that would tear her apart more than it's tearing me apart if it happened, if I went through with it. After a while, she leaves me again and I stay in bed, wanting to scream.

'We should go.'

'What?'

I turn and stare at Colin from my seat by the fire. I know I look pale and shaken to him. I know I look like a bundle of nerves and anger, the very woman he met in St Brigid's so long ago. It's as if nothing in this trip has changed me, yet I'm so utterly different at the same time. He's standing by the door, as if he really means what he's just said and that he wants to leave this instant. But his boots sit on the floor by the bed and his coat is still hanging on the rack beside him. He watches me, eyes dark, standing out of the light the fire and lanterns cast. Like a ghost, an apparition telling me to turn back, that I'm not safe.

'You're slowly killing yourself being here for so long.'

'The snow has kept me here, not my indecision.'

'Don't blame the snow, Blair,' he says quietly. 'I can't stand seeing you like this; you're torturing yourself and you don't deserve it.' He points in the direction of the house that we both can't see. The house of Russ Gaitwood and his wife and son. 'That man no longer deserves it, either. You're getting nowhere and I dunno if I can let you do this to yourself anymore. I know I said I'd support you with whatever decision you came to, I'd draw my gun and do the act myself if you wished, but I ain't letting you keep this up no more. You need to go back home; you need to accept what's happened and live a happy life. You deserve that more than anyone, darling.'

I'm shaking in my chair, tears spilling down my cheeks. I turn my face away from him and stare at the flames as they dance. His words make me want to disappear. I don't want to be here anymore; I don't want to have to be alive in order to come to the decision. I know that either one will hurt me and they'll hurt him and they'll hurt Marcia and Pablo and even Russ Gaitwood himself. I know I can't leave without doing anything, I know that deep within my soul and I don't think Colin understands that. Or maybe he does, but he doesn't want me to kill him, no matter what he says about supporting me. I feel hollow. I feel alone.

Something within me forces me to stand up and I start to put on my boots and I see Colin watching me, still in the doorway, as I do. When I go towards him and take my coat from the rack, shrugging it on, he puts his hand on my arm, frowning.

'Blair...'

'I just want to go for a walk.'

He shakes his head. 'The snow is almost waist deep, just stay here; we can talk about it.'

I stare at him. 'I don't want to *talk*, Colin. Not to you. You don't understand, you say you do, but you *don't*.'

'How can I? I haven't been through what you've been through and I'm so sorry that I can't fully comprehend what you're going through, but I'm here. I've always been here, I've always *tried*—'

'Please.' I shake my head. I can't be around him.

'Stay inside, it's too cold out there, you'll freeze.'

'Then let me freeze!' The words burst out of me, in a shriek that's filled with nothing but raw emotion. 'Let me die, let me not have to be here, dealing with all of this!'

He grabs me and pulls me against his chest and I struggle, shaking my head, telling him to leave me, that I don't want comfort, that even his comfort can't bring me content any longer.

'Blair,' he hushes, grasping my face, pressing his forehead against mine, 'Blair, c'mon, it's alright, please.' He moves his thumbs over my tears, shushing me. 'A bad man deserves to die; he deserves to be killed by anyone who thinks they've been wronged by him. A bad man, who is still bad, should expect that sort of justice. A man who's good, who has been bad in the past, but has repented and made a life for himself, who understands his wrongdoings, what does he deserve? We don't know, but surely you don't think it's death? Surely? He's just like me, Blair. He's just like me.'

I pull away from him and I'm surprised when he lets me. 'He needs to know how much he's hurt me, how much he ruined my life.'

With my back to the coat rack, I feel for the gun-belt I hung there when we first arrived. The revolver is still in it, fully loaded. My fingers grasp the cold handle and I pull it out. I see Colin's eyes widen. I see his heart break just by the look on his face and I turn away from him and open the door. A storm of emotions rushes through me. I'm tuned out from the rest of the world, driven purely by them and nothing else. I'm running through the snow, pulling myself through it towards the house, my breath forming in clouds before my face, blurring my vision. It's so cold and it bites through my clothes and into my skin. I'm numb to it. Nothing else matters but getting to Russ Gaitwood and pulling the trigger.

The kitchen door is close. I see it in my desperate attempt to get there. I'm moving as fast as I can through the snow. I can feel the blizzard in my eyes, in my open mouth, suffocating me, blinding me. I'm sobbing, running away from Colin, even though I can faintly hear his voice over the sound of the rushing wind. I reach the back steps and climb up them. I'm shaking, wet through. I push the door open and move inside. My hand is gripping the gun so tightly, I don't think there's any chance of anyone prying it from my frozen fingers. The kitchen is warm and the fire in the hearth flickers when the door opens, a rush of wind and snow coming in behind me. There's a man sitting at the table in the almost-dark, drinking by himself. His head is hung and he looks lost in thought. When he lifts it and gazes at me, I see that it's the man that executed my husband. And the look on his face almost breaks me from the raw and desperate delirium. It's like he's expecting me. I see his eyes go down to the gun in my hand.

'Ms Ryan,' he says quietly and there's no shock in his voice, just a quiet deadliness that clenches at my heart like a fist.

'Your name is Russ Gaitwood, isn't it? Brother of Joseph and Edwin Gaitwood, leader of the Gaitwood gang.'

He lifts his hand slowly and finishes his drink, keeping his eyes on me. I step further into the room, keeping the gun by my hip. I'm shaking.

'*Is* and *was* are two very different words.' He sounds sad when he says it, as if mourning something. Perhaps himself. 'If you would believe me, I would say I *was* that man, but I am no longer. I also would not blame you if you refused to see my side of it.'

'You know who I am, don't you?'

'You are the wife of the last man I killed, yes.'

I nearly fall to my knees. 'When did you find out?'

'I knew as soon as Mr McCarthy introduced you.'

'So, you never forget the names of the men you kill? You knew my husband's name and still killed him as if he were nothing but a lame horse?'

'Murdering him changed me... I no longer wanted to be Russ Gaitwood the day I killed him. I became a repenting man, a man who loved his family and was sorry for all the things he did.'

'Is that supposed to make me forgive you?'

He stares at me. I see him slowly rise from his chair, keeping his hands in sight. 'I'm sorry, Ms Ryan. From the bottom of my heart, I cannot tell you how sorry I am. I was hoping you would see that I am no longer the man that killed your husband. I was hoping you would realise that a man can change, that killing and getting revenge fixes nothing.'

'What do you know about revenge?' I snap.

'I've killed countless men that have killed people dear to me, my life was built on the bodies of those men.'

'What did Thomas do to you?'

'Nothing. Killing him was a mistake. A grave, grave mistake. One that I will hold with me until my last breath.' His eyes go to the gun again and I see the sadness in them. 'And that may be this very moment.'

'Why?' I yell through my tears. 'Why did you think it was in your power to kill an innocent man?'

'I was reckless. I was evil. I was selfish.' He nods at me. 'You know what it's like, don't you? Killing? I heard word of my brother's death in Memphis. I know it was murder, that the perpetrator got away, and I can only assume it was you. I'm not blaming you, but killing him tore you apart on the inside, didn't it? It's something we do so mindlessly, so savagely, without any thought of how it slowly tears us apart. I've connected with those emotions now. I've realised we're not made to kill. We're made to live, to love.'

'Blair.'

I jump and turn around. Colin is standing behind me in the doorway. The snow and wind continue to blow in. He slowly steps inside and closes the door.

'Colin, don't, I need to do this. I need to hear why he thought it was necessary to murder Thomas.'

He holds up his hands. 'I ain't gonna do anything. I just want you to know I'm here. Just… please, listen to him.'

'I won't try to talk my way out of this, Ms Ryan,' Russ tells me and I turn back to him, trembling. 'I completely understand if you think it's crucial to you that I die tonight. I just want you to know the man that you're killing isn't the man that killed your husband and he is very, very sorry.' His face creases and I see his eyes shine with tears. 'But perhaps I can suggest we do it out in the barn and away from my family?'

'Jesus…' I hear Colin swear.

'What's going on?' Marcia comes out, wrapped in a shawl, her hair in a long dark plait over her shoulder. She sees me and smiles and then it slowly fades when she sees the revolver in my hand. '*Chica*? What are you doing?'

'Marcia, my love, go back to bed,' Russ says carefully, keeping his eyes on me. 'Ms Ryan and I are having a talk… it won't take long.'

'No…' She stares at him, her voice cracking. 'What did you do, *mi alma*?'

'He killed Thomas Ryan, my husband. And he needs to answer for what he did.'

Marcia throws herself in front of him, shaking her head. The shawl falls off her shoulders and she stares at me across the room, eyes wild.

'You can't have him,' she says harshly. 'You'll have to kill me, too. You can't have him. I *refuse*.'

I see myself in her. The animalistic desperation to protect the man she loves. I see Colin standing behind me as I shield his body with my own. I see myself dying while trying to protect him from those who think they have the right to kill him because they believe he deserves to die after what he did so long ago.

'This isn't fair,' I whisper, shaking my head. I slowly fall to my knees, the strength seeping from me.

Colin is behind me, holding my shoulders. 'Blair, please...'

'Don't kill him, *chica*, please,' Marcia says, voice strained. 'Please!' She starts to speak in Spanish, crying out, voice tight with emotion.

'Mama?' Pablo comes out and she screams, running to him.

'Go back to bed, Pablo! Go back!'

Colin holds me to him, murmuring to me, trying to block the sounds out so I don't have to hear them. Protecting me from the sounds of the people who were so close to being my victims. I'm a monster.

'You're my beautiful girl, I love you. I love you more than anything. You don't have to do this anymore. Let's just get you home.'

I'm cradling the revolver in my lap, sobbing so hard I think my ribs are going to break. Colin's arms are wound tight around me, desperately trying to hold me together as I fall apart against him.

'Ms Ryan.'

It feels like hours have passed. My eyes can no longer shed tears and I feel close to vomiting, dizzy and exhausted. When I lift my head, Russ Gaitwood is kneeling in front of me. I see Marcia standing where she was across the room, Pablo in her arms. Perhaps only seconds have passed. Colin still holds me, quiet.

'I cannot tell you how sorry I am for what I did to you. I won't ever be able to repay you for what I've done, but I hope you seeing what I do here — how I help these unfortunate men, how I raise my family, how I treat everyone as respectfully as I can — shows you that I have repented and I'm no longer the murderer that I was. If you disagree — if you must see me receive the justice that I deserve — take me to the sheriff's office in Fargo in the morning and I will willingly go with you—'

'*No!*' Marcia cries.

He holds up a hand and glances at her. 'Dear, please.' He turns back to me. 'I don't want you to kill another man, and I don't think your Colin does either. I don't really think you do. No one should have the death of another person on their shoulders and if I shall save you from that by going to hang, then so be it.'

'No,' I say quietly, weakly. 'I'm done.'

I let go of the gun and it clatters to the floor. Colin kisses the side of my head as I collapse into him. He lifts me up and I feel the room spin. It feels as if the whole world collapses as I lose consciousness and I'm suspended over an empty void.

22

Galway City is clouded by rain and from the ocean it resembles a lurking leviathan, hidden amongst a crest of rocks and waves, its eyes, hundreds of shimmering lights. It looks almost dreamy, blinking at me as I stare at it from the deck; as if trying to recognise who I am from the distance between us. I can hear it say, *I know you, but I do not know from where,* and I can't blame it. The Blair Ryan that left this city is nowhere near the woman I am now. I am but a stranger to this place and it too is somewhat strange to me, the familiarity somehow wrong and distorted. Whatever memories I have here are for that woman I was before and I don't feel as if I belong to them anymore. They're not for me, but for someone who died in America and the very moment that woman died was when she dropped the revolver that was meant to kill the man who murdered her husband.

This place I used to adore and call home is but a distant memory to me, one that doesn't seem to serve any purpose in my life anymore. The rolling hills of the Connemara, the great cliffs of Moher, and the city itself — the blinking, tired beast it seems to be from here — has been outgrown by me. I can no longer fit in the cobbled streets, smelling of burning peat and salt, the great rush of the Corrib somewhere underfoot. I'm too large for the house Thomas and I bought, too open-eyed for the dreary life that running a distillery would give. I wish to explore, to find a place in the green wilderness of my country and settle, take a great sigh of relief and hear nothing in response but the sound of the wind in the leaves. The sound of a child laughing. The sound of tobacco sizzling somewhere close, the smell comforting.

I no longer want the memory of Thomas to be filled with anger and hatred of the men that took him from me. I want to believe people can change, simply because I've seen it first hand, even in myself. I want to think of my past husband and only smile, thank him for the time he gave me, and continue on in my life.

Leaning against the railing of the ship, I slowly pull the Claddagh ring off my finger. The ship cuts through the water below me, creating waves that lap up the sides, skirting about one another in a dance. My fingers lift the ring to my lips and I kiss it gently. And then I hold my arm out and release the ring and it falls down. The splash it creates gets lost amongst the white foam. I let out a deep breath and close my eyes. It's as if surrendering my ring to the Atlantic takes a weight off my shoulders and I feel myself grow more content. Thomas will always be a part of my history and he'll always be someone who contributed to the shaping of the woman I am now. But releasing his ring into the waves is my way of finally letting go of the resentment, of accepting and letting his spirit free. Whatever demons and monsters that lurked amongst the shadow I cast, have now fled. It's as if the act of forgiving has given me the very contentment I went to America seeking. It didn't come through the death of the men that murdered him, as I believed it would, but through the growth I went through realising that wasn't what I needed at all.

A hand falls within mine and I grasp Colin's fingers instinctively, lifting them to my mouth as I did the ring. He kisses my forehead as I kiss his hand and pushes my hair from my face as the wind picks up.

'Good to be home?' he asks and his voice is as deep and soothing as it's always been.

'Let's live just outside Clifden,' I tell him quietly. 'On a plot of land, where there's no one but us for miles.'

I see the corner of his mouth quirk upwards. 'What about your business?'

I think of Martin and how happy he'll be to hear he no longer has to deal with me.

'I'll sell my share to my partner and he can do what he pleases. It's not my business anymore.' I look back out to Galway as it grows closer and closer. 'It never really was.'

'I'll do whatever you wish, just name it,' he murmurs and I meet his eye again. He's watching me, earnest.

'I love you, Colin McCarthy.'

This time he does smile and it's wide and beautiful and he kisses me softly in reply.

⊢•—◦—•⊣

The house I used to be so in love with, sitting along a cobbled road, close enough to the ocean to hear it but not so close to be weathered by its salt spray. I stand within its threshold, gazing into the kitchen that I covered with white blankets before I left. I see the outline of Thomas' chair amongst the throng of white, the chair I used to protect so savagely after he died. That feeling is gone from me now, a subtle bittersweetness left in its wake. My bags at my feet, I stare at the flagstones I used to lovingly wash down, the hearth fire, always warm, now dead cold and silent. I step over to where the table is and move the sheet away from it so I can see its marred surface, the very surface that knew the goings on of my life ever since I was a child. I run my fingers over the nooks and gouges; I have memories of how some were formed, but others belong to the Blair I no longer am, forgotten. I close my eyes and imagine that small plot of land closer to my home province again. The green fields, the sweet smell of fresh peat.

And then I turn around and I gaze at the man that I want to come with me. So long ago he stepped into this kitchen for the first time and sat at my table, as I stared at him with hatred. Now I only hold love in my eyes and it's so deep and wonderful that I can barely grasp it without feeling the need to weep. We're both strange in here, cramped in the confines of this place, so used to the open air of the American plains. We've grown so large, the both of us, that this small kitchen can scarcely keep us. Our knowledge of life and its hurt, its joy, stretched out far more than what this house could ever encompass. The both of us need a place where we can love, where we can pass on the knowledge to the life that we create, where we have room to live on and heal.

Shawline Publishing Group Pty Ltd
www.shawlinepublishing.com.au

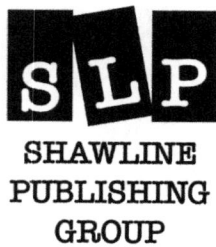

SHAWLINE
PUBLISHING
GROUP